═══ TRAILBLAZERS ═══

FEATURING

DAVID LIVINGSTONE

AND OTHER CHRISTIAN HEROES

Find us on the Web at . . .

TrailblazerBooks.com

- Meet the authors.

- Read the first chapter of each book—
  with the pictures from the original
  editions.

- Track the Trailblazers around the world
  on a map.

- Use the historical timeline to find out
  what other important events were happening in the world at the time of each
  Trailblazer story.

- Discover how the authors research their
  books, and link to some of the same
  sources they used, where
  you can learn more
  about these heroes.

- Write to the authors.

For books for older readers and adults by Dave and Neta Jackson,
visit *www.daveneta.com*.

DAVE & NETA JACKSON

TRAILBLAZERS

FEATURING

DAVID LIVINGSTONE

AND OTHER CHRISTIAN HEROES

BETHANY HOUSE PUBLISHERS

Minneapolis, Minnesota

Published by Bethany House Publishers
11400 Hampshire Avenue South
Bloomington, Minnesota 55438

Bethany House Publishers is a division of
Baker Publishing Group, Grand Rapids, Michigan.

Printed in the United States of America by Bethany Press International, Bloomington, MN.
October 2009, 1st printing

ISBN 978-0-7642-0729-7

DAVE and NETA JACKSON are an award-winning husband-and-wife writing team, the authors or coauthors of more than a hundred books. They are most well-known for the TRAILBLAZERS, a forty-book series of historical fiction about great Christian heroes for young readers (with sales topping 1.7 million), and Neta's popular YADA YADA PRAYER GROUP novels for women.

Dave and Neta also brought their love for historical research to the four-volume series of HERO TALES. Each book features fifteen Christian heroes, highlighting important character qualities through forty-five nonfiction stories from their lives.

The Jacksons make their home in the Chicago metropolitan area, where they are active in cross-cultural ministry and enjoy their grandchildren.

Books by
Dave & Neta Jackson

Heroes in Black History

Hero Tales Volume I

Hero Tales Volume II

Hero Tales Volume III

Hero Tales Volume IV

*Trailblazers: Featuring Harriet Tubman
and Other Christian Heroes*

*Trailblazers: Featuring Amy Carmichael
and Other Christian Heroes*

*Trailblazers: Featuring William Tyndale
and Other Christian Heroes*

*Trailblazers: Featuring David Livingstone
and Other Christian Heroies*

*Trailblazers: Featuring Martin Luther
and Other Christian Heroies*

ESCAPE FROM THE SLAVE TRADERS

DAVID LIVINGSTONE

Authors' Note

All the named characters in this book are real. Though greatly simplified, the story draws from events in David Livingstone's second trip to Africa, the Zambezi expedition, and concludes by incorporating elements from his third expedition. Further details on how history has been condensed and simplified may be found in the "More About David Livingstone" section at the back of the book.

CONTENTS

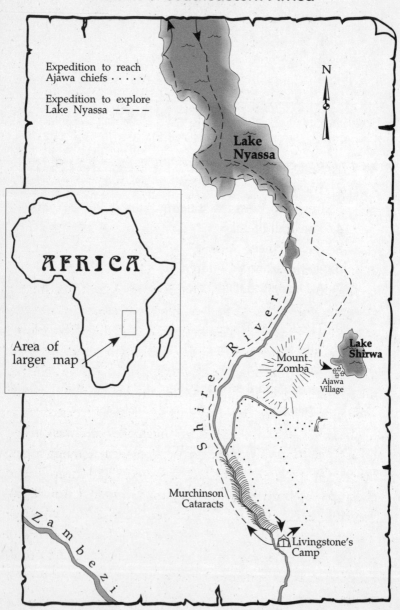

1861 in the area now known as Malawi in southeastern Africa

Expedition to reach
Ajawa chiefs · · · · ·

Expedition to explore
Lake Nyassa – – – –

N

Lake Nyassa

AFRICA

Area of larger map

Shire River

Mount Zomba

Lake Shirwa

Ajawa Village

Murchinson Cataracts

Livingstone's Camp

Zambezi

CHAPTER 1

RED CAPS IN THE MIST

"Chuma! Chuma!"

The urgent call cut through the morning mist that floated along the shores of Lake Shirwa. *Why is Wikatani yelling at me again?* wondered Chuma. He thought the older boy bossed him around too much, especially so early in the morning. What was the hurry this time? They would get the village sheep to the pasture soon enough, well before the African sun rose high enough to drink the dewdrops off the tender blades of grass.

"Chuma, help . . . !" And then Wikatani's voice was choked off as though he were gagging on a ball of wool. Chuma swung his staff at the heels of the last lazy sheep. The sheep leaped ahead to catch up with the flock that stretched around the bend of the lakeshore and disappeared into the mist. *Wikatani is always in a hurry,* Chuma thought. *What difference does it make whether the sheep eat along the trail or in the pasture?* Still, he couldn't remember Wikatani's voice ever sounding so urgent.

11

Instead of trying to push his way through the flock of sheep, Chuma ran out into the shallows of the lake to get around the woolly animals. The cool water splashed high over his body with each step until he hit a hole and suddenly sunk in water up to his neck. Chuma was a good swimmer, and there was no danger, but he grabbed quickly at the folds of his clothes to make sure the yam he had hidden there for lunch was still safe. He also checked to see that his drinking gourd still hung from the cord around his neck.

He swam strongly until his feet touched bottom again, and he waded to shore. With a brief scramble that dislodged sand and gravel, he made it to the top of the bank and plowed through the tall grass to a point where he could again meet the trail. He paused to scan the trail and listen for Wikatani. Straight ahead of him, through the fog, he thought he could make out his friend, but who were the strange men, and what was wrong?

Wikatani looked as if he were fighting for his life! One man held him securely from behind while another man tried to bind the boy's feet with cords. Frightened, Chuma barely held back a scream. What should he do? Should he rush to the attackers and try to free his friend or hold back until he figured out what was happening? Just then Wikatani must have bitten the hand of the man who held him because the man yelped, and Wikatani began yelling again: "Chuma! Chuma! Run for help!" Quickly the man clamped his hand back over Wikatani's mouth and looked at Chuma.

Chuma stared in disbelief and shock as the stranger's fierce eyes locked on him, but only for a moment. Chuma spun around to run back down the lakeshore to their village—but he was not fast enough. A third man who had hidden in the tall grass jumped out and faced him with a spear pointed right at his heart. Chuma froze in his tracks before he noticed that the man's spear had no point and looked more like a sawed-off canoe paddle with the handle pointed toward him.

Chuma thought of diving into the lake; not many people could outswim him. But before he could move, the man poked him hard in the chest with the pointless spear. It did not cut, but pain shot through his bones. Chuma decided not to make a run for it. Then the man began speaking to him in a strange language and motioning with his pointless spear. Chuma understood that he was being ordered to join Wikatani and the two strangers, so he turned and slowly walked through the deep grass to the trail.

When Wikatani saw that Chuma had been captured, the older boy's shoulders sagged. One of the men quickly tied Chuma's feet and then left both boys sitting helplessly on the ground by the trail while the men spoke to each other in their strange language.

Swallowing his fear, Chuma studied the features of the unusual looking men. He had never seen anyone who wore bright red caps or pants or vests. He knew they weren't from his tribe, the Ajawa. And they didn't look like Manganja tribesmen either. Even though the Ajawa tribe had sometimes feuded with the Manganja, they were the only two tribes in the area. The Ajawa villages were primarily situated around Lake Shirwa, while most of the Manganja villages were to the west, near Mount Zomba. So who were they?

One of the men near Wikatani stood up and raised his pointless spear to his shoulder. He pointed it toward one of the sheep that was grazing along the trail. Suddenly the pointless spear made a terrible boom, and white smoke shot out of the end. Both boys cried out with the thunder, then opened their eyes. There lay one of their sheep—dead!—while the others ran off. That was bad. The village elders would be angry at the boys for having lost a sheep, but what if the strangers stole or killed the whole herd? Fear gripped Chuma's stomach.

And what about the stranger's awesome weapon? To Chuma, it looked like the pointless spear had killed the sheep without the stranger having thrown it. "Very powerful magic," Chuma whispered to Wikatani.

"They are guns. I have heard of them," said Wikatani. "They can kill from far away."

"Of course . . . guns," said Chuma. He did not like to admit it when Wikatani knew something he did not know, even though Wikatani was thirteen and he was only twelve years old.

Then Chuma was surprised to notice the man pick up a regular spear. He could see by its tribal markings that it was a Manganja spear. The man walked over to the dead sheep and wiped some of the sheep's blood on the spear. He broke the spear over his knee and brought the pieces back and threw them on the ground near Chuma and Wikatani. Then he ordered one of the other men to pick up the dead sheep and carry it over, too.

Seeing the other man obey his order convinced Chuma that this man was the leader of the group, maybe even a chief, though they were all dressed the same.

When the other man brought the sheep back, he let some of the blood drip on the sand and grass around the area where the boys were bound. Chuma did not understand these strange actions, but it was getting scarier by the moment. Were they performing some kind of magic?

Next, the leader grabbed the drinking gourd that hung by a thong from Chuma's neck. With one jerk he broke the thong and then smashed the gourd on the ground. Chuma stuck his chin out at the man defiantly. He could make another drinking gourd. He only carried the gourd with its fresh water because it was convenient when he was watching the sheep on the hills around Lake Shirwa.

But the man also ripped the family bracelets from Wikatani's arms and threw them to the ground not far from the broken gourd. He gave more orders. One man tied Chuma's hands behind his back while the other tied Wikatani's behind his back, and then they cut the cords on their legs.

Finally, the leader of the Red Caps started up the trail while the other two men prodded Chuma and Wikatani to follow. *Now what's happening?* thought Chuma with alarm. *They are not stealing our sheep; they are taking us!*

One of the men carried the dead sheep over his shoulder. It was still dripping blood on the trail as they walked. In a short distance, they turned off the main trail along the lakeshore and marched west, away from the lake. The path was barely visible as it wound uphill through the thick grass toward the jungle.

Chuma looked back anxiously. The mist was lifting from the lake, and before they entered the jungle he could see its peaceful surface shining in the morning sun. Far back along the shore were wisps of smoke rising from their village. That was home, and they were being taken away. *No one will know where we are!* worried Chuma. *They won't even miss us until tonight when we don't return with the sheep. By then we'll be so far away that they will never find us!* Below, their sheep were wandering away from the trail along the lakefront. Suddenly a hopeful thought came to him: *Maybe some sheep will wander home. Someone will certainly notice and know something is wrong and come looking for us. Or else,* and his spirits fell, *or else they'll just think we've been careless.*

As they entered the jungle, Chuma could no longer see the lake. The dew that had clung to the grass of the open fields now dripped like rain from the trees and vines overhead. Monkeys screeched and swung from limb to limb as the boys and their captors passed beneath. As the Red Caps hurried the boys along under the dark trees, Wikatani said in a hushed voice, "They had a Manganja spear. Do you think they are from the Manganja tribe?"

"I don't think so," answered Chuma. "Why would the Manganja take us away?"

"They're our tribe's old enemies."

"Yes," said Chuma, "but it is a disgrace to send others to fight your battles. These aren't Manganja, and we are only boys. What could be gained by capturing us?"

"Well, I am a chief's son," said Wikatani, lifting his head proudly. "Much trouble will come from attacking *me*. We are headed west into Manganja country. The Manganja must be behind this, and they will pay!"

"But the Manganja have no reason to attack us," said Chuma again.

At that point a Red Cap slapped Chuma on the back of the head so hard that he stumbled and fell. With his hands tied behind his back, he was unable to catch himself, and his face plowed into the dirt. Fortunately the ground was soft, and Chuma was not hurt. He quickly got up spitting bits of leaves and dirt from his mouth.

"No talking! Just march," shouted the Red Cap angrily, gesturing, and raising his hand as though to strike again. Chuma was as surprised that this man could speak their language as having been hit on the back of the head. *What'd I do? What's so wrong with talking?* Chuma wondered.

Wikatani said, "Don't hit him. He didn't do anything."

"I said, 'No talking,' " yelled the Red Cap again, this time at Wikatani. He spoke the boys' language well enough for them to understand him, but his accent was very thick. Then the Red Cap swung his gun at Wikatani like a club. Wikatani dodged out of the man's reach and hurried on up the trail. Chuma followed as quickly as he could.

By noon Chuma was feeling hungry and thirsty. Safely tucked in the folds of his loincloth was the small, cooked yam that his mother had set aside for him to eat while he herded sheep. He longed to take it out and eat it, but his hands were tied. Besides, he was afraid that the Red Caps would throw it away as they had his drinking gourd.

Plodding along the jungle trail, Chuma's thoughts kept returning to the house with its sturdy mud walls and thatched roof where he lived with his father and mother and three little sisters. He wanted to be brave, to face this difficulty like a man, like his father . . . but he kept thinking of his mother. *Who'll fix my food?* he wondered, even though he knew that wasn't his worst problem at the moment.

CHAPTER 2

WAR DRUMS

As the sun dropped lower, its warm rays pierced the jungle roof only occasionally. But when they did, the golden beams sliced through the forest to turn various ferns a bright green or the trunk of a tree a rich, brick red.

Chuma no longer knew where they were. The country was turning hilly, and Chuma felt certain they were headed toward Mount Zomba, but he had never been this far west. Would they soon arrive at a Manganja village? He had no way of knowing, but he almost wished that they would. He was so tired he thought he would drop, and he was hungry.

Then suddenly, without any warning, they stepped out into a small clearing and the Red Caps stopped. It seemed to be their camp. There were two simple shelters made of palm branches under which supplies were piled high. And there were two other Red Caps already there, sitting near a smoldering fire while they smoked rolled leaves of tobacco.

The man carrying the sheep dropped it on the ground by

the fire, and the leader gave more orders in the strange language. Soon the men by the fire butchered the sheep and put it on a spit over the fire to cook it.

The man who had slapped Chuma herded the boys over to the edge of the clearing and tied a rope tightly to each boy's ankle. The rope was also tied securely to a tree. He cut the cords that bound their wrists together, then left to join the others near the fire. Chuma and Wikatani tried to make themselves comfortable on the ground between the great roots of the tree and waited to see what would happen.

Nighttime in the jungle can be very dark; very little starlight makes its way through the dense roof of leaves. Even at the edge of the clearing it was dismally dark. Chuma and Wikatani sat dejectedly watching the five Red Caps around their small fire feasting on the roasted sheep and passing a jug of some sort of liquor. *Those men have no right to be eating our sheep!* Chuma thought angrily. Hunger kept him hoping that the Red Caps would bring them some of the mutton, but soon the men were so drunk they fell asleep.

With the pain mounting in his stomach, Chuma finally dug into the folds of his loincloth and pulled out the cold yam. He took a bite. It was *so* good . . . or maybe it was just that he was so hungry. He took another bite, then nudged Wikatani: "Want some yam?"

"What?"

"You want a bite of my yam?" whispered Chuma.

"Where'd you get that?" said Wikatani, groping in the dark until he found the yam.

"My mother. It was wrapped in my clothes."

"I never knew a yam could be so good," Wikatani sighed, handing the remainder back to Chuma. "Do you think we can get these ropes off our ankles?"

"I don't know," said Chuma, taking another bite and then putting the rest of the yam back into his clothes. He went to work trying to wiggle his foot out to the loop that held it firmly. But the harder he pulled, the tighter the rope seemed to hold him. "I can't get it off."

There was a quiet moan from Wikatani. "I made it."

"Then help me."

Wikatani pulled and tugged. He used his teeth to try and tease the knot loose, but it was no use. The rope held Chuma fast to the tree.

"See if you can find something sharp to cut the rope," said Chuma.

Wikatani slipped off into the dark, and suddenly Chuma felt terribly alone. He waited a long time. *Wikatani ought to be back by now*, the boy thought, his heart beating fast. *Maybe he got lost. What if he never comes back?*

And then, as if he had never been away, Wikatani was at his side. "I can't find anything sharp. Only a few stones around here, and they're all smooth. I can't see a thing in this darkness."

"What about a knife from the Red Caps?" asked Chuma.

"Are you crazy? What if they woke up?"

They sat in silence for a while. Finally, Chuma said, "Maybe you should go for help."

"In the dark? I'd get lost for sure and the hyenas would find me."

It had been a bold suggestion, and Chuma shivered. The short time that Wikatani had been away had been enough to let him know how much worse it was to be a captive alone. But it seemed the only way. "How about just before it gets light? You could hide in the jungle until you can see and then find your way home."

"I guess so," admitted Wikatani. "But for now, let's get some sleep."

———

The constant chatter of jungle birds and monkeys woke Chuma. He had been dreaming about his three sisters playing at the edge of the lake. *Home. Home is so good*, he thought, and a heavy sadness spread through his heart when he remembered where he was.

A faint light tinged the sky above the clearing. They had slept longer than they should have! He shook Wikatani, and they both sat up. But in addition to the jungle noises, they could hear something else: the *thump, thump, thumpity-thump* of distant drums.

"Chuma, listen—Ajawa drums."

"You're right." Chuma imagined some of the head men of his village beating the hollow logs that sent their messages for miles through the jungle. Their rhythms could announce many things, but this beat meant. . . ." War. It's war against the Manganja," concluded Chuma in a hoarse whisper.

"Because we're missing?" his friend asked.

"Maybe." Chuma thought for a moment. "That broken Manganja spear and the sheep's blood did make it *look* like the Manganja had captured us."

"And now Ajawa warriors will attack them."

"Yes. I think the Red Caps set it up that way. But why?" wondered Chuma out loud.

"Right now, who cares? I've got to get out of here."

"Take care," said Chuma, putting his hand on his friend's shoulder. "And come back soon. I don't like being a prisoner."

As Wikatani slipped away, Chuma could barely see him

moving through the dense jungle as he tried to get around the campsite and find the trail by which they had entered the small clearing.

Then suddenly a terrible howling erupted. Wikatani must have come upon some baboons that were trying to raid the Red Caps' camp. The baboons screeched and yelled as they scampered up the vines to reach the safety of the trees.

Chuma held his breath and wished he could silence the baboons, but it was no use. Two of the Red Caps sat up and spotted Wikatani running down the trail. They grabbed their guns and tore down the trail after him.

"Run, Wikatani, run," urged Chuma under his breath, his fists clinched in fear. If Wikatani did not escape, they might not be rescued. And if they were not rescued, there might be a war, and many Ajawa would die.

Chuma wanted to pray to the spirits, but he knew the spirits didn't care. Their help could only be obtained by a sacrifice, and he had nothing to give. Then he remembered the small scrap of yam left from the night before. He dug it out. *It's my only food*, he thought. *If I throw it to the spirits, I might die. But if I don't, Wikatani might not escape*.

Before he could decide, a gun boomed in the distance. Chuma's heart sank. *Had the Red Caps killed Wikatani?* He waited but heard no more booms, just the sounds of the jungle coming alive in the morning—birds singing, insects buzzing, and still in the distance the talking drums.

When he felt he could wait no longer, he heard footsteps coming up the trail. The sight of Wikatani staggering back into camp was a tremendous relief. At least he was alive! One of the two Red Caps who followed him had cut a stiff vine and was using it to whip Wikatani every few steps if the boy did not move fast enough. The boy's arms were tied behind him. When they arrived at the tree where Chuma was tied up, the Red Caps gave Wikatani a shove that knocked him to the ground. The man was yelling at the boys in his strange language as he retied the rope around Wikatani's ankle, leaving some extra rope to tie around his other ankle, too. Then he gave Chuma's rope a big yank to see that it remained tight. Chuma's ankle throbbed with pain, the rope was so tight.

"What happened?" Chuma asked as the Red Cap went back to his camp. Then he realized what bad shape his friend was in. He was smeared with mud, and he had scratches and scrapes up and down both legs. There was a cut across his forehead that was oozing blood and beginning to swell. "What happened to you?" asked Chuma again anxiously.

"They caught me," pouted Wikatani, tears welling up in the corners of his eyes.

"I can see that," said Chuma. "But how?"

"I don't know," Wikatani said, looking away into the jungle. "I ran and ran. I knew they were behind me. I ran down a little hill and crossed a stream. I was climbing the other side when they shot at me with a gun. I did not want to die, so I stopped. When they caught me, they beat me."

Chuma asked no more questions.

By noon the Red Caps still hadn't given the boys anything to eat or drink. Chuma began to worry. He'd been thirsty before, but this was serious. His mouth was completely dry, and his tongue had swelled up so that he talked funny. His head felt light, as if he might fall over if he stood up. And Wikatani looked worse as the hours passed.

Finally, he decided they must do something, even if the Red Caps got angry. So he began to yell. "Give us food! We need water!" He knew that at least one of the men understood the Ajawa language. But when the Red Caps looked over at him, they just pointed and laughed. Still, Chuma kept yelling. Maybe their captors would get tired of the noise and give them what they needed.

One Red Cap grabbed a leg bone from the sheep they had feasted on the night before. Chuma eagerly saw that there were still some shreds of meat on it. The Red Cap walked toward the boys, and Chuma sat quietly in expectation. The Red Cap stopped a short distance away and gave Chuma a wicked grin. Then he dropped the bone to the ground, kicked dirt on it, and said, "Hungry?" When he made a gesture for Chuma to come get it, Chuma lunged, but the bone was out of reach. He pulled hard on the rope that bound him to the tree, got down on the ground and stretched out on his belly reaching as far as he could, but the bone was still beyond his reach.

The Red Cap broke into a great laugh, and the others joined in. The more Chuma stretched and groaned, the more the Red Caps roared until they were bored with their game.

But Chuma refused to give up in defeat. He crawled back to the tree and began looking around until he found a small stick. Then, attracting as little attention as possible, he scooted back toward the bone and reached out with the stick.

It just reached, and he began rolling the bone toward him. He got it rolled half way over, then it rolled back. He tried again, but just when it was about to come a full turn, he slipped and bumped it back—even farther away! After that, he could not reach it at all.

"Chuma, Chuma," Wikatani whispered. "Try this." It was a longer stick with a little branch on the end.

Using it like a hook, Chuma was able to roll the bone back and finally retrieve it.

Back at the tree, the boys eagerly pulled the remaining meat from the bone. It may have been too dirty even for the dogs back in the village, but they were so weak from hunger, they didn't even care. They ate it anyway, and it tasted good.

As Chuma was gnawing the last bit of gristle from the bone, Wikatani said, "Where did they go?"

In their excitement over having something to eat, the boys had not noticed that the Red Caps had left camp. "Ah, they're around here somewhere," Chuma said.

"I don't think so," said Wikatani. "I think they've left. Look. The supplies under that far shelter are missing. They've gone somewhere."

"Now's our chance!" said Chuma. "We've got to get free and get out of here!"

CHAPTER 3

IN CAMP
WITH THE "ENEMY"

Try as they would, however, the knotted ropes would not give. And soon the boys' hunger and thirst became a nightmare that overshadowed their desire to escape. Wikatani hurt everywhere from his beating, and his cuts were already infected. Chuma hated the thought of dying tied to a tree. He and Wikatani lay on the ground, weak with hunger, dehydration, and exhaustion. What seemed like an eternal day of torment finally blended into the night and the boys drifted off into a fitful sleep.

In the middle of the night, something woke Chuma. At first he was confused. *What was happening?* Then he yelled, though the sound came out more like a squeak. "Rain! Wikatani! It's raining!"

Cupping their hands, the two boys caught the sweet water, satisfying their thirst again and again. The shower did not last long, and soon they were both asleep again.

The next morning the clearing was still deserted. "Are the Red Caps going to leave us here to die?" asked Chuma.

"No, they will come again," Wikatani assured Chuma. "Some of their supplies are still here."

The water had renewed their strength, but the hunger grew worse. As the day wore on, Chuma had a thought. He reached over and picked at the bark of the tree they were tied to. Then he began ripping off the bark as fast as he could. Termites! And grubs! *Why hadn't they thought of it sooner?* Wikatani helped him, and the boys popped the insects and little white grubs into their mouths as fast as they could. It took a lot of termites, but the terrible pain in their stomachs finally settled into a dull ache. Both boys hoped their meal stayed down, but it was not their last meal from the tree.

Two days went by before the Red Caps returned to camp with dozens of new captives. Men, women, and children were tied together with stout ropes. Many of the children were younger than Chuma and Wikatani. The Red Caps frequently hit the men with the butts of their guns and slapped the women and children. The younger children were wailing with fear.

The Red Caps cracked real whips this time, not just vines like they'd used on Wikatani. The whips whined through the air and cracked on bare skin, raising huge welts and sometimes cutting the skin open as the people were pushed into the center of the clearing.

Chuma and Wikatani stared open-mouthed. "Look!" Chuma whispered as he noticed the tribal markings tattooed on the bodies of the captives. "They're all Manganja."

"You're right. And some of the men are wounded."

"Not gun wounds . . . spear."

The boys watched as two of the Red Caps set to work attaching Y-shaped poles to the necks of the men. Each pole was about six feet long and branched into a Y at the end. The Red Caps put a Y around a man's neck and fastened it by driving a long metal spike through the tips of the open ends of the Y. This left the man with a huge pole sticking out in front, or to his side or back. It made any fast movements impossible because the poles had a tendency to catch on things, giving the wearer a sharp and painful jolt in the neck.

"They're making slaves of them!" Wikatani said in shock. "Those poles keep slaves from running away. No one can run through the jungle with one of those things around his neck." Just then one of the captured men spit on his captors after they'd put the Y on his neck and began kicking wildly. A Red Cap grabbed the pole and flung the man to the ground without getting close enough to be kicked or hit.

Chuma stared in awe. He, too, had heard of this practice for controlling slaves. In fact, once he had seen a thief treated this way as a punishment.

When the Red Caps had attached Y-sticks to all the men, they set to work retying the frightened women together with strong ropes from one woman's neck to another's, creating a human chain.

Chuma counted a total of eighty-three captives. Several of the children couldn't be more than five years of age, and there were a few who were still in their mothers' arms. Some of the Manganja carried personal belongings—cooking pots, water gourds, and bags probably containing cornmeal or cassava root flour.

Many of the women were crying with grief and fear, their tears mingling with their children's who clung to them. But as evening approached some of the people began trying to make the best of their situation, arranging a family space to sit down and huddling everyone together. At first this activity created a great deal of confusion because of the women who were tied together. One wanted to go one way, and the next woman wanted to go another. Finally, things got sorted out so that they weren't continually pulling at one another's throats.

The children began gathering wood for fires while the men stumbled around in their neck yokes putting water and cornmeal in the cooking pots and setting them over the small fires to make the familiar porridge *nsima*.

With the situation under control, the Red Caps stayed back and allowed the captives to prepare their food without yelling and using their whips, except when one of the men got too near the edge of the clearing where he might try to run away into the jungle.

Wikatani and Chuma tried several times to talk to the new captives. The Ajawa language was similar enough to the Manganja language so that the boys could understand them speaking to one another. But the only response they received was angry glares; one woman close by spat on Wikatani.

"I know our tribes are enemies," Wikatani pouted, wiping off the spittle, "but *we* can't hurt them. Why are they so nasty to us?"

"I don't know," Chuma said, watching a Manganja girl in the glow of the light from the many small fires. She was about their age. "We are all captives of the Red Caps; we should help each other."

"Yes. We both have the same enemy now. The Red Caps don't belong here; they are outsiders." Wikatani was watching the same girl. She was pretty and not tied up like the older women.

When the girl looked their way, Chuma motioned to her to come over to them. She looked around to see if any Red Caps were watching, but she did not come. A few minutes later she looked at them again. Wikatani smiled, and she smiled back. He, too, motioned, but she shook her head.

Then she casually walked away from her people and began gathering wood near the edge of the clearing. Slowly she made her way around to the tree where Chuma and Wikatani were tied. "What do you want?" she asked when she was within hearing range.

"Water," they both said. "And food," added Chuma.

She walked on, picking up sticks until she got back to her family's fire.

In a few minutes the girl returned with a small gourd of water. "Have they not fed you?" she asked.

"Just a bone," said Wikatani.

"If this tree didn't have termites in it and a few grubs, we would have starved."

The girl looked closely at the boys. "You're not Manganja," she said in surprise.

"No. We're Ajawa," said Chuma. "The Red Caps captured us three days ago when we were taking our village sheep to pasture."

"The Ajawa are hyenas," the girl snapped. "They attack when one's back is turned." And she grabbed the water gourd and started to walk away.

"Wait!" said Wikatani. "Why do you say that?"

The girl turned slightly and gave them a hate-filled stare. She spoke in a tone of deep anger: "The Manganja and the Ajawa were supposed to be at peace. We kept the peace, but your people attacked us! In the dark I did not see that you are Ajawa, or I would never have brought you water."

Chuma thought fast. Their people had attacked the Manganja? He began to understand what had happened.

"But it was a mistake!" Chuma pleaded as the girl started

to walk away again. "Our people thought *you* had captured us. That's why they went to war with you. They knew nothing about these Red Caps."

The girl hesitated.

Wikatani continued. "That's right. If our people had known that the Red Caps had captured us, they would have come here to rescue us."

The girl faced them again, still angry. "Why did the Ajawa think it was us?" she demanded.

"Who else?" said Wikatani.

"No; there's more to it than that," said Chuma. "The Red Caps broke a Manganja spear and left it on the trail where they caught us."

"And they spread blood all around to make it look as if we had been killed or badly hurt," added Wikatani.

"But why would the Red Caps do all that?" asked the girl skeptically.

"We think they *wanted* the Ajawa to attack the Manganja, so they made it look as if your tribe had captured us."

"But we don't know why," Wikatani admitted. "Why start a war between our two tribes?"

"If what you say is true," said the girl, "their reason is clear. They wanted to buy slaves. There are only five of them. So this was the only way to get many unarmed slaves."

"What do you mean?" asked Wikatani.

"We were captured by your people and taken to an Ajawa village. The Red Caps came the very next morning and bought all of us and brought us here."

"Bought you? With what?" asked Chuma.

"Rolls of bright colored cloth, pieces of copper wire, new cooking pots—white men's things," spat the girl.

Neither boy had ever seen a white man, but they had heard

plenty of stories about them. Far down the Shire River, where it joined a larger river—the Zambezi—white men traveled on the water in their gigantic smoking canoes. Rumor said they had a village named *Tete* many miles up the Zambezi.

"Slave traders," breathed Wikatani. The only source of the brightly colored cloth, wire, and iron pots was white men. Often they traded those things for slaves.

A new fear shone in Wikatani's eyes. "Will we be sent away to the white man's land?"

"*We* won't," said the girl proudly. "Manganja warriors will soon rescue us."

"Yes. I'm sure they will try," said Chuma slowly, pondering the situation. "But they don't know where you are. They will attack Ajawa villages and take more captives in revenge—"

"And probably sell them to the Red Caps, too," added Wikatani.

The girl stared at the two boys in dismay. "Then . . . we might never get home!"

CHAPTER 4

THE TRAIL OF TEARS

Hoot—hoot—hoot!

Chuma woke up with a start to the terrible racket. When he sat up, he saw one of the Red Caps walking among the captives blowing loud blasts on a bright tin horn.

Wiss-crack! Wiss-crack!

Another Red Cap followed the first one cracking a whip over the heads of the people. "Get up! Get up! Today we march," he yelled in the Manganja language, kicking those who weren't quick enough to rise.

The Red Caps then took the men to the shelter and loaded them with the remaining supplies stored there: more rolls of cloth, copper wire, iron cooking pots, heavy boxes, and bags of grain.

"Let's go! Let's go!" yelled the Red Cap, cracking his whip and letting it land on any captive who was not moving fast enough to suit him. The other Red Caps were going among the women making sure that the ropes that linked them together were still securely tied.

With the Manganja men loaded down by the Red Caps' supplies, the women had to shoulder all their own supplies. Several women had a huge bundle balanced on their head, a child in one arm, and a cooking pot or some other item in the other.

Hooting on his tin horn again, the leader of the Red Caps started off down the trail while the other Red Caps whipped the rest of the people into line to follow.

Chuma and Wikatani remained silent under their tree. "Maybe they will leave us," whispered Chuma. "Then we could escape."

"How?" answered Wikatani. "We haven't managed to get free yet. We'll starve tied up here if we don't have anything more to eat than these termites."

"We'll figure out something. I just hope they don't take us and sell us to the white men."

But the last Red Cap in the caravan stepped over to their tree and cut their bonds. "Hurry up. Catch up with the rest of them," he barked in his strange accent.

The boys started off down the trail at the back of the caravan. Children were crying, the Red Caps' whips were cracking—sometimes causing a captive to yell out in pain. And through it all, the women were trilling their grief: a high-pitched cry made by moving the tongue back and forth rapidly, creating a mournful wail. Chuma remembered his grandfather's funeral, and the feeling stuck in his throat.

The men were having a terrible time managing the Y-yokes. The poles seemed to catch on every bush, and when the caravan climbed a little hill, the poles constantly jabbed into the ground in front of the men almost knocking them over backwards.

The progress of the caravan that morning was very slow, and the constant whipping of the captives' backs made it all the worse. Shortly after noon, the strange company worked its way down a hill like a long centipede to a lush, green valley. There, tall sugarcane plants lined both sides of the trail, and the Red Caps were obviously worried that one of their captives would dart from the trail and disappear into the cane. They kept running back and forth along the line making sure every one remained right in the center of the path.

But one man did make a break for it. In spite of the cumbersome yoke attached to his neck, he spotted a small game trail going off into the cane and tried to run into the tunnel before the Red Caps saw him.

A Red Cap near Chuma and Wikatani saw the man. He laughed loudly and yelled, "You cannot escape us. Go ahead and try, and you will all see that no one can run from us." Just then the Y-pole on the man's neck caught in the cane and threw him back onto the path. He choked and coughed as he struggled to his feet trying to untangle the pole and swing it around behind him while he desperately pushed into the cane. Then the Red Cap lifted his pointless spear to his shoulder and—just as it happened to the sheep—there was a loud boom, a lot of smoke, and the runaway crumpled to the ground, bleeding from his back.

He gasped once and died.

Many of the captives screamed, and a woman who must have been the man's wife tried to run to his side, pulling other women with her by the rope between their necks. But the Red Caps beat her back with their whips. "Move on! Move on, or you will die with him," they shouted to the terrified string of captives.

Chuma and Wikatani stared in horror at the man who had

been shot as they silently walked past his body. The Y-pole remained stuck in the cane, holding his head up off the ground in a half-way sitting position. His eyes were still open, and they stared, unseeing, into the sky.

"Get moving," snarled the closest Red Cap.

The column of stunned people marched on in silence except for quiet sobbing by some of the women. No longer were they trilling the traditional grief songs. Their spirits were broken.

In the afternoon black clouds piled high in the sky, and thunder signaled a heavy downpour. The rain made walking on the muddy trail difficult, but still the downpour was welcomed by many of the captives. They had been traveling since the Red Caps woke them so roughly at dawn, and many had not had time to get anything to eat or drink. The heavy rain at least provided a little water. The storm did not last long, however, and soon the sun broke through the clouds to warm the travelers from the chill of the rain.

As the clouds drifted away, the march continued without relief until the sun slipped behind the hills. With night falling on the strange caravan, the Red Caps chose a small meadow with a stream flowing through the middle to set up camp. The stream was a welcome place to soak sore, tired feet that had been scratched by thorns or cut by sharp stones during the day's long march.

However, the meadow had one disadvantage. It contained very little wood for fires. The few fires that were started had to be fed with bunches of twisted grass. But the recent rain had dampened the grass so much that it made a heavy smoke and gave off very little heat for cooking—when it burned at all. The Red Caps would not allow the children to venture into the forest to gather wood. This meant that most people could not cook their food and had to make do with raw cornmeal or other tidbits they had with them.

The Red Caps did not supply any of their own provisions for their captives, so the only food for the slaves was what they had managed to bring with them. Chuma and Wikatani had none, and with the Manganja blaming them for their captivity (because they were Ajawa), no one offered to share.

Chuma closed his eyes against the sharp pain in his stomach. He felt weak all over and knew he could not walk again tomorrow without food. He sat for a long time, trying not to think, then was startled when he heard someone call his name.

His eyes flew open. It was almost dark and at first he saw no one. Then he saw the girl. She had brought each of the boys a leaf with a scoop of cold cornmeal mush on it. Both Chuma and Wikatani ate eagerly. Not having been cooked, one could not say it was real *nsima*, but it did ease the gnawing pains in their stomachs.

"How did you know my name?" he asked the girl.

She nodded at Wikatani. "I heard him call you. And you call him Wikatani."

"What is your name?"

"Dauma." The girl sat on the ground near the boys. "Do you know where they are taking us?"

"We've been traveling southwest most of the day," said Wikatani. "We should be deep into Manganja country by now. I thought you would know where we are."

"My people do not know this land," the girl answered. "They fear we are being taken to the white men at Tete on the Zambezi River. We will never see our homes again!"

———

The next day the captives made sure that they got up before dawn so that they could prepare something to eat, gather their belongings, and be ready to move out before the Red Caps started cracking their whips.

Several of the Manganja men invented a smart way to ease the pain on their necks caused by the Y-shaped poles. With twine woven from meadow grass, pairs of men tied their poles together. The man in front arranged his pole to extend straight out behind him, and the man following swung his pole around to stick straight out to the front. Then, with the ends of each pole overlapping, a third person wrapped twine around the poles, tying them together. This bound each pair of men together as though there were just one pole between them with a Y on each end. The invention kept the ends of the poles from flopping around and getting caught on things. Apparently the Red Caps did not think it made escape any easier, because they did not object.

That day and the next several people got sick and could hardly walk, but the Red Caps had no mercy on them. The whip fell just as harshly on their backs as on the backs of those who were still healthy.

In the afternoon of the third day on the trail, one of the men stumbled and fell. His bag of corn—belonging to the Red Caps—broke open when it hit a log. Chuma saw the corn come spilling out and dove for a handful. The corn had not been ground, but he stuffed his mouth with the hard kernels anyway and grabbed for more. By then more people were reaching for the food. Some of the women pulled others to the ground with them because of the ropes connecting their necks. Pretty soon a huge pile of people were scrambling to get a bite to eat.

As Chuma tried to wiggle his way out from under the

pile, he could hear a Red Cap yelling at the people. The whip whistled through the air and landed with a crack on someone's back. It whistled again, and this time the stiff rawhide cut into Chuma's leg. He yelled, spewing the corn from his mouth, and pulled himself from the pile of people. Quickly, he ran down the trail before he caught another lash from the whip.

He squeezed his eyes hard to keep the tears from coming; a few trickled out, which he wiped on the back of his arm. Then he realized that he still had both hands full of corn. He looked around fearing that a Red Cap might notice, but none were nearby. Instead, he saw Wikatani and Dauma running to catch up to him.

"What happened?" they cried. They had been farther back in the line and had not seen what had taken place.

Chuma told them about the bag of corn ripping open. "And look what I got," he said, holding out his clenched fists. Chuma poured a little corn in the eager hands of his friends, and then put some of the kernels in his mouth.

"Aiee! Your leg is bleeding!" cried Dauma. "What happened?"

Chuma looked down. "The whip got me," he said.

Funny . . . before Dauma had mentioned it, Chuma had not noticed the torn skin on the back of his leg, but now the pain seemed to increase to the point where there was no stopping the tears. And the throbbing got worse before the caravan stopped for the night.

All night the burning ache stole Chuma's sleep. The next morning, he could not stand on that leg.

"Here," said Wikatani, "let me help you. We don't want to attract another taste of the whip."

When it was time for the caravan to get going, the two

boys hobbled off down the trail near the front of the column, staying away from the Red Caps.

They had not traveled more than an hour when they came around the top of a hill and saw below them a valley with a river winding through it. A strange village lay by the river's edge. It was strange because it was not made up of the usual mud houses with grass roofs. This village had canvas tents, something the boys had never seen before, but something that filled them with dread.

The Red Caps gestured excitedly to one another, and the leader of the Red Caps got out his tin horn and began blowing on it, announcing their arrival to the camp below.

The boys saw people stop what they were doing and look up the hill to see who was coming; others came out of the tents. Suddenly, among the people coming out of the tents, Chuma and Wikatani saw their first white man.

CHAPTER 5

DELIVERANCE

Several men from the camp came running up the trail to meet the slave caravan. Following them came a white man.

The leader of the Red Caps was tooting his horn and waving and shouting his greetings. The Red Caps seemed very proud of all the slaves they were leading down the trail. The captives now numbered eighty-four—eighty-two Manganja (after the man who had tried to escape was shot) and the two Ajawa boys. But several slaves, like Chuma, were either injured or seriously sick and barely able to travel. If the trip continued much longer, several would die.

But to the boys' surprise, as soon as the first men from the camp met the leader of the Red Caps, they grabbed him and took away his gun. Two strong men held his arms while several other men ran on up the trail and tried to catch the other Red Caps. But seeing what had happened to their leader, the other Red Caps disappeared into the forest.

"Wha—what's happening?" asked Chuma, bewildered.

By then Dauma had caught up with the boys. She stood behind Wikatani, looking around him like a child hiding behind her mother.

"I think the white man is stealing us from the Red Caps . . . and without paying for us, either," said Wikatani. "He has double-crossed them!"

Chuma was glad to see the Red Caps run off. But if the white man was stealing the slaves, it didn't help them any; a slave was a slave whether someone paid for you or not. The white man might even be crueler. "I hope we don't have to travel anymore until my leg gets better," he grumbled. He hopped around on his good leg, keeping his balance by holding on to Wikatani's shoulder.

The black men who held the leader of the Red Caps were yelling at him, demanding to know where he had gotten the slaves, from what tribe they came, and for whom he worked.

"Quiet!" ordered Wikatani as Dauma started to say something. "This might be our chance to escape." The older boy began guiding his friends back through the crowd that was gathering around the Red Cap and the new strangers who held him.

"Wait," said Dauma, pulling away from Wikatani.

The white man had arrived at the top of the hill and was also questioning the Red Cap. Chuma thought Dauma was only interested in seeing a white man for the first time. He was curious, too, but Wikatani interrupted his observation. "We can't wait," the older boy said. "This may be our only chance to get away."

"No," insisted Dauma. "Listen! The white man is not stealing us." The stranger was speaking Manganja; she could understand him better than the boys and was listening closely, trying to figure out what the white man was doing. "He's telling the Red

Cap that taking slaves is wrong. . . . He says his God is against slavery. . . . He is talking about letting us go free!"

"It's a trick," said Wikatani. "We have all heard that the white men buy slaves."

"Then just look what's happening," said Dauma.

Some of the men from the tent village were tying the Red Cap's arms behind his back. Others started going among the slaves, cutting the ropes that bound the women together by their necks. As the truth of what was happening began to dawn on the weary travelers, shouts of joy spread through the column, and the people began to run forward to be released. In their eagerness, many who were still fastened by the neck rope got tangled up. Some fell to the ground, others were choking or calling for help. Dauma ran to her mother and tried to help her get untangled; then the girl guided her mother to one of the strangers with a knife.

A cloud of dust soon concealed the eager slaves.

"I don't like it," said Wikatani. "I don't trust the white man. He is evil!" He pushed Chuma away from the trail toward the forest. "Let's get out of here before he can do whatever he's up to. Look—he's got the Red Cap's gun!"

Chuma's leg hurt fiercely as the bushes at the edge of the forest tore at it. "I don't think I can keep going," he told Wikatani. "Can't we just hide here for a little until we see if the white man is lying?"

"That won't do much good if they start looking for us."

"But why would they look for us?" Chuma sat down and rubbed his leg gently. "Look. Even if the white man is planning to take us for slaves, he doesn't know how many captives there are, and since we're not Manganja, no one else will miss us, either."

Still not convinced, Wikatani sat down beside Chuma.

"Well . . . most of the Manganja think this whole thing is our fault anyway, so, if we're gone, maybe that will just make them *sure* we were involved." Wikatani remained quiet for a few minutes. Then he said, "But I don't want Dauma to think that."

"What do you mean?"

"She trusts us. I don't want her to think we lied to her."

Chuma moved some branches aside with his hands so he could look out. "I don't think you need to worry about that," he said. "They really are letting the captives go. Look, they're cutting the yokes off the men."

Wikatani peered through the bushes. Several of the strangers were gathered around as the white man used a saw to cut the yoke that held one man's neck. Suddenly it gave way, and the yoke was pried off the man's neck. A great cheer went up among the men as the freed slave jumped to his feet and began dancing around. Other slaves were calling, "Me! Me next!" The white man gave the saw to one of his men who proceeded to free the rest.

As the boys watched from the shadows of the forest, several of the newly freed women and the children began gathering wood for fires and setting up the heavy metal pots to cook food . . . right there along the trail. Then the boys noticed that the white man was walking among the people giving instructions. They could hear his booming voice as he spoke in the Manganja language: "Set up another pot over here. Sure, go ahead and use the Red Caps' corn. Use any of their supplies! You need food, and they were making you carry it. So eat up. Have a feast."

A little farther up the trail the man knelt down beside a woman who was sitting in the dust with a sick child in her lap. With kind hands, the man felt the child's forehead and then pressed gently at different points on the child's stomach. He talked quietly to the women for a few minutes, then opened a large pouch that hung from his shoulder and poured a thick brown liquid from a bottle into a small cup, which he held to the child's lips.

The child coughed as he drank it and then made a sour face. The white man laughed and stood to his feet.

Chuma struggled to get to his feet. "He's not going to make slaves of us," he said. "I'm not staying here in the bushes anymore."

"Wait," protested Wikatani. "Maybe he poisoned the child. You saw how he laughed. It's better to stay hidden a little longer until we are sure."

"Maybe for you," said Chuma, "but my leg hurts, and he's a medicine man." He hobbled out onto the trail. "Doctor! Doctor!" he called out to the white man. "Would you fix my leg?"

Chuma followed the white man as he attended to other people who were sick. Finally the doctor noticed the boy behind him and turned. "What's the matter, son? I've never seen slavers take cripples before."

"I'm not a cripple. My leg's been hurt," said Chuma, turning so the strange man could see the back of his calf. He tried to stop his leg from trembling, but it hurt too much.

"My! What happened to you?" the man exclaimed as he stooped down to get a closer look.

"It was a whip," said Chuma.

"Mmmm, yes. But it's also infected. It looks very nasty." He withdrew a small silver tube from his bag and squeezed something from it that looked to Chuma like white grease and smeared it on the wound. Then he wrapped the boy's leg with a clean strip of cloth. "There," he said as he stood up. "Now run over there and get yourself something to eat."

But Chuma didn't move. Standing next to the tall white man he took a long look. The man wore a blue suit and blue hat, like nothing Chuma had ever seen before. His face was rough, and his sharp eyes were set deep below bushy eyebrows. *Very strange*, Chuma thought. "Doctor," Chuma said, working up courage to speak, "the Red Caps tied us up and starved us, but you cut the ropes and tell us to eat. What sort of a man are you? We thought all white men took slaves. Where do you come from?"

"Sadly, you are right, young man. Many white men buy slaves, and the Red Caps have been helping them. But I was sent to Africa by God, the great God who created everyone and wants you to be free."

"Your God does not like slavery?" asked Chuma. By then Wikatani was standing beside him.

"He hates it," said the man as he stroked a large mustache that completely covered his upper lip. "If you want, I will tell you more about God later. But now I must see to the others."

As the boys gathered with some of the other freed captives around one of the pots bubbling over a hastily built fire, they were distracted by a commotion down the trail. Chuma turned just in time to see the Red Cap leader running at top speed into the jungle. Two of the men from the tent village ran after him but the white doctor called out in his loud voice, "Let him go. He'll never bother these people again."

CHAPTER 6

"LIVINGSTONE'S
CHILDREN"

When all the men were free and everyone had eaten, the people gathered up their belongings with the remains of the Red Caps' possessions and headed down to the valley. The white doctor had invited them to set up a temporary camp along the river until they were ready to return to their home villages.

When the newcomers got to the valley, they discovered that the doctor was not the only white man in the area. From snatches of conversations he overheard, Chuma figured out that the tent village was really a temporary camp, and there were several more whites traveling with the doctor, along with the black men who were working as his porters.

As the boys dropped the bundles of supplies they'd carried down the hill, three new white men came into the little camp from the other direction. They had been up the river, bathing. The doctor went to them quickly, and the white men stood together talking seriously in low voices.

"I don't like it," said Wikatani. "They fooled us into coming to their camp, and now they will keep us as slaves. Don't forget that so far no one has tried to leave. These white men have guns and so do many of their porters. We have no chance to escape."

"You're too afraid," said Chuma. "The doctor is a *good* medicine man. My leg feels better already. I believe him."

"Well, if your leg feels better, I think we should leave tonight and go home."

"Home? That's a four-day trip! I said my leg felt better. I didn't say it was completely healed. Besides, how would we find our way?"

Just then the white men ended their discussion and the little group broke apart. They came toward the former slaves. "Gather around, please gather around," called the doctor. Then he climbed up on the stump of an old tree and started speaking.

"My name is David Livingstone, and this is Bishop Mackenzie," he said, pointing to one of the other white men. "The bishop and his assistants have come to the Shire Valley to build a mission station to tell you about the great and good God who loves all people.

"We were happy to set you free you today, and we are ready to help you return to your villages as soon as you wish. However, you are also welcome to stay here and be the first members of Bishop Mackenzie's mission station. You would be able to learn about God the Father and His Son Jesus. The bishop would teach you. You could build a village right here on the banks of the Shire River. The land is good, and we would teach you how to grow new crops, crops that you could trade for many goods. You could have a good life and help in the great work of the bishop.

"The bishop will also build a school and teach you to read and write," the doctor continued. The Manganja people nudged one another and spoke in loud undertones, shrugging their shoulders. Chuma was confused too: what did "read and write" mean? The doctor stopped, realizing that the people did not know what it meant to read. He tried to explain: "When you hear the drums, you understand the message. Right?" The people murmured their agreement. "And when you follow a trail in the jungle, you read the signs and know which animals have passed that way—a footprint here, a broken reed there, fresh droppings. In the same way, the bishop will teach you how to read little marks on paper to get the messages put there long ago by other people."

"Why would we want to learn to read such old and small signs?" someone in the crowd asked.

"They will give you much wisdom," the doctor said. "They will tell you about things and people far away; they will teach you about the one true God. God has spoken, and His words are written in a book for you to understand. Reading is very useful." He looked around the crowd. "Take time to think carefully about this offer to be part of the new mission and give us your answer in a few days."

He then got down from the tree stump, and he and the bishop strolled among the people, greeting them.

The white men and their helpers gave the former slaves machetes to cut palm branches, and the people quickly set about making temporary shelters. Chuma and Wikatani offered to help Dauma's family, but her mother said coldly, "We don't need any Ajawa help to build a hut. You have already done enough damage. Now get away from here!" And then she turned on Dauma and yelled, "I thought I told you to stay away from those Ajawa brats. If I ever see you talking to them again, I'll beat the—"

But by then Chuma and Wikatani were running down the trail away from the Manganja camp.

"She still thinks it's our fault they were captured as slaves!" Wikatani grumbled.

"It's probably hard for her to believe anything else. After all, our Ajawa warriors did attack their village and take them captive and sell them into slavery."

"But the Red Caps set it all up!" argued Wikatani.

"We know that, but how can she?" asked Chuma.

"We told Dauma, and she believes us."

"Yes, but it's not always so easy to convince adults. That tribe truly hates us."

At the edge of the clearing the boys made themselves a small lean-to. It wasn't much, but it was enough to keep off the rain.

When they finished, they went exploring. Down by the river they both gasped when they discovered the white man's smoking canoe. No smoke was coming out of the top of it, but it was so big that at first the boys thought it was a strange island in the river. There was a bridge that went from the bank to the boat, but they did not risk going up the ramp. The boat was so big that if it floated away with them, they knew that they could not paddle it back. Instead, they waded into the river and touched the side of the great boat. It was hard and cold, and when they tapped on it with a stick it sounded like a strange drum.

"It is made of iron," said Wikatani. "But that is strange; everyone knows that iron cannot float."

"It must be filled with wood," offered Chuma. "Wood floats."

"Yes. Maybe so. Maybe so."

Just then the boys heard someone coming. They quietly slipped away from the boat and swam downriver for a short distance, then climbed out to dry on a warm rock.

———

Three days later, when the friendly white men came to visit the camp of the former captives, they discovered that most of the Manganja men were missing. Chuma and Wikatani knew where they had gone. The men had returned to their homeland to join in the fight against the Ajawa. "We could follow behind them until we got close to home, then we could slip away," Wikatani had suggested the evening the men had departed.

"Sure," Chuma had countered, "but if they noticed us, we'd be dead." Still, Chuma felt deeply homesick as the men had walked single-file out of the camp.

But now the Manganja who remained—mostly women and children—were ready to give their answer to the bishop's invitation: They would stay and become part of the mission.

The bishop could not yet speak an African language that the people could understand, but when he understood the people's decision, he began talking excitedly to Doctor Livingstone. The doctor interpreted to the people: "Bishop Mackenzie is very happy with your decision. He says that you will not be sorry you have chosen this way. You will have a fine village here, and God will bless you."

Blessings or not, Chuma and Wikatani were not happy. "How will we ever get home?" said Wikatani as the boys walked away from the gathering of people.

"I don't know," admitted Chuma. "I guess we could walk by ourselves. My leg really is a lot better now. But how would we find our way? And what if there are still slave traders about?"

"Or what if we got caught in the middle of the war?" added Wikatani. "The Manganja will not think twice about killing us."

"But I don't think we can stay here in the new village," said Chuma. "I am afraid of these Manganja. Some night they might cut our throats."

"You're right, but what can we do?"

The boys had wandered away from the gathering and without intending to, came to the white men's camp. Some of the porters were working around the camp, cooking or cleaning various things. Others lounged under trees or in their own huts, which were set up alongside the white men's tents.

"What if we moved over here?" said Chuma. "Then we'd be safe."

"They'd send us back," said Wikatani.

"But why? If we talked to the doctor, maybe we could help him. Then they wouldn't send us away."

It was an idea worth trying, and the boys stayed near the edge of camp so as not to attract any attention until the doctor came back into camp. The bishop was not with him. Wikatani hung back, but Chuma ran right up to him. "Doctor, Doctor," Chuma said, "can we help you?"

"Well, if it isn't my boy with the sore leg. How's it doing? Let me have a look." The doctor stooped down and removed the well-used bandage from Chuma's leg. At this, Wikatani came closer to watch. "That looks a lot better. Does it hurt anymore?" the doctor asked.

"I hardly notice it," said Chuma, grinning.

"Good. You don't need this bandage anymore, but try to

keep the wound clean. Now you run along, and get to work on that mission station for the bishop."

"But Doctor, we want to help *you*."

"No, no, no. I don't need any more porters. Besides, you boys are a little small to carry heavy loads on the trail."

"But we could run errands for you," said Chuma eagerly.

"And we could clean things for you," offered Wikatani, "and build your fire in the morning, and—"

"And," interrupted Chuma, "we're good sheepherders."

"Sheepherders?" said Doctor Livingstone, raising one of his bushy eyebrows skeptically. "I didn't think the Manganja kept sheep."

"Oh, they don't," said Wikatani. "But we do. We're Ajawa."

"You're from the Ajawa tribe?"

"Yes. See?" Chuma said, pointing out his tribal tattoos.

"Yes, I see," said Livingstone. "Hmm. Come over here, and tell me about your village." The doctor walked over to his tent and sat on a chair. The boys had never seen a wooden chair before and inspected it carefully to see how the sticks held the man up without tipping over.

Livingstone interrupted their exploration. "Tell me where you live. How did you end up being with the Manganja?" he asked, pulling at the corners of his large moustache.

Carefully, the boys told the doctor how they were caught by the Red Caps as they were herding sheep near Lake Shirwa. They also explained how the Red Caps made it look like they had been captured by Manganja. "That started a war between our people and the Manganja," said Chuma.

"Why would that start a war?" asked the doctor.

"Because Wikatani is a chief's son," explained Chuma.

Wikatani looked distressed with the idea that the war had started because of him, and hastened to say, "But the Manganja and the Ajawa are old enemies. In almost every generation war breaks out."

"But this time it started when the slave traders made it look like the Manganja had captured you?" asked Livingstone.

"Yes," Chuma said, "and when our warriors attacked and took many captives, the Red Caps came the next day and bought them for slaves. Dauma told us so."

"Who's Dauma?"

"She's a Manganja girl," explained Wikatani.

"She's the only one who gives us any food," said Chuma. "Everyone else thinks we are the enemy."

"That's why we can't stay in the Manganja camp," explained Wikatani. "Someone will kill us—just because we are Ajawa."

The doctor didn't respond. Instead, he leaned forward with his elbows on his knees and his head in his hands. He sat that way so long the boys thought he might have gone to sleep. When he finally raised his head, there were tears in his eyes. "I'm very sorry," he said. "I'm so sorry."

"That's all right. You don't need to cry," said Chuma, unable to understand why the good doctor was so upset about their situation. "We'll be fine if you will allow us to live in your camp and help you. We won't be any trouble."

"Of course, you can stay here for now," Livingstone said, sighing heavily. "But my heart is very sad at what you have told me. I feel partially responsible for this terrible situation." The white man stood up and looked to the north, frowning. "I have come to Africa from my country to find new tribes—like the Manganja and the Ajawa—so that missionaries like Bishop Mackenzie can establish missions and schools, to tell people the good news about the great God in heaven, and His Son Jesus, who loves them. I have only recently made contact with some of your people, the Ajawa. Before my visit, the Ajawa would not allow *any* outsiders to come into their area. But as soon as I gained their trust and opened the door, other outsiders like the Red Caps have followed me and brought death and slavery with them."

Chuma and Wikatani didn't know what to say. They weren't sure that it was the doctor's fault, but they could see it was very upsetting to him.

That night in the white men's camp the boys had a good meal and slept soundly for the first time in many days.

However, the next day some of Livingstone's men intercepted another slave caravan coming through the area. This time they captured and held the Red Cap in charge and brought him to be questioned by Livingstone. It turned out that this Red Cap was the head servant for the Portuguese commander in that part of Africa.

"Does the commander know that you are buying and selling slaves?" Livingstone yelled at him.

"No, no. He does not know anything about this. He thinks I have gone to visit my relatives."

Livingstone looked at him a long time and then said, "I do not believe you. I think the Portuguese are fully aware of this terrible slave trade." Turning away, the doctor snapped, "Get him out of my sight."

"What shall we do with him?" asked one of Livingstone's men.

"I don't care."

"Shall we release him, Doctor?"

"Yes, yes. Just get him out of here."

Wikatani and Chuma followed Livingstone as he doctored and talked with the newly freed slaves, but the news they heard was very disturbing.

All the villages to the northeast were at war. Many of them—both Manganja and Ajawa—had been completely destroyed. Most of the people were either dead or had been taken captive and sold as slaves.

"The Red Caps move freely through all the area," said one old man. "They call themselves 'Livingstone's children.' But I do not know who this Livingstone is."

Livingstone winced as if he had been struck. "I am David Livingstone," he said as he cleaned a wound in the man's forehead. His voice hardened into a snarl. "But it is a lie. The Red Caps have no right claiming they are connected with me."

CHAPTER 7

A DESPERATE PLAN

"Oh, God," moaned the doctor as he walked back to his camp. The two boys following along behind were the only people to hear the pain in his voice. "Why, God? Why have you let my work lead to such tragedy for these people?"

The white man stumbled on a tree root, but hardly seemed to notice. Chuma and Wikatani weren't sure who this God was he was speaking to. "I came to Africa to bring the good news of your love. I have risked my life and worked hard to get these tribes to allow me to enter their territory. But wherever I go, the evil slave traders follow. And now they have the brashness to use my good name to gain access into tribes that were once safe from all outsiders!" He raised his voice until he was almost shouting. "My God! It's not fair! What should I do?"

The boys had never heard anyone talk to a god like this, but they knew this God must be different than the gods of their tribe.

The tall man walked along in silence for a few moments,

then suddenly turned to the boys as though he had been talk-ing to them all along. "You boys live near Lake Shirwa, don't you?"

"Yes, Doctor," answered Chuma. "Our village is right on the shore of the lake."

"My father is chief of our village," added Wikatani proudly. "Often he has taken me in his canoe on Lake Shirwa."

"That's right . . . you said you were a chief's son," said Liv-ingstone with interest. "Then I must speak to him." He turned and strode resolutely back to camp.

The boys looked at each other, startled, then hurried to catch up with the doctor. "Are you going to our village? You will take us with you?" they asked breathlessly.

The man did not answer but busied himself looking through his maps and books on the table outside his tent.

"Doctor," Chuma tried again, "can we come with you?"

Finally, the doctor stopped his rummaging and turned to the boys: "I don't see how you can. This will be a very fast trip—and dangerous, too, if all these reports of war are cor-rect. We will be heading right into the middle of the conflict. And—"

"But this may be our only chance to return to our village!" Chuma interrupted.

The doctor gave the boys a kindly smile. "I know how you must feel—you are far away from your home and family. But I will be taking only my best porters and moving fast. However, I promise that if I see your families, I'll tell them that you are here and that you're safe. Maybe they can come get you."

The boys were deeply disappointed, and their faces showed it. Certainly their families would send for them . . . if Living-stone found them. But they did not want to wait. They wanted to go home—now! Chuma started to beg the good doctor to take them, but Wikatani put his hand out and cautioned him to be quiet while Livingstone continued to study his maps.

When the doctor looked up again, he seemed surprised to see the boys still there. "What are you standing around here for? Run along and find something useful to do." They did not move. He stared at them a few more moments, then he said, "I'd like to take you home, but . . . Say, have you boys ever seen my steamboat?" He grinned at the boys as he changed the subject. "Tell you what. I'll give you a tour of the *Pioneer*. I'll bet you've never been on board a steamboat before. I've got to go down there anyway, so come on. Maybe I can find something useful for you to do."

The boys followed the doctor reluctantly. They knew he was trying to distract them from their determination to return home with him. His smoking canoe might interest them at some other time, but if he thought they would forget their longing to return home, he was mistaken.

When they were on board, the boat seemed even bigger than before. It didn't even move when all three walked up the ramp and stepped on deck. "See how big it is," said the doctor. Chuma noted the size of the deck, but all he could think about was his home: *A whole herd of sheep could fit in back and there'd still be room for all the boys in our village to play a game up front.*

"In the rainy season, when the water is high, I can travel up the river in much less time than if I were trying to go overland through the swampy lowlands. And of course, it would take hundreds of porters to transport what the boat can carry," explained the doctor. "On the other hand," he laughed, "if the water in the river is too low, the boat gets stuck on sandbars, and it takes forever to make the trip."

A house was built in the middle of the boat while a canvas

awning sheltered the front and back decks. On each side of the boat were huge wheels with paddles on them. "The engine makes these wheels go around and they push the boat along," explained Livingstone. *Just like paddling a canoe on Lake Shirwa*, thought Chuma.

"This is a very wonderful boat," said Wikatani politely, trying to sound grateful for the doctor's attention.

"The fact is," said Livingstone, "this old tub is nearly ready to sink. We've patched it up so many times, you can't tell what's the boat and what's a patch. I've ordered a completely new riverboat built in England—spent every last penny I own to do it, too. It will be taken apart, and the pieces will be loaded on a great seagoing ship and brought to Africa by the end of the year. Then we'll put it back together and have something worth traveling in. Maybe I'll take you boys on a trip in it. Would you like that?"

What we'd like is to go home, now, with you, thought Chuma, but he didn't say it. Instead he politely asked, "Where is the smoke for this smoking canoe?"

" 'Smoking canoe,' is it?" laughed the doctor. "Well, there's got to be some fire before we get any smoke. Come with me." Taking the boys into the engine room, he showed them the big boilers that made the steam to drive the boat. The boys had never seen so much metal, all of it shiny like silver and gold.

"How would you boys like to polish the brass on this engine?" offered Livingstone. "It'll give you something to do."

The boys just stared at him sadly.

The doctor let out a long sigh and ran his fingers through his unruly hair. "Listen, you boys must understand one thing: my most important objective is to get this war stopped." He pointed a bony finger at Wikatani. "The fact that your father is a village chief may be of some help—if I can find him. . . ."

The doctor stopped and stared at the boys for a long minute. Then he broke into a big smile and clapped his hands together as he said, "Why didn't I think of that before? Of course, of course. You boys are the key. You are the ones who can prove that the Manganja did not steal you—that there is no cause for this war. And with you along to tell your story, I can stop these rumors that the Red Caps work for me. Of course you can come!"

"Thank you, Doctor! Thank you!" both boys said gleefully.

"We leave in the morning—overland," the doctor said abruptly as he headed out the engine room door and stomped off the boat.

The boys followed him, playfully punching each other on the shoulder. "I didn't see any wood to keep this thing afloat," whispered Wikatani as they ran up the ramp.

"Well, the doctor said it is about ready to sink. That's probably why," noted Chuma.

———

The boys were up before the sun rose the next morning. "I'm going down to the river to bathe," announced Chuma. "It seems like a good thing to bathe before such an important journey."

"You go ahead. I'm going to see Dauma," said Wikatani in a secretive whisper.

"But what about her mother?" asked Chuma.

"She won't catch me."

"You want me to come?," asked Chuma.

"No. You go on down to the river. I'll be there as soon as I tell Dauma good-bye."

"Then tell her good-bye for me, too," said Chuma, and the boys went off in different directions.

"Today we leave for home. Today we leave for home," Chuma chanted quietly to himself as he walked down to the river.

The eastern sky was a bright pink, casting an eerie glow everywhere, silhouetting the doctor's boat like a great mountain against the sky. Somehow the strange light made everything look unfamiliar, or maybe it was because today he was going home, and that made the whole world look different. But there was also an odd smell in the air, like sour smoke—not the smoke that rose in thin wisps from last night's campfires.

The boy slid down the bank to the river's edge. The tied-up steamboat sheltered the water near the bank from the river's fast current and only small waves played along the muddy bank. Chuma jumped in the water and glided toward the side of the steamer. Two ducks scurried around the back end of the boat, trying to get away without having to take to the air.

Then Chuma noticed two strange objects bobbing in the water under the boat's huge paddle wheel. Whatever they were, they were caught there by the river's current. They were round, dark, and smooth, floating just at the surface of the water. *Probably just pieces of driftwood*, he thought. He'd seen driftwood worn smooth and shiny by bumping along the river rapids mile after mile. He swam toward the paddle wheel, thinking he would remove the logs so they wouldn't jam when the big wheel turned.

He touched one of the objects and it rolled over.

"Aieee!" he screamed at the top of his lungs and swam for the shore. He kept on screaming as he scrambled up the bank and ran for the camp.

Instantly everyone in camp was awake and coming out of their tents. Some of the men had picked up their guns.

"What's the matter, Chuma?" boomed David Livingstone when he saw the boy running toward him.

Chuma pointed back toward the river. His mouth hung open, his eyes wide. Finally he said in a hoarse whisper, "A body . . . two of them—in the river."

The men ran down to the shore. As they pulled the bodies from between the paddles of the riverboat, Wikatani noticed the tribal markings and whispered, "Ajawa."

The doctor sighed. "Probably war victims. Call the bishop; we must bury them. Then we'd better get on our way. Things aren't getting any better between the Ajawa and the Manganja."

Chuma and Wikatani looked at each other in horror. For the first time, Chuma realized his own family might be in serious danger.

CHAPTER 8

AMBUSH!

The sun had already begun to slide toward the horizon when Chuma noticed the same sour, smoky smell he had whiffed that morning. The little party had been traveling at a good pace all day. The group included Doctor Livingstone, six porters—each carrying a load of supplies and trade goods—and the two Ajawa boys.

"I don't remember any of this country. Do you?" asked Wikatani.

"No. It must be a different route than the Red Caps took."

"I hope the doctor knows where he's going."

"He's got maps," assured Chuma.

They worked their way down a steep, wooded hill to a small river. On the other side, several canoes were grounded on a small beach beneath a steep cliff.

"There's a Manganja village up there that I visited when I came through here two years ago," said Livingstone as they waded across the shallows. "The canoes are still here, but where are the children? Why aren't they coming out to meet us?"

Climbing the trail to the top of the cliff, Chuma worried whether the Manganja would welcome them when they realized the boys were Ajawa. But the village was empty; every house had been burned. Chuma then realized that the strange smell came from burning huts. On the still night air, the smoke had drifted throughout that part of the Shire River Valley.

"Where are the people?" asked Wikatani.

"Dead . . . or fleeing the war," said one of the porters grimly.

In the ruins of one of the houses they found the body of a woman—possibly someone too sick or old to flee. They buried the body and then sat under a tree near the edge of the village while Livingstone studied his map. After a time he looked up at the boys and said in a very tired voice, "I think if we are going to find your village, we'd better turn east here and go around the bottom of Mount Zomba and approach Lake Shirwa from the south.

"We had a good march today," he announced to everyone. "My guess is that the Manganja who lived here are either captured or still on the run and too afraid to return. And since the Ajawa know this village has already been defeated, I doubt that they will return. So, let's stay here for the night."

But the porters let out a loud protest. The idea of sleeping where people had been killed and homes burned terrified them. So the party hiked east until darkness forced them to stop and make camp.

That night, however, they built no fires, not wanting to attract any attention. They also posted two guards all night. Chuma and Wikatani took their turns on guard, though not at the same time.

"What was it like? Did you fall asleep?" asked Chuma when Wikatani woke him for his turn in the middle of the night.

"Are you kidding?" said Wikatani. "I was too scared that someone would sneak up on our camp."

The next morning as they hiked east they began meeting Manganja fleeing the war. At first there were just one or two at a time, but soon they passed whole families. Some people had wounds that Doctor Livingstone tried to treat as quickly as he could. But his greatest urgency was to get to the front and make contact with the leaders of those who were fighting in the hope of achieving peace.

Around midday they came to another deserted, burned village. No dead were found, but corn was dumped out of the storehouses and spilled all over the ground. A few scraggly chickens pecked at it but flew away, squawking when anyone came near.

In the afternoon the little party saw the smoke of other burning villages. In the distance they could hear shouts of victory mixed with the cries of women mourning over their dead. They had traveled a few miles out onto an open plain with high grass, huge boulders, and occasional trees when one of the porters pointed out a line of Ajawa warriors coming down a distant trail with Manganja captives.

"This is our chance," said Livingstone. "Maybe I can reason with them and arrange a meeting with the chiefs."

But when the two groups met, one of the Manganja captives recognized Livingstone and started yelling, "Our general has come! The white man will free us! The white man will free us!" Other Manganja joined in, and for a few moments there was great confusion. The Ajawa warriors panicked and fled, yelling, "War! War!" Then the Manganja also ran off in the opposite direction, toward the distant hills, leaving Livingstone and his party standing alone in the open country, unable to talk peace with anyone.

"Why did he start yelling that I was their general and liberator?" said Livingstone, taking his blue cap off and slapping it on his leg in frustration. "Where did he get that idea?"

"Excuse me, Doctor," Wikatani offered, "but I think I recognized the man. He was one of the slaves of the Red Caps. We traveled together before you freed us."

"Of all the . . . I should have known," said the doctor in disgust as he sat down on a rock. "He was one of those men who did not stay to help build the mission. They probably told the story to every Manganja they met. And he thought I was going to free him again. Now we'll never make contact with the Ajawa."

But he was wrong.

The white man and his companions had traveled only a short distance when a much larger number of Ajawa warriors appeared, closing in on the little group from both sides. "Down!" yelled Livingstone. Chuma and Wikatani dropped to the ground and crawled behind an enormous ant hill; Livingstone and the porters took cover in the tall grass and behind the few rocks at hand. As the Ajawa came closer, Chuma caught glimpses of movement as the warriors darted skillfully through the tall grass from rock to bush to tree. When they were within a hundred yards, they began shooting their arrows at Livingstone and his men.

Their accuracy was amazing and would have been deadly if the travelers had not taken cover so quickly. The porters had their guns ready and would have shot back, but Livingstone kept saying, "Hold your fire! We don't want bloodshed." Then he called out in a loud voice, "Ajawa warriors! We have not come to fight, but to talk peace!" But the number of arrows flying toward them seemed only to increase.

Finally, in desperation, Wikatani scrambled onto the ant hill, stood up, and yelled in the native Ajawa language, "Don't shoot! Don't shoot! I am Ajawa!" Chuma was ready to join him when Wikatani let out a yell and fell back down to the ground with an arrow through his left arm.

"We've got to get out of here," said Livingstone, moving quickly to Wikatani's side. He pulled the arrow from the boy's arm and pressed hard to stop the flow of blood. "They're not going to listen to reason."

Chuma raised his head and saw the Ajawa warriors advancing on their position more quickly, doing a wild war dance as they came to within fifty yards. One of the porters shouted, "Doctor, they are surrounding us! The trail is cut off!"

Livingstone was tying his handkerchief tightly around Wikatani's arm. "Then we'll have to fight our way out," he said grimly. It was exactly what the frightened porters had been waiting for. They opened fire with their guns and soon the Ajawa warriors pulled back.

"I hit two!" one of the men cheered. "I got one!" said another. In all, the porters claimed to have shot six Ajawa, but when the doctor climbed to the top of the ant hill and surveyed the area, no dead or wounded could be seen.

"Let's go before they return," he ordered, and the group moved warily back up the trail toward the protection of the forest.

As they reached the safety of the jungle trail, Livingstone walked between the two boys with a hand on each of their shoulders. "I'm very, very sorry," he said. "I did not want to shoot at your people."

Chuma felt uncomfortable. He had been afraid and was

glad when the fighting stopped. But he had also felt angry when the porters began shooting their guns at Ajawa warriors—his own people. But seeing how discouraged the doctor looked, he finally said, "You couldn't help it."

"Maybe not," Livingstone said. "But I have been in Africa for twenty years; I have been face-to-face with some of the fiercest chiefs in the whole land; I have been within an inch of losing my life . . . but I have never before had to shoot at an African. I have always found another way." The doctor walked in silence for a few minutes, then said, "It feels like the end of my work here. Word will spread; how will the people ever trust me?"

Chuma looked at Wikatani; pain etched the other boy's face from the wound in his arm. But both boys seemed to realize that their friend the doctor was also struggling with pain.

Toward evening the travelers came upon a group of Manganja refugees fleeing for their lives. Livingstone invited them to share their fire, hopeful that the increased numbers would be sufficient protection from attack.

"What do you know of the fighting around Lake Shirwa?" the white man asked their guests, gently cleaning Wikatani's wound in the firelight and putting medicine on it from the shiny tube.

"There is no fighting there," said the head man.

"Is it possible to get there from here?"

"No. Terrible fighting is between here and there; there is no way through."

"How do you know that there is no fighting around Lake Shirwa?" asked Wikatani, wincing as Livingstone bandaged his arm.

"Because Manganja hold all of Lake Shirwa now," the man said proudly. "We have taken it from those treacherous hyenas, the Ajawa." The man snarled out the last words, staring directly at the boys. Both Chuma and Wikatani shivered. Did he know they were Ajawa?

The doctor frowned. "What happened to the villages around the lake?"

When the man answered, he did not turn to the doctor but continued staring at the boys. "All—Ajawa—villages—have—been—burned." He spat out each word distinctly. "The only Ajawa near Lake Shirwa are dead ones whose bones are being picked clean by buzzards. Soon that will be the fate of all Ajawa."

CHAPTER 9

THE RAGING RIVER

"I know both of you want to return to your families," Living-stone spoke to the boys the next morning as they prepared to leave the camp of the Manganja refugees, "but I cannot risk repeating what happened yesterday. If what the Manganja say is true, the villages around Lake Shirwa have been destroyed, and the likelihood of finding your families there is not good. . . . And even if we did," he said, seeing the fear in their eyes, "it wouldn't be safe for you to remain in this part of the country right now."

"But . . . what will we do?" Chuma asked, disappointment sticking in his throat.

"Come back to the mission station with me. If I had been able to avoid bloodshed, we might have arranged safe passage through the war zone to reach the chiefs. They are the only real hope for bringing peace to this senseless war. But now . . ." Livingstone shook his head. " . . . we are likely to be targets for their arrows whenever we encounter Ajawa."

It was a dejected and weary band that cautiously set out down the trail. No longer did they march along with confidence. Livingstone decided that the only safe way to travel was by stealth if they did not want to have to use their guns again. So he sent out a man to scout the trail ahead, and only when it was clear would the rest of the party silently follow.

Once, when the scout discovered a party of Ajawa warriors resting beside a stream, Livingstone decided they should leave the trail and cut through the dense jungle to circle far around the warriors. It was an exhausting detour. At times they found themselves in the middle of brambles with seemingly no way out. The thorns caught and would not let go. If each one was not carefully unhooked, it would tear skin or clothes. Worse, the bramble vines were so tough that they required several hacks from a machete before they would give way.

"Quiet! Quiet!" Livingstone would whisper when someone would yelp or curse with the difficulty. "We must not announce our presence."

Finally they came upon the trail of a herd of elephants and followed along with more ease where the beasts had beaten down the jungle in their passing.

The second night of their return trip was spent without any shelter or fire while a hard, chilling rain fell. "But Doctor," protested some of the porters, "no warriors will be moving about in weather like this."

"Good warriors will endure anything. Good peacemakers must do the same. No fires here!"

It rained most of the next day and only let up in the evening as the tired party trudged into the burned-out village on the cliff above the river.

"I still think this village is safe," said Livingstone. "If you can find dry wood that makes no smoke, I think we could have a small fire tonight. But try to shield it from view."

The porters did not want to spend the night in the burned-out village, but the prospect of sleeping in the cold, wet jungle again drove them to brave it. They found a couple of huts with their roofs still in place.

Later, Livingstone spread his map by the fire and said, "I think this little river dumps into the Shire River just a few miles above the mission station. If those abandoned canoes are still down there on the beach, we could use them. It would be farther—two legs of a triangle, to the west and then south rather than cutting directly cross-country—but it would be safer than traveling through the jungle."

"Yes, but Doctor," said one of the porters, "the great rapids and waterfalls begin just above the mission station. They go on for many miles. Once we hit the Shire River, we'd be in the worst of them."

"Indeed, the Murchison cataracts are too rough to take my steamboat up, but don't you think canoes could come down quite safely?"

"Doctor, they are terrible. Many people have lost their lives in them."

"Well," said Livingstone, folding up his map, "if it gets too bad, we'll just put ashore and walk."

———

Travel on the small river the next morning was a pleasant change from hacking through the jungle. After assuring Doctor Livingstone that they were skilled in handling a canoe, having used one often on Lake Shirwa, Chuma and Wikatani were allowed to share a small canoe of their own. Three other canoes made up the remainder of their flotilla. Livingstone and two porters were in one, while the other two canoes carried two porters each plus most of their supplies.

"We still must travel in silence," warned the doctor, and it was good advice. An hour later they were gliding through an area where the jungle hung far out over the river from each bank, almost touching the water. Suddenly there was yelling from both sides of the river just behind them, and a shower of arrows sailed after them. One arrow landed harmlessly in the bottom of the last canoe as the whole party paddled hard to get out of range.

"That was too close," murmured Wikatani as they sprinted around a bend in the river.

"If they had heard us coming and been ready, we would have been like big fish in a little pool. No one could have missed," said Chuma.

Where the small river joined the Shire River, a herd of hippopotami were swimming in the shallows. The paddlers steered well out of their way, knowing that the round, gentle-looking animals are some of the most dangerous animals in Africa. They do not like to be disturbed and can easily crush a canoe with a single bite of their powerful jaws.

But by watching the hippopotami, the travelers were taken by surprise when the four canoes suddenly swept out onto the angry Shire River. Instantly, they were shot downstream with a force that the paddlers couldn't resist. At that point there were no rapids, so the surface was deceptively smooth, but the speed with which the water moved was far beyond anything the boys had ever encountered. They could feel the powerful water drawing them this way and that with a will of its own.

Within less than a mile, they came to the rapids. They were so steep and turbulent that as their canoe came upon them, it looked like they were ready to slide down a white mountain.

"Look out!" yelled Chuma, who was sitting in the back. But there was nothing Wikatani could do as a huge wave of water came over the bow of the canoe and landed in his lap with the weight of a bag of corn being dropped from a tree. The gallons of water in the bottom of the canoe made it heavy and even more difficult to handle.

"Straighten us out," screamed Wikatani over his shoulder as the current swept the canoe sideways toward a huge rock sticking out of the river. Chuma paddled hard, knowing that if the canoe hit the rock broadside, it would break in half like dried reed. But the current was too powerful; he could do nothing to straighten the canoe. And then, at the last moment, the bulge of water rising up before the rock swung their canoe around, and they shot past it down into the trough beyond like an eagle swooping down on its prey. But then they faced a mountain of water. The little craft rose on the curling wave and seemed to hang in midair for a moment and then came down, dumping both boys into the raging river.

The water around Chuma churned white with bubbles, and the strong current sucked him deeper into the darkness below. He kicked hard as he fought for the surface, but there was no resisting the cold monster that clutched him in its grasp. Down, down he went until all was blackness, and he had no idea which way was up. Suddenly something raked the length of his back like the claws of a lion, and his head crashed into stone. He tumbled helplessly over and over along the bottom of the vengeful torrent. The river was intent on knocking every bit of breath out of him.

It began to get lighter, and Chuma noticed bubbles swirling around him. Were they his air, knocked from his lungs, or was he rising to the foaming surface? And then the river spat him out, and he flew into the air, face up with legs and arms outstretched toward the dazzling blue sky. For an instant he looked back over his shoulder and saw what must have happened. Above him was a roaring waterfall. Somehow he had plunged over it and been driven to the bottom of the pool below, then was coughed up by the river.

He landed back on the water with a stinging splat and righted himself quickly. *Where is Wikatani? Where is the canoe?* He looked around desperately. Twenty yards downstream he caught a glimpse of Wikatani, clinging to the bottom of their overturned canoe as it bobbed on down the river. Chuma took a big breath and then struck out, swimming toward his friend. *At least he is alive,* Chuma thought.

Something rose to the surface to his right. It was someone's clothes—dark blue, like the doctor's. *I should get them for him,* the boy thought. But he was too exhausted and had swallowed too much water. *I better just save myself, otherwise I might not make it.* And then Chuma realized that it was more than the doctor's blue jacket. It was the doctor himself, floating face down in the swirling water!

"Help!" Chuma yelled to anyone who might hear. He altered his course and swam for the blue patch, hoping it would not be sucked under before he got there. But the river was playing more tricks on him and kept moving the doctor away.

"Oh, God," gasped Chuma, "if you are the black man's God, too, as the doctor says, don't let him die. Help me . . . help me reach him in time." Finally, in one last sprint, Chuma reached out and grasped the back of the blue jacket. He rolled it over and pulled the doctor's face above water. There was a wound over one eye, and the older man didn't seem to be breathing. Chuma got a big handful of the white man's lank hair and tried swimming toward the western shore.

But the river bank was too far away; he would never make

it. Every time he tried to take a fresh breath, a wave slapped him in the face, leaving him coughing and gasping. He seemed to take in more water than he spat out. Then, when he was about to give up, a rock island appeared right in front of him. He maneuvered to get his feet around in front of himself to catch his weight so they wouldn't crash into the rock too hard. When he hit, he got a footing on the upstream side, then reached for a handhold to pull himself up onto the slab of rock. He really needed two hands, but he was holding on to the doctor with the other. Grunting and straining, he pulled and pulled on the handhold and finally rolled to safety just as the current caught the doctor's body and swung him around downstream. Chuma almost lost his handhold. With all his might he wrestled the doctor out of the grip of the terrible current, then dragged the doctor up onto the smooth stone beside him.

The boy lay panting for a moment, but knew he couldn't wait if the doctor had any chance of living. He rolled the soaking man over onto his stomach; the doctor's legs still hung in the river, buffeted by the rushing water. Chuma sat on top of the man and pressed all his weight into the middle of the man's back. Chuma raised himself then pressed back down. Again and again he did the same. Suddenly a great stream of water gushed out of the doctor's mouth and he began coughing and choking. Chuma rolled off and collapsed on the rock beside him.

Then everything went black.

CHAPTER 10

THE SECOND JOURNEY

Chuma awoke in the shade of a spreading acacia tree, its flowers giving a sweet smell to the warm air. Faces etched with concern were staring down at him. He looked from one to the other: the doctor—his clothes still dripping wet; Wikatani; and all six porters. Everyone had survived.

"How did I get here?"

"All our canoes were lost—except one, thank God," said the doctor. "With it some of the men were able to come over and take us off that island."

Chuma sat up, but quickly wished he hadn't moved. His back burned like fire.

"I want to thank you. You saved my life . . . at a great risk to yourself. But," the doctor said as he turned Chuma to look at his back, "I'm afraid I lost all my medicine and have nothing to put on those scratches on your back. Looks like you tangled with a lion," he chuckled.

"I think it was just a river—but it almost won," said Chuma.

"Well, I think you'll be all right until we get something for it. But we'd better get going, if you feel well enough to walk. It's going to take another full day or maybe even longer to get back to the mission station."

———

In the days and weeks that followed at the mission station, Chuma and Wikatani often worried about what the Manganja warriors had said about their village. "What if our families are all dead as that Manganja said?" said Wikatani one day. Both boys had been afraid to put their worst fears into words.

Chuma thought for a long time. When he broke the silence, there were tears in his eyes. "If they are, I will stay with the doctor and be a Christian. But we do not know that. We cannot give up hope."

"Besides," said Wikatani. "The Manganja like to boast. He was just trying to scare us. But . . . we must go back and let our families know we are alive."

It was only a couple of days later that Livingstone called the boys to him while he was sitting outside his tent studying his maps.

"I have heard reports of another lake to the north of your homeland. It is said to be a very great body of water. Do you know of it?" he said, looking up at the boys standing beside his table.

Chuma shrugged, but Wikatani said, "I have heard of it. It is called *Nyassa*."

"Yes, Lake Nyassa," mused the doctor, pulling at the corners of his moustache. "Have you ever seen it?"

"No, Doctor, but my father has."

"He has? Did he tell you anything about it?"

"Only that it is very, very long. One old man told him that if you started as a boy, you'd be an old man before you finished walking around it."

"Really?"

"He said it, but everyone else laughed and said it would take two months to walk around it—but it can't be done."

"Why not?"

"I don't know."

"That's still pretty big. I must explore this Lake Nyassa. It may be the key to stopping the slave traders."

The boys did not understand.

"You see," the doctor continued, punching a point on the map with his finger, "if we could get a steamboat onto Lake Nyassa, we could bring in the supplies and people to set up a mission station there. I could claim that part of the country for England, and it would be out from under the control of the Portuguese slavers. *Then* we could be much more effective in stopping this terrible slave trade."

"But, Doctor," said Chuma, "how would you get your steamboat beyond the rapids?"

David Livingstone shrugged. "That's why I must explore the lake. If it is as big as you say, then it has to have another outlet besides the Shire River." Livingstone got up and started pacing around his camp, slamming his right fist into the palm of his left hand with each step. He whirled and pointed at Wikatani. "Did your father say anything about a river running out of the lake to the east all the way to the sea?"

"No."

"Well, there must be one, and I will find it. The whole geography of the region demands one."

As the boys left the doctor's camp, Wikatani turned to Chuma and said excitedly, "Did you look at the doctor's map?"

"Yes. What about it?"

"We could not get home from the south because of the terrible fighting between us and Lake Shirwa. But what if we approached Lake Shirwa from the north?"

"There might not be so much fighting up there."

"Right," said Wikatani eagerly. "If we could go on this expedition with Doctor Livingstone, we could travel up the Shire River, around all the fighting to Lake Nyassa to the north—"

"From there," interrupted Chuma eagerly as he saw the plan, "we could come down to our homeland."

———

The boys had to do some fast talking, but three days later they were again part of the doctor's expedition. They did not, however, tell him their real hopes for wanting to go along.

The Murchison cataracts that began just above the mission station on the Shire River did not allow for any boat travel. So four porters carried a four-oared rowboat as they headed north along the west bank of the river. Two more men went ahead and cleared the way with machetes. Livingstone preceded them, trying to scout out the easiest path—which was never very easy as they were always going steeply uphill. Chuma and Wikatani followed, loaded down with the heavy oars, the sail, and an awning. "When we get on that lake, we'll be glad for this sail," the doctor had said. "And the awning will protect us from the sun day after day."

When the men were exhausted, they put the boat down and everyone got a rest—if you could call it that—while all but two (left as guards) hiked back to pick up their supplies. Then everyone hoisted boxes and bundles onto their backs and carried them up to the point where they had left the boat. Then they did it all again.

On a good day, this routine was repeated three or four times.

Along the way, the boys marveled that they had ever tried to come down the river in canoes. Often they would hike for miles along the top edge of a deep gorge with the raging river at the bottom and no shore at the water's edge where they could have sought safety or taken a rest.

Once Livingstone showed the boys the map. "The Murchison cataracts on the Shire River are forty miles long. I think the Lord God was protecting us by getting us out of that river as quickly as He did," the doctor admitted.

Soon they passed the point where their canoes had come out of the small river onto the Shire. But it took a total of three weeks of torturous work portaging the rowboat overland before the party arrived at a point where they could safely put it in the river.

Having finally arrived at calm water, they took a day to rest, hunt for fresh meat, and prepare for the next leg of their journey.

Travel on the river the next day was a pleasant relief from the constant toil of carrying their heavy loads uphill. The water was relatively smooth, and their rowing—while hard work—made good progress.

Along the rapids they had not seen any signs of the tribal war. But that day, in the rolling hills to the east, a great pillar of black smoke rose high into the silvery sky. Since the area was mostly green jungle, it did not seem likely that the fire was accidental but probably a village that had been put to the torch.

That night they camped at the base of a cliff in a damp,

marshy area. "No fires tonight," said Livingstone. "We don't want to attract any attention."

Later, as everyone slapped at the mosquitoes that would not let them eat in peace, Chuma decided it was time to bring up their plan.

"Doctor Livingstone, when we get to Lake Nyassa, won't we be almost straight north of Lake Shirwa?"

"Almost, Chuma. Why do you ask?"

"Wikatani and I were thinking that it might be safe to travel to Lake Shirwa if we came down from the north since the battles we ran into were south of the lake."

The doctor sat silently for a few moments, a deep frown creasing his forehead as he pulled at his mustache. "It might be possible," he finally agreed. "But here we are almost straight west of Lake Shirwa and we saw that burning village today. So the fighting is not only in the south. But why do you ask?"

"We were wondering," jumped in Wikatani, "whether, when you got that far north, you might decide to go south to meet the Ajawa chiefs."

"And you could take us with you to find our families," added Chuma.

Livingstone got up and walked down to the water's edge. The boys did not know whether he was angry or not. Finally, he strode back to the rest of them. "I *had* hoped to bring a quick end to this fighting by trying to reach the Ajawa chiefs," he explained. "But we failed. Since then, I've come to feel that God has a larger purpose for me: I believe we *must* establish a mission base in the interior. It's the only way to break the back of this wicked slave trade—"

"But you wanted to stop the war. Remember?" said Chuma.

"Yes, and I would still give my life to accomplish that. But

I must not be shortsighted. I do not know how much longer the Portuguese will allow me to remain in this part of Africa. We must establish a permanent base farther north—around Lake Nyassa—and the only hope is to find a waterway from it to the sea. Then I can get a steamboat with supplies into the interior."

All the porters were quiet and listening intently.

"You see, as terrible as this tribal war is," Livingstone went on, "there is a more serious mission. The bishop and others like him want to bring the Gospel—the story about God's Son, Jesus—to all these tribes. Jesus showed people a new way to live with one another. He forgave His enemies; He showed that everyone—old and young, men, women, and children, black and white—is important to God. Most important, Jesus died to take the punishment for our sins, so that all of us can live with God in heaven forever."

No one spoke. This was something to think about.

"You see, the only real way to stop the slavers and the fighting is to change people's hearts. If the people hear the Gospel, maybe they will obey God's commandments and stop warring with one another and selling people into slavery."

Livingstone looked kindly at Chuma and Wikatani. "I'm sorry, my young friends. I must try for the greater purpose first. We must go on to Lake Nyassa and find the river to the sea. Then maybe we can make another attempt to reach the Ajawa chiefs."

CHAPTER 11

LAKE NYASSA

In the afternoon of the next day a breeze arose along the river; Livingstone put up the sail, and they moved along even faster than the men could row. What a welcomed rest! Chuma and Wikatani had never seen a sailing vessel, let alone ridden in one. "We are like kings with invisible slaves rowing us along," Chuma grinned.

Three days more they traveled with much the same routine, rowing in the morning and sailing in the afternoon, until— four weeks after leaving the mission station—the river mouth widened and they came out onto Lake Nyassa. It was so big, the water seemed to run right into the sky. Doctor Livingstone was even more excited than the boys; he wrote the date in a little book and read it to the boys: "We found Lake Nyassa on September second, 1861."

Beaching the boat on a gentle bank, the travelers were met by hundreds of Africans who had never seen a white man before. Even the men were very curious, wanting to touch Livingstone's skin and feel his strange, limp hair.

The people were friendly and eagerly provided plenty of food for the newcomers, including fish from the lake. However, they did not speak a language that any of the travelers could understand, so communication was very difficult. But Chuma and Wikatani were impressed with the doctor's skill in learning a new language. Before the evening was over he had mastered dozens of words and could put together a few simple sentences to the great amusement of the local people.

Each day the little boat of explorers traveled farther north on the great lake and spent the evening in a new village on the shore. As soon as Livingstone was able to communicate with the people, he began telling them about Jesus, how He was the Son of the only true God, and that He had come to earth to tell everyone of God's love and forgiveness of sin. The people listened attentively, but few responded. "That's all right," said the doctor. "I planted a seed."

At every stop Livingstone also asked if there was a river that flowed east out of the lake. But every person he questioned gave a different answer. One man declared positively that they could sail right out of the lake on such a river; but the next man said, no, they would need to hike overland fifty or even a hundred miles before reaching a river of any size.

"We're going to have to see for ourselves," Livingstone said stubbornly.

But as they made their way along the shore of the great lake, trouble began to develop. One night robbers crept into their camp while they slept and stole nearly all their supplies. The most serious loss was their food and trade goods. The trade goods were important in making friends with new tribes and in paying tolls to the chiefs for permission to pass through their territory.

The next night no one met them when they beached their boat. Pushing into the surrounding jungle, the travelers found a village burned to the ground and strewn with rotting bodies. "More tribal warfare," Livingston muttered, poking through the ruins. "I'll bet the slavers are behind this, too."

Once again the porters insisted that they leave the place of death; they rowed by moonlight until they saw a deserted beach and pulled toward shore.

But no sooner had they landed than a large group of warriors ran out of the jungle, painted for war and waving their spears fiercely. "Mazitu!" one of the porters cried fearfully. As the warriors advanced, the porters immediately raised their guns. With nothing to trade, Chuma was sure they would have to resort to their guns again to avoid being killed.

"Wait!" Livingstone ordered. At the last minute he rolled up his sleeves and opened his shirt, exposing the whiteness of skin that had not been tanned by the sun. In the moonlight his skin shone pale and ghostly. The warriors stopped in their tracks. Cautiously, one moved forward, his spear extended. He brought the tip to Livingstone's chest and drew it down slowly across the skin. The tiny trickle of blood that followed the sharp point looked black, rather than red, in the strange, pale light.

Suddenly the warriors let out a frightened cry, turned, and fled back into the jungle.

Startled, the little group stood staring at the dark edge of the jungle that had swallowed up the fierce warriors.

One of the porters finally broke the silence. "We must not continue!" he declared. "We have no food and nothing to trade for more. The next war party may not be so scared by your trick. It is time to go back."

"Yes. Yes. We must go back," the others insisted.

But Livingstone protested and there was a big argument. Finally he convinced the men to go on one more day in hopes of moving out of the war-torn area.

They posted guards that night as had become their custom wherever trouble threatened, and it was Chuma's lot to draw guard duty with Doctor Livingstone. Because they had set up camp on the open beach, no one could approach the camp without being seen. The guards did not have to patrol so much as watch over the camp in the moonlight. Chuma and the doctor chose the top of a small dune near their sleeping companions and sat down.

When all was quiet, Chuma said, "Doctor, I would like to become a Christian like you, and follow your God."

"That's good, Chuma. But tell me, why do you want to do this?"

"Well, you could have ordered those warriors shot tonight, but God gave you great courage to do a good thing."

"Yes, He did, Chuma. But what if I had not had that courage?"

Chuma thought for a while. "I still think you would have *wanted* the good thing. I think you really love the African people."

"But *why* do you think I love Africans?"

"Because you love God, and God loves all people. That's why God sent His Son, Jesus, to die for us." Chuma grinned, remembering what he had heard the bishop and the doctor say.

"That's right, Chuma. And you must remember that. Even if I completely fail to do what's right, Jesus did not fail. Put your trust in Him, not in how well other people behave."

They listened in quietness to the waves gently lapping at the beach, then Chuma asked, "But, how do I become a Christian?"

"Well, you know that we're all sinners. And that's more than occasionally doing an evil thing like lying or stealing—those, of course, are sins. Even when we try hard to do good—like I'm trying to find a way to stop the slave trade—it doesn't always work out. And sometimes we make things worse, and people get hurt. Then we realize how badly we need someone to save us."

"I know that, and that's what I want. I want Jesus to save me. But how?"

"The Bible says, 'As many as received him, to them gave he power to become the sons of God, even to them that believe on his name.' Do you believe that, Chuma? Do you want to give your life to Jesus?"

"Yes."

They talked some more, and then Chuma prayed. The next morning before setting out, Doctor Livingstone baptized Chuma in the lake as a new Christian while the others watched.

———

That night, when the explorers stopped, they were met by local people who laughed at them and thought they were fleeing from the Mazitu. For some reason—Chuma never found out why—a shoving match started between the porters and the villagers that soon broke into a fight with sticks. Livingstone did his best to stop it, and the local people finally withdrew sullenly. The travelers made camp, but decided not to sleep by the fire. Instead, they made beds filled with grass to look like sleeping people and crawled away into the nearby tall grass to sleep. Once again they posted guards to watch over the camp.

In the middle of the night, warriors snuck into the camp and stabbed their spears into the fake sleepers. When they realized they had been fooled, they ran away, thinking that the trick was an ambush.

The continual obstacles and constant threat of harm from tribal warriors was too much for the porters. "We must go home," cried all the porters in the morning. "If we do not, we will all die!"

Reluctantly, Livingstone agreed. They had traveled nearly two hundred miles up the lakeshore, but still the water to the north seemed to run on into the sky. They had not yet discovered a river flowing east to the ocean . . . on the other hand, they had not proved that a river didn't exist, either.

As they sailed back down the lake, Chuma noticed that the doctor said very little. Clearly he was discouraged by their failure. It made Chuma sad, too. They had come so far—for nothing! The more the doctor had talked about finding a river going to the ocean so he could start a mission, the more the boy had wanted to help make it happen. Like Livingstone, Chuma had been happy when they had a good day traveling or made friends with the local tribespeople, and he was sad when things went wrong.

Chuma thought about this as the boat creaked under the sail. Just last summer he was a sheepherder. Now he was traveling with the white doctor who wanted to stop the evil slavers. He didn't understand everything the doctor said, but he did know that Livingstone wanted all the tribes to live peacefully with one another. He was a good man. Chuma was only a boy . . . but he wanted to help Livingstone, too.

As they journeyed southward on the lake, the explorers

avoided the areas where they had encountered problems before. But they faced a new problem: the weather. One morning Wikatani said, "The big winds are coming; we must not go out on the lake today."

Everyone looked up at the sky and wondered what he saw. While there was some haze in the sky, the sun was bright, and the day seemed like any other. If anything, the breeze was a little lighter than usual. "What do you mean?" laughed Livingstone. "It's a beautiful day." He proceeded to get ready to shove off.

Chuma knew that Wikatani had gone out frequently on Lake Shirwa with his father, and was probably more familiar with the weather in the area than anyone in the group. But even Chuma thought his friend was mistaken.

"The windy season is starting," Wikatani insisted. "It will blow today, and it will blow so hard that we could sink." The boy was truly frightened and at first refused to get into the boat, even after everyone else had climbed in and actually pushed off from shore.

From a few yards offshore Doctor Livingstone called back, "Come on, Wikatani. We don't want to leave you, but we *are* sailing this morning. So get in the boat."

With fearful eyes the boy waded out to the waiting craft and reluctantly climbed in. He actually shook with fright as he sat down in the bottom of the boat and looked up at the sky.

They traveled almost two hours under a good breeze and sunny skies when suddenly the wind shifted. Within minutes it turned into a gale. The waves in the shallow lake grew enormously, driving the little boat toward an angry surf crashing on a rocky shore. Livingstone and the boys immediately lowered the sail, and the men began to row with all their might. But still the wind drove them directly toward the rocks. Finally

Livingstone ordered, "Drop anchor! It's the only way to keep us out of those breakers."

But with the anchor out, the waves broke over the side and filled the boat, threatening to sink it. Everyone bailed out the water as fast as possible. Chuma and Wikatani had nothing to scoop water, so they used their hands. Hour after hour the little band struggled to keep the boat afloat. Many times Chuma clung terrified to the side of the boat, sure it was going to tip over or sink, and they would all drown.

But six hours later the wind finally slackened; exhausted, the men rowed slowly away from the rocks and beached on a sandy shore.

From then on, Doctor Livingstone listened to Wikatani's advice when he said a wind was coming up. As a result, they spent many miserable days on shore waiting for the waves to go down. But in Chuma's mind, it was a lot better than bailing water.

On October 26, they arrived again at the south end of the lake. That night as they all sat dejectedly around the fire, Wikatani said, "Doctor, now can we try going south to Lake Shirwa?"

A hush fell over the whole group as everyone's eyes turned toward the doctor. Finally, he said, "All right. In the morning we'll find a place to hide the boat and set out on foot."

But in the morning, the doctor and the boys awoke to a terrible shock. During the night all the porters had run away.

CHAPTER 12

HOME AND BEYOND

"What will we do now?" asked Chuma.

"Well, we can always sail the boat by ourselves," said the doctor. "Even one man can sail it."

"But you said we'd go to Lake Shirwa," said Wikatani.

Livingstone laughed wryly. "It would be foolish without any porters. They took the guns. What if we were attacked?"

"But Doctor, you said you didn't want to use guns, anyway," protested Chuma.

"I don't, but it's never good to appear weak in the face of danger."

"Won't God protect us if we are doing His work?" asked Chuma sincerely.

The doctor turned away from the boys and looked north across the lake shimmering in its morning light. When he turned back, he sighed deeply. "I'm not sure I know what God's work for me is anymore," he confessed, pulling the ends of his moustache. "I was so sure, but . . . everything I try seems to fail."

He got up and set to building a fire. When it was crackling its comfort into the chill air, he turned to the boys again. "I guess there is still one thing I know to do." He looked into the fire and tossed a twig at it. "I should take you boys home. You've risked your lives for me, and even though I may not be able to save all of Africa from this evil slave trade, I can pay my debt to you. Let's go."

The boys were elated. But first they rowed the boat up a small stream flowing into the lake until they came to a marsh where they concealed the boat among tall reeds.

"There," said Livingstone. "Unless someone knows right where it is or comes on it accidentally, it'll never be found. I may not come back this way to explore Lake Nyassa again. But if I do, I'll have a boat." And his craggy face broke into a grin.

Then the doctor and the two boys waded out of the marsh and headed south.

———

It was near sunset three days later when they came over a hill and saw in the distance the shining mirror of Lake Shirwa. This country was more open—rolling hills, groves of forest, and open grassland.

The three travelers were hungry and bone-tired. Along the way, they had avoided other people and all villages. They did not want to announce their presence. But that also meant that they had no way of getting more food except for what they could gather along the trail.

And the land to the north of Lake Shirwa had not been free from warfare, either. From a distance they had seen burned villages, and on the trails they frequently came across a warning sign: a skull atop a spear that had been driven into the ground.

But as they looked at their lake in the distance, Chuma asked, "Can we keep on going so we can get home tonight?"

Livingstone surveyed the lake glistening in the distance and then looked at how close the sun was to the horizon. "The lake is still several miles away. Where's your village?"

"Around the lake, on the west shore," offered Wikatani.

"It's a pretty big lake; it could take quite a while to get there. I think we ought to wait until morning."

Though the boys were greatly disappointed, they did not complain. They knew the doctor was very tired and had already taken great risks in bringing them this far. But when they made camp, the boys could hardly sleep.

"I wonder if our sheep all wandered back to the village?" whispered Chuma as they stared up at the bright stars.

"Our sheep? They are too dumb. If someone didn't go out and round them up, they'd wander right off the earth."

"You think our families think we are dead?"

"Probably," said Wikatani. "Won't they be surprised when we come marching in?"

"I'm going to have my mother make a big feast for Doctor Livingstone." Chuma could hear the man already snoring softly near them.

"Maybe my father will assign some men to be new porters for him," said Wikatani.

In their excitement, the boys left unspoken any fears they had about the Manganja boast that all the villages around Lake Shirwa had been burned out. After all, it was just a boast; the Manganja had been trying to frighten them.

Finally they dropped off to sleep. But they were up early

in the morning, and, with the doctor in tow, they covered the distance to the lakeshore while the air was still cool.

"Look!" shouted Wikatani. "That's our village across the lake. See the white strip of beach and the little trail of smoke rising in the air. My mother is probably baking bread for breakfast."

Several times the doctor had to urge the boys to slow down as they traveled around the edge of the lake. After they had gone about five miles, Chuma pointed out that they were now on the trail that they often used when they took the sheep to pasture.

In another quarter hour, he said to the doctor, "Right down there, that is where the Red Caps got us."

"They tied me up," said Wikatani, "and broke a Manganja spear and shot one of our sheep."

"And I came running through the shallows to help him," said Chuma. "But another Red Cap was waiting for me, and he had a gun."

A few minutes later, when the boys came in sight of their village, they began to race each other for home. Chuma was two strides behind Wikatani when Wikatani suddenly stopped short. Chuma ran ahead in glee, looking back over his shoulder as he shot past his friend. But Wikatani was staring strangely ahead. Chuma also slowed down as he looked down the hill toward the village.

Something was wrong. There were no canoes on the beach. Some of the houses had been knocked down, some burned. Chuma pushed the panic away and forced himself to walk. There were no joyful sounds of children shouting and playing. No dogs came out to bark at them. But the village was not deserted. A few people could still be seen moving from hut to hut.

Again he began to run. He tore past the old sheep pen. There were no sheep in it. *Of course, someone else is out herding them,* he reassured himself. He turned right after the first house. Its thatched roof was caving in. In the doorway of the next house sat a strange woman. *Who's she? I know all my neighbors. I know everyone in the village,* he thought. *Maybe she's a visitor.* His own house was next, but as Chuma rounded the corner of his neighbor's house, he faced a burned-out pile of rubble. Half of one mud wall was still standing, and a few roof beams lay haphazardly against it like a blackened logjam on a river after a spring flood.

He turned to the right and left. The only building belonging to Chuma's family that still stood was their corn crib. He ran over to it and around to the door, thinking his family might be taking shelter within, but that whole side was knocked out. Not one single ear of corn remained.

"Mother! Father!" Chuma yelled. "Mother, where is everyone?" He ran to the next house—just a hut, really—but it was completely empty. He ran on from house to house. All had been badly damaged; many had been burned to the ground.

Panic completely engulfed him. He ran up behind an old grandmother—finally, someone he knew! He grabbed her, and spun her around. "Where is my mother?" he demanded. But the old woman didn't say a word. She just stared at him as if he were a ghost.

He ran to the other side of the village to Wikatani's house. As he approached, he saw with relief that it was standing and that people were home. Wikatani was standing outside, talking to someone standing in the dark doorway.

"Where's my family?" he insisted as he skidded to a stop.

Wikatani turned to him with horror on his face. "They're

dead. Almost everyone is dead!" His voice came out in a high-pitched whisper.

"No. It can't be! Who are these people?" Chuma pushed past the woman standing in the doorway of Wikatani's house. He looked around. There were several others in the dark interior, but he recognized no one. "Who are these people?" he demanded as he came back out into the blinding sun.

"They say they are my cousins," said Wikatani. "They're from another village . . . over the hills." He pointed back toward the north.

"But what has happened?"

The boys looked at each other in silence. Finally, the woman standing in the doorway spoke up. "The Ajawa had many great victories, but then the battle turned and the Manganja overran this village. Many warriors from our village in the hills came down to help, but we were too late."

Wikatani sat down in the dust and began to rock back and forth, moaning quietly. Chuma just stood there. He knew that war killed people, but he had refused to believe that his family might die, not even when the Manganja man had said that the villages around Lake Shirwa had been defeated.

"But all are not dead," said the woman as she came out and put her hand on Wikatani's shoulder. "Your little brother is still alive."

At first it seemed that Wikatani had not heard. Then he looked up slowly and said, "What?"

"I said, your little brother is alive."

"Where?"

"He is with your uncle, down at the lake."

Wikatani jumped up and ran toward the water. Chuma turned and followed along slowly, walking as though he were in a dream. Suddenly Doctor Livingstone was walking beside him. The white man put his arm around the boy's shoulder and pulled him close.

At the lakefront, Chuma and the doctor stood at a distance while Wikatani and his little brother hugged each other and cried. They stood there in silence a very long time. Finally, the doctor said, "You know, Chuma, you *could* come with me."

———

That night the two boys went for a walk along the lakeshore. They followed the path they had taken with the sheep that fateful day and stopped again at the point where they had been ambushed. They sat on the sand thinking about all that had happened in the last months.

"Chuma, when you get back to the mission, try to talk to Dauma again. Tell her that I'll never forget her kindness to us."

"Without her, we might have died," agreed Chuma.

Soon a new moon rose. It was nothing more than a golden fingernail of light, but it laid down a shimmering path across the placid, black waters.

"The doctor saved our lives, too," added Wikatani.

"Yes," said Chuma. "He's been like a father to us."

"You know, I think he knew what we might find here . . . and he didn't have to bring us back."

"But I'm glad he did. I had to know."

"Me, too."

Somewhere in the distance a hyena howled its hideous laugh. In a few minutes Wikatani continued. "You once said that if our families were dead, you would become a Christian and stay with the doctor. Is that why you are going with him?"

Chuma thought before answering. "No. I became a Christian when I still thought our families were safe . . . and I would still be a Christian even if the doctor hadn't offered for me to go with him."

"Yes. I think you would. And I believe in Jesus, too. Do you think he would baptize me before you go?"

Chuma grinned at his friend. "Of course! Ask him—first thing in the morning!"

"But I wish I could help the doctor, too," said Wikatani wistfully. "He *is* doing a great work, even if he can't see the benefits."

"That's true," agreed Chuma. "How else would we have heard about Jesus? Someone had to come tell us."

A slight breeze turned the path of moonlight on the lake into a field of glittering diamonds. Again, Wikatani broke the silence. "I just wish I could go with you."

"Me, too. But you need to take care of your brother, and we don't want our village to die out."

"No. I guess not." After a moment Wikatani turned to Chuma. "You wouldn't desert the doctor like those porters did, would you? Promise me!"

Chuma grasped Wikatani's wrist, as his friend's hand clasped his own wrist in a sign of friendship.

"As long as God gives me the strength and courage, I will remain with Doctor Livingstone and help him in his work," Chuma vowed. "You can count on that, my friend."

CHAPTER 13

EPILOGUE

Chuma remained at Doctor Livingstone's side for seven more years of missionary exploration in Africa's interior. When the good doctor died from exhaustion and fever, Chuma and others carefully preserved his body and then carried it across half of Africa to the coast where it could be sent by ship back to England for burial.

Chuma was also invited to England to help tell the story of Livingstone's life to all those who had admired and supported his great work.

Though Livingstone never had the privilege of seeing the fruit of his efforts, he opened the way for hundreds of missionaries to enter central Africa and establish mission stations there. One of the most important was located on Lake Nyassa and named Livingstonia. And within fifteen years of his death, through the influence of the Gospel, as well as other factors, the slave trade was brought to an end in central Africa.

MORE ABOUT
DAVID LIVINGSTONE

David Livingstone was born on March 19, 1813, on an island off the coast of Scotland. He grew up in a Christian home where his father was a tea merchant.

After receiving a degree in medicine from Glasgow University in 1840, Livingstone became connected with the London Missionary Society. With the Society's support he went to South Africa in 1841. He ventured north by lumbering ox-wagon on a ten-week trip. But what he saw troubled him. The mission stations he visited seemed more interested in creating comfortable British outposts than pressing on to reach the unreached peoples of the interior. He also discovered that some of the missionaries were racist about the very people they were trying to reach with the Gospel. They did not think the Africans were suited for much more than servants or field hands.

Livingstone's complaints to the mission headquarters earned him the disapproval of some, and he was not granted permission for an extended missionary journey for several years. So he spent his time learning everything he could about

Africa and its people. He became convinced that when English missionaries founded a mission station, they should set about training African converts to take it over as soon as possible. He quickly mastered several African languages and learned the customs of the people.

On one shorter foray into the bush, Livingstone was attacked and severely mauled by a lion. It took months for him to recover, and the injuries to his shoulder bothered him the rest of his life. However, while he was recovering, he got to know Mary Moffat, the daughter of Dr. Robert Moffat, Bible translator and mission director.

Shortly after they were married in 1844, the Livingstones set out to establish a new mission station on the frontier. From there it was Livingstone's intention to make journeys deep into Africa to reach people who had never heard the Gospel before.

This he did in three dramatic expeditions.

The first expedition extended north across the eastern edge of the Kilahari Desert to the River Zouga and then west; he become the first white man to see Lake Nagami in 1849. He then went on to reach the Zambezi River in 1851.

Before long he came to realize that he wasn't an evangelist but had been called by God to explore and open up new areas for other missionaries to follow. Between 1853 and 1856 he made a most remarkable Trans-Africa journey, first out to the west coast, then back across Africa, down the Zambezi River to sight the Victoria Falls, and then on to the east coast.

It was on this first journey that he became aware of the devastation of the slave trade in Africa. When he returned to England in 1856, he was honored by the Royal Geographic Society as a major explorer and commissioned by the government to return to Africa as a British Consul.

He went back to Africa on his second expedition and started up the Zambezi River by riverboat. There he intended to establish Christian mission stations in the hope of spreading the Gospel and stopping the slave trade. That situation provides the setting for this story.

Though greatly simplified, this story follows the events of the Zambezi expedition with the following exceptions: (1) It is only conjecture that Chuma and Wikatani were the spark the Red Caps used to ignite the tribal war. (2) While at least two freed slaves accompanied Livingstone in his attempt to contact the Ajawa chiefs on his Nyassa exploration, they are not named. (3) Livingstone's rescue from the Shire River is fiction, though he had an equally close call with death earlier when coming down the Zambezi River. (4) Chuma and Wikatani did not return to their homeland for another five years. For the sake of this story, the time frame was condensed. What actually happened in the meantime was that Livingstone's second expedition came to a tragic end.

Livingstone's wife as well as the wife of Bishop Mackenzie and some other women came to join the men at the mission station. However, when Livingstone was away exploring Lake Nyassa, the bishop made a canoe trip on which he foolishly carried most of the mission's medicines. The canoe capsized and all the medicines were lost. By the time Livingstone got back, everyone was so sick with malaria that the bishop and all the women died—including Mary Moffat Livingstone.

Shortly after that, even in the middle of his great grief, Livingstone came across an official dispatch that conclusively proved that the Portuguese were involved in the slave trade. He sent off this proof to England, thinking the government would put international pressure on Portugal to stop the trade. However, it was more important to England to maintain good relations with Portugal at that time than to embarrass their ally by exposing Portugal's violation of the treaty. To avoid any further "incidents," England ordered Livingstone out of Africa.

Heartbroken and discouraged, Livingstone withdrew, vowing to return at his own expense as soon as he could. Rather than allow his riverboat (it was his third one by this time) to fall into the hands of the slave traders, he sailed it across the open sea to India. Chuma and Wikatani—as well as some other African and white sailors—volunteered to accompany him on this wild and dangerous voyage in which all nearly lost their lives. In India, Livingstone enrolled Chuma and Wikatani in a mission school and sold his boat before returning home to England.

Several years later Dauma was reported to be a fine teacher in a mission school in South Africa. She had been among some of the women and children Livingstone brought down the river to safety on his boat before he sailed to India. He arranged for them to be cared for at the mission station on the island of Zanzibar.

Three years after leaving Chuma and Wikatani in India, Livingstone returned to take them back to Africa for his third expedition. They faithfully accompanied him until they arrived in their homeland. There Wikatani stayed—probably to get married—but Chuma continued on with Livingstone.

Livingstone went deep into the interior of Africa and lost all contact with the outside world. Many thought him dead until the *New York Herald* sent newspaper reporter Henry Stanley on an expedition to find him or bring back conclusive news of his death. In March 1871, Stanley started his search from Zanzibar. In the fall he finally located Livingstone. The doctor was sick and out of supplies, but in good spirits. Their meeting is remembered by Stanley's famous words: "Doctor Livingstone, I presume?"

Though grateful for the visit and the fresh medicines and supplies, Livingstone would not come out of Africa. So Stanley returned to worldwide fame for having found the great missionary/explorer.

When Livingstone died on April 30, 1873, Chuma and some other faithful companions carefully embalmed and wrapped his body and carried it to the coast. There, Chuma went with the body to England where Livingstone was buried with great honor. Chuma met with the Queen and toured the country telling others about the expeditions of Livingstone.

TRAITOR IN THE TOWER

John Bunyan

Authors' Note

The Winslows of this story are fictional, as are Elder Barnabas of the secret London church and John White's wife, whom we called Agnes. All other named characters and events in this story are real. John White served as the under-jailer at the Bedford jail during the time when John Bunyan was imprisoned there. Not only did White nearly lose his position because of the liberties he granted Bunyan, but he was so strongly influenced by Bunyan's witness that he got in trouble for refusing to pay the state church tax.

Also, the details surrounding Bunyan's imprisonment were somewhat more complex than we were able to portray in this book.

The stories told by John Bunyan are adaptations of his allegory *Pilgrim's Progress*.

CONTENTS

CHAPTER 1

THE MIDNIGHT RAID

Bang! Bang! Bang!

The crashing yanked Richard Winslow out of a sound sleep. Or was he still dreaming? Was he in a castle with the enemy at the gate? No. As his wits came to him, he realized that he was in his own bedroom, and the banging and yelling came from the front door of his house just below his bedroom.

Bang! Bang! Bang! "Open up in the name of the king!"

A flickering yellow light came through Richard's window and danced on the ceiling of his room. Then he heard his father calling out for the butler. "Walter! Walter—what's happening? Who's at the door? Someone light a candle."

Richard jumped out of bed as he heard his father run past his door and scramble down the stairs. Richard followed partway down the stairs in time to see his father open the heavy front door of their London house.

In barged two of the king's men with swords drawn.

As Richard hesitated on the landing of the stairway, he

5

could see other soldiers outside. One had a torch in his hand, and its light cast a flickering glow into the dim hallway.

"I am the captain of the king's guard," barked the older of the two soldiers inside the house. "Is this the home of Obadiah Winslow? Are you Winslow?" He took a threatening step toward Richard's father.

"It is, and I am," said Mr. Winslow as he pushed his nightcap back on his head and stood up straighter. But it was hard to appear as a dignified gentleman in a wrinkled nightshirt and bare feet.

"Who else lives in this house?" demanded the captain as he ducked down to peer up the dark stairway toward where Richard crouched on the landing. Richard crept back from the edge and tried to make himself invisible.

Obadiah Winslow also glanced up the stairs, then stammered, "J-just my family—my wife and children."

"Is that all?" The soldier looked toward the back of the hall. "What about back there?"

"Well, there's the maid . . . and the butler," Mr. Winslow said as the side door swung open and the old butler tottered into the hall holding a candle high with one hand. The old man's mouth hung open, and in the dim glow of the candlelight he appeared dazed.

"Who are these people?" he muttered. "I am the butler here, and I have not given you permission to enter this—"

"Silence, old man!" shouted the captain. "This is none of your business." He turned back to Richard's father. "Obadiah Winslow, I arrest you in the name of the crown for high treason. You will come with us."

"Treason! B-but this cannot be," stammered Obadiah. "I have done nothing wrong. Who is making these outrageous charges? What led to them?"

"I cannot say," said the captain. He tilted his head back and looked down his nose at his prisoner. "I am neither judge nor prosecutor. However, I do recall that you had a rather long and close association with that traitor, Oliver Cromwell. You were his assistant secretary, weren't you?" The captain smiled slyly.

Shock spread across Obadiah's face. "W-why, yes. But, but—he died in 1658, over two years ago, before young King Charles returned to England. Besides," said Richard's father, trying to regain some control over the situation, "I thought that the king granted amnesty to anyone associated with Cromwell. He promised it in his Declaration of Breda. Everyone knows that."

"What the king promised or didn't promise is none of my business," said the soldier. "The king *is* the king, after all." The captain slid his sword back into its scabbard and looked Richard's father up and down. "You're a sorry sight to be going to the Tower," he snarled. "Go put on some clothes, but make it quick. We don't have all night."

Obadiah sucked in his breath. "The Tower? Why the Tower?" But seeing that he could not evade the king's soldiers, Obadiah Winslow took a candlestick off the mantel, lit it off the butler's candle, and trudged up the stairs. When he got to the landing on which Richard crouched, he put his hand on the boy's shoulder and said, "Come along, son."

The bewildered butler was left downstairs facing the soldiers—as though such a feeble old man could stop them from invading the Winslow house any farther.

Upstairs, behind closed doors, Richard's mother, Eunice, and his three younger sisters pelted Obadiah with anxious questions. On the far side of the room, Molly, the maid, stood holding her skirt up to her mouth as she cried bitterly.

"Just calm down," Mr. Winslow said firmly. "I don't know what's happening. It's some mix-up about Cromwell. But before the king was even allowed back into England, he promised freedom to all his enemies—though I have never considered myself an enemy of the crown. I'm sure I'll be released in the morning as soon as we get this mess sorted out. Don't worry about me. Just calm down and put yourselves back to bed."

Sensing the fear in their mother, the girls began to cry as they clung to their mother's nightdress. The whole thing seemed like a nightmare—the banging on the door, soldiers arresting their father.

Richard found that he was shivering uncontrollably even though he didn't feel cold, but he gritted his teeth and refused to cry. He was tall for twelve, with a shock of dark, wavy hair that would have gone to curls had he let it grow long. His face was square with a strong jaw for his age. He watched nervously as his father pulled on his trousers and buckled his shoes.

"Keep a stiff upper lip," his father said as he patted him on the shoulder. Richard knew that meant he wasn't to cry; it would only upset his sisters even more.

Once his father had been taken away by the soldiers, Richard's three weeping sisters crawled into bed with their mother, but Richard was much too old for that. He went back to his own room.

The June night was warm, but his bed felt cold, and he continued to shiver. It all seemed so unreal. Maybe none of it had happened; it was nothing more than a bad dream. But no . . . dreams wandered from one scene to another, and even in the most vivid dreams there were always things that didn't fit—like the stairs turning into a waterfall.

But the midnight raid had been one continuous sequence,

and the only thing that didn't make sense was *why*. Why had soldiers come for his father? It made no sense.

It was true that his father had worked closely with Oliver Cromwell as he led his armies against old King Charles. And after the king had been defeated and executed, Obadiah Winslow had assisted Cromwell when he ruled England for five years as the "Lord Protector." But all that was in the past. Cromwell had died, and now Charles II, as he was being called, had been brought back from Europe to sit on the throne.

All the old quarrels were supposedly put to rest, everyone pardoned for earlier allegiances. It had all been politics, and politics made enemies, but who could tell right from wrong?

So why *had* his father been arrested?

Richard thought about the Tower with a shudder. The Tower of London was about two and a half miles down the Thames River, across London from where he lived. He had been by it several times. There were two high stone walls—one inside the other—that surrounded a tall, square "keep" with turrets on each of the four corners. This structure was "the Tower." Earlier, it had been used as a castle by the king or queen—something no enemy could invade. However, when someone realized that invaders could not enter and prisoners could not escape, it became a prison. But it was not a prison for common thieves and mischief makers. This prison housed only major criminals and enemies of the king. Very few prisoners who went through its gates came out alive.

Richard moaned and pulled the covers over his head.

At some point he must have fallen asleep, because the events of the midnight raid merged into a dream . . . or nightmare, as it became. The king's soldiers were after him, but the faster he tried to run, the more difficult it was to move his feet. The street seemed to turn into a muddy field, and with every step his boots gathered more mud until his feet were so heavy that he could hardly pick them up. He became exhausted, and the soldiers were just about to grab him when he finally woke up.

———

It was morning. Birds were chirping and the fishmonger was coming down the street calling out, "Eels, two a penny! Fresh eels! Get 'em now or let 'em go! Salted herring. You need it? I got it!"

Richard got out of bed and pulled a blanket with him, wrapping it around his shoulders as he shuffled to the small window overlooking the street below. As his blue eyes gazed down, the night's horrors came back to him: His father had been arrested and taken to the Tower!

Quickly, he threw on his clothes and ran downstairs. "Has my father come home?" he blurted to Walter as he burst into the kitchen.

"No, Master Richard," Walter said as he set down the coal bucket by the open fireplace. "We haven't seen a whisker of him."

"I'm going out to see what I can learn," announced Richard.

"Oh no. You mustn't. After last night, it's not safe," clucked Molly, pulling a large loaf of fresh bread out of the oven.

The Winslow family did not have a large household staff— only Walter, who was called the butler, but he did many other chores as well, and Molly, who also served as a cook and nurse for the children when necessary. In spite of Obadiah Winslow's close association with the former head of the English government, the family was not wealthy. So they made do with what they had.

Richard looked at Molly as she set the fresh bread on the table. "Can I have some bread and butter?" he asked.

"Certainly, but I don't think your mother would want you running around in the streets."

Richard cut a thick slice of the hot bread and spread butter on it. The butter melted immediately and smelled delicious. He didn't want to argue with Molly. She'd just call his mother, and then he would have to stay home. So he took such an enormous bite that no one could have understood him when he mumbled, "I won't be gone long," and rushed out the back door.

He ran down the alley, then ducked between two buildings and came out onto the street. The day was already warm. Not far away, the leaves on the trees around Westminster Abbey, the great church, still had the yellowish green of new growth. But Richard had no sooner started to enjoy the beauty of the day when his thoughts slammed against the memory of his father's arrest.

Westminster Abbey . . . Oliver Cromwell was buried there, inside the stone cathedral. The boy clenched his fists angrily. His father was not a traitor for having worked for Cromwell! Richard wished the old man were still around to explain to the king or the judge or the soldiers that his father was a good man.

As Richard approached Westminster Hall, he became aware of a crowd, restless and murmuring. The faint smell of something musty and old wafted on the morning breeze. He stopped in shock.

Hanging from a tall pole was a dark and twisted shape wrapped in what seemed to be old clothes. It looked like a skeletal corpse had been hung from a gallows. Richard pushed his way through the crowd until he could read a sign mounted on top of the pole: "Here hangs the remains of Oliver Crom-well, guilty of treason. Let all traitors beware! This will happen to you!"

Horrified, Richard backed out of the crowd and tripped over a stone and fell. But the jolt of hitting the ground was not nearly as great as what he had seen. Scrambling to his feet in panic, he ran for home.

CHAPTER 2

ESCAPE FROM LONDON

Richard ran into his house yelling, "Mother! Mother! They've hung Oliver Cromwell!" He skidded to a stop in the kitchen where his mother, sisters, and the butler and maid were eating breakfast.

Normally, Molly served breakfast to the family on trays in their bedrooms. But given the frightening events of the night before, everyone had gathered in the kitchen.

"What do you mean?" said Eunice Winslow. "Cromwell's been dead for over two years. No one hung him. He died a natural death, and we all know that his body is buried in the tomb at Westminster. So sit down, catch your breath, and speak sensibly."

"But they did hang him!" insisted Richard. He did not sit down but stood behind a chair, gripping its back and nervously tipping it back and forth as though it were the handle of a pump. "They hanged him! I saw it myself in front of Westminster Abbey. He's still there."

"Possibly," offered Walter in a voice tuned for speaking to a child much younger than Richard. "Perhaps what you saw was an *effigy*. Maybe someone made a dummy and dressed it up to look like Lord Cromwell. Could that have been it, Master Richard?"

"I'm not a baby," protested Richard, objecting to Walter's tone of voice. "Do dummies smell like . . . like . . . ? I found an old dead cat once. I know what dead smells like. He was dead! I could see his skull with brownish skin stretched over it. There were eyeholes, and yellow teeth, and he had long, stringy gray hair just like when he was alive. *Someone took him out of the tomb and hung him up*."

"Eeaah," said Anne, his oldest sister, making a sick face.

But Richard looked around at the unbelieving adults. "Go see for yourself. There was a whole crowd of people gathered there. You can ask anyone."

Suddenly, the expression on his mother's face changed from disbelief to concern. "What else was happening?" she asked. "Were there any soldiers about?"

"No, no soldiers. But there was a sign on the pole. It said, 'Here hangs the remains of Oliver Cromwell, guilty of treason.' " He frowned as he tried to remember. " 'Traitors beware!' or something like that."

No one spoke for almost a minute. Then Eunice Winslow said gravely, "If this is true, Richard, then what happened to your father last night is far more serious than I realized. If the winds of politics have changed again, we may no longer be safe."

"What's going to happen to Papa?" wailed Chelsea, Richard's middle sister. A whimper escaped her throat, and her face screwed up as she began to cry.

"We don't know yet," said Mrs. Winslow soothingly, brushing

her daughter's hair out of her eyes. "But one thing is certain. We must not cause Papa greater concern by having to worry about us. I think we'd better get out of London."

"Out of London?" said Richard. His mind swirled. He wasn't sure he wanted to leave this familiar house and his friends. "But . . . where will we go?"

"I don't know," said his mother as she looked back and forth between Walter and Molly. "Maybe . . . maybe we could go to our relatives in Scotland. I'm sure they would be glad for a visit. And then when this thing blows over we'll come back." She smiled bravely at the young girls.

"But that would take over two weeks, madam," said Walter with a knowing air.

"Only if we go by land. By ship we should arrive in less than a week."

"A ship! We're going by sea?" Richard felt a thrill of excitement—then immediately felt guilty. What about Papa? They couldn't just leave him behind in the Tower.

"Shall I begin packing, ma'am?" asked Molly.

"Yes, if you would, please."

"Then I'll get the carriage prepared," offered Walter.

"I don't think we should take our own carriage," said Mrs. Winslow. "It might attract too much attention. People recognize it, you know. We'll hire a public carriage, but not until dark. What I'd like you to do, Walter, is go down to the docks and arrange passage for us. Make sure it is on a decent ship and that we can board tonight after dark. We don't want to be seen by any more people than is necessary."

"Very well, madam," said Walter.

"And Walter," continued Mrs. Winslow, "when you come back, I want you to shut up the house as though we have gone away on holiday. I think that would be best. I want Molly to come with us, but will you stay here to look after things?"

As the family servant, Walter never objected to the instructions given him, but he often let his opinion be known by a smile if he approved, or by raising an eyebrow or straightening his neck if he disapproved. This time, he both straightened his neck and raised his eyebrow, but Mrs. Winslow continued without hesitation. "I want you to enter and leave only through the back, Walter. And light no candles or lamps in the front part of the house at night. We want everyone to think we are gone. However, someone needs to remain here in case—" she paused and glanced at the children—"for *when* Obadiah is released."

Richard noticed her hesitation and realized that his mother feared the worst: Obadiah Winslow might not come home from the Tower.

They worked all day packing and preparing the house for their absence. Supper was cold—just bread and cheese, some apples, and cider. At the table, Mrs. Winslow finally spoke the thought that had been on everyone's mind. "I hate for us to all be so far away from Obadiah. What if he needs us?"

"I will be here, Mrs. Winslow," said Walter. He sounded hurt and indignant.

"I know, I know, Walter, but I don't think you could get in to visit him. Sometimes they admit only immediate family members."

The thought crossed Richard's mind that he could stay. Possibly he could get in to see his father. But if he stayed, he would miss traveling by ship to Scotland. Once, when he was about seven years old, his father had taken him on board a ship that was anchored in the Thames. Ever since, he had dreamed of traveling by sea! But a sea voyage without his father—with his father in *danger*—felt wrong, somehow. No, he chided himself, helping his father was the greater necessity.

"What about me, Mother?" he finally said quietly.

Mrs. Winslow looked at him thoughtfully. Then, "No, son. I couldn't risk your staying in London. That would be unwise."

"Well then," Richard thought for a moment, "what if I went to stay with Uncle John and Aunt Agnes in Bedford? I'd be safe there, and I could come back to London and visit Father when things are safer."

At first, Mrs. Winslow's head shook firmly from side to side. But then it slowed, and thoughtful lines appeared in her brow as she reconsidered. "Possibly. Bedford is only about fifty miles northwest of London, and John White is not one of the gentry. I doubt that anyone is paying any attention to John and Agnes." She put the palms of her hands to her cheeks, thinking aloud. "I could take the whole family there, but that would be too obvious. However, you—I suppose you would be safe. But I don't know about you trying to come back to London. That could be too risky."

Richard swallowed. On the one hand, he wanted to travel on board the ship with his mother and sisters. But staying with his uncle and aunt would be almost like being on his own. He felt pulled both ways. His father needed a family member near, and he was the oldest. It was a grave responsibility . . . was he brave enough to take it?

"Let me stay with Uncle John and Aunt Agnes," he finally said in his calmest, most adult-like manner. "I'll be careful."

Finally it was settled. Mrs. Winslow and the girls would go to the ship during the night, and he would catch the next day's mail stage for Bedford. His mother went to her room to write a letter for him to take to his uncle explaining the danger and also the need for a family member to remain as close to London as possible.

It was dark when Mrs. Winslow, the girls, and Molly got into the carriage to be taken to the dock. Walter went with them for protection and to handle the luggage. But he would return as soon as the family was aboard ship.

Richard went back into the dark house and was immediately struck with how gloomy and empty the place seemed. He did not envy Walter's staying there alone. The chaos of the night before haunted him. He remembered vividly being rudely awakened when the soldiers banged on the door and arrested his father. In such a short time his whole life had turned upside down. Now he was going away to a strange town to stay with relatives he had not seen for several years. It was exciting . . . and scary.

———

The next morning Walter took Richard to catch the mail coach to Bedford at a pub on the north side of London. To get there, they again traveled by rented carriage. Richard knew that Walter disapproved of the plan because all morning he had said no more than necessary.

"What's the matter?" Richard finally asked as they jostled along through the streets of London.

"Nothing, Master Richard," grumbled the old man. "It's just . . . it seems to me that a boy of your age ought to be with his mother. I don't know what this new generation is coming to. This certainly would not have happened when I was your age, at least not among respectable people."

Richard knew that Walter's little comment about "respectable people" was intended to scold him for being so brash. He didn't know how to respond. He wasn't going off to his uncle's because he thought he was such a big shot. It was just the necessity of the situation.

He tilted his chin, trying to sound confident. "Things are different now, Walter. Lots of things are different. Nothing seems safe. Who knows what tomorrow will bring? I must do what I can." He didn't mean to be rude. But the midnight raid by the soldiers had changed everything—and he was scared.

CHAPTER 3

THE JAIL KEEPER

The next afternoon as the mail coach plowed through the muddy rural roads, Richard braced himself and stared straight ahead at the man in a powdered wig who sat in the seat across from him. Richard had never experienced such a rough ride. Foot-deep ruts created by heavy summer rains yanked the coach's wheels this way and that with no warning.

More than once Richard had been looking out the window at the lush green countryside when the coach had lurched so violently that his chin had smashed onto the windowsill. And now, to make matters worse, the constant jostling had caused him to feel sick to his stomach.

He had heard people speak of seasickness. Was this how his mother and sisters were feeling on the ship to Scotland?

But the thought of them so far away while he was becoming sicker by the moment made him feel worse rather than better. If there ever was a time to be home in your own bed with people who loved and cared for you, it was when you were sick. Richard was trying to be a man, to do the grown-up thing—but right now all he wanted was his mother to soothe his head with a cool, damp cloth.

He broke into a sweat and clenched his lips tightly together. He would not throw up. Whatever happened, he would not let himself throw up on the coach!

"What's the matter, lad?" said the man across from Richard. "You look a little green around the gills. Do you want me to signal the driver to stop?"

Richard didn't dare open his mouth. He shook his head, no. But even that extra movement brought another wave of dizziness.

The man across from him looked out the window and then turned back to Richard. "Just you hang on a bit longer. We'll be in Bedford soon. Then you can take a break."

Bedford. The trip was almost over. Nearly two days on the road would wear anyone out. But these last couple hours—ever since they had turned off the Great North Road—traveling had been torture. Richard couldn't wait to put his feet on solid ground again.

———

Bedford was a sleepy town, the county seat of Bedfordshire. Richard was grateful when the road became smoother and he noticed that he was riding past houses. For the most part, they were small townhouses with partially exposed timbers at the corners and crossing as braces. Between them brick and stone was plastered as a rough stucco. The roofs of the buildings were generally thatch, though some buildings had red tile roofs.

But the thing that amazed Richard was that behind the rows of houses that lined the streets, there were open grain fields and orchards as though the houses made a picket fence around the field in the center of each large block. This was so different than London where, except for the gardens of the very rich, buildings covered every inch of space not taken up by the narrow streets.

Richard stared out of the window as he rode by a large church.

"That's Saint Mary's Church," offered the man sitting across from Richard. "We'll be crossing the Ouse River in a moment. Then I'll be home, and you, my young traveler, can take a break."

"Oh, this is as far as I am going, too," said Richard. "Do you live in Bedford?"

"I most certainly do. I am Edmund Wylde, the sheriff of Bedfordshire. So you better mind the law, young man." But his proud smile indicated that he was not issuing a threat. The man turned and looked out the window. "Oh, here we go, across Great Bridge. Now, don't you think it is a fine structure for a small town like this?"

Richard looked out as the wheels of the coach clattered across the stonework. In the middle of the bridge there was a tower with an arch in its center through which they rode. Richard was not all that impressed having seen much more impressive structures in London.

As soon as the coach was off the bridge, the driver yelled *whoa!* to the horses, and the carriage came to a swaying stop.

"That's it," said the sheriff as he opened the door and stepped out.

Richard climbed out shakily. They had stopped in front of a public inn.

"Old Swan Inn," said the sheriff pointing up to a sign on the door that displayed a large white swan swimming in a dark pond. "Not a better place for board and room in the whole town. Well, good day to you," he said as he turned and walked toward the inn's door.

"Excuse me, sir," said Richard, still feeling a little unsteady on his feet. "Would you happen to know where John White lives?"

"Do I know him? Of course I know him. He works for me! Now," he said as he wiped his hands down the front of his coat and took a deep breath. Then he pointed with an outstretched hand. "Just go right up High Street here—let's see, one, two, three—to the third street. On your left is Silver Street. On the northwest corner of High and Silver streets is the jail. John White lives just west of the jail. Can't miss it."

Richard grabbed his bag from the boot of the coach and headed up the street. Bedford seemed like such a strange place compared to London. The dirt streets were wide and open. And he still marveled at the fields and orchards right in the middle of town.

He walked along, past another large church on the left, and passed two small boys chasing a hoop with sticks.

At the third street—Silver Street—he noticed what had to be the jail. It was a two-story stone building with three narrow windows, each covered with an iron grill.

———

Richard did not recognize the man who answered the door in the house west of the jail. He was not much taller than Richard, round in the middle, and balding. What hair he still had was black and pulled back where it was tied at the back of his head in a limp ponytail. His clothes were rust-colored and typical of most merchants—no excessive lace and frills. But one thing was unusual. Though his britches stopped at the knees, and stockings extended below them, he did not wear the common shoes of the day. Instead, he had on a pair of boots, like a farmer or dock worker.

"I'm looking for John White," said Richard, feeling much better after his walk in the fresh air.

"You're looking at him," said the man in a rather brusque manner, his brow knitting together. "But if you've brought something for one of the prisoners, you'll either have to leave it with me or come back tomorrow about noon. I'm not running a public hostel here, so I don't have time to open the gate at everyone's beck and call."

"Uh—Uncle John?" Richard ventured, not certain whether this was his uncle or not.

"Uncle? Who are you, lad?" He squinted at Richard. "You can't be Eunice's boy, can you?"

"Yes, sir. I'm Richard Winslow."

"Well, well." The man's face smoothed into a smile. "Come in, my son. Come in! But what brings you all the way to Bedford? Where is your mother?" He looked up and down the street as though he expected to see some sort of carriage with the rest of the family in it.

John White pulled Richard through the door and called excitedly to his wife. "Agnes! Agnes! Come see who is here. You will never guess."

Agnes White came bustling in, middle-aged, round-cheeked, wiping her hands on her apron. "Richard," she cried, recognizing him immediately. "My, how you've grown. The last time we saw you, you were only half as high." She threw her arms open wide and embraced him in a warm hug.

"Where's my sister? Where's Eunice and the babies?" she bubbled.

Richard snickered inside. He wished his sisters were there to hear themselves called "babies."

Soon the three of them were sitting around the kitchen table with mugs of tea as Richard told his story.

John and Agnes White had no children, and because they were simple working people, they did not have any servants. But their snug cottage was warm and welcoming all the same.

As Richard finished his tale with what he'd seen at Westminster Abbey, Uncle John shook his head and frowned. "I don't know what this country is coming to," he said. "My jail is full and overflowing these days. And it's not with criminals, mind you—at least not what *I* would call criminals. Most of these are good, Christian people who just happen to be on the wrong side of the king. Though I don't think some of them even oppose him."

"You're the jail keeper?" asked Richard in surprise. Then he remembered what the sheriff had said about his Uncle John working for him.

"Oh yes," said Uncle John proudly. "We've been here about three years now. My back just couldn't take working the flour mill anymore. Too much lifting, ya know. Now I'm a *king's* man!" Then, realizing what he had said, he added quickly, "But that doesn't mean I have anything against your good father. I'm sure he's done nothing wrong, and that'll all come to light soon enough."

Finally, Richard asked the main question on his mind. "Uncle John, would it be all right if I stayed with you and Aunt Agnes for a while?"

Uncle John grinned. "Well, that all depends. I've been looking for a strong lad who can help me around the jail. You think you are up to such work? There's hauling hay and water and dumping the prisoners' waste buckets over in Saffron Ditch. It's not a pleasant task. You got a strong stomach?"

Richard remembered how he had almost lost his lunch

riding in the coach that afternoon. The thought of having to empty waste buckets brought on another wave of nausea. But he took a deep breath and said, "I'm up to it."

"Good," said Uncle John as he clapped Richard on the shoulder. "A jailor you shall be!"

"Now, John," murmured Aunt Agnes. "He's just a lad. You mustn't work him too hard." She turned to her nephew and beamed. "Of course, you can stay with us for as long as you like—and if he works you too hard, you just let me know."

"Don't you go buttin' in, Agnes," growled Uncle John. "It'll do the lad good. He's nearly grown up, and a little hard work will make a man of him."

———

That night, after a simple meal of barley soup and hard, black bread, Richard had the best sleep he had had since his father was taken away. The little upstairs room under the thatch roof had a small window that looked out over the town of Bedford. A silver moon illuminated the shops, cottages, fields, and churches, making it seem as peaceful as the ripples on a pond—nothing like the hubbub that always filled a London night.

But the next morning, Richard got his introduction to the county jail of Bedfordshire. It had two floors above an underground dungeon. His Uncle John lifted the bar from the massive oak door, unlocked the iron bolt, and pulled it free with a clank. The door swung open, and he led Richard within.

"Here on the ground floor," said Uncle John, "is where we keep your average criminal—those waiting for trial or already sentenced to prison. There are two open rooms surrounded by several sleeping cells. As you can see, we are greatly overcrowded. It used to be nearly empty, just a thief now and then, especially around the time of the county fair. But now we've got close to fifty people in here, mostly religious nonconformists— Puritans, Baptists, Quakers, and a couple Presbyterians. I don't see any good reason for putting most of them in jail, myself, but then I don't make the laws."

They went through another heavy door and climbed the stairs to the second floor.

"I've had to put some of the nonconformists up here, but usually this floor is reserved for debtors."

On the second floor there was one common room and four sleeping rooms, much larger than those downstairs. Also, instead of the windows being narrow slits with iron grates over them, the windows on this floor were larger and covered only by bars.

When they came downstairs, Richard's uncle lit a torch and opened another door. This one was bolted as securely as the front door had been. They went down eleven steps into the dungeon.

"Is there anyone down here?" asked Richard nervously, looking around the dingy place.

"That there is, in both cells," said Uncle John. "In there"— he pointed to a heavy door with no window in it—"we have John Fox. He's raging mad and accused of murder. We feed him through that slit under the door. He'll probably hang."

"How 'bout in there?" Richard pointed to the other door. It had a small window in it with an iron grate over it.

"You can look in there. That cell has one small window up at ground level. We keep a woman named Elizabeth Pratt in there. They say she's a witch, but I can't believe she ever did anything so bad."

Richard looked through the small hole in the door that was covered with an iron grate. In the far corner, in the dim light from a tiny slit window near the ceiling, he could make out a lump under a blanket on a pile of straw.

"Now, she ain't dangerous," said Uncle John, "not unless you are afraid of her casting a spell over you. So every few days you'll be replacing her straw and doing what you can for her. I wouldn't keep her in there, except the court requires me to. It's a terrible thing."

"Why do you do it then?" asked Richard.

John White shrugged. "I don't make the law. It's just my duty to uphold it."

Richard frowned. "But why carry out an unjust law?"

"Ah-ha! You're thinking of your father being thrown into the Tower. Why didn't some good-hearted guard turn his head the other way and let him flee? But what good would it have done? That would have made a fugitive of your father . . . and a criminal of the guard. I don't doubt that your father's an honorable man, and I've known the law to be unfair more than once. But—" John White paused and looked back up the dark dungeon steps. He stood there staring as though he could see through the stone walls of the jail to some scene miles away. Suddenly, he shook his head and brusquely continued, "It is a terrible thing to land in prison. Workin' here you'll see that for yourself, and you'll want to stay out . . . by obeying the law, even the parts you *don't* like."

CHAPTER 4

THE PAROLEE

The very next day Richard began his job carrying food and straw to the prisoners and emptying the stinking waste buckets. It was hard work, and at first he resented it. Criminals, after all, were lowlife sorts, a class of people far below himself. He avoided their eyes, did his job as quickly as he could, and got out of there. But one day as he brought back the empty waste buckets, he had a startling thought: his father hadn't landed in prison for being a lowlife.

These were real people in this jail; some of them like his father.

He began to take more notice of the prisoners. Theirs was a hard life, made harder by the crowded conditions. There was no means of taking a bath in the jail and no fireplaces or brazier pans holding burning coals for warmth. This made life easier for Richard since he didn't have to haul coal or firewood. But he couldn't imagine how the inmates warmed themselves in the winter.

"They don't," his uncle said when Richard asked. "Sometimes prisoners get what's called jail fever, and since we don't have an infirmary, some of them die. It's too bad, but with no heat, the place never really dries out."

Each prisoner received a quarter of a loaf of bread per day, and for that the prisoner had to pay. Any other food had to be brought in from the outside by family and friends.

After working in the jail awhile, Richard began to recognize the family members who stopped by regularly to visit their imprisoned loved ones. He tried not to think about his father alone with no visitors in the Tower. There was nothing he could do about it yet. Soon, though, he would have to think of a way to return to London and attempt a visit. What if his father had nothing more than bread and water to eat? What if he needed someone to bring him better food like these prisoners got from their families?

One of the regular visitors at the Bedfordshire jail was a girl about Richard's own age who came each day at noon with a widemouthed jug of soup for one of the prisoners. His uncle let her into the jail with a friendly welcome, calling her Mary.

She was an attractive girl with thick, dark hair and clear skin the color of cream. Richard was watching her intently one day, trying to figure why she walked in a slightly stiff manner and never spoke to him. *Maybe she's too embarrassed*, he concluded. He knew that feeling, not wanting other people to know that his father was in prison.

Seeing him watching her, his uncle said, "Interesting girl, that Mary Bunyan. She lives a block up Mill Lane on the corner of Cuthbert Street. More dependable than a sundial. A sundial requires the sun to be out, but she's here *every day*—by noon—sunshine or rain. You'd never know she's blind."

"What?" exclaimed Richard. "She can't see?"

"Not a bit, but it doesn't stop her. She goes all over town."

Astonished, Richard watched the girl as she moved across the crowded common room to the far side where a man sat on a bench working intently with his hands. She moved in that slow, stiff manner he had previously noticed, looking straight ahead. And then he saw it. She was feeling her way with her feet, and when her toe touched the leg of a man sleeping in the middle of the floor, she easily turned to the side without losing her balance.

It was amazing! Richard remembered times when as a younger boy he had pretended to be blind, trying to walk around and do things with his eyes closed just to see what it was like. His game had never lasted more than a few minutes before he squinted one eye open and peeked. It was just too hard.

But this girl seemed to manage with only the slightest stiffness.

The next day when she arrived, John White was away from the jail taking care of some business. "Hello, Mary," Richard said boldly as he let her in.

"Good day," the girl said tentatively. "I don't think I know you. You sound young. Are you a—?"

"No, I'm not a prisoner. I work here, helping my uncle. I'm Richard Winslow . . . from London," he added as an afterthought.

"Oh."

"I've seen you bringing soup every day. Is that tinker your father?" Richard pointed to the man who spent his days working over a small bench. His uncle had told him that the man was a tinker, but of course, he couldn't repair pots and pans or make knives in jail. So he had found some small craft with which to make money.

"Yes." She started to move on into the common room.

"What's his name?" asked Richard, eager to learn more about this remarkable girl who could walk all around town even though she was blind.

"His name is John Bunyan, and he doesn't belong here."

"Well, why is he here then?" Richard said in a rather challenging tone of voice.

"He was preaching without a license." She took another step, then turned back and said, "Why don't you come and meet him? He can tell you all about it."

Richard tentatively followed the girl into the common room and over to the bench where her father sat and worked. The man was average height, in his early thirties, his shoulder-length light brown hair hiding his face as he bent over his task. It was the first time Richard had paid any attention to what the tinker was doing, but he quickly saw that the man was making laces for women's corsets. He had piles of them bundled together. He cut them to length and crimped brass tags on each end to keep them from unraveling.

"Mary!" said the prisoner with warm joy in his voice, lifting his face. It was a broad, open face, with wide-set brown eyes and a strong nose. One eyebrow arched slightly higher than the other. "It's so good to see you. Here, let me take that jug. Hmmm, it smells so good." John Bunyan took a sip. "Thank you, Mary. Here, sit down." He moved his things off the bench, and the girl sat beside him.

Richard stood by awkwardly during this family greeting. Finally, Mary said, "Father, this is Richard Winslow. He wants to know why you are in prison."

"Oh, he does, does he? Why, for preaching God's Word, lad," said Bunyan, looking up at the lanky boy standing near him.

"What's wrong with preaching?"

The man grinned ruefully. "That's what I'd like to know. The Bible plainly says, 'Preach the word,' and that's all I was doing. But, now that the king has returned and the state church is back in power, we nonconformists aren't tolerated. One would think that some of the freedoms gained under Cromwell would last. But I guess he made too many enemies. So, since I didn't have a license, they said I couldn't preach."

Mary added, "Father could get released today if he would promise not to preach anymore, but he won't."

Richard frowned. The girl spoke with pride rather than resentment in her voice. It confused Richard. "Why not promise, Mr. Bunyan?"

"How can I promise *not* to do something my Lord has commanded me to do?"

"Well . . ." Richard fumbled for an answer. "For the sake of your family, obviously! My father is in prison, too, and I know what grief it brings," he blurted out.

"Is he, now?" said John Bunyan with a broad smile. "And why might he be held?"

Richard froze. He had not intended to tell anyone other than his aunt and uncle about his father's imprisonment. Personal information in the hands of the wrong people could be dangerous, and he did not really know whether this John Bunyan was trustworthy or not. "It was nothing," said Richard stiffly, "just some political confusion that will soon be straightened out."

Bunyan's eyebrows went up. "Yes," he said, "political confusion can be nearly as bad as religious confusion."

Richard withdrew and went back to his work of distributing new straw to the sleeping cells. Later, when Mary was ready to go home, he let her out but did not speak to her.

The next day was Sunday, and Richard went early to carry a bucket of water around to the prisoners. Suddenly, he was surprised to see his uncle come into the jail and release John Bunyan.

Richard hurried to his uncle's side. "Is he free?"

"Oh no. He just wanted to go to church this morning—some special meeting or something."

"But aren't you afraid that he will escape?"

"Bunyan? Not in the least. He could get out of jail any day if he would just promise not to preach, but he won't make such a promise. Says he has to obey God rather than man." John White shrugged. "Since he's in jail by his own choice, I have no reason to think he will flee the county. Besides, as I told you the other day, his wife and family just live over on Cuthbert Street. So where would he go?"

Richard returned to his chores, feeling confused and unsettled. *So it's true,* he thought. *This man Bunyan could be released any time simply by promising not to preach anymore.* The information nagged at Richard's thoughts. Why would a man abandon his family and choose to rot in jail if he could get out simply by making a promise not to preach? The more he thought about it, the more upset he became, until he realized that he was outright angry at the man.

John Bunyan returned to jail that afternoon, just as Richard's uncle had said he would, and with him came his daughter Mary. Richard admitted them both into the jail, then followed them into the sleeping room Bunyan shared with three other men who were out in the common room at the time gambling with homemade dice carved from bones.

Richard had to say something—for the sake of Bunyan's blind daughter, he told himself. "As I told you yesterday," he blurted, challenging, "my father is in prison, too. If I knew he could get out simply by making a promise, I'd be very upset if he refused to do so." He looked at Mary, who was staring in his direction, but with her unseeing eyes, she did not focus on his face. "You can't imagine how hard it is on my poor mother for him to be in prison." In spite of himself, Richard's voice quavered.

"So you think I should make the promise?" said Bunyan.

Richard shrugged, but it was a shrug that said absolutely yes.

John Bunyan squinted, and Richard saw tears gather in the man's eyes. "I've thought very hard about that myself," he said, "but maybe I can explain myself by telling you a story. Mary, would you like a story?"

"Oh yes, Father." The girl's face lit up. "You tell such good stories."

"Both of you—sit down here on the straw, and I'll see what I can do."

A story? What kind of answer was this? Richard hesitated a moment, knowing fleas and lice infested the prison, especially the straw bedding. But he handled it every day, and he was curious so he sat down.

"Once upon a time," began John Bunyan, "there was a man—we'll call him Pilgrim.

Pilgrim had a tremendous pack on his back that he could not take off. But he also had a book in his hand. He opened the book hoping for some instructions for how to remove his burden. But as he read, he began to cry and tremble.

Soon he let out a great moan and said, "What shall I do?"

In this sad state, he went home and tried—as long as he could—to keep his feelings from his wife and children. But he could not keep silent for long. Finally, he said, "My dear wife, and you my own dear children, I'm very upset because of this burden I'm carrying on my back. It is made of sin, and I must find a way to become free of it."

His family looked at the pack on his back and shrugged. Everyone in the city carried some sort of a burden, and no one had ever thought of taking it off, so why should Pilgrim?

Then he said, "I have also learned that this city of ours shall be destroyed with fire from heaven for all its sin. If we cannot find some way to escape, we shall all be destroyed."

The more Pilgrim talked, the more his family frowned. They did not believe what he was saying, and so they became more and more concerned that he might be going crazy.

As it drew toward night, they whispered to one another the hope that sleep might settle his brain. "Come, Dear," said the woman, "it's time for bed. Have a cup of warm milk and get some sleep. Tomorrow you will feel better."

But the night was as troublesome to Pilgrim as the day. Instead of sleeping, he spent it in sighs and tears. In the morning his children said, "How are you feeling now, Papa?"

"Worse and worse," he said. "We must all leave this place and find a way to get these burdens off our backs."

But the more he talked, the more they resisted. Finally, they tried to drive away what they thought was craziness by scolding him to straighten up. When that didn't work, they tried begging him to come around.

Finally, the wife said, "Let's just leave him alone, and maybe he'll come to his senses on his own." So they left his bedroom and carried on their life as normally as possible.

Pilgrim took the opportunity to pray for them and read his book, for the book he had was the Bible. It was, in fact, from the Bible that he had learned that the burden on his back was sin and that the sin of the whole city would lead to destruction.

The standoff continued for several days. Sometimes Pilgrim prayed and read in his room, and sometimes he went for walks *in the fields outside the city. When he was by himself, he would cry out loud, "What shall I do to be saved?"*

One day when Pilgrim was walking in the field praying, a man approached and said, "Hello. My name is Evangelist. You seem upset. Why are you crying?"

Pilgrim answered, "Sir, in reading this book, I discovered that I am going to die and after that I must face judgment. I'm afraid to die and even more afraid to face the judgment."

Evangelist rubbed his chin. "Why are you so afraid to die? Isn't this world full enough of troubles that you'd be glad to get out of it?"

"Oh, no," said Pilgrim. "This burden upon my back would sink me lower than the grave, and I would slip into hell. I don't think I could take that. Why, I wouldn't last a day in prison. So how could I stand hell? It's the thoughts of these things that make me cry."

Then Evangelist said, "If this is your condition, why are you standing still?"

"Where should I go?" asked Pilgrim.

At that, Evangelist handed Pilgrim a parchment scroll with the words, "Flee from the wrath to come!" written on it.

"But to where?" cried Pilgrim in great confusion.

Evangelist pointed across the plain and said, "Do you see that gate almost to the horizon?"

"Can't say as I do," answered Pilgrim.

"Well, can you see that light in the sky—like a star?"

"Yes."

"Go directly toward it," continued Evangelist. "And when you get across the plain, you'll come to the gate. Knock at it, and you will be told what to do."

So Pilgrim began to run. But he had not gone far when his wife and children, seeing what he was doing, began to call after him begging him to return. But Pilgrim put his fingers in his ears and ran on, crying, "Life! Life! Eternal life!" And he would not look back but fled across the plain.

John Bunyan stopped talking and leaned back against the wall of his cell, crossing his arms on his chest. The story was obviously over.

"But, Father," cried Mary, "did Pilgrim get rid of his burden? What happened to him?"

CHAPTER 5

INTO ENEMY TERRITORY

John Bunyan smiled at his daughter's questions. "I guess you'll have to wait for some other time to find out what happened to poor Pilgrim," he said as he reached out and patted Mary's hand. "I was trying to tell a story to answer Richard's question. Does that help you understand, son?"

Richard furrowed his brow as he thought about the story of Pilgrim leaving his home and family. It was such a mysterious story, as though the prisoner had been telling a riddle. He felt there was more meaning in it than he realized. But as far as the man leaving home . . .

"I guess," he ventured, "if Pilgrim knew something that no one else would believe—not even his family—he would have to act on that knowledge."

"Very good," said John Bunyan. "The story is an allegory, a pretend story that symbolizes spiritual truths. And you figured out the exact point I was trying to make. Now, my wife and children have not 'cried after' me like poor Pilgrim's family did. They have been completely supportive. As you can see, Mary brings me food every day, and my dear wife, Elizabeth, comes with the other children to visit as often as she can. But with or without their support, I would have to obey God's call just as Pilgrim did."

"Seems kind of disloyal to me," Richard muttered. "They need you!"

John Bunyan was silent for several moments, and again Richard saw tears come to his eyes as he looked at his blind daughter. Finally, in a husky voice he said, "Yes, they do need me. Some men leave their families for their own selfish reasons, but for me, there is no greater sacrifice. I take no pleasure in my condition. But what do you think Jesus meant when He said, 'He that loveth father or mother . . . son or daughter more than me is not worthy of me'?"

"I'm . . . not sure," Richard admitted.

"I think He meant that there are times when we all must choose between what other people want us to do and what God wants to do. Whenever we face one of those choices, we must obey God rather than other people, even our own families. That's why I'm in this jail, you know. In my case it wasn't my family who opposed my call, it was the king."

Richard got up. He was feeling awkward with what John Bunyan was saying, but he didn't know why. "Thank you for the story," he said lamely and walked out of the tinker's cell. Aunt Agnes would want him home for tea, anyway.

———

Richard did not talk to John Bunyan for the next few days, and when next he did, it was at Bunyan's request.

"Take a break, lad," the tinker said as Richard raked up the old straw. "I have something to ask you." They were in the common room, and Bunyan was again working at his bench cutting and tagging laces. By selling them for a few pennies per hundred, he earned enough for food for himself and his family. Richard had learned that Elizabeth Bunyan also took in laundry and mending to help ends meet.

"Here, lad, sit down," said Bunyan. "I've been wanting to ask you about your father. Would you mind telling me why he is in prison?"

Richard looked around at the other prisoners. Several were within earshot. "Out in the exercise yard," he said. There was a small, walled courtyard that the prisoners were allowed to walk around in when Richard or his uncle had the time to guard them.

Security in the Bedford jail was not as tight as it might have been in a large city prison. The chances of escape were slim. Most prisoners had no place where they could run to evade the law. In the English countryside, everyone was attached to some landowner either directly as a servant or as a tenant renting a farm from the landlord. Even the landowners considered the king their "lord." In one way or another, everyone had a master, someone to whom he was accountable. Any "masterless" men roaming the English countryside were suspect and could be immediately arrested by a local lord. In towns, things were a little different. There were craftsmen and shop owners and other merchants who weren't directly responsible to an overlord. But they belonged to the town where everyone knew them and could vouch for them.

Because fleeing was so difficult, it was easier to keep someone in jail than it might seem. Nonetheless, the wall around the small courtyard was tall and impossible to climb over while a jailer was on duty.

As Richard and John Bunyan walked in the exercise yard,

Richard related how his father had been arrested in the middle of the night because of his association with Oliver Cromwell. Then he told how he'd seen Cromwell's body taken from its tomb and hung near Westminster Abbey, and how his mother had concluded it was too dangerous to remain in London.

"So that's why I came here," said Richard. "My mother and sisters went to Scotland by ship. It's been almost a month. As soon as I get a chance, I'm going back to London to visit my father and see if there is some way I can help."

"If your father worked closely with Oliver Cromwell," asked Bunyan, "was he a Puritan?"

Richard shrugged. He had heard the term used often, but he didn't know exactly what a Puritan was.

"Well, I am a Baptist myself, but Puritans are not all that different," said John Bunyan. "They want to get back to the *pure* Gospel, you might say. The Church of England has gotten so caught up in politics and ritual that the souls of the common people have been neglected. But it is not just the common people. The king and many of the lords and nobles live such wicked lives that they provide no fit example."

Bunyan laid a hand on Richard's shoulder as they walked. "The Bible says, 'All have sinned,' but the state church does not guide the people to conversion. How can one become acceptable to God? How can one live a pure and holy life? These are the central questions of a true and pure religion."

Richard nodded thoughtfully. "Yes, my mother often said the same things. My father took us all to church services every Sunday—it was the thing to do, I guess—but at home, it was my mother who read the Scriptures to us and prayed with us each night. My father thought that was taking religion a bit too far—but that doesn't mean he deserves to be in prison," he added quickly.

"No. I'm sure he doesn't," agreed John Bunyan. The two walked in silence for several moments, then Bunyan said, "I am planning on going to London next week. Do you want me to ask around about your father?"

"What? London?" Richard said in shock. "I know Uncle John allowed you to go to church for a few hours last Sunday, but—London? You'd be gone for several days! He would never allow that."

Bunyan pursed his lips. "I'll allow that you might be right, but then again, I think he will trust me with the trip. He knows I'll return. There's no question about that."

"If he does let you go," said Richard, hardly daring to trust the eagerness he felt, "I would be most grateful if you would check on my father." He stopped with a worried look on his face as he remembered. "However, our butler didn't think anyone but family could get in to see him. But maybe, maybe"—he was thinking fast—"maybe I could go with you. If I were to go along, Uncle John would be more likely to let you go, wouldn't he? And when we got there, I could try to visit my father. What do you say about that?"

"Hmmm, I don't think having his nephew along would make much difference for your uncle. Either he'll let me go on my good word or not." Bunyan stopped walking and looked Richard in the eye, being only slightly taller than the boy. "You might have a chance to see your father. But what if someone traces you back to me or the underground church in London? It's not safe these days to be connected to someone in prison."

"What underground church? I don't know of any underground church in London or anywhere else."

"Ah, of course not. Excuse me for mentioning it. Furthermore, it's best you don't know anything about it, either, so don't ask any more questions."

———

To Richard's amazement, his uncle not only agreed to John Bunyan's trip but allowed him to accompanying the tinker. He even said, "Richard, you're becoming a man. I'll make you my unofficial deputy to see that this man returns as promised."

His going *had* made a difference. Richard looked over at John Bunyan with a smug grin on his face. Bunyan shrugged and smiled back, and then Richard began to wonder whether his uncle was just humoring him, trying to make him *feel* grown-up. Oh well, it didn't make any difference; at least he was going to visit his father.

They caught a ride on the weekly postal coach on Tuesday afternoon. This time, the trip over the rough country road from Bedford to the Great North Road did not make Richard sick. Maybe the road was a little smoother, or maybe he had his mind on other things. In any case, the two-day trip went by quickly, and he and John Bunyan arrived in London tired but eager.

In London, Bunyan took Richard to a house in a part of the city that Richard had never visited. "Elder Barnabas," Bunyan said once they had stepped inside, "I'd like you to meet—" He paused as though he were uncertain what to call Richard. "Yes, well, I'd like you to meet Brother Richard."

Richard shook the older man's hand, and they were led into a small sitting room crowded already with about thirty people. Everyone was introduced simply as Brother or Sister, with no last names. Food was brought in for the two visitors from out of town, and Richard suddenly realized that they had been expected. The whole group had gathered because John

Bunyan was visiting. It had to be the secret church Bunyan had mentioned.

Soon someone started the group singing hymns, and then, when John Bunyan had finished eating, Elder Barnabas stood up. "O Lord," he prayed, "we thank Thee for sustaining our Brother John, and we ask your blessing on him now as he brings us Thy word. Amen."

The room was warm, and Bunyan had only begun to speak when Richard's head began to nod. Embarrassed, he jerked awake and tried to listen. But he was so tired from the trip that he couldn't pay attention.

Finally, a woman touched him on the shoulder and whispered, "Would you like to go to bed? It's all right."

CHAPTER 6

THE TOWER OF LONDON

The room to which Richard was shown was small with two hard cots in it. As he sat down on one of them, he couldn't help but think that this would probably be the best bed John Bunyan had slept on for months.

But surprisingly, as soon as Richard lay down to sleep, he felt wide awake. In the morning, he would go to the Tower and try to see his father. But what if the guards wouldn't let him in? What if someone wanted to capture the rest of the family? What if his father was sick? What if he had already been condemned to death?

The questions were too many and too big to cope with, and they swirled around inside his mind, chasing away every hint of sleepiness.

In about an hour, John Bunyan came into the room carrying a small candle and noticed Richard's eyes open. "I thought you'd be in dreamland long before now. What's the problem?"

Richard shrugged and sat up, swinging his feet to the floor.

"Thinking about tomorrow?"

"Yes, I guess so. I—I just don't know what's going to happen. What if they arrest me?"

John Bunyan looked at Richard for a few minutes, then sat down on the cot across from him, setting the candle on a bedside table. "You remember that story I told you and Mary?"

"Yes, the one about Pilgrim?"

"Exactly. Let me tell you another story about Pilgrim." John Bunyan sat back on his cot so that the wall became a support for his back. He pursed his lips and looked up toward the ceiling as though the story were written there in the dark for him to read. Then he began.

After many difficulties and delays, Pilgrim succeeded in crossing the plain to find the gate that Evangelist had described. The gate opened onto the long, narrow road leading to the Heavenly City. And at the gate, as Evangelist had promised, Pilgrim received instructions for continuing his journey.

Not far beyond the gate, he went up a small rise to where a cross stood. Long ago on that cross, a Man had taken the punishment Pilgrim deserved for all his sins. As Pilgrim gratefully knelt at the base of the cross, his burden fell from his back and rolled down the hill.

Pilgrim leaped up in joy, tears streaming down his face. Then he saw three shining beings. The first said, "Your sins are forgiven." The second took his rags and gave him new clothing. The third gave him a scroll to present at the gate of the Heavenly City.

Even though his burden of sin was gone, Pilgrim's journey was not over, because he had determined to travel on to the Heavenly City where he would find safety and peace. So on he went through many hardships and trials. He met various companions on his trip. Some were faithful and true and helped him on his way. Others led him astray or discouraged him.

One day as Pilgrim was climbing a particularly steep mountain, he stopped to rest under a pleasant tree. It had been planted there by the Lord of the mountain to refresh weary travelers like Pilgrim.

While he was resting, he pulled his Bible out of his pocket and read to comfort himself with the promises he found within. At last, he fell asleep, and his Bible slipped out of his hand.

When he awoke a short time later, the words of the last verse he had read were fresh in his mind: "Go to the ant, thou sluggard; consider her ways and be wise." Immediately, Pilgrim jumped to his feet and hurried on his way so as to not waste the precious hours of daylight that remained.

When he got up to the top of the mountain, there came two men running to meet him. The first introduced himself breathlessly as Timid, and the second said, "And I am Mistrust."

"But, sirs," said Pilgrim, "what's the matter? You run the wrong way."

"Oh," moaned Timid, "we were going to the Heavenly City and had gotten past so many difficult places, but the farther we go, the more danger we meet with. So, we turned around and are going back again."

"Yes," said Mistrust with wide eyes of fear, "not far ahead of you lie a couple of lions in the way. We couldn't tell whether they were asleep or awake, but we knew that if we came within reach of them, they would pull us to pieces."

"This is frightful," said Pilgrim. "But where can anyone run to be safe? If I go back with you to my old town—a town that I now call the City of Destruction—that's exactly what will happen to me. I will certainly be destroyed. But if I go forward and succeed in reaching the Heavenly City, I will be safe. But you say the path gets harder. So what am I to do?"

Pilgrim tested his choices, describing them again: "To go

back is nothing but death. To go forward involves the fear of death, but if I make it, there is life everlasting beyond it." Pilgrim clapped his hands and declared, "I will go forward!"

No sooner had he made his choice than Mistrust and Timid ran down the hill heading back to the old country. Thinking again of the warning they had given him, Pilgrim felt in his pocket for his Bible so that he could read a few words of encouragement.

It was not there! In deep distress, Pilgrim felt around. Could he have put it someplace else? But no. It was missing. This was serious. He had wanted simply to read a few words of comfort, but not having the book was far more serious. For it told him how to get to the Heavenly City. He had to have it!

Finally, he calmed himself enough to recall the last time he had it, and then he remembered his nap under the tree. "I must have left it there," he moaned. What carelessness. There was nothing to do but go back for it. So back he started, resenting the time he wasted in retracing his steps.

When he got to the tree and saw his little Bible lying there on the ground, he had mixed feelings. "One should never sleep in the midst of difficulty!" he scolded himself. "Look at all the time I have wasted." But he was also very joyful at having found his little Bible. He snatched it up and stuffed it in his pocket securely so as never to lose it again. "Thank You, God," he murmured, "for directing my eyes to the place where I found it."

Then he turned around again and scurried back up the hill. But before he got to the top, the sun went down, and he was again reminded of his foolishness for sleeping during the day. "Now my pathway is dark, and there are all sorts of noises out there that I won't be able to identify."

He remembered the story that Mistrust and Timid told him about the fearful lions. Pilgrim said to himself, "These beasts roam in the night for their prey, and if I meet them in the dark, what will I do? How will I escape being torn in pieces?"

But he did not turn back, and in a short time, he looked up and saw not far ahead a beautiful inn that stood beside his path. "Ah," he sighed, "if only I can reach that inn, then I will gain a safe night's rest." So on he slogged.

But before he had gone far, he entered a narrow canyon. Suddenly, he spied two lions. Now, thought he, now I see the dangers that caused Mistrust and Timid to turn back. Maybe I should go back, too. Fear caused him to tremble. It seemed that nothing but death lay before him.

Just then the porter came out of the inn and put his hands to his mouth. "Good traveler," he called, "do not fear the lions, for they are chained, and are placed there to test the faith of those who come this way. Those who have no faith always turn back, but if you will keep in the middle of the path, no harm will come to you."

Then, trembling for fear of the lions, Pilgrim followed the directions of the porter and moved on through the canyon. The lions roared and leaped at the ends of their chains. But their tethers held fast, and he proceeded unharmed.

His heart was beating wildly once he had reached safety at the end of the canyon, but he clapped his hands joyfully and went on up to the gate of the inn.

"Good sir," said Pilgrim to the porter, "is there room for me to spend the night here?"

"That there is, my young friend," said the porter as he opened the gate wide. "The Lord of the mountain built this house for the very likes of you. Come in, and take your rest."

While John Bunyan was telling the story, Richard had lain back down on his cot, and as the storyteller concluded with the phrase, " . . . and take your rest," Richard's eyes closed and he fell asleep.

———

During the night Richard woke up, uncertain where he was. Then he heard the London night sounds and remembered the journey . . . and John Bunyan's story about Pilgrim.

As he stared into the darkness, he thought, *I'm like Pilgrim, away from my family . . . on a journey with dangers and uncertainty ahead . . . but am I still carrying that pack of sins on my back?* As he thought about the story, he remembered kneeling at his mother's knee as a child, asking Jesus to forgive his sins. He felt a leap of recognition. Hearing Pilgrim's story, he understood more what his mother had been teaching him and his sisters.

Richard turned his head toward the cot where his companion slept. He wanted to tell John Bunyan that he, too, was a believer . . . but the man was snoring softly.

———

The next day, with the fantastic images of Pilgrim's journey still floating in his mind, Richard headed for the Tower of London. On the way through London's narrow streets, he imagined himself passing through the canyon where Pilgrim approached the inn. Of course, he was not headed to a pleasant inn for some rest and relaxation, but the temptation to turn back out of timidity and mistrust were just as real.

Suddenly, to his utter amazement, Richard noticed a huge stone building—some government building or something—with two enormous lions sitting on either side of the columned entrance. He had to look twice to reassure himself that they were only stone. The sight was awesome. They had been carved to look frightening, but Richard took courage in seeing them. The Lord would be with him just like He had been with Pilgrim. All he needed was a little faith.

Did John Bunyan know what streets I would be walking down

on my way to the Tower? Richard wondered. *Did he remember those lions and build his story around them just for my sake?*

The guard at the gate to the Tower was nowhere near as welcoming as the porter of the beautiful inn where Pilgrim stayed. But after asking a dozen questions, he did swing the creaking gate open and allowed Richard to enter.

"Wait here," he commanded, pointing to a small alcove in the prison's wall.

Richard waited and waited and waited. Finally, another guard arrived and said, "Are you here to see Obadiah Winslow?"

"Yes, sir," said Richard in a pleasant voice. The man looked like he had had all the unpleasantness he could stand for one day, and Richard knew that he needed his good will.

They passed through locked door after locked door and down long, stone passages and up many stairs. By the time the man stopped before a cell and fumbled for his keys, Richard had no idea where he was.

"You have twenty minutes," the guard barked and swung open the heavy door.

For a few seconds, Richard just stood in the doorway, trying to adjust his eyes to the dim light.

"Richard!" said his father's familiar voice, taking three steps across the small cell and embracing his son. "It's so good to see you!"

Richard hugged his father for a long time. His father felt much thinner, but his embrace was strong, and his voice sounded firm. When his father finally held him at arm's length, Richard noticed that his father had grown a short beard. He had never seen his father with a beard, and this one was not trimmed but just rough whiskers. There was gray in it, too, something Richard had never noticed in his father's hair before.

Richard started to pepper his father with questions about

how he was doing, but Mr. Winslow dismissed his questions by saying, "Oh, I'm doing all right. They feed me and bring me things to read, but I can't seem to get any writing material. I guess I fall between the cracks." He gave a short laugh. "I was too important to ignore but not important enough to get any special treatment."

Richard looked around. The cell was about six feet wide and ten feet long. High on one end was a small slit window. There was a sleeping mat on the floor and a table, chair, and candle. Briefly Richard wondered whether it was better to be crowded into a common jail like the one in Bedford or to have a cell all to one's self—with the obvious loneliness of being alone.

"Tell me about yourself, and your mother and the girls," his father insisted.

Richard told him about his mother and sisters going to Scotland the day after his arrest, while his father nodded approval and asked a few questions. Then Richard told about his being in Bedford, living with Uncle John and Aunt Agnes. He did not say that he was working in a jail.

"But what's happening with your case, Father? Is there anything I can do?"

His father's shoulders fell in discouragement. "I don't know," he said. "Everything takes so long. I have not yet even spoken to a lawyer. I don't even know why they are holding me. It has something to do with my working for Oliver Cromwell."

Mr. Winslow got up and paced back and forth in his tiny space. Richard sensed that he had already put in many miles on that short path. Then his father slammed his fist into the palm of his hand. "If only Cromwell were still alive," he said. "He could prove that I don't belong here."

"What do you mean, Father?"

Just then the door of the cell swung open and the jailer barked, "Time's up! Come along, boy."

The guard grabbed Richard by the arm with an iron grip and pulled him toward the door.

"Wait!" protested Richard. "What were you saying, Father? What could Cromwell do?" He looked back over his shoulder as the guard pulled him out of the cell, and at the last moment saw his father shaking his head in caution with a worried frown on his face.

"Cromwell can rot in his grave, for all I care," his father called after him.

But as Richard walked through the dingy passages of the Tower, he was certain that was not what his father had meant to say.

CHAPTER 7

THE CLAMPDOWN

The day after Richard and John Bunyan got back to Bedford, there came a loud knock at the jail door. Richard answered it and found a familiar-looking man in a powdered wig standing in the rain.

"Well, well, if it isn't my traveling companion," the man said as he shook the water off his broad-brimmed hat and stepped into the small entry room. "Have you recovered from that awful coach ride yet?"

"That I have, sir," said Richard, recognizing the sheriff of Bedfordshire who had ridden in the coach with him when he first came to Bedford. "I expect you'll be wanting to speak with my uncle. He's over at the house. But I was on my way there just now. Can I take you?"

"I'd be most pleased. I hear you are helping your uncle around the jail these days. Do you think you will make a life of it?"

Not likely, Richard thought as he opened the door, let the guest out, and locked the jail tightly behind himself.

A few minutes later, when all three were seated around the table in the White family's house drinking tea, Edmund Wylde turned to John White and said seriously, "John, I don't usually interfere with your running of the jail as long as everything goes smoothly. But recently some of the magistrates got wind of the liberties you're allowing John Bunyan, and they don't like it. I've been told to instruct you to keep him on the premises under lock and key. No more going to church or whatever you've been allowing."

John White pursed his lips and frowned, looking down into his teacup as though he were counting the leaves. "Excuse me for saying so, sir, but I hardly see why that's necessary. You and I both know that Bunyan's not going anywhere. His word's good as gold. Why, this past weekend I let him go to London, and he came back just as he promised."

"You . . . you *what*? You let him go all the way to London?" The sherriff looked like he might have a stroke. "Oh, John, this could mean big trouble."

"Why? He's in the jail right now, working on his tagged laces or writing one of his tracts. You can go see for yourself."

"That's not it, John. The magistrates think he may be part of those Fifth Monarchy men. And if they hear that he went off to London, they'll be sure he was talking with some secret group to conspire against the king."

John White snorted. "Edmund, I don't even know what this so-called Fifth Monarchy group is, but Bunyan's just a simple tinker. He was born over in Elstow. You even knew his parents. He's lived here for years. He's no conspirator. You know that as well as I do."

"All the same, John. We have no idea what he did in London. Who knows what he was doing there!"

"Well, Richard here knows. He went with him." John White

smiled broadly at his nephew, then turned back to Edmund Wylde. "If any of those stuffy magistrates complain, you tell them that Bunyan didn't go to London alone. He went under guard. I sent my deputy with him."

Edmund looked over at Richard and scowled. "John, I don't mind you using the boy around the jail, but he's not a king's guard, and you have no authority to deputize him." His face had become red with emotion, and he was speaking louder, almost angrily, right into John White's face. "This is serious! Either you keep Bunyan in jail, or you are out of your position. Is that understood?"

John White shrugged and said, "Of course, you're the sheriff . . . but I still don't think any harm was done. He just went to some church meeting or something. You know Bunyan. If he's not preaching to a congregation somewhere, he'll gather up the mice in jail to hear him give a sermon."

Edmund Wylde sighed with relief and he leaned back more easily. "I suppose it wouldn't hurt if the mice got a little religion. Seems like they are always thievin' and robbin'." He laughed, easing the tension.

Then he leaned forward again and said, "So your nephew, here, went to London with him, did he?" Then he turned to Richard. "What happened while you were there, lad? Did he meet with any secret groups or anything?"

Richard swallowed hard. It felt like all the blood had drained out of his head, and for a moment he thought he was going to faint. He swallowed again, and finally his voice came out in a kind of squeak. "He just preached." It was all he could say.

" 'Preached'?" said the sheriff as though that were an unbelievable activity. There was silence as he waited for Richard to explain more.

But Richard was thinking about the meeting of the secret

Puritan church. He remembered the singing and the warmth of the room after his long and tiring journey. John Bunyan had begun to speak when Richard had nodded off to sleep. The next thing he had known, a woman had tapped him on the shoulder and shown him up to his bed. And then it had been some time before Bunyan came up. He couldn't say for sure what had gone on at the meeting. *Could they have been conspirators?* he wondered.

But before he was required to answer, his uncle came to his rescue. "Of course, he preached, Edmund. What else would Bunyan do? Isn't that what got him into this jail in the first place? He's a preacher, not a revolutionary. You know that. Now leave the boy alone."

"Yes, yes, John," said the sheriff, holding his hand out to calm John White, but he wasn't finished questioning Richard. "But was this a regular church like Saint Cuthbert's or Saint Paul's?"

"No. It was just in someone's house," admitted Richard. He didn't know what was happening. He had grown to like John Bunyan, and he didn't want to say anything that might get him into trouble.

"Does he ever talk about strange things around you, like he was speaking of some other country or something?" pressed the sheriff.

Richard remembered the Pilgrim stories. Yes, John Bunyan had spoken of strange things—of the very "lions" he had seen on the way to the Tower—but did that make him an enemy of the king? No. He couldn't believe it. Finally, Richard cleared his throat and said firmly, "No. He speaks only of the Christian life and the trials and troubles we all face as we try to obey God's Word. There's nothing sneaky about him."

"There, see, Edmund?" offered Richard's uncle with relief. "What did I tell you? Bunyan's just a preacher."

"Well, be that as it may. You are to keep him inside the Bedford county jail from now on. No exceptions! You understand?"

———

That afternoon Richard and his uncle returned to their work in the jail. Richard was busy scrubbing the walls, attempting to remove some of the damp, musty smell from his uncle's work space when John White said to him, "Well, Richard, I guess I had better tell John Bunyan about Wylde's visit. Can't put it off forever."

With his brush in his hand, Richard followed his uncle to the preacher's cell and listened while John White broke the news to Bunyan. He spoke in a matter-of-fact tone of voice, downplaying the importance of his message. "Bunyan, I have received orders not to let you out of the jail for any purpose at any time . . . from here on out. So, no more trips. Understand?"

John Bunyan stood there staring at the jailer through the bars of his cell door with his mouth slightly open. He glanced over at Richard, who turned away and pretended to clean the wall. But of course, his mind was totally on the conversation between his uncle and John Bunyan.

"I'm sorry, John," said the jailer, "but that's just the way it is."

"But why? Who gave you this order?"

"The sheriff brought word from the magistrates, John. It's their ruling, and there's no way of getting around it."

"But what are they trying to do? How did the magistrates find out?"

"I don't know, John. Apparently, someone's been informing them about your activities, and they are all in a tizzy about them."

"But why?"

"Don't ask me! I don't know. They seldom trouble themselves with matters as small as this, but someone has been telling them what you've been doing, and so I guess they feel obliged to respond."

"But who would tell them? Who cares?"

"Don't speak to me as though I were on trial. I don't know, but obviously someone who knows about your activities has something to gain by reporting them to the authorities."

"You speak as though the person were a traitor, but what is there to betray?"

"I'm not sure, John," said the jailer in exasperation, "but they suspect you of being a conspirator against the king. So they don't want you going off to any more of your meetings. There's nothing I can do about it."

Without further comment, John White turned and went back to his office. Richard also walked away and didn't see Bunyan again until the next morning. But by then the clampdown had done more than restrict his activities. It had dampened his mood as well.

At first Richard tried to stay away from him. The gray look to his skin and the haunted stare in his eyes scared the boy. But when he walked by the old tinker who was again busy at his workbench in the common room, the man reached up and grabbed his sleeve. "What else do you know, lad? Did they say any more yesterday?"

Instinctively, Richard pulled away. "No, nothing that I can remember. What's the matter with you?"

"I guess I'm worried. They arrested me to stop me from

preaching without a license. Until now, I considered this imprisonment something of a tug-a-war. I've been insisting on the freedom to preach, but my opponents were not willing to grant me a license. Now it seems as if they are out for blood, saying that I am some kind of conspirator or something. That could get me hung."

"Oh, I don't think so," protested Richard. "If you stay here in the jail, they know you can't do anything against the king from here."

"But last night I had a dream," Bunyan continued in a thin, far-off-sounding voice. "In it I kept seeing the old gallows out at the Caxton crossroads—I've passed it a hundred times in my life. In my dream, I was mounting the steps to have the rope put around my neck. But then my knees seemed to give way, and I started to beg for mercy like a common coward. I've prayed for courage. If I must die, I don't want to die a coward. It would be a denial of Christ, the very hope I've preached to others."

"You need to tell yourself one of those Pilgrim stories," Richard suggested, trying to draw Bunyan out of his dark brooding. "Pilgrim would never let himself be defeated by a thing like this."

"I guess you're right," said John Bunyan with a wry grin. He brushed a strand of limp brown hair back out of his face. "I need to get my eyes on the Heavenly City."

But the next time Richard passed with a bundle of straw in his arms, Bunyan stopped him again. "This is more than a struggle with my own fears," he said urgently. "I'm ready to stay in this jail as long as they want to keep me here. But what about my wife and poor children—especially dear Mary. I can't leave her in the world alone, unable to see. If I were to be put to death, what would she do?"

Richard felt uncomfortable with such questions. How was he supposed to answer them? How was he to comfort a grown man, a preacher at that? He thought again of his father in prison. Maybe if he tried to help the person God put before him, God would send someone to comfort and encourage his own father. "Mary? Why, she'd do just fine," Richard said, not knowing if that would help, but believing it was true, nonetheless. "No one's pluckier than she is. You don't have to worry about her."

John Bunyan smiled faintly. For the moment, Richard's words did seem to give him some encouragement.

———

The next day when Bunyan's wife, Elizabeth, and daughter, Mary, came by the jail with his food, Richard noticed them talking urgently together in quiet voices. Elizabeth was at least ten years younger than her husband, only about twenty or twenty-two—a second wife. Her golden hair—a stark contrast from her stepdaughter's dark tresses—was mostly hidden under a plain white cap.

Then Richard realized that Bunyan was calling him over to them.

"Richard," the tinker said matter of factly. "I've got to get these charges against me dropped. I'm not willing to promise to never preach again—that would be going against God's instructions—but there may be some legal steps I can take. I wasn't legally charged when I was arrested. If Elizabeth can deliver a petition of acquittal to Lord Barkwood at the House of Lords in London, I might be released."

He looked fondly at his young wife. "But it's not proper for a woman to travel alone. However, if you were to go to London with her, Richard . . . would you be willing?"

CHAPTER 8

THE PETITION TO
LORD BARKWOOD

As Richard Winslow and Elizabeth Bunyan rode in the public coach toward London, Elizabeth reviewed the events that had led up to her husband's arrest. Richard listened intently; it was a story he had not heard before.

When Charles II had returned to power more than a year earlier, the laws of England began to change. Fearing that someone would try to stir up another revolution and throw him out of power as Oliver Cromwell had thrown his father out, King Charles decided to restrict public meetings where revolutionaries might organize and communicate their ideas. In one sense, he had good reason to be afraid because there was a secret group calling itself the Fifth Monarchy that was plotting to remove the king.

But it was not so easy to prohibit all public meetings, so the king decided to try to control what happened in meetings. Therefore, the government required all preachers to be licensed by the Church of England. This, the king thought, would silence anyone with revolutionary tendencies. As a result of this law, the free meetings of the nonconformist believers were restricted or stopped because they had no preachers licensed by the state.

Since John Bunyan was one of these unlicensed preachers, he had been warned that he could no longer preach on the streets of Bedford or in the small churches that met in various homes around the countryside because he had no license. "Stick to being a tinker," he was told, "and let the official clergy tend to the preaching." Bunyan, of course, believed no government had the right to prohibit him from carrying out God's command to preach the Gospel. God's law came first, then human laws.

So, when he was invited on November 12, 1660, to preach at a friend's farm some thirteen miles south of Bedford, he eagerly accepted. But when he got there, the group of believers gathered in the old farmhouse were strangely subdued. Finally, his friend took him aside and said, "John, there is a warrant out for your arrest if you preach here tonight. I happen to know that the constable will not be here for another hour; maybe we ought to dismiss the meeting and all go home."

"By no means," John had said firmly. "I will preach the Word as God has commanded me." Then he turned to the whole group and said more loudly, "Come, let's all cheer up. It is time to praise the Lord."

And so the service began as scheduled.

Before long, the constable arrived, and as expected, he interrupted the meeting and searched everyone present. He was a little apologetic when he found no weapons—these people were not the dangerous revolutionaries his superiors had told him he might find there. But he had his warrant, so he arrested John Bunyan as he had been told to do.

The next morning, Bunyan was brought before a local magistrate, Francis Wingate, for a hearing. Wingate was a hard-nosed man with a chip on his shoulder, but some of Bunyan's friends convinced him to give Bunyan a second chance. "See if you can get him to promise not to preach, and then let him go," they urged.

So Wingate questioned Bunyan and asked him if he would promise to quit preaching.

Bunyan said no, he would never make such a promise. This angered Wingate. Who did this country tinker think he was to reject leniency and refuse to promise to obey the law! In his anger, Wingate sent Bunyan off to the Bedford county jail—not for having preached the night before, but for refusing to promise not to preach again. After that there were other efforts to secure Bunyan's release, but they all required his agreement not to preach anymore, which he steadfastly refused to promise.

When his case finally came to trial in January, the technical charge against him did not involve his preaching at all. Instead, the indictment accused him of "not coming to church to hear divine service"—meaning the official Church of England—but rather taking part in "several unlawful meetings"—meaning the unofficial house churches.

Normally, sentencing did not take place until an accused person pled *guilty* or—if he or she pled *not guilty*—until a trial proved the person guilty. However, in John's case, he avoided pleading either guilty or not guilty by engaging the judges in an argument about what the charge against him actually meant. He pointed out that he regularly did attend church, and told about the worship services he and his fellow Christians often held. The judges then got sidetracked into trying to prove that Bunyan's church wasn't a real church. In the end, the exasperated judges simply sentenced him to prison until he would promise to not preach anymore.

Therefore, Elizabeth pointed out to Richard, John Bunyan had been arrested for something other than what he was charged with and sentenced without having been convicted.

"On the basis of these legal mistakes," she said, holding on to the window ledge of the swaying coach, "John is being held in jail illegally. I intend to petition Lord Barkwood at the House of Lords for his acquittal."

Richard listened admiringly. He was as eager to help secure John Bunyan's release as he was to see his father again.

———

In London, Elizabeth Bunyan and Richard stayed with Elder Barnabas, the same elder of the secret Puritan church where he and Bunyan had stayed on their first trip. That night Elizabeth told some of the church people all that had happened in Bedford, especially how John's freedom of travel had been restricted and that his enemies seemed to be getting bolder. "We can't figure how John's enemies heard that he had so much freedom. It's as though someone informed them," she said.

The members of the church looked knowingly at one another. "Things have been getting worse here in the city, too," said one of the men. "There is a secret society calling itself the Fifth Monarchy. . . ." At the mention of the group, Richard paid particular attention. There would be no falling asleep for him during this meeting. He had to know who these Puritans were. "Anyway," continued the man, "those Fifth Monarchy people have brought much trouble to all true believers. They claim to be religious, but they really are revolutionaries."

"My John has been accused of being associated with them, but what makes them revolutionaries?" asked Elizabeth.

"Well," said Elder Barnabas, eager to instruct his country friends with the latest news from the big city, "it's their notion that all earthly kings should be overthrown so they can take over. They say that the Assyrians, Persians, Greeks, and Romans were the first four monarchies, and now it is time for Christ to come back to earth and reign for a thousand years. Of course, *they* are the ones to set up this new government."

"Well, we are to expect Christ's return," said Elizabeth innocently.

"Yes, but these rascals would take over the country by force. Not long ago they started a riot here in London in which many people were killed. The government is truly afraid of them."

The more Richard listened to this conversation, the more assured he became that John Bunyan and these Christians had nothing to do with anything revolutionary.

"The problem is," continued Elder Barnabas, "many people accuse us Puritans of being part of this group like they did your John. It has put pressure on us all."

———

The next day, when Elizabeth Bunyan went to meet with Lord Barkwood, Richard set out to visit his father.

However, instead of going straight to the imposing prison, he stopped by his family's old house.

Everything was dark and shut up as he expected. He snuck around to the back and quietly let himself in the rear door with his key. There was a strange musty smell to the quiet house that did not remind him at all of home.

He crept through the kitchen and into the hall and was just passing the library when a pitiful yell came from the room, followed by a loud crash. Richard spun on his heels to make his escape when out of the corner of his eye he saw old Walter, the butler, sprawled on the floor trying to get his feet back under himself.

"Walter, what are you doing down there?" he gasped.

As the old man pulled himself up by the back of a chair and shakily regained a nearly upright stance, he blubbered, "I might be asking you much the same thing, young man. Why are you here without so much as a civil warning? You nearly frightened me to death."

"I didn't mean to frighten you," said Richard, hurrying forward to assist the old man. "I'm sorry. I guess—" Suddenly he stopped. Why should he have to issue a warning before entering his own house? "I'm sorry I frightened you," he finished simply.

Walter sat down in the chair that he had used to help himself up and took several deep breaths.

"Why don't you have some light in here? Then I'd have known you were home."

"Where else would I be?" the old man grouched. Then he waved his hand as though to dismiss the question. "I don't use lights because I don't wish to attract any attention to the house. Things are bad, Master Richard," said the butler. "When I heard you in the hall, I thought you might be the king's men come for me. I guess I tripped over something." He peered at the dark floor to see what might have caught his foot. "I expect them any day, you know. You should not be here in the city."

Richard stayed within the darkened old house most of the morning trying to rally enough courage to go to the Tower. He really didn't want to go to that awful place, but—his father was there, and maybe if he went he could help his father in some way. Besides, what had his father been saying the last time he had visited—something about Cromwell being able to prove that he didn't belong in the Tower?

Richard reviewed that conversation over and over in his mind, but he couldn't make any sense of it. What difference could Cromwell make? He was dead.

It was afternoon before Richard emerged from the old house and headed toward the Tower. As was his custom, he came out the back door, ran down the alley, then ducked between two buildings to emerge on the street. He walked briskly up the block with his shoulders hunched and head down, hoping that no one would recognize him. He peered this way and that out of the corners of his eyes, and then, just as he turned the corner, he caught a glimpse of someone half a block behind him. The figure ducked out of sight into an alcove along a garden wall—but why? Richard knew that wall well. There was an old gate there, but it hadn't been used for years.

The person had no reasonable business turning in there. It was simply someplace out of his sight. *But why hide from me?* Richard wondered. The obvious answer was, he was being followed!

CHAPTER 9

SHADOWS IN THE ALLEYS

Richard dashed down the street and skidded to a stop as he rounded the corner. Was the man really following him? This was no time to get carried away with unreasonable fears. It was his chance to visit his father.

He returned to the corner and peeked around. There came the same stranger at a brisk walk. He was young, and though he did not look like a nobleman, he was dressed better than the average working man. Long, curly, dark hair tumbled down below a large-brimmed hat pinned up on one side with a sweeping red feather. His waistcoat and breeches were dark green, his hose burgundy. *At least*, thought Richard, *those bucket-topped boots of his won't let him run very fast.* But the man kept coming at a quick pace, turning his head right and left, obviously looking for someone as he hurried along.

He's looking for me! There's no question. Richard lost no time and took off at a run.

When he got to the Thames, he headed east along the river

until he came to London Bridge. He would have darted across it, but the drawbridge was up. So he slid behind a wagon filled with wine barrels to see if his pursuer was still on his trail.

Richard wasn't far from the Tower; maybe he ought to run straight there. Certainly this man, whoever he was, couldn't follow him within its walls—that is, not unless the man was a government official, and the whole plan was to catch him and take him to the Tower, too.

Just then, he saw the man's dark hat with the red feather bobbing along through the people waiting for the bridge to open. Richard took off running again, past the Tower and on along the river until he came to the Docklands. There he made his way between the warehouses and through the alleys until he was sure he had lost his "shadow."

All afternoon he was afraid to go out on the main streets or return to the Tower for fear his pursuer would be waiting for him. He hid until dark, then made his way by a longer route back to Elder Barnabas's house, his opportunity to see his father lost.

When he knocked on the door and was admitted, he realized that Elizabeth Bunyan had arrived only a few minutes before him because she was still removing her cloak. Their host invited both guests into the simple dining room where crocks of thick soup were brought and placed before them. It seemed that there were always several people at the elder's house. Richard hadn't yet figured who was a part of the family, who were church members living there, who were overnight guests like himself and Mrs. Bunyan, and who were just visiting for the evening. All seemed to pitch in as though this were their home.

Two women and an old man crowded into the room and sat at the table while Richard and Mrs. Bunyan ate. Elder

Barnabas came and stood in the doorway. Looking directly at Richard, he said, "Well, give us a report. What did you accomplish today?"

"Not much," sighed Elizabeth, thinking he was speaking only to her, which he might have been, but at the time Richard had felt that the man had been asking *him* to give an account of his day. In any case, Elizabeth looked up at the elder and continued. "I had to wait several hours before I had an opportunity to speak to Lord Barkwood. Finally, I caught him in the hall as he was coming out of some committee meeting."

With a gasp, one of the women said, "What was he like?"

"Oh, my. I'd be much too timid to speak to a lord, especially right in the House of Lords," said the other woman.

"Quiet down, now," said Elder Barnabas. "I'm sure we all admire Mrs. Bunyan's courage, but let's give her a chance to tell us what happened. Please continue." He nodded to Elizabeth.

"Well, there's not much more to say. He was courteous enough, but once I explained the situation, he said there was nothing he could do—"

"What do you mean?" Richard butted in. "I thought a lord could do just about anything."

Elizabeth shrugged. "I had hoped so, but Lord Barkwood said that if John was wrongfully arrested, then we needed to get the circuit court in Bedford to rule on the matter. It would not be proper for him to interfere."

A quiet moan of disappointment escaped those in the small room. "I am sorry your petition didn't produce any fruit," said the old man. "But you certainly are a brave person to attempt this for your husband."

"Yes," said the woman closest to Richard. "To go right to the House of Lords and wait for Lord Barkwood. Why, that's as brave as Daniel walking into the lion's den."

"My, yes," said the other woman. "And to think that you traveled all the way here by yourself. I admire you, Mrs. Bunyan."

Wait a minute, thought Richard. *She didn't travel here by herself. I came with her. Don't I count?* But he wasn't feeling like he counted for much. The more everyone admired Elizabeth Bunyan for what she had done that day, the more Richard began to feel like a coward for having given up on visiting his father. His thoughts spun off to the streets of London and the shadowy person who had been following him.

Suddenly, he realized that Mrs. Bunyan was speaking to him. "I say, Richard, how did you find your father today?"

"How?" he mumbled, thinking at first that she was asking how he found his way to the Tower. But obviously she was asking whether his father was all right. "Oh . . . well, he is doing as well as can be expected—for being in prison."

He hoped she wouldn't ask more, but she pressed on. "Is there any news of his release?"

"No. Things are about the same," he mumbled, then quickly changed the subject. "I say, is there any more of this soup?"

His face felt hot, and he was certain that he must be blushing with embarrassment. He had just told a lie, causing everyone to think he had visited his father when, in fact, he hadn't had the courage to go to the Tower at all.

More soup came, but he couldn't eat it.

Soon the little group was busy talking about other things, but Richard couldn't help but think that Elder Barnabas was looking at him very closely. *Somehow he knows*, thought Richard. *He knows that I didn't go to the Tower.* But there didn't seem to be anything he could do about it at the moment.

———

The trip back to Bedford was grim. The day was dark and

rainy, and Richard and Elizabeth's spirits were gray. What was going to happen to their loved ones? The question hung over both of them like the stormy clouds in the sky, and there didn't seem to be much reason to talk about it.

The coach was a fast one in spite of the rain, and they arrived that evening. Together they went to the Bedford jail, sloshing through the muddy streets with their wraps pulled tightly around them.

In the jail, John Bunyan greeted them hopefully. And even when Elizabeth reported her failure to get any help from Lord Barkwood, he was still able to say, "The Lord knows our need. He will provide." Then Bunyan turned to Richard. "And how did your visit with your father go?"

Having already told a lie that Elizabeth Bunyan had heard, Richard repeated it by saying his father was satisfactory. Then he added, "He is well, but I think he is losing hope for any release."

"I'm sorry to hear that," said John Bunyan. "Very sorry. But we must not despair. Here, sit down and have a piece of my bread. Let me tell you another Pilgrim story that I've been thinking about. Maybe it will revive your spirits. Elizabeth, you can stay a few minutes, can't you?"

They sat together on the straw, and a few other prisoners gathered around. John Bunyan's stories were becoming a valued form of entertainment in the jail.

"On his journey to the Heavenly City," began Bunyan, "Pilgrim picked up a worthy companion named Hopeful. But one day they strayed off their path and nearly became lost. Before they recovered, a storm hit—much like the one raging outside this evening." Bunyan gestured toward the small window through which they could hear that the rain was coming down much harder.

Finding an old shed, Pilgrim and Hopeful crawled into the rough shelter and soon fell asleep.

Now, not far from the place where they lay, there was a castle called Doubting Castle. It was owned by Giant Despair. Unknown to our two travelers, it was his property where they were now sleeping.

When morning broke, Giant Despair got up early and went for a walk in his fields. There he caught Pilgrim and Hopeful asleep in his small shed. He picked them up with his mighty hands and with a grim voice said, "Wake up, you vagabonds! Where are you from?"

"We are Pilgrim and Hopeful," answered Pilgrim, "and we are on our way to the Heavenly City, but in the storm last night we lost our way and were waiting out the weather before continuing on."

The giant said, "Well, you have trespassed on my property, trampling through my fields. Therefore you must go along with me."

So they were forced to go, because he was so much stronger than they. They also didn't have anything to say because they knew they were at fault.

The giant carried them to his castle as though they where rats and threw them into a dark dungeon, very nasty and stinking. Here they lay from Wednesday morning till Saturday night without one bit of bread or a drop to drink or any light.

Giant Despair had a wife named Distrustful. When he went to bed, he told her what he had done. "What do you think I should do with them?"

"You should beat them mercilessly. We can't trust any strangers," she said.

In the morning, he went to the dungeon and at first started calling them dogs. Then he beat them until they couldn't rise.

That night Distrustful told Giant Despair that he ought to kill them. But when he went to do so the next morning, he had a fit and couldn't use his hands. Fortunately for the travelers, he staggered out of the dungeon without hurting them worse.

But they were so shaken by what he had planned to do that they wondered if it would be better if they took their own lives rather than wait for him to torture them to death.

"Brother," said Pilgrim, "what shall we do? Is it better to live to be tortured or die at our own hand? It seems to me that the grave would be better than this dungeon."

"Indeed, our present condition is dreadful," said Hopeful, "and death would be welcome. But what would God say? He said, 'Thou shalt do no murder.' Certainly that applies to killing ourselves. And Giant Despair doesn't always have the last word. God is still in charge, and others have made it out of this dungeon. Maybe the giant will die or forget to lock us in. As long as there is life, there is hope. Let us not be our own murderers."

For the time, that restored their courage.

But when night came, the giant's wife asked him about the prisoners.

"They are sturdy rascals," he said. "They would rather bear all hardship than to take their own lives."

"Tomorrow take them into the castle yard and show them the bones and skulls of those you have already killed. Then they will give up rather than wait for you to tear them in pieces."

So in the morning, the giant took Pilgrim and Hopeful to the castle yard. "This is what happened to other travelers whom I caught on my land. I tore them in pieces, and so I will do to you." Then he beat them all the way back to the dungeon.

In their misery, the travelers renewed their conversation about giving up and bringing an end to it all by taking their own lives. But about midnight, they began to pray, and continued in prayer till almost break of day.

Now, a little before daybreak, Pilgrim suddenly sat up and said, "What a fool I have been. I have a key in my pocket, *called Promise, that will, I am sure, open any lock in Doubting Castle."*

"Well, let's try it," said Hopeful.

And when they did, they discovered that the key called Promise did indeed open the door of their dungeon. Out they walked and continued on all night until, by morning, they were back on the King's highway on the way to the Heavenly City.

As John Bunyan finished his story, there were murmurs of appreciation and a little clapping from several of the prisoners as they rose to be about the little tasks by which they passed the time in jail.

But not Richard. He was looking around dumbfounded. "Wait a minute," he blurted. "I thought these Pilgrim stories were about truth—allegories, you called them—but that's not realistic." He looked around at the ragged men and women of the Bedford jail. "None of you carries a key around your neck that will open these doors. And neither does my father," said Richard, feeling like the story somehow mocked the seriousness of his father's plight.

John Bunyan lowered his head slightly, then spoke in a gentle voice. "I was not speaking of these stone walls"—he gestured around him—"or the Tower in London, young Richard. Instead, I was referring to another dungeon many of us have been in and out of more than once during our time in this jail, a dungeon in which I sensed you were in danger of being trapped even now. And for that prison we do carry a key."

"What do you mean?"

"The giant in the story was named Giant *Despair*. His wife was *Distrustful*. And the pilgrims were caught in the dungeon of *Doubting* Castle. There is only one key out of such a trap.

Not even the giant himself could have freed poor Pilgrim and Hopeful."

"Why not?"

"Because the key out of despair and discouragement is not something any human can do for you. In fact, you can't even get out yourself. Wishful thinking is of no value."

"I don't understand," said Richard. "You said they had the key."

"Indeed. But it had been given to them. It was not something they created. The key was the promise that they had received, a promise that has been given to each of us."

"What promise?"

"God's promise. The promise in the Bible that says, 'And we know that all things work together for good to them that love God.' "

Richard's eyes drifted slowly toward the heavy oak door of the jail.

"No, Richard," said Bunyan. "It won't open *that* door, but it will open the door in here." He patted his chest. Then he gestured toward both Richard and Elizabeth. "When the two of you came in here tonight, I was afraid that the door of despair was closing on you. I hope you'll use the promise 'key' to keep it open."

"Thank you, John," said Elizabeth, her cheeks flushed. "It's true, I was very discouraged." She gave her husband a kiss. "We'll try, but right now I need to get home to the children. Poor Mary has taken care of them for four days. And I'm sure Richard needs to get to bed, too. I'll see you tomorrow."

Richard rose obediently, not daring to speak. How did John Bunyan know he was close to despair?—not only at his father's imprisonment, but at his own cowardice that kept him from seeing his father when he had a chance.

CHAPTER 10

THE BATTLE IN
THE SWAN CHAMBER

That night in bed, Richard thought about Bunyan's story and the promise. Suddenly, what had sounded like a riddle at the time became clear to him. If God was really in control of all things, and if He had made a promise that everything would work out for those who loved Him, then there wasn't any reason to despair and feel discouraged.

Things might *seem* to be going badly, but God would take care of the final outcome. But the more Richard thought about God, the more uncomfortable he became. He had lied about visiting his father, both to Elizabeth and Elder Barnabas in London and to John Bunyan. It was such a little lie, slipping out of his mouth like wiggling fish from his hand. He knew God didn't like lying, but how was he to get back that lie? It seemed gone forever.

Would God keep His promises to someone who lied?

———

Three days passed before Richard saw Mrs. Bunyan again.

"Well, Richard," Elizabeth said as she arrived at the jail with the little jug of soup that Mary normally delivered, "I've decided to take John's advice and not give in to despair. I'm going to trust God to care for John." She was wearing a plain gray dress that brought out the blue in her eyes.

Richard smiled without much enthusiasm, and Elizabeth perceived his skepticism. "That doesn't mean I'm going to quit doing what I can do. I'm going to try to get John Bunyan a hearing in the local circuit court."

Doing something—almost anything—seemed like a good idea to Richard. By then he was feeling pretty low. Not only had he been a coward, but he had lied to cover it up. *Maybe I can also do something that would make up for my lies,* he thought. *Then maybe the promise would be mine.*

"Could I help you, Mrs. Bunyan?" he asked.

"I suppose. All I can do right now is deliver some petitions to the judges of the circuit court. They are in town right now, so I'm going to ask them to grant John a hearing. But I'd be glad for you to come along. Do you have some time this afternoon?"

"Soon as I get a couple buckets of fresh water," he said.

When Richard finished his chores, he and Elizabeth Bunyan headed down High Street to Guildhall, which served as the county courthouse when court was in session. Within it they found Sir Matthew Hale, one of the judges who would rule on John Bunyan if he were granted a hearing. Sir Matthew had served as a judge under Cromwell and was therefore inclined to grant a sympathetic ear to religious dissenters.

Sir Matthew had a pale, gentle face from which his deep-set

eyes gave a somewhat sad expression beneath dark eyebrows. He glanced over the paper that Elizabeth handed him. "You are, I take it, Mrs. Bunyan?"

"Yes, my lord," Elizabeth said with a small nod of her head.

"And is this your brother?" said Sir Matthew, glancing at Richard. "You appear far too young to have a son of this age."

"Oh no, my lord. He's neither son nor brother." Elizabeth turned to Richard to let him speak for himself.

"I am Richard Winslow. I work for my uncle, John White. He's the jailer."

"Ye-e-s-s"—Sir Matthew drew the word out as he rubbed his clean-shaven chin—"John White. He's rather too lenient, I'm told. I wouldn't think working in a jail is a suitable place for a young boy such as yourself. Is that why he grants so many liberties to his prisoners—to make the place more pleasant?"

"I don't think so, sir," Richard said, but added nothing more. *Better to say little and be thought a fool than to say too much and prove it so*, he thought, remembering his father's advice whenever important guests came to the house.

"Well, never mind." Sir Matthew looked back at Elizabeth and smiled slightly. "I will consider your petition, madam, and do my best for you."

With that, he put aside the petition and picked up some other papers. Richard and Elizabeth realized that their meeting was over.

The next day Elizabeth and Richard went looking for another judge, Sir Thomas Twisden. "He's not going to be so agreeable," said Elizabeth. "They say he's a hanging judge, quick to give out the harshest sentences. But we must give him a copy of this petition because he will also sit on the bench if John is granted a hearing."

When they stopped by the courthouse, a clerk said Judge

Twisden was having lunch at the Swan Inn. But as they went down the street and approached the inn, they saw an older man come out of the building fancily dressed in a long red coat trimmed with white fur. He had a heavy, fat face with a large red nose and a mouth that turned down at the edges in a permanent frown. Gray, stringy hair fell to his shoulders.

"Sir Thomas!" called Elizabeth loudly enough for him to easily hear at the forty-foot distance. "Sir Thomas Twisden, I must give you something."

But the man didn't even look in their direction. Instead, he climbed into his ornate carriage and ordered the coachman to drive away.

Richard grabbed the petition and ran after the carriage, which was not heading over the bridge but was in the act of making a U-turn to head back up High Street. Richard easily overtook it before it finished its turn and threw the petition in through its open window.

In a glance, Judge Twisden saw what the paper was and threw it out of his coach, yelling back, "He'll not be released unless he promises to stop preaching."

As Richard walked back toward the forlorn wife of the jailed preacher, he said, "How are we ever going to get him to consider the petition?"

"I don't know," she sighed, "but we can't give up. God will just have to make a way." But Richard noticed that there were tears in her eyes.

While they were standing in the middle of the street, not knowing what to do next, Sheriff Edmund Wylde came out of the Swan Inn. Richard recognized him immediately as the man he had shared a coach with when he first came to Bedford and who had come by the jail some time later to tell his uncle that John Bunyan was not to be allowed any more unusual liberties. "I saw what happened," the sheriff said as he approached Elizabeth and Richard. "Don't mind him. He's a sour old goat."

"But I needed to deliver this petition to him," said Elizabeth, smoothing out the crinkled paper Richard had rescued from the street.

"Really? What do you have there?" said the sheriff. He read it over, then said, "Don't give up. This evening when court is adjourned, both Judge Hale and Judge Twisden will probably be right up there." The sheriff turned and pointed to the window of an upper room in the Swan Inn. "They usually meet with several of the local gentry to review the day's court proceedings and discuss other business of the shire."

"But how should we ever be admitted to the Swan Chamber?" asked Elizabeth, naming the classy dining room to which the sheriff referred.

"Oh, I wouldn't worry about that," said the sheriff with a wink. "I imagine someone as pretty as you could walk straight in there. The worst they can do is tell you to leave. In the meantime, you might get a chance to make your request."

———

Richard had waited in the town square all afternoon while Elizabeth went home to care for the children. While he waited, he had seen Sir Thomas Twisden return in his carriage and go into the courthouse. Then, when court was over, both judges and several other men came out and walked down the street to the Swan Inn, just as the sheriff had said they would. As time passed, others went in as well.

Richard hardly recognized Elizabeth when she arrived. She wore the same plain gray dress, but she had put on a clean white collar and cuffs and had brushed her hair into a knot at the back of her head from which beautiful golden ringlets fell.

"Let's pray," she said when she got to where Richard was standing. Richard bowed his head and listened respectfully as the young woman said, "O Lord, you know John is innocent of all wrongdoing. He was only trying to serve and obey you. Please grant us courage now as we plea for justice. But more importantly, let your will be done."

She took Richard's arm as they walked toward the inn. He could feel that she was trembling, but her step was sure and steady. Just inside the door, she quickly guided Richard toward some stairs. They followed a barmaid up the steps as she carried a basket of bread in one hand and a large pitcher of beer in the other. "Let me through. Clear a way," said the barmaid to those who blocked the steps and the interior of the dining room.

By following closely behind the maid, Richard and Elizabeth managed to get all the way to the main table where both judges and several other gentlemen sat in conversation.

"My lord," Elizabeth began in a clear, loud voice as she addressed Sir Matthew Hale. "I come to you again to ask your lordship what can be done for my husband."

The conversation stopped, and all the important men of Bedford looked up at her.

"Woman," said Sir Matthew in a much less friendly tone than he had used the day before in the courthouse. "Your husband pled guilty. There's nothing I can do to help him."

"My lord, that is not so. He did not plead guilty. He was only answering questions put to him about the *nature* of the charge against him."

Suddenly, Judge Twisden interrupted with a face red with anger. "Do you think we can do what we want? Your husband is a lawbreaker, and we are bound to uphold the law. Even if we wanted to, we couldn't release him. And I, for one, certainly have no desire to release him until he agrees to quit preaching. Why, just the other day, our justice of the peace, Sir Henry Chester, reported to me that Jailer White was giving this man special liberties. But did he use them to spend time with his family? No. He ran off to preach in London. Sir Henry actually saw the man in London. But I wonder, was it preaching he did there or conspiring with those revolutionaries calling themselves the Fifth Monarchy? This man belongs in jail."

"But my lords, he was not lawfully convicted," said Elizabeth, gaining confidence. Then she told about going to London and speaking with Lord Barkwood. At the mention of a member of the House of Lords, the judges became far more attentive. "Lord Barkwood advised me to petition you for a proper trial. So I am here on his advice."

There was a moment of silence. Then Judge Twisden said, "Will he quit preaching?"

Elizabeth's shoulders sank. "My lord, he will not quit preaching as long as he is able to speak."

"Then why are we wasting our time on such a fellow?" And he grabbed his flagon of beer as though the matter was over.

But Judge Hale turned to some of the other men and said, "What's this man's occupation, anyway?"

Several spoke up at once, saying that he was just a tinker, though all agreed a good one. At that, Judge Hale also turned away as though the issue was over.

But Elizabeth was not ready to give up. "Is it because he is a tinker that there is no justice for a poor man in England?"

Her words seemed to strike a nerve. England prided itself on its system of justice—as unjust as it sometimes was.

"That's not the point," said Sir Matthew in a much more

kindly tone. "It's just that because his statements were recorded as a confession of guilt, he is considered guilty. There is nothing we can do, madam. Maybe he could apply to the king for a pardon. I am truly sorry. Now leave us in peace."

Elizabeth did not move for a full minute. Then, realizing there was nothing more she could say, she turned and followed Richard down the steps into the darkening street.

CHAPTER 11

LETTER FROM
THE PAST

The next day, Richard returned to his work at the jail with a heavy heart. It was not just that Elizabeth Bunyan had failed to secure a new hearing for her husband. It was that things *didn't* seem to be working out for good according to the promise. *If God won't rescue someone noble and good like John Bunyan from trouble, what hope do I have for things turning out good for me and my father?* he wondered. The memory of his lie continued to trouble him.

Later that day, a thick letter arrived at the Bedford jail addressed to John Bunyan. Richard delivered it and thought nothing more about it until that afternoon when Mary brought her father's jug of soup.

Richard let her into Bunyan's cell and started to go on about his work when the tinker said, "Richard, when Mary leaves, could you stay a few minutes? Something arrived in the mail that I want to discuss with you."

Richard shrugged agreeably and went on about his duties, but he kept wondering what could have come in Bunyan's letter that involved him.

Once Richard had said good-bye to Mary and returned to Bunyan, the preacher said, "Richard, is there any chance that you have lied to me in the past?"

A wave of shock rolled over him. How could John Bunyan have found out that he hadn't visited his father? For certainly that must be the lie that Bunyan wondered about. It was the only lie he had ever told the prisoner.

But just as he was ready to confess, the thought struck him that maybe Bunyan *didn't* know about his not visiting his father. Maybe he was asking about something else entirely, something that had not been a lie. So Richard approached the subject cautiously. "Why do you ask?" he said, hoping he could wiggle out of admitting his untruthfulness.

"The letter I received today came from London, and it caused me to wonder."

Richard's heart sank. Somehow John Bunyan had learned the truth. There was nothing to do but come clean. With deep embarrassment, Richard said, "I didn't . . . I mean, I didn't mean to," he stumbled. Then he blurted it all out in one stream. "It's just that when Mrs. Bunyan asked me, I said yes, and Elder Barnabas heard me, so when you asked me, I had to say the same thing to you."

"You lost me in a swirl of snowflakes, lad. What did Elizabeth ask you? And what did you say yes to?"

Slowly, Richard made his confession. He had not visited his father on his last trip to London because someone was following him, and he was afraid. "Everyone was making so much over how brave Mrs. Bunyan was when she went to talk to Lord Barkwood, I was ashamed to admit that I got scared and didn't go see my father."

"I thought as much," mumbled Bunyan, shaking his head. "Well, if you didn't visit him, what did you do?"

"I hid." Seeing the puzzlement on Bunyan's face, he explained. "I was going to see him, but Walter said it was very dangerous, so . . ."

"Wait a minute, wait a minute. Who is this Walter chap—a friend of yours? And where did you meet him?"

"Walter is our family butler. I went by our house—he still lives there—and nearly scared him to death. He said it was very dangerous in London these days. When I left to see my father, I was very wary. And sure enough, someone started following me. I ran and ran until I finally got away. But then I had to hide in an alley in Dockland. By the time it was safe to go back on the main streets, it was too late to go to the Tower. So I returned to the elder's house."

Bunyan nodded somewhat skeptically. "It's not uncommon to lose one's courage, especially in times like these," he admitted, rubbing his forehead with the tips of the fingers of one hand. He looked out of the sides of his eyes at Richard and said, "I have one more question, Richard. Were you the one who told the magistrates about my liberties from jail? Did you report to one of them how John White was letting me out from time to time?"

"No, never!" Richard protested. "I didn't say anything to anyone."

"You know that someone reported to them about my travels, don't you? You were here when the sheriff came and told your uncle to end such liberties, remember? At first, it seemed as though we had a traitor among our church brothers and sisters. But maybe it was you. Were you the one who gave me away?"

"No, no! It wasn't me. *But I know who it was*," said Richard. He felt suddenly relieved as he remembered something that had been said in the Swan Chamber the day before. "It was Sir Henry Chester, the local justice of the peace. He knows about everything that happens here in Bedford. And yesterday in the Swan Chamber—you can ask Mrs. Bunyan—Sir Thomas Twisden said Sir Henry was the one who reported on you. In fact, when he went to London, he actually saw you there, too. It wasn't me. You've got to believe me."

"I do believe you," said Bunyan with a sigh of relief. "I didn't ever think you would betray me, but when I discovered that you had lied, it naturally caused me to think that I didn't know you as well as I thought I did."

"Yes, sir." Richard hung his head. "I'm sorry. I'm truly sorry for lying." Richard sat silently for a few moments. Then his curiosity got the best of him. "How did you know that I had lied about visiting my father?"

"First of all," said John Bunyan with a broad smile, "let me say that I forgive you. But learn this lesson: 'Be sure your sins will find you out.' That's from the Bible. As to how I discovered your lie, it was that letter you brought me today. It was from Elder Barnabas in London. And you were right; someone was following you around London."

Richard's eyes widened. "Really? Who?"

"When Elizabeth told the believers in London that someone had reported my unusual freedoms, it sounded to Elder Barnabas—as it did to me—like someone had betrayed us. So, Elder Barnabas asked one of his young men to check on you, to see where you went."

"But why? Why would he suspect me?"

"Because he had heard about your father before and therefore had reason to think you might be spying on me."

"My father, Obadiah Winslow?" gasped Richard in bewilderment. "But why my father? What would cause him to think
that my father—or I—was a traitor? My father is in the Tower
because he worked for Oliver Cromwell. That makes him kind
of on your side since Cromwell was a Puritan. He's there
because the king's men don't trust him. So why would Elder
Barnabas doubt us?"

Bunyan held up his hands to calm Richard. "Let me explain,"
he said. "Apparently, shortly before Oliver Cromwell died, he
sent Elder Barnabas a letter asking for advice. Cromwell considered Elder Barnabas his pastor and valued his wisdom. Anyway,
Cromwell had discovered that his trusted secretary, Obadiah
Winslow—your father—was spying for General George Monck
in Scotland. Monck was dedicated to returning Charles II to
the throne, which, of course, you know he succeeded in doing
two years after Cromwell's death."

Richard was speechless.

"Along with his own letter to me," John Bunyan continued,
"Elder Barnabas sent me Cromwell's letter to him concerning
your father. This is it." He handed the tattered, yellow sheet
to Richard. "There's no doubting it. You can see Cromwell's
seal right there on the bottom."

Richard stared at the letter in amazement as John Bunyan
continued. "When Elder Barnabas learned you were Obadiah's
son, he had reason to be cautious about you, especially when
he heard that there seemed to be an informer in our midst.
Therefore, this last time when you were in London, he had
someone follow you."

"He thought I was meeting with some of the king's men?"

asked Richard in surprise. "To report on you and the other believers?"

"He wasn't sure. He was only checking. The man followed you to a strange house, and when you came out several hours later, you ran, finally losing him in the alleys near the docks. Knowing that you said you were going to the Tower to see your father, he went there and waited, but you never showed. Elder Barnabas realized that all of that could have been chance and proved nothing amiss. But later, when you lied, saying that you *had* visited your father, he became even more suspicious."

"But now you know why I didn't visit my father," protested Richard.

"True enough," assured Bunyan, putting his hand on the boy's arm. "But at the time, that wasn't clear. We usually lie thinking we will avoid trouble. But in this case, the lie got you into trouble. It caused your actions to *look* suspicious. So, he wrote me to warn me, thinking that if you were an enemy, you might do more damage. He sent Cromwell's letter along as proof and told me to do with it as I please."

Richard again stared at the letter. "So, what are you going to do?" he asked in a small voice.

"I have already forgiven you, and I am satisfied that you did not betray me. There's nothing more . . . except for that letter. It's yours to do with as you please. It was sent to me because of the suspicions your lies created, but now that you have repented, God can use it for good. Do you realize its significance?"

"No."

"Son, that piece of paper is your father's ticket out of prison."

"But . . . how?" asked Richard, bewildered.

John Bunyan leaned back against the cold stone of the jail

and looked up at the beamed ceiling. "The winds of change blow to and fro," he said philosophically. "One day we have revolution. The next day the king is back in power." He shrugged and looked Richard in the eye. "I am more interested in eternal things. I feel no malice toward your father no matter which side he took. He probably had his reasons. Cromwell could have hanged him as a traitor. But that was yesterday, and he did not. Who knows why?

"Today, that letter proves your father is no enemy of Charles II. It should get him out of the Tower as soon as you show it to the right people."

Richard looked again at the well-worn paper in his hands. He could hardly comprehend what had just happened. His father—a spy? Richard didn't know what he thought of that—but he did know one thing.

Now his father could be free.

CHAPTER 12

ONE OUT, ONE IN

With a bounce in his step, Richard threw his bag over his shoulder the next morning and said good-bye to his Aunt Agnes. The childless woman's round face was blotchy, and her chin quivered as she hugged her nephew good-bye.

Next Richard stopped by the jail where he found his uncle already hard at work. "I guess my vacation is over," his uncle teased as he brought in a load of straw. They talked for a while, then Richard went to speak to some of the prisoners. He especially wanted to thank John Bunyan for providing the letter he hoped would lead to his father's release from jail.

John Bunyan sat on his little bench in the corner of the ground floor open room. He was not cutting and tagging the laces as he so commonly did, hour after endless hour. Instead, he was leaning slightly to one side so that the light from the small window above him would fall across the pages of his tattered Bible.

Suddenly, Richard was overcome by the contrast between

his own situation and that of this country preacher. He stood there bag in hand, ready to ride to London where the prison gates would soon open for his father. But Bunyan sat at his bench in a dingy jail where the heavy doors had recently slammed all the tighter.

At that moment, Bunyan looked up and smiled across the room. "Richard, my boy, come here. I understand you're headed to London today. I'm going to miss you."

Richard went over and dropped his bag to the floor as Bunyan made a space for him to join him on the bench. "I'll miss you, too," said Richard. His voice sounded pinched.

"Say, now, what's troubling you, lad? You don't sound as though this was your day of jubilee."

Richard shrugged, then finally blurted, "I've been thinking, Mr. Bunyan. Remember when you told Mary and me about the promise, how God will work all things out for good?"

Bunyan nodded and waited for Richard to continue.

"Things are turning out good for me—and my father—but what about you? How can your rotting in jail week after week be good? Nothing seems to be going right for you."

Bunyan grimaced his face and stretched his arms as high into the musty air as he could. "Now that's a tough one," he admitted with a sigh as he ended his stretch. "But who am I to judge what God considers good? We don't always see the end from the beginning."

He turned so that he faced Richard and clapped his hands. "You remember the story about Joseph in the Bible?" Richard nodded, and Bunyan continued. "His brothers sold him into slavery down in Egypt. There Joseph was falsely accused and thrown into prison—for years. Finally he was released and became an important ruler after God helped him interpret the Pharaoh's dreams about the coming famine.

"After suffering for thirteen years, God used Joseph to save the lives of his father, brothers, and their families. And when that happened, do you remember what Joseph said to his brothers?"

Richard shook his head.

"Joseph said, 'You intended evil against me; but God meant it for good.'" John Bunyan stopped and smiled at Richard, waiting for him to catch the point of this ancient story. "Don't you see?" he finally asked. "For thirteen years everything seemed to be going badly, and in fact, the brothers intended it all for evil. But that wasn't God's view. He used it for good and in the end saved the whole family, even a whole nation."

"So you're saying," said Richard, "that even though you are in jail now, God might be making something good come out of it?" He shook his head. "I've worked here long enough to know that jail isn't what you'd call *good* for anyone."

"Don't confuse easy and comfortable with good, lad. I'd be the last one to tell you I enjoy it in here, but I do believe God has me here for a purpose."

Bunyan reached out and put his arm around Richard's shoulder. "I confess," he said, "from our human point of view, things don't look so good for me. But what's 'good,' my boy? How do we measure true goodness? I may want out of prison, but God may want to do something more important by letting me remain here for now . . . though I can't imagine what it might be," he sighed. "I must not let myself be defeated by circumstances!"

The two friends—one young and headed off for more joyous prospects, the other older and locked in jail—looked at each other in silence. Then Bunyan said, "Tell you what, that mail coach of yours won't be in for another hour or so. Why don't you run over to the house and get Mary—it's about time for my soup anyway—and when the two of you get back, I'll tell you both another Pilgrim story. It'll be a kind of going-away gift to you."

————

At the small Bunyan cottage, six-year-old Johnny flung open the door to let Richard in. Then he ran off to continue his play so quickly that he forgot to close the door until his mother called him back.

Within, Richard found Mrs. Bunyan fanning some damp, barely glowing coals in the family's small fireplace. "Let me help you with that," Richard offered.

"Oh, thank you, Richard," Elizabeth Bunyan said as she got up. "When you get it going, could you swing that pot over the fire? It's time for Mary to take John's soup to him, and it's not even hot. I don't know what's happened to my time this morning."

Richard looked around the room. "Where *is* Mary?"

"She's out back with Thomas. I hear you're on your way back to London."

Richard told her the good news about the letter from Cromwell and the high hopes he had for getting his father out of jail. When he had finished, Elizabeth said, "I'm glad for you." She turned her back to Richard and busied herself with pouring the now-hot soup into the jug. When she turned back around, her voice cracked as she said, "You've been a good friend . . . going with me to London and helping me try to get a hearing for my John. Thank you, Richard, and may God be with you."

She called Mary, put the jug into her step-daughter's hands, hugged Richard briefly, and pushed them both out the door.

The two young people walked in silence. Richard still marveled at how well Mary got around without her eyesight. It was as though she had memorized every tuft of grass, root, and mud puddle on the path to the jail. Not once did she stumble or hesitate.

"Do you really think your father will get out of prison?" said Mary, breaking the silence between them.

"It's almost certain," said Richard excitedly. "The letter your father gave me proves my father has always been supportive of King Charles. I can't wait until our family can be back together."

"I'm happy for you," said Mary in a thin voice as they arrived at the jail and knocked. While they waited for Richard's uncle to open the heavy oak door to let them in, Richard noticed that tears were welling up in Mary's eyes. For some reason, he hadn't thought before about blind people crying. It bothered him deeply.

———

When Richard and Mary were seated on the straw in the old Bedford jail and John Bunyan had taken the first sips of his noon meal, he leaned back against the stone wall and rubbed his chin. "Last time I told you about how Pilgrim and Hopeful escaped Giant Despair," Bunyan began.

Overhearing that a story was beginning, three other prisoners drifted over and joined them, for there was no privacy in prison, and many had grown to enjoy the preacher's stories. "But this story is about a time when Pilgrim was traveling alone on the road to the Heavenly City." Bunyan paused until everyone was settled. Then he continued.

You know, we cannot always have faithful companions to help us. Even though God gave us the church, we sometimes are alone and must rely on God's other gifts.

For just such a time, Pilgrim had been given the whole armor of God. He had on the breastplate of righteousness and the helmet of salvation. And he carried the shield of faith in one hand and the sword of the Spirit, which is the Word of God, in the other. But there was no armor to protect his back.

So when, one day as he trudged along, he saw a dragon coming toward him over the fields, he knew that he would have to stand his ground. He couldn't turn and run.

This hideous monster was covered with scales like a fish. He had wings like a dragon, feet like a bear, and the head of a lion. Out of his mouth came fire and smoke.

When he had come up to Pilgrim, he looked at him and sneered. "Where do you come from?" the dragon roared. "And where are you headed?"

"I have come from the City of Destruction, and am going to the Heavenly City," answered Pilgrim in a trembling voice. But he did not run!

"Then you are one of my subjects," belched the dragon in a great cloud of black smoke, "for all this country is mine, and I am its prince. Why are you trying to run away from your prince? If I didn't think you could still be of some service to me, I would strike you to the ground this moment with one blow."

"It is true that I was born in your kingdom," said Pilgrim, "but your service was hard, and no one can live on your wages, for it is written, 'The wages of sin is death.' Therefore, when I grew up, I did what any wise person would do. I changed my ways and left your realm."

Dragon snorted. "There is no prince that will lose his subjects so lightly, and neither will I let you go. However," he said, changing his voice to the sweetness of syrup, "since you complain about your service and wages, I'll make you a deal: I hereby promise, if you come back under my rule, I will give you whatever my country can afford."

"But I have promised myself to another," said Pilgrim, "to

the King of princes. So how can I, in fairness, go back with you without being hanged as a traitor to Him?"

"You did the same to me," roared Dragon. Then he quieted himself, took a deep breath that sucked all the smoke out of the air around him, and continued in as gentle a voice as his scaly throat could manage. "I am a generous master. Though you have broken your pledge to me, I am willing to forgive all . . . if you will but turn again and come back to me."

Pilgrim sighed. "What I promised you, I did as a child, and besides, I'm sure the King under whose banner now I stand will forgive me for whatever I did when I was so young. Besides, Dragon, to tell you the truth, I like His service, His wages, His servants, His government, and His company better than yours. Therefore, quit trying to persuade me further. I am His servant, and I will follow Him."

Then Dragon broke out into a monstrous rage, bellowing, "I am an enemy to this King. I hate His person, His laws, and His people. Therefore, I am come out to destroy you!" Two blasts of flame shot from Dragon's nostrils and singed Pilgrim's eyebrows.

"Beware, Dragon, what you do; for I am on the King's highway, the way of holiness, and I am under His protection."

Then the scaly monster straddled the path and said, "I don't care what He might do. Prepare yourself to die, feeble traveler! For I swear by my infernal den, that you shall go no farther. Here I will spill your soul!"

And with that he hurled a flaming dart at Pilgrim's breast. But Pilgrim threw up his shield and deflected it with no harm to himself.

Then Pilgrim drew his sword, for he saw it was time to take the offensive. Dragon lunged at him, firing fiery darts as thick as hail.

Dodging and weaving and using his shield to every advantage, Pilgrim fended off the darts, but his efforts were not perfect *and three missiles got through his defenses to wound him in his head, his hand, and his foot.*

Seeing Pilgrim fall back a little, Dragon followed up his attack with even greater fury. But Pilgrim did not lose heart and rallied his courage to resist as manfully as he could.

This fierce combat lasted for half a day until Pilgrim was almost exhausted. For his wounds caused him to grow weaker and weaker.

Then Dragon, seeing his opportunity, moved in on Pilgrim and, wrestling him tooth and nail, gave him a dreadful fall. Pilgrim landed so hard that his sword flew out of his hand.

"Ah-ha," roared Dragon, "I have you now," and leaped upon him to crush him to death. The weight of the foul-smelling beast was so great that Pilgrim thought he was done for.

But just as Dragon was rising to deliver his last blow, Pilgrim stretched out his hand for his sword and caught it, saying, "Don't count me out yet, you rotten brute. For though I fall, I shall arise again." Then Pilgrim gave him a deadly thrust, which made Dragon fall back as though he had received his mortal wound. Seeing his advantage, Pilgrim made at him again with his sword, saying, "It is written that 'in all these things we are more than conquerors through Him that loved us.' "

And with that, Dragon spread his leathery wings and with much flapping and wheezing managed to rise unsteadily into the air. Pilgrim watched as the smoldering monster careened over the fields until he was no more than an oily smudge against the evening's sunset, never to trouble Pilgrim again.

But from this battle, Pilgrim learned one lesson. Never again did he go about with his sword in its sheath. For as the Scriptures say, "The Word of God is quick, and powerful, and sharper than any two-edged sword."

"Hear, hear," cheered the prisoners who had gathered around to hear the story. "Very good. Very good."

"You ought to put those stories in a book," said Richard as he stood up.

"Oh, I don't know," laughed the preacher. "I'm glad you like them, but what good would it do to write them down?" Then he also stood and dusted his hands off. "Well, it's probably time for you to get down to the Swan to catch your coach." He clapped Richard's shoulders with his hands. "May God go with you, my boy, and don't forget to stand your ground. Things look cheery today, but life will bring its troubles. Remember to use your Sword!"

In a matter of moments, Richard's uncle had opened the doors and was waving good-bye to him as he went on his way. But as the boy trudged down the dusty street of Bedford toward the Swan Inn, he couldn't help wondering, *What kind of a man is this John Bunyan who has found such peace in jail?*

He thought about the two men he knew best who were in prison: his father, a political prisoner; the other, a simple preacher who told stories. One would soon be free; the other would remain behind bars simply because of his convictions.

I wonder, Richard thought, turning back to look at the Bedford county jail, *what kind of a man will I become?*

MORE ABOUT JOHN BUNYAN

John Bunyan was born in 1628 in the small town of Elstow, near Bedford, in southern England. He was the son of a tinker, someone who repaired pots and pans, sharpened knives, and did other metal work that did not require a large forge. Such a trade—and the necessary tools—was passed down from generation to generation.

On his sixteenth birthday, Bunyan reported for duty in the parliamentary army. Though he did not have strong political views, this did pit him against King Charles I. In about 1648 he married. Some think his wife was called Mary, after whom their first child was named, but that is uncertain. Daughter Mary was born blind and received John's deep tenderness and affection.

John's wife was a Puritan and inspired within John a powerful religious conversion. This led to his becoming a lay preacher in the nonconformist congregations of Bedford.

His style was powerful and direct, and he became a favorite preacher in the surrounding towns. However, except for the rise of nonconformist churches under the rule of Oliver Cromwell, it was unheard of for a lowly tinker to presume to preach. And once the monarchy was restored, the government did everything it could to stamp out these independent churches and preachers.

John's first wife died in about 1658 after bearing four children. As someone who thrived on married life, this left him devastated and in need of help in raising four small children, the oldest of whom was only eight years old and blind. Within a year John married Elizabeth, who some have suggested was John's much younger second cousin and thereby knew John and the children well.

Whatever the case, she became a devoted wife and mother and bore two more children. Throughout his life, she loyally supported him and his ministry.

In the meantime, big changes had been happening on the political front. In 1640, the English Revolution had erupted in the form of a series of political alliances and bloody battles essentially between King Charles I's army and the parliament's army, the one into which John Bunyan and most young men in his county were recruited. For ten years the civil war raged back and forth, pitting family against family and town against town. Loyalties frequently changed, and just as frequently treason was charged.

Finally, the parliamentary army won, essentially under the leadership of Oliver Cromwell. The monarchy was suspended, Charles I having been executed, and reforms were instituted, loosing the grip the Church of England had on the common people.

Oliver Cromwell emerged from the warfare and political turmoil as the Lord Protector of England and a powerful ruler for the next eight years.

As a devout Puritan, he allowed religious freedom for Puritans, Quakers, Baptists, Presbyterians, and other nonconformists. Several Anglican bishops (many of whom had sided with the king during the civil war) were removed from office, and some churches fell into the hands of the nonconformists. "Religion of the people" spread like revival. It was this populist movement that gave John Bunyan the chance to become a preacher.

Of course, all this change made enemies of many powerful people who waited for the day when they could turn the tables and return to power.

When Cromwell died on September 3, 1658, the country drifted toward anarchy under his inept son, Richard, until General George Monck, commander of the army of Scotland, invaded England, marching all the way into London in February 1660. The revolution was over.

General Monck recalled the Long Parliament, and it then contacted Charles II, who had been in exile on the continent in the town of Breda, Netherlands. In April 1660, in a proclamation known as the Declaration of Breda, Charles II promised that if Parliament allowed him to return to the throne, he would accept a parliamentary form of government and grant amnesty to his enemies. He was brought back to England and finally restored to the throne on May 8, 1660.

He did not, however, keep his promise, and soon simple preachers as well as actual political enemies were being thrown in prison all over the country. In fairness to Charles II, there was an active revolutionary group afoot that he had reason to fear. They called themselves the Fifth Monarchy and wanted to throw out the king and establish a government under "King Jesus" with, of course, themselves in charge.

The specific reason John Bunyan was jailed involved his preaching without a license. Of course, being a nonconformist, he could not get a license even though he had pastored a church for several years. As this story shows, the details of the arrest and sentencing were legally questionable, and Bunyan had good reason to petition for a new trial.

During his first few months in prison, John White, his jailer, often allowed him out on informal parole to attend services. And on one occasion, Bunyan even went to London. Then the magistrates cracked down, and he spent most of the next twelve years in the Bedford county jail.

Near the end of his time there, he probably wrote the majority of his masterpiece, *Pilgrim's Progress*, as well as several other tracts and books. He was released in 1672 and returned to his life as a pastor. However, his writings, which finally numbered more than sixty books, caused him to be much in demand as a preacher all over southern England.

He died in London in 1688 from pneumonia, which he apparently caught after riding far out of his way through a chilling rainstorm to help settle a quarrel between a father and son.

FOR FURTHER READING

Brittain, Vera Mary. *Valiant Pilgrim, the Story of John Bunyan and Puritan England*. New York: Macmillan, 1950.

Bunyan, John. *Pilgrim's Progress*. London: J. M. Dent & Sons, 1962 (the public domain edition from which scenes were adapted for this book).

Hill, Christopher. *A Tinker and a Poor Man*. New York: Knopf, 1989.

Talon, Henri. *John Bunyan, the Man and His Works*. Cambridge, MA: Harvard University Press, 1951.

Venables, Edmund. *Life of John Bunyan*. London: Walter Scott, 1888.

Winslow, Ola Elizabeth. *John Bunyan*. New York: Macmillan, 1961.

RISKING THE
FORBIDDEN GAME

MAUDE CARY

Authors' Note

This story about Maude Cary, missionary to Morocco, takes place in the spring of 1925, when Abd el-Krim, "the Desert Prince," fomented rebellion against the French. The German deserter, Sgt. Joseph Klem, who aided the rebellion, as well as all dates and battles are documented in fact.

Into this historical time frame we weave a fictional story about a "forbidden game" to highlight the tensions between the Muslim population and their French "protectors," and between three faiths: Islam, Judaism, and Christianity.

Jamal Isaam and his friend Hameem are fictional characters loosely based on two real Muslim boys in Sefrou—Mehdi Ksara and Mohammed Bouabid—who attended Miss Cary's school and eventually became Christians and co-workers with her. The soldier, David Hoffman, is also based on a true character named Leon Feldman, a Polish Jew who deserted the French Foreign Legion in Morocco, was converted, and also became one of Maude Cary's faithful co-workers. (See "More About Maude Cary" for more information about these historical characters.) However, the relationship between the boys, the soldier, and their game is entirely fictional.

CONTENTS

CHAPTER 1

THE DARE

An overloaded donkey heaved an annoyed *eee-aww! eee-aww!* in the narrow cobblestone street below the second-floor window, waking Jamal from his dreams. But as soon as the boy popped his eyes open, he heard the familiar call of the *muezzin* from the tall minaret of the mosque in the square: "Allah is great! There is no God but Allah!"

The morning call to prayer already? Jamal sat bolt upright on the soft rugs and cushions that served as his bed and squinted at his uncle Samir's bed in the semi-dark room. Empty.

Jamal groaned and felt around for his trousers and cloth shoes. Why hadn't he heard Uncle Samir leave for prayer? He had wanted to get up in time to grab a handful of dates and drink some water before the gray fingers of dawn revealed "the difference between a black thread and a white thread"—the traditional way in the Muslim world to tell when another day of fasting had begun during the month of Ramadan. Now there would be nothing to eat or drink until nightfall.

Winding his cloth sash around his already rumbling belly, Jamal hurried out on the balcony that ringed the second floor of rooms above the open courtyard of the Isaam home. The household was quiet. His father, grandfather, and uncle were probably already at the mosque where his father led prayers five times a day. His younger sisters were probably still asleep— still "babies" needing to be cared for by their mother.

Jamal hurried down the steps to the lower courtyard, pad- ded across the cool tiles and through the dark hall to the front door. It wasn't easy not to eat or drink all day long during Ramadan, but he was twelve now, no longer a child for whom exceptions could be made. Well, he'd just have to tough it out till his family broke the fast at nightfall . . . but all the more reason to play The Game today. It helped distract his mind from his empty stomach.

A smile tugged at the corners of Jamal's mouth as he slipped out the door and ran down the narrow street to the mosque. No one else knew about The Game except his friend Hameem. It all started a couple weeks back when the two boys, playing along the river that flowed down the mountain and watered the town of Sefrou, had found a military canteen stuck in the mud of the riverbank. . . .

Jamal snatched up the canteen, looking around to see if anyone had seen him. One of the French soldiers occupying the town must have dropped it.

Hameem's eyes grew wide as Jamal dipped the canteen in the cold, rushing river, then raised it to his lips to drink. "What are you doing, foolish boy! That belongs to the infidels!"

Jamal, a wiry contrast to the stocky Hameem, shrugged. "It's mine now."

"But if they catch you with it, they will think you are a thief!"

Jamal considered. He knew the rules. French property was French property and should be returned to the commanding officer. But why should he help the French? The French didn't belong in Sefrou—or anywhere in Morocco, for that matter. That's what Uncle Samir said. Jamal's uncle agreed with the rebel tribes out in the desert who refused to accept the Treaty of Fez the sultan had signed in 1912, which made Morocco a French Protectorate. For the most part, French, Arab, African, and Jew mingled side by side in the walled cities and towns along Morocco's fertile coastal plains. But the wild Berber tribes—who barely accepted the sultan's authority, much less a foreign power—kept the spirit of rebellion alive. One day Morocco would be independent once more.

Jamal decided. "It's my trophy—the spoil of war!" He held the canteen high.

Hameem sneered. "Do you think your uncle will let you bring that into your house? Your mother will make you wash your hands and say ten prayers of penitence."

That was true, too. The sultans of Morocco might be pro-European, with their phonographs and railroads and electric lights. And ordinary Muslims tolerated and cooperated with their French "protectors." But many devout Muslims would not allow *anything* belonging to the infidels in that most sacred place, their homes.

Jamal pulled Hameem down into the scrubby bushes, where they could not be seen by the women washing clothes in the river. His dark eyes shone with an idea. "Hameem! We can pretend we are rebels, fighting alongside the Desert Prince." Uncle Samir had often held the boys spellbound with stories about the exploits of Abd el-Krim, the notorious rebel leader among the Berber tribes. "It will be a contest—just between you and me—to see who can collect the most things belonging to the enemy." Jamal looked at Hameem's dubious face. "I dare you! Here—you can have the canteen to start your collection. Now you're ahead. But I'm going to win!"

And so The Game had started. Already Jamal had a plastic comb, a leather strap from an officer's horse, two empty bullet casings, and a metal fork in his treasure box, hidden under the bed pillows in his room. The boys had agreed on a point system: one point for something found; five points for something taken from the buildings the French occupied at the far end of Sefrou; and ten points for something lifted right off a French soldier.

As Jamal slipped into the big open room of the mosque where his father was leading the morning prayers, his mind was already plotting how he could add to his collection after school. But catching the disapproving look in his grandfather's eye, Jamal quickly washed his hands for the ritual cleansing, then slipped to his knees facing the *mihrab*, the niche in the far wall that pointed the way to Mecca, the Holy City.

———

Jamal was afraid he'd be scolded for being late to morning prayers, but his father, grandfather, and uncle were already arguing as the Isaam men headed back to their household—as if morning prayers had interrupted a conversation already in progress.

"Samir, you see a rebellion under every rock in the desert." Jamal's father, the *imam*, or leader of prayers in the mosque, waved a hand as though brushing off Samir's words.

"And *you* wouldn't recognize a rebellion if it sat in your courtyard and ate from your dish, Mirsab!" scowled his brother. Uncle Samir was the younger of the two Isaam brothers, but his muscles were big and hard and he walked with a swagger. Jamal had always thought of him as a giant of a man.

"My son, *why* do you think el-Krim is planning a major attack?" said Grandfather Hatim mildly. "We hear rumors all the time. Nothing comes of them."

"Because of *that*." Uncle Samir pointed to a piece of paper tacked to the wall of the corner house on the square. Jamal ran over to look. The face of a French soldier stared from the poster. The writing beneath was in both French and Arabic: "WANTED—for desertion and treason. Sgt. Joseph Klem, 2nd Régiment Étranger d'Infanterie. REWARD." The poster was dated April 1925—the European calendar.

"So?" shrugged Jamal's father. "French soldiers desert all the time."

Uncle Samir lowered his voice. "But *this* one has joined forces with Abd el-Krim. He knows weapons—now el-Krim's forces can be trained to use the machine guns and artillery they took from the Spanish."

Jamal's father snorted. "Ha. Not very likely."

Grandfather Hatim's voice was still mild, soothing. "But the last we heard of el-Krim, he was far to the north in the Rif Mountains. And besides, surely no one would mount a major offensive during Ramadan." Jamal's grandfather was a respected judge in Sefrou, and he approached all of life with a calm reason. He alone of the Isaam family had made a pilgrimage, a *hajj*, to Mecca, the holy city in Saudi Arabia.

"An excellent time in my opinion!" growled Uncle Samir. "We are not distracted by our bellies or women. Don't say I didn't—"

"Come, come, no more talk of war and rebellion," said Grandfather. The men had arrived at the blue door in the whitewashed wall that led into the spacious home within. "We do not want to upset Faheema and the little ones. Mirsab, I will not be back until time for *iftar* this evening—the French magistrate and I have a full load of cases today. . . . Jamal? Can you be ready in half an hour? I will walk you back to school."

————

Jamal tried to concentrate as the thin-faced teacher paced back and forth in front of the schoolroom, part of the mosque in the square, chanting that day's verses from the Koran. " 'This is why when Allah prescribed fasting, he says: "O you who believe! Fasting is prescribed to you as it was prescribed to those before you, that you may learn self-restraint." ' "

" 'This is why when Allah prescribed fasting . . .' " the roomful of boys repeated.

"Where is it found?" demanded the teacher.

"Al-Qur'an, 2:184," said the boys dutifully.

The teacher continued to pace, his brown striped *jellaba*, the long hooded robe worn by most Muslim men, moving back and forth across Jamal's vision like a long loaf of bread. Jamal shook his head. He mustn't think about food.

"Get out your number boards."

The room erupted in a shuffle as boys pulled clay-covered boards from beneath their benches. Jamal glanced at Hameem. His friend was already at work with a thin wooden stylus, pressing the number problems given by the teacher into the soft clay. Jamal sighed. Why was the morning going so slowly?

The last lesson of the day was French. Jamal groaned silently. Arabic was hard enough. Why did they have to learn to read and write French? The letters and words didn't even use the same alphabet!

Finally the call of the *muezzin* floated through the windows:

"Allah is great! There is no God but Allah!" Time for midday prayers. School was over.

Benches were hurriedly moved aside, prayer rugs laid side by side, and the teacher, also an *imam*, led the boys in the second set of the daily prayers.

Then, like horses released from a starting gate, the boys poured from the schoolroom into the square and galloped eagerly toward freedom. Jamal grabbed Hameem and pulled him down the congested street. "Want to back out?"

Hameem shook his head, and the boys took off running. Since there was no noon meal—the main meal for most Muslim families—during Ramadan, the boys had agreed to scout out the French quarters today to see what they could find to add to their "booty" collections. So far, pointwise, they were neck and neck. It was time to take The Game to a new level.

As usual, the streets were full of merchants selling their wares in the daily *suqs*, or markets, along with jugglers, musicians, and storytellers. Some merchants were shutting down until after midafternoon prayers, when business would pick up again. Each street market boasted different goods for sale—baskets in one *suq*; grains, herbs, and spices in another; bolts of cloth and embroidered clothing in another. Jamal deliberately avoided the market selling fresh food. The smell of *couscous* and *tajins*—a savory stew of mutton and vegetables—simmering in their pots could be his undoing. *I can wait till nightfall,* Jamal muttered to himself.

"Hey!" said Hameem. "Look."

The boys stopped to check out the small crowd that had gathered around two brown-haired men standing on wooden crates right in the middle of the basket *suq*. One was wearing a traditional *jellaba*, but the other had on long trousers and a long-sleeved shirt. Not far away, a middle-aged woman sat in the doorway of an abandoned barbershop, passing out picture postcards to a group of boys. She wore a blue caftan like most Moroccan women, but her hair was brown, her face uncovered and pale. Probably American.

Curious, the boys stood on tiptoe at the back of the crowd, trying to hear what was going on. The brown-haired men spoke in careful Arabic, as though the language was unfamiliar.

"Ever since the time of our father Abraham, the prophets in the Old Testament spoke of a Messiah, who would save the people from their sins. Jesus Christ, the Son of God, came to—"

Jamal poked Hameem and snickered behind his hand. He knew most European or American foreigners were Christian—at least, they weren't Muslim. But he'd never heard any of them actually talk about the Christian God.

"Son of God?" challenged a voice in the crowd. "There is only one God, and Allah is his name!"

"You are right, my friend—there is only one God. But God has revealed himself in three persons—the Father, Jesus Christ the Son who lived among us, and the—"

"What nonsense is *that*?" another man called out. "One God, or three gods? The Koran says that Allah is God and Mohammed is his prophet."

"The Jews still wait for the Messiah!"

Jamal couldn't see the last speaker, but he was probably from the *mellah*, the Jewish section of Sefrou.

The noises of merchants shutting down their shops and the clatter of donkey carts on the cobblestones made it hard to hear what the men were saying. Behind him, Jamal heard the woman's voice rise and fall, as though telling a story—a common pastime in the marketplace. Losing interest in the men's argument, Jamal pulled Hameem over to hear what the woman was saying. She was holding a large picture of a bearded man dressed in a *jellaba* and carrying a lamb on his shoulders. One of the boys dropped his postcard, and the wind skittered it against Jamal's foot. He bent down and picked it up. It was a copy of the same picture.

"The Good Shepherd looks for His lost sheep until He finds it, just like the shepherds here in Morocco count their sheep and goats each day and know if one is missing," the woman was saying in Arabic. But just then her pleasant voice was drowned out by the now-familiar *tramp, tramp, tramp* of soldiers marching through the marketplace.

Immediately the crowd parted and made room for the French Legionnaires. The soldiers wore blue caps with black bills and a square of fluttering cloth from the back that covered their necks from the hot Moroccan sun. Marching two abreast, they carried rifles over the left shoulder of their short, blue jackets, and their white pants were tucked into the top of black, shiny boots. A sergeant marked time at the head of the column: *"Un, deux, trois, quatre . . . Un, deux, trois, quatre . . ."*

The men in the market stared, then began to murmur among themselves. Jamal knew what they were thinking. Were these new recruits being assigned to Sefrou? Why? Did that mean the rumors of a rebellion in the Rif Mountains were true? Was Abd el-Krim on the move?

Jamal absently stuck the postcard in the folds of his sash just as something bright caught his eye—a loose button on the jacket of one of the French soldiers marching past him. It bounced on its threads, shining gold in the midday sun. *One point for something found, five points for something taken from the soldiers' quarters, ten points for taking something right off the soldier's person.*

With a sudden movement, Jamal darted close to the soldier, grabbed the button, and pulled. The button came off in his hand.

"Run!" he yelled to Hameem.

CHAPTER 2

THE FORBIDDEN
PICTURES

Ten points! Ten points!" Jamal danced gleefully around Hameem, waving the prized button in his friend's flushed face.

Still panting after their mad dash, the stocky Hameem rested his hands on his knees. Someone had yelled in French, "*Arrêtez! Stop!*" as the boys took flight. But they had zigzagged through the marketplace, cut through a long alley, and lost themselves in another street full of copper pots, gleaming jewelry, and decorative metalwork. The coppersmiths' *suq*. At last they'd stopped to catch their breath.

Hameem did not join in Jamal's celebration dance. "If you're going to get us in trouble, you could at least give me some warning," he sulked.

Jamal just grinned. "Ho, ho! Pulled this button right off his jacket. How are you going to top *that*, eh? . . . Hey! Where are you going?"

"Home. I've got to help *Om* fill the water jugs."

"Huh. You didn't say anything about helping your mother when we were going to scout out the French quarters."

Hameem just shrugged. "See you tomorrow."

Jamal watched his friend make his way through the *suq*, which was emptying out for the midday rest period. Stubborn donkey. He'd won his ten points fair and square.

The midday sun was hot, even for early spring. Jamal was suddenly aware of how thirsty he was. A drink of water from the jugs his mother filled each day rose up in his mind like an oasis in the desert . . . and just as rapidly disappeared. No. No water to drink. Not until nightfall. The month of Ramadan was only ten days old, and he would have to learn to wait.

Jamal sauntered lazily toward his own house. From the outside, the Isaam home—like all the other homes along the narrow cobblestone street—looked blank and bare, a long whitewashed wall extending from one end of the street to where it opened into the square, punctuated with painted doorways. Behind the plain blue door, however, the Isaam home had welcoming cool, decorative tiles along the passageways, soft rugs, low tables, and bright cushions in the main family room, pots of green plants decorating the sunny courtyard, and waterfalls of ivy spilling from the balcony railings looking down into the courtyard from the second floor of rooms.

Jamal's little sisters pounced on him as he entered the courtyard, giggling. He picked up three-year-old Jasmine—"little flower"—and tickled her till she screamed with delight. Seven-year-old Jawhara's cheeks were stuffed with dates, and she sucked the sticky fruit off her fingers.

Lucky little goats. They didn't have to fast during Ramadan until they'd reached their womanhood.

Jamal untangled himself from Jasmine's clutches and ran up the courtyard stairs to the sleeping room he shared with

Uncle Samir. Good. The room was empty. Jamal dug beneath a pile of cushions and blankets stacked in one corner and dragged out a small wicker chest with a rounded top. He opened the lid and dropped the button inside, where it nested with the black comb, empty shell casings, leather strap, and metal fork he'd found scouting the stables and barracks of the French Foreign Legion. He grinned. That button was worth more points than all the rest of them put together.

As Jamal closed the chest, a white postcard fluttered to the floor. What? He picked it up and turned it over. It was the picture of the shepherd carrying a lamb across his shoulders. He'd forgotten he'd tucked it into his cloth sash.

Jamal squinted his eyes and studied the picture in the dim light. Who was the bearded man? Must be a Berber tribesman—the man was out in the wild, with craggy rocks and scrubby bushes on all sides. He was wearing a long robe, a cloth head-dress, and sandals on his feet.

Why was the American woman telling stories about a Berber shepherd? Who was she, anyway? How long had she been living in Sefrou? Was she the wife of one of the men who'd been preaching Christianity?

Jamal shrugged to himself and dropped the picture into the chest along with the button. Maybe it would count for one point, since he'd found it in the street and it belonged to an infidel.

———

Jamal dipped his flatbread into the big bowl of steaming *tajins* in the middle of the low table and scooped up a mouth-ful. *Ahhh*. His mother's mutton stew, fragrant with onions and dried raisins, tasted especially good after going hungry all day. He quickly dipped again, fearing Uncle Samir and the friend

16

he'd brought home with him after evening prayers might finish it off before he'd stilled the gnawing in his belly.

Faheema Isaam gave her oldest child a gentle scold with her eyes, then she smiled. Jamal relaxed. He knew what that smile meant: *Do not worry, there is plenty.* Of course. His mother always made a lot of food each evening during Ramadan, as it was common to invite guests to share *iftar,* the breaking of the fast.

Finally Grandfather Hatim leaned back against the cushions, content. It was the signal to clear the table of the big bowl they all ate from and bring out the tea. Jamal watched as his mother poured the steaming mint tea from the tall silver teapot and handed the small cups first to Samir's guest, then to the rest of the household. The tea was already plenty sweet, but Jamal snitched another sugar cone and dropped it into his cup.

After-dinner tea was the time for conversation. Uncle Samir's friend wiped the sugary tea from his shaggy beard. "The Christian missionaries were preaching in the marketplace again."

Jamal nearly choked on his tea. Hot liquid splashed on his shirt and up his nose. He forced a cough or two to cover up his alarm.

"Jamal! Are you all right?" Grandfather leaned toward him in concern.

"I—I'm fine, Grandfather." Jamal wiped his mouth with his sleeve and took another casual sip of tea. But his mind was racing. Had someone seen him rip that button off the uniform of the French soldier?

But the dark-eyed young man at Uncle Samir's side did not even glance at Jamal. "All their talk about a three-headed God—what blasphemy."

"One God in three persons, Mateen," Grandfather Hatim said gently to their guest. "If you are going to criticize another religion, at least get it right."

Uncle Samir snorted. "With all due respect, Father, you are too patient with these infidels! The Christians say they worship the one true God, but they are nothing but barbaric idol worshipers. Haven't you seen the statue in the chapel at French headquarters? Their Jesus is nailed to a cross, dying like a common criminal. They even wear the gory image around their necks!"

Jamal was all ears. So *that's* what hung on a chain around the necks of some of the Legionnaires. He shivered in fascinated horror, just like the time he'd seen the heads of some Berber tribesmen hanging from the gates of Fez after clashes with the sultan's troops.

But he wasn't prepared for Mateen's next verbal shot. "*I* have heard that the Christians kill Muslim children if they catch them alone."

"All right, Mateen, that's enough!" said Jamal's father, gruffly. "You are a guest in our home, but I will not have my children frightened by careless rumors." Mirsab Isaam pointed a finger at his brother. "Samir, you and your friends do Islam no favors by refusing to get along with the foreigners among us. If we wish the Jews and the Christians to treat Islam with respect, we must respect their beliefs, as well. Debate is healthy! But it must be based on truth, not rumors."

"Truth?" Samir snorted. "I don't need the infidels' 'truth,' Mirsab. This is Morocco, and the Koran tells us all the truth we need to know."

————

The next day during school, Jamal was still thinking about

what Uncle Samir and Mateen had said about the Christians, when he noticed that Hameem kept looking at him from the next row of benches. Was Hameem still mad at him for getting that ten-point button? But his friend had a silly grin on his round face, as though he had a secret to tell. Jamal shot him a look: *What is it?* But Hameem ducked his head just as Jamal heard the whistle of the teacher's cane and felt its stinging *whack* on his shoulder.

"Pay attention to your own work, Jamal Isaam!" the teacher barked, then continued pacing up and down among the rows of benches. Jamal's face turned red as he struggled to keep tears from springing from his eyes. The sting in his shoulder was nothing compared to the fear that the teacher might tell his father he had misbehaved in school. Mirsab Isaam expected strict obedience from his children, and Jamal's punishment would be severe if the teacher complained about him.

Finally the sweet notes of the *muezzin* called them to midday prayer. Once the stampede of boys had emptied the schoolroom, Hameem fell into step beside Jamal. "I am sorry the teacher caned you."

Angry words leapt to Jamal's tongue, but Hameem truly looked sorry. "All right," he relented. "We are even now." More than even, Jamal thought. Making Hameem run from the French man yesterday wasn't half as bad as getting caned by the teacher.

Relieved, the same grin sprang to Hameem's lips.

"Why are you looking at me like a camel about to spit?" demanded Jamal.

Hameem's grin widened. "Come on, I'll show you!"

Curious, Jamal followed Hameem as he led the way through the heart of the *medina*, the "old city," then stopped triumphantly outside an ordinary house. But strangely, the door stood open, and Jamal could hear children singing.

"What is this? It sounds like a school." Jamal tried to peer inside the open door into the dim passageway.

Hameem pulled him aside. "It is! It's the American woman's school," he hissed in Jamal's ear. "And I'm going in to see what it's all about. Now *that* ought to be worth ten points!" Hameem crossed his arms and tilted his chin up defiantly.

So that was what this was about—Hameem was trying to top the button episode yesterday. "Don't be a fool!" Jamal grabbed Hameem's shirt and tried to pull him away, but Hameem's stocky build did not budge. Instead, Hameem jerked away, gave Jamal a cocky grin over his shoulder, and disappeared into the open door.

Jamal stared after his friend, open-mouthed. School? What kind of school? The Islamic school was the only kind of school he knew about. He had an urge to march in after Hameem— after all, *he* was usually the one who dared to bend the rules and take a few risks for the sake of The Game.

But he hadn't had time to think this through. The American woman was probably a Christian—which made her an infidel. He was sure his father would say it was one thing to listen to the Christians in the open market, but quite another to go into their homes and attend their schools!

What *was* Hameem doing? As the minutes crawled by, Jamal paced up and down the street, though avoiding the front of the American woman's house. He was half mad at himself for not going in, too—would Hameem think he was a coward?—and half worried for Hameem. What if . . . what if the rumor about what happened to Muslim children if Christians got hold of them was true!

The sun had moved a good hour and Jamal was hot, thirsty,

and irritable before Hameem appeared again in the doorway, along with several other Muslim and Jewish boys. The same American woman who had been telling stories in the basket *suq* yesterday came to the door and waved. "*Ma'a el salama!* Good-bye!"

This time Hameem allowed himself to be pulled along as Jamal grabbed his arm and towed him out of sight of the house. "What happened! Tell me!"

"Ten points?"

Jamal rolled his eyes. "All *right*. Ten points."

Hameem strolled slowly down the street. "Well, school today was called Sunday school—it is the Christians' holy day, the first day of their week."

Jamal frowned, puzzled. Islam's holy day was Friday. And that was the only day they did *not* have to go to school. "What did you do?"

"Well, she talked about the Christian Bible—"

"You mean you memorized verses from the Bible?" Memorizing verses from the Koran took up a major part of Islamic school.

"No. She just told us a story—about Jesus. The one they call the Son of God." Hameem dug in his sash and pulled out a postcard. "I got a picture, too."

Jamal sucked in his breath. "Hameem! You better be careful! What would your father do if he found out you had gone inside the infidel's house and attended their Sunday school?"

Hameem shrugged, trying to look unconcerned, but Jamal caught the uneasy frown. "What else?" Jamal demanded.

"Well, Sunday school only meets on Sunday. But Miss Cary—that's her name—told us that she runs a school every afternoon for anyone who needs help with their regular school studies so they can pass their exams. She can speak three languages—English, French, and Arabic. And some Berber, too."

The boys walked in silence for a few moments. Then Hameem said, "Do you want to see the picture?" He thrust the postcard at Jamal.

Jamal studied the picture postcard. The bearded man—the same one who looked like a Berber shepherd—was holding a handful of mud and putting a mudpack on a man's eyes who was kneeling in front of him, his face upturned.

"That man was blind," Hameem offered helpfully. "Miss Cary told a story about how Jesus healed his eyes. She said if I come back she has lots more stories . . . and pictures, too."

Jamal wished he'd heard the story—but even as he studied the picture, a sly idea began to form. Hameem may have earned ten points for going to Miss Cary's Sunday school . . . but he, Jamal, could top *that* by collecting *all* the Jesus pictures! There had to be more. But he had to be careful—he would be in big trouble if his parents found them, not to mention Uncle Samir. But what was The Game if it didn't involve a dare? He already had one picture, and here was another. . . .

"Hameem." Jamal laid a hand on his friend's shoulder. "You really played The Game today—you earned that ten points! But don't take the Jesus picture home, or your parents may discover what you did. I don't want you to get in trouble because of The Game. Here—I'll get rid of this for you."

Before Hameem had time to think about it, Jamal tucked the picture into his sash and hollered, "Come on! I'll race you home!"

CHAPTER 3

THE INFIDEL'S SCHOOL

There was only one way to get the American woman's Jesus pictures—Jamal would have to go to her afternoon school.

The more he thought about it, the more he was confident he could pull it off. After all, nothing had happened to Hameem, and he had gone to *Sunday* school. Jamal could go between prayer at noon and midafternoon prayer, when the boys were usually free to roam the marketplace or play outside the city gates anyway. No one would miss him as long as he showed up for the daily prayers.

Besides, hadn't Hameem said that Miss Cary offered to help with their regular studies—Arabic, French, and numbers—so they could pass their exams? Both Grandfather Hatim and his father were expecting him to go to school in Fez after he passed Islamic school examinations. But Jamal often worried: what if he didn't pass?

The next day, the twelfth day of Ramadan, Jamal caught

Hameem after school. "I want to go with you to the American woman's school today."

Hameem's eyes narrowed. "Copycat. The first one to do a dare gets points. I already got the ten points for going into her house—you said so yourself."

"I know, I know. But you said she can speak three languages and is willing to give help with our regular studies. I"—Jamal had to swallow his pride. "—could use the help. I'm not as good at numbers as you are. And my French is terrible." That was true—even if it wasn't the *only* reason he wanted to go to Miss Cary's school.

Hameem scratched his head. "Well, I hadn't really planned on going again. I only did it to get points."

"Come on, let's just go see what it's like—no points."

Hameem gave in, and the two boys found themselves once more before the open door of Miss Cary's house. Jamal hesitated, took a breath, then stepped inside. He'd never been inside the home of a Christian before—or a Jew, for that matter, even though a lot of Jews lived in the *mellah*, their own section of Sefrou. The only place the Jews and the Muslims really mixed was in the marketplace.

To his surprise, the house was not that different from his own—but smaller, simpler. A dim passageway opened into a small courtyard, where a handful of other boys Jamal only vaguely recognized sat on the floor around the American woman. Probably from one of the other Islamic schools around Sefrou.

Miss Cary looked up. "*Ahalan.* Hello. *Ma ismok?* What is your name?"

Jamal suddenly felt tongue-tied. He wasn't used to seeing a woman other than his mother without a headscarf and face covering. Miss Cary's hair was brown, like the mud of the

24

riverbank, with streaks of gray and pulled back into a knot at the back of her neck. She wasn't a particularly pretty woman, but her smile was warm and welcoming.

He swallowed. "Jamal Isaam. I—" He didn't know what to say next. He felt very uncomfortable. After all, this was the house of an infidel!

"I am glad you came. Please sit down. I am ready to begin a story—then we will practice our French."

Jamal and Hameem sat.

Miss Cary held up a large picture—the shepherd in the *jellaba* again. Except this time the man was sitting down, with a lot of children crowded around him. "One day," Miss Cary began, "Jesus was walking with His disciples—the men whom He was teaching to carry on His work—when a group of mothers brought their children to Jesus so that He would bless them. But the disciples told them to go away."

Of course, thought Jamal. The mothers and children shouldn't bother a *khatib*—a preacher or teacher.

"But Jesus said, 'Let the children come to me.' And He blessed them. Then He told the disciples that they should have faith like little children."

Jamal poked Hameem and rolled his eyes. Everyone knew that babies like his sisters didn't know anything. It was the old men like Grandfather Hatim who knew everything about faith and God. Miss Cary must have told the story wrong.

But true to her word, Miss Cary drilled the small group of boys on their French verb forms and their vocabulary. At first, Jamal was afraid to answer for fear he would give a wrong answer and get a caning. But when one of the other boys gave a wrong answer, she simply said, "*Non.* Does anyone else know the right answer?" Realizing that Miss Cary had no cane, Jamal ventured an answer—the correct one—and was

25

rewarded with, "*Bon!* Good! See me after class, and I will give you a picture."

What? She wasn't going to just pass them out? He had earned one, but how would he collect in front of Hameem? He couldn't—not after telling Hameem to get rid of his picture yesterday.

The hour went by quickly. Miss Cary closed her French book. "I must get ready for my next class. . . . *Ma'a el salama,*" she said in Arabic. "Good-bye."

Jamal removed his blue-and-white crocheted cap. "*Ma'a el salama.*" He turned to go, casually dropping the cap as he went out.

Outside, Hameem seemed impatient to leave. "Come on. I have had enough school for today. It's almost time for prayers."

"Wait." Jamal felt his thick crop of black hair. "I forgot my cap. I will be right back."

A new group of boys were going into Miss Cary's house— Jewish boys. Did they need help with their schoolwork, too? He slipped in, found his cap, then singled out Miss Cary. "I answered correctly. Could I have a picture, *min fadilak*—please?"

He took the small picture she offered, tucked it into his cap, and pulled the cap tightly down on his head before running out to join Hameem.

———

Jamal got back home just in time to slip into the mosque in the square for midafternoon prayers. A quick glance around located his grandfather and father. As usual, Mirsab Isaam was getting ready to lead the prayers. In row upon row, men and boys kneeled side by side on the prayer rugs, hands on their knees. As his father intoned the first prayer, Jamal lowered his forehead to the ground to the rustling sound of everyone else doing the same. Most Muslim men and boys wore snug-fitting caps that allowed them to do this ritual unhindered. Even the red fez and tassel worn by rich men had no brim, allowing them to bow to the floor in prayer.

Jamal had seen newspaper pictures of European and American men wearing hats with wide brims. How could anyone pray with a hat like that?

As Jamal relaxed in the familiar ritual of the prayers, he felt a little guilty. Had he disqualified himself from the benefits of the fast by attending the infidel's school? In his mind he could hear his teacher listing the five things that were particularly offensive during Ramadan: slander; criticizing someone behind his back *(no problem with those two)*; a false oath *(clear conscience there)*; greed *(hmm, did talking Hameem out of his Jesus picture count as greed?)*; telling a lie *(ouch!—he hadn't actually told a lie, but he wasn't telling the truth about going to the infidel's school.)*

"As-salaam Alaikum." He heard his father give the final blessing. "Peace be upon you." The crowd of men and boys spilled out of the mosque and into the square. Jamal hurried home and immediately ran up to his room. Uncle Samir was nowhere to be seen. Jamal hadn't seen him at the mosque, either. His uncle was a wheelwright by trade and often got called to other towns and villages to repair carts and wagons. He might be gone for days.

Jamal pulled off his cap and fished out the picture post-card he'd put inside. He smoothed the bent edges and looked at the children crowded around the man. Then he noticed something he hadn't seen before: the children were all different colors! Black hair and yellow hair, brown eyes and blue, dark skin and light skin—and every shade in between. Who *were* these children?

He'd have to ask Miss Cary . . . if he went to her school again. His insides tightened—he wasn't sure if it was hunger pangs from fasting or guilt about doing something his parents might not approve of. Should he tell them about the American missionary?

———

That evening when they broke the day's fast at *iftar,* Uncle Samir was still absent. Good—this was Jamal's chance to say something without his uncle jumping all over him. His mother had made *harira,* a spicy lentil soup with meat, beans, and tomatoes, thick enough to scoop up with the flatbread.

Jamal took a deep breath. "I saw the Americans in the marketplace, too. The woman is a teacher."

His father looked up and frowned. "What kind of teacher?"

"Uh, French, Arabic . . . and numbers. She tutors children who want help before taking their exams."

"Miss Cary? The Christian missionary?" said Jamal's mother, feeding Jasmine, who sat in her lap. "She helped Shu'a Serraj deliver her baby two months ago—I heard the women talking at the river. They said she is very kind."

Jamal stared. He hadn't expected her to be an ally.

Mirsab Isaam looked keenly at his son. "Where did you hear about the American teacher?"

"Hameem told me." That was certainly true.

Jamal's father frowned. "Meddlers," he grumbled. "We can deliver our own babies and teach our own children. Sometimes I think Samir is right. They should take their foreign religion and go home."

Grandfather Hatim chewed thoughtfully. "On the contrary. It strengthens our religion to know what the Christians and Jews believe and how to answer. When I studied Islamic law in Marrakesh, we had many good debates with foreigners. It made us think."

Jamal decided to take the plunge while things were going his way. "I could use the extra help with my studies." He caught the look his father sent his mother; his father was not pleased. But his mother gave a slight shrug and started to clear the table of the nearly empty bowl of *harira*.

Grandfather settled back. "Christians teach many things that are true—about the holiness of God, about loving your fellow man, about the good deeds of Jesus. But you must be alert. They also claim that Jesus was God—how can that be? He was a man. A good man, a saint—but not God's representative. As you know, Jamal, our prophet, the great Mohammed, is the only true representative of God."

Inspired by his grandfather's confidence in him, Jamal blurted, "And the Koran is God's holy word given through our prophet."

Even Jamal's father nodded approvingly. Just then Faheema arrived with the teapot, and Jamal settled back with his cup of sweet mint tea. The conversation turned to other things, but he was satisfied. He had told his family about Miss Cary's school. They hadn't said yes, but they hadn't said no, either. And hadn't his grandfather said it was good to know what the infidels believed so one could make a good argument?

———

"Jamal! Come on! We're going to watch the Legion do their drills outside the city gates! Some French prisoners are making bricks along the mud banks, too—must be deserters who got caught, poor worms."

Jamal felt torn. It would be fun to run off with Hameem and the other boys—maybe they could even snitch some loot for The Game. But he had been attending Miss Cary's school for over a week now—except for the Friday Holy Day—and even his Islamic teacher seemed surprised at Jamal's new grasp of French verbs.

Not to mention that his collection of the forbidden pictures was growing.

He steeled himself to his resolve and went to Miss Cary's school. He recited all his verbs correctly and got another picture—Jesus standing in a fishing boat surrounded by frightened disciples during a fierce storm. According to Miss Cary, Jesus commanded the storm to stop, and it did. *Hmph*. Maybe Jesus was just braver than His followers.

When Jamal got home, he heard male voices talking in excited tones in a corner of the courtyard. Uncle Samir was back, along with Mateen and a couple of other friends. The men didn't seem to notice him, so Jamal quickly ran up the courtyard stairs to the second floor balcony. Pulling the small wicker chest from behind his bed cushions and dropping the picture inside, he looked around the sleeping room. He needed a better hiding place for his collection of forbidden treasures— but where? Finally he pushed the chest under the low table that stood along the wall. Uncle Samir wouldn't go looking under there.

But he felt anxious as the family broke the day's fast at *iftar* that night. What if Grandfather or his parents asked him about Miss Cary's school in front of Uncle Samir? But he needn't have worried. Samir's friends had stayed for the meal, and only one thing was on their minds: Abd el-Krim and the rebellion.

"I tell you, Mirsab," Uncle Samir said to his brother, dark eyes gleaming, "we shall see action before the end of Ramadan. Out in the villages, there is talk of nothing else. The Desert Prince has amassed a great army from among all the tribes."

"The French know something is up," Mateen agreed. "The number of troops in Sefrou has doubled."

"*Na'am*—yes. They march and drill outside the city gates every day," Jamal chimed in.

Uncle Samir lowered his voice, as though the walls might have ears, and looked meaningfully at Jamal's father and Grandfather Hatim. "We must be alert. One of these days we will have to choose where we stand—with the infidels . . . or el-Krim."

CHAPTER 4

THE DESERT PRINCE

By the time Jamal got to school the next day—the twenty-second day of Ramadan, or April sixteenth on the Western calendar—reports and rumors were already on the tongues of the farmers and tradesmen coming to sell or buy in Sefrou's markets.

"The Desert Prince has thousands of horsemen, heading toward Fez!"

"They say the French deserter rides with him!"

"Klem? He's not French—even if he did make sergeant in the Legion. Calls himself 'The German Pilgrim,' claims he's a convert to Islam."

"Convert? Huh. Maybe, maybe not. But he knows weapons. Taught el-Krim how to use the guns they captured from the Spanish."

"Ha! No wonder the French want his head!"

Even Jamal's teacher seemed to have el-Krim's rebellion in mind as he drilled them on that day's verse from the Koran again and again: "Sura 61:11—To believe in God and His messenger . . ."

"To believe in God and His messenger . . ." recited the class in unison.

". . . and to fight hard in God's cause with your property and your persons," the teacher intoned.

". . . and to fight hard in God's cause with your property and your persons," the class repeated . . . and on it went, back and forth, through the whole passage.

Later Jamal surprised himself when the teacher called on him to divide two numbers—he was able to do it in his head and he gave the right answer.

Miss Cary's classes were paying off.

Still, he dragged his feet on the way to her street after midday prayers. Uncle Samir had warned that they would have to choose between the infidels (meaning the French occupation) or the rebellion. Miss Cary wasn't French—but it was well known that the American missionaries lived in Moroccan towns under French protection. She didn't have any "idols" in her house—but she told stories from the Christian Bible. Even Grandfather Hatim had said he must be alert to their false claims.

Was he being a traitor to Islam by going to school in Miss Cary's house? He knew Uncle Samir would think so. Maybe he should quit. . . .

Even though his mind felt divided, Jamal's feet took him into Miss Cary's courtyard. After all, he argued with himself, his parents hadn't said no, and his schoolwork was improving. And, he admitted to himself, Miss Cary's class was his only source for the collection of forbidden pictures.

Forbidden. That was part of the excitement of The Game—collecting stuff that belonged to the infidels.

Miss Cary was passing out a small leaflet with Arabic words on both sides, limping as she did so. Jamal had noticed that she limped when she was tired, but when one of the students had asked if she was hurt, she just laughed and called it "the rheumatiz."

"Who would like to start our reading lesson today?" she asked.

Another boy's hand shot up. He stood and began reading. To Jamal's surprise, the reading lesson was about Jesus—a terribly sad story about religious leaders who wanted to kill Him because He claimed to be God's Son—just like God.

Jamal's ears pricked. This was what Grandfather Hatim had warned him about.

Another boy read about Jesus' trial, and still another read how He was sentenced to death by crucifixion—hanging alive on a wooden cross to die a slow, horrible death.

The final reader, however, read that after Jesus was buried, He came alive again on the third day. Jamal's face grew hot. He should not be here listening to this heresy.

Miss Cary held up a large picture of Jesus hanging on the cross. "The death of Jesus was part of God's plan," she explained. "Our sins keep us away from God, and the punishment for sin is death. But God loved you and me so much that He sent His only Son, Jesus, to earth to take the punishment for our sins. If you ask Jesus to forgive your sins, He will come to live in your heart, and you can go to live forever with God in heaven."

Jamal jumped up. This was blasphemy! "The Koran says there is no God but Allah! The Koran tells us the way to heaven is to pray five times a day, to keep the fast of Ramadan, to take care of the poor, and make a pilgrimage to Mecca at least once in a lifetime. *That* is the way to heaven!"

His eye caught the brazier that kept Miss Cary's pot of

water hot at all times. With a burst of self-righteous anger, Jamal thrust his copy of the blasphemous leaflet onto the coals. It burst into flames and the edges curled up. Then he stalked out of Miss Cary's house. He was proud of defending Islam. Uncle Samir would be proud of him, too.

No one came out after him. He looked back inside, where he could hear the rise and fall of Miss Cary's gentle voice. He felt cross. The other boys should have walked out, too. They were Muslims, weren't they? Didn't they know blasphemy when they heard it?

Pacing up and down in front of Miss Cary's house, Jamal told himself he was going to set the other students straight. From time to time he stopped and tried to listen, but all he could hear were boyish voices and occasional laughter. Were they laughing at him? He felt foolish, but he angrily pushed out his chest and stuck his chin into the air. No, *they* were the fools!

With a sudden pang, he also realized he had walked out without getting a copy of the cross picture. Maybe that one was *too* risky, but of all the pictures he had, wouldn't a picture of the infidel Jesus on the cross be worth the most points in The Game?

At the end of the hour, the other boys filtered out of Miss Cary's house. Some of them had a picture postcard in their hands. A few of the boys hesitated when they saw Jamal. "Foolish boys!" he barked, snatching the picture out of one boy's hand. "Don't you know these pictures are blasphemous?" He snatched another picture, and another. "I will get rid of them for you—now go!"

The boys backed off slowly, then turned and ran.

Triumphantly Jamal watched them go. Tucking the pictures into his cloth sash, he ran for home.

———

Jamal spent the twenty-third day of Ramadan—the weekly Holy Day—with his family and at the mosque. But after school on Saturday, he yelled, "Hameem! Wait for me!"

Hameem, ready to go off with the other boys, raised a skeptical eyebrow. "Aren't you going to the Christian school?" Jamal's daily attendance at Miss Cary's school had been a sore point with his friend.

"No." Jamal gave a shrug. "I got what I wanted."

Hameem grinned. "Good! Come on! We've been playing war games with the French soldiers when they drill out in the fields—except they don't know it."

Laughing, the boys ran after their friends, but slowed as they picked their way through the basket-weavers' *suq*. The marketplace was abuzz with the latest news:

Abd el-Krim was attacking the string of French outposts between "occupied" Morocco and the western border of Algeria.

"I heard the Desert Prince has captured five, maybe six, of the French forts already!" said a bearded merchant, more interested in talking than selling his stacks of baskets.

"*I* hear he is not taking prisoners." The seller in the next stall winked knowingly.

Jamal eyed Hameem grimly. No doubt the heads of French soldiers were decorating the gates of those forts.

More sober now, the boys threaded their way through the crowded streets and out the city gate. Sefrou in the spring was lush with sprouting olive, date, and almond trees fed by the river from the nearby mountains, swollen from the spring rains. Newly planted fields of barley and corn were surrounded by large plots of vegetables and pungent mint plants. Sefrou was one of the last oases before the stretching desert.

The French Foreign Legion had tramped out their own parade ground close to the city gates. "Hope you don't think I've been sitting on my hands while you've been feeding verbs and numbers into your head," said Hameem, giving Jamal a playful shove. "With all these soldiers running around getting ready to fight, I've been picking up a *lot* of their stuff for my collection."

"Like what?" Jamal demanded. Of course it was only fair that Hameem had continued to play The Game—hadn't he been getting points for himself by pocketing Miss Cary's pictures? But was it possible that Hameem had gotten more points than he?

Hameem shook his head. "I'll show you when we *both* show our collections and count points. When?"

Jamal considered. "After Ramadan. How about the first day of Shawwal?"

Shawwal was the tenth month of the Muslim year—only one week away.

"Agreed," said Hameem smugly.

———

The French Foreign Legion in Sefrou was on high alert. Guards were stationed at the city gates, and other soldiers patrolled the top of the city wall. Reports and rumors continued to feed into the town from camel trains and nomadic Berbers selling sheep's wool: El-Krim had captured nine French outposts; the French had abandoned thirty others and pulled back; overtaken at some of their posts, French soldiers—true to tradition in the Legion—had saved their last bullet for themselves. The latest report—coming right after *Lailat al-Qadr*,

37

the "Night of Power," when Muslims commemorate the night the Holy Koran was revealed to the prophet Mohammed—had tongues wagging at *iftar* in every household in Sefrou:

Abd el-Krim was heading for Taza, only one day's march from Sefrou.

A new contingent of French soldiers poured into Sefrou. Curious, Jamal followed them as they marched past the mosque just after midafternoon prayers. Besides, with only three more days of Ramadan, Jamal had to get more points—*high* points—if he wanted to win The Game.

But as the new soldiers reported for duty at headquarters office, Jamal realized it wouldn't be easy to sneak off with something. Soldiers in blue coats and white pants were *everywhere*. Some were on duty; others waiting for orders. But no one seemed to pay any attention to a mere boy, so he loitered and watched.

A soldier sitting off by himself in the shade of the sleeping quarters caught Jamal's attention. The young man—he couldn't be more than twenty—had a long, angular face and was reading a book. Jamal sidled closer, wondering what the soldier was reading. Then he noticed an empty place on the soldier's uniform where a button was supposed to be. Startled, Jamal stared at the soldier's face.

It was *his* button Jamal had ripped off that day in the basket-weavers' *suq*.

Jamal had an urge to flee. It wouldn't be smart to get caught for thieving! But the soldier's attention seemed diverted by the new arrivals who were going in and out of the sleeping quarters, storing their gear. Jamal saw him shake his head and heard him mutter, "Why don't we just let these people *have* their old town. It's their country, anyway."

Jamal's ears pricked up. The soldier had spoken French, but

his accent was Polish or Czech—something eastern European. Jamal shook his head. He never had understood why the French Foreign Legion had so many *foreigners* in it.

One of the recent arrivals stopped abruptly, then took a step or two toward the reading soldier. "I wouldn't say that too loudly if I were you," he whispered sharply. "I've heard what the Legion does to traitors." Then he raised his voice and spoke loudly. "Say, would you show me where I'm supposed to bunk? I don't know my way around yet."

With a friendly nod, the first soldier closed his book, stuck it in his knapsack, and got to his feet. "You sure have a lot of gear," he said, tipping his chin toward a pile of bedrolls and canvas bags.

The new soldier snorted. "Not all mine—my buddy had to go take care of the lieutenant's horse." Just then he caught Jamal observing them. "*Hé, garçon!* Hey, boy! *Parlez-vous Francais?* Come help us take these bags inside."

Not believing his luck, Jamal sprang to life. These soldiers were *taking* him inside! He slung one knapsack over his shoulder and tucked a bedroll under the other arm. Trotting obediently behind the two soldiers, he glanced around him furtively, trying to memorize every detail. The first soldier led the newcomer and Jamal up a set of rough wooden stairs to a large open room, filled with low wooden beds in row after row.

"This is my bunk," said the soldier in French, throwing the knapsack with his book inside on the military-neat bed. "You can take that empty one there. The way things are going, you'll only be sleeping in it one night."

The other soldier rolled his eyes, then remembered Jamal. "Here, boy. *Merci.*" And he flipped him a coin.

"*Merci beaucoup!*" Backtracking down the wooden stairs,

Jamal hoped he'd remembered the right French words for "thank you very much."

As he came out again into the late afternoon sunshine, his eyes shone with an idea: the book. If he could get the soldier's book right out of his backpack—now *that* was a ten-pointer. Hadn't he seen where the soldier's bed was? But he didn't want to get caught. He'd have to plan very carefully—no, wait. Something the soldier said hinted that the Legion might be leaving for Taza in the morning.

If he wanted to get the book for his collection, he'd have to do it tonight.

CHAPTER 5

MIDNIGHT RAID

Jamal was impatient for the household to blow out their oil lamps and go to sleep. He brought water without being told and poured it into a large brass basin so that his mother could give Jasmine and Jawhara a bath. Then Faheema Isaam swept the wet little girls into the folds of her caftan and disappeared into the "women's rooms" on the second floor.

Grandfather Hatim excused himself soon afterward. Uncle Samir had been strangely quiet and brooding at *iftar* that evening, but he stayed up a long time with Jamal's father, lingering over their mint tea and talking politics and war in low voices.

Jamal checked to make sure that his wicker treasure chest was safely stowed out of sight beneath the low table, then rolled out the soft rugs that served as his bed and lay down. It wasn't unusual to sleep in his loose clothes—no problem there. But what if he fell asleep? Even if he didn't, could he get out of the house without anyone hearing him?

The last light down in the courtyard was blown out, and a

moment later Uncle Samir's dark shape appeared in the dim doorway and lay down on his own bed. Jamal didn't move. He waited and listened, hoping to hear the deep, regular breathing—even a snore or two!—that would tell him his uncle had fallen asleep.

Instead, he heard nothing. As though Uncle Samir was lying awake, too.

Well, he'd just have to wait—and not fall asleep, or his golden opportunity would be gone. As he lay there in the dark, Jamal realized he missed going to Miss Cary's house. Her school was so peaceful, and she always had a warm smile and greeting for each of the boys. She didn't seem to have any children or a husband—at least it looked like she lived alone. Did she have a family? Were the American men he saw in the marketplace her brothers? He hadn't seen them since that day he'd pulled off the soldier's button—where had they gone?

Jamal liked the Jesus stories, too—even if He was an infidel. Jesus had been kind to children and lost lambs; He gave food to thousands of people who got hungry while listening to his teachings. The different pictures in the wicker chest floated in his mind—Jesus healing the blind man . . . Jesus healing a little girl . . . Jesus healing a man who couldn't walk. For a man like that—why didn't His followers rise up and fight when His enemies captured and killed Him? Why, Abd el-Krim would—

A rustling noise in the room startled him. Uncle Samir was getting up! Jamal couldn't see in the darkness, but it sounded like his uncle was putting on his *jellaba* and sandals. Sure enough, his uncle's form appeared in the dim light of the open doorway, then Jamal heard soft footsteps going down the courtyard stairs.

Where was he going? Scrambling to his feet, Jamal moved

quickly to the wooden railing just outside his room and looked down into the open courtyard. As his eyes adjusted to the muted moonlight, he caught movement disappearing into the passageway that led to the front door.

Uncle Samir was leaving the house!

This was Jamal's chance. Trying to be as quiet as possible, he hurried down the stairs, grabbed a handful of figs from a bowl—at least it was nighttime and he could eat—and silently eased the door open. Poking his head out, Jamal looked up and down the dark, narrow street. His uncle was heading toward the square, the same direction Jamal wanted to go.

Moving as swiftly and quietly as he could, Jamal followed his uncle, keeping to the shadows. A quick glance at the night sky showed a thin cover of clouds, barely letting the glow of the moonlight sift down over the town. Where *was* his uncle going? He seemed to be heading straight to the French garrison.

As they turned onto the last street before reaching the garrison, Jamal saw his uncle pull back into the shadows. Two guards were making their rounds; they passed each other, then continued in opposite directions. Jamal drew closer, stepping into deep doorways along the way, then held his breath until he reached the safety of the next one. Uncle Samir was still standing in the shadows at the end of the street—he seemed to be watching the doorway of the Legion's headquarters.

To Jamal's surprise, a soldier in a French uniform appeared seemingly from out of nowhere. Had he come out of the dark office? He started walking in their direction. Jamal wanted to cry out and warn his uncle—he was going to get caught! But to his amazement, Uncle Samir stepped out of the shadows and met the soldier in the middle of the street.

What was going on? Uncle Samir had no love for the French Foreign Legion. Jamal crept closer, still keeping to the shadows.

Now he could see that the soldier wore sergeant's stripes, and his hair and beard were light—probably a "yellow hair." Jamal strained his ears—what were they saying? He couldn't make out any words, but it didn't sound like French *or* Arabic. It almost sounded like one of the Berber dialects that he sometimes heard in the marketplace.

The two men moved farther away. Jamal started to follow, then realized this was his chance to complete his own mission. While his uncle was distracted, he ducked behind the headquarters office and slipped between buildings until he located the soldiers' sleeping quarters. The guards were nowhere to be seen—good. They must still be making their rounds.

Carefully Jamal pushed at the door he'd entered earlier that afternoon. It opened a few inches, just wide enough for the agile twelve-year-old to slip through. Should he leave it open to give him some light? No, the guards on their rounds might notice it.

Moving slowly in the pitch dark, Jamal counted his steps: one, two, three, four, five . . . right. The stairs going to the second floor were right where they should be. Feeling his way up the rough stairway, Jamal climbed. Halfway up, a loud *creeeeeak* protested under his foot. Jamal froze, his heart pounding. But he heard no movement from above or below, so he stepped over the offending stair and continued upward five more steps till he stood at the edge of the large open room.

The room looked different in the dark. What if he couldn't remember where the soldier's bunk was? Again he tried to count the long bumps in the room as he moved between the rows of wooden beds . . . was this the one? Or was it the next?

Uncertain what to do, Jamal hesitated. Some of the dark lumps moved as men grunted and turned over. Snoring started and stopped. He had to act or someone was going to wake up, and he would be caught!

Taking a chance, Jamal moved alongside the bed he thought he remembered, knelt down, and felt around with his hand. There! A knapsack. But was it the right one? Stealthily he fumbled with the leather straps and buckles. But just as he was about to get it open, the man on the bed turned over and flung out his arm. Jamal flattened himself on the wooden floor in the knick of time, his arms around the knapsack, hardly daring to breathe. Now he was trapped by the soldier's outstretched arm!

But the man's breathing settled into a slow, deep rhythm, so Jamal began fumbling around inside the knapsack. His fingers closed around . . . a book.

Grinning to himself in the darkness, Jamal slowly withdrew the book, then crawled beneath the soldier's arm and hand dangling over the side of the wooden bed. He glanced at the soldier's face—now that his eyes had adjusted to the darkness, he could make out the angular jaw and nose of the book reader. Keeping his body low, he felt his way back toward the stairs, down to the first floor—again stepping over the offending middle step—and poked his head slightly out the door.

No one in sight. He began to breathe easier. Either the guards had not come back this way, or they'd already passed and were gone again.

Giddy with success—oh, how he wished Hameem knew what he was doing!—Jamal tucked the small book into his sash and started to run. He had to get home before Uncle Samir, or he'd be one plucked chicken! Pausing slightly as he came around the small building that housed Legion headquarters, he looked up and down the street. It was empty. Dashing across the open space, he darted into the safety of the shadows—and crashed right into the body of a man he had not seen standing there.

A strong arm grabbed him across the chest and a voice snarled in his ear. *"Sie kleiner spion!"* Panicked, Jamal struggled to free himself. He didn't understand the words—they were neither Arabic nor French—but they sounded sharp and guttural, like German. *Another* foreigner in the Foreign Legion. Twisting to see his captor's face, Jamal recognized the light-colored hair and beard: the French Legionnaire his Uncle Samir had been talking to! At close quarters, the man's face looked familiar . . . where had he seen him before?

Jamal was suddenly aware of a second man standing behind the first. "He's not a spy. C'*est mon neveu*—my nephew." Uncle Samir's voice!

He stopped struggling, but his mouth went dry, and his heart felt like it was pounding in his throat. The sergeant let him go, but Uncle Samir immediately grabbed his arm in an iron grip and marched him down the narrow street away from the garrison.

"What are you doing here?" his uncle hissed in Arabic between clenched teeth. "Why are you spying on me?"

Jamal's feet were flying over the cobblestones as his uncle hustled him along. He licked his dry lips and tried to find his voice. "I—I didn't mean to be spying on you!" he blurted. "I mean—I saw you leave the house, and—and I was curious. So I followed you, but—"

Uncle Samir pulled him up short and shook him roughly. "You followed me? What did you see? What did you hear?"

"N-Nothing, Uncle! I—I—I lost you, so I wandered around trying to find you, but I gave up and was on my way back home when—when—"

They had reached the edge of the square where the mosque

46

stood. Jamal could barely see his uncle's face in the deep shadows of the tiny street that spilled into the square, but he could feel the tension in his uncle's body relax slightly.

"Hmph." Uncle Samir dropped his grip on Jamal's arm. "Schoolboy prank," he muttered. Then his voice got hard again. "Go on home and keep your mouth shut, and I won't tell your father *this* time—understand? Now go! Go!"

To Jamal's surprise, Uncle Samir gave him a push. Relieved, Jamal ran across the square. He could hardly believe his good fortune! He hadn't planned to tell anyone, anyway. How could he tell on Uncle Samir without telling on himself?

Then a strange thought made him turn around and look back. Uncle Samir had disappeared. Why wasn't Uncle Samir coming, too?

———

Back inside his own home, Jamal tiptoed into the room the Isaam family used for eating and visiting and felt around on the shelves where his mother stored necessary foodstuffs and supplies. His adventures had made him ravenously hungry, and after being up half the night, he could not count on waking up early in the morning to eat before morning prayers. His probing fingers found what he was looking for: leftover flatbread wrapped in a cloth, and a candle and matches.

Back in his room, Jamal lit the candle and set it carefully on the floor before tearing off bites of the flatbread. While still chewing and swallowing, he fished his prize out of his sash: the soldier's book.

Jamal wanted to laugh with glee. What a coup he'd pulled off! He had walked right into the sleeping quarters of the French Foreign Legion *while the men were sleeping* and made off with a book from the personal knapsack of one of the soldiers!

What a rebel soldier he'd make! If his father or grandfather found out, they'd only see it as a foolish, risky game and probably punish him for hoarding stuff belonging to the infidels and desecrating the sacredness of the house. Even Uncle Samir might not understand . . . but Jamal knew one person who would probably praise him: Abd el-Krim, the Desert Prince!

Feeling pleased with himself, Jamal took another bite of bread and turned the book over in his hand to the front cover. He stopped in mid-chew . . . what was this? The words on the front cover were written in Hebrew letters!

He knew it wouldn't be Arabic—few of the ordinary soldiers bothered to learn the language of the country they occupied. But he had expected French—at least he'd hoped so, so he could figure out what the book was about—or maybe the language of whatever eastern-European country the soldier had come from. But Hebrew? Only Jews read or spoke Hebrew. He had no idea what the letters meant, but he recognized the Hebrew writing from signs he saw in the *mellah*, the Jewish section of Sefrou.

He felt confused. An eastern-European Jewish soldier in the French Christian Foreign Legion?

And then he worried. What if it was a Jewish holy book— the Torah? Maybe The Game had gone too far. The button and the canteen and bullet casings he could maybe get away with, even if they did belong to the infidels. But all those Jesus pictures of stories from the Christian Bible, and now maybe a Jewish holy book.

If discovered, Jamal could be in big trouble with his own people.

CHAPTER 6

THE DESERTER

It wasn't the call of the *muezzin* that woke Jamal the next morning, but the *tramp, tramp, tramp* of boots on cobblestones in the distance. Jamal bolted upright. The French troops were moving out! This he would like to see!

Dawn had not yet invaded the sleeping room, but as he felt around for his shoes, Jamal realized that Uncle Samir had not returned to his bed. Maybe he had to walk to a distant village to repair a cart wheel. But why didn't he want Jamal to say anything to Father or Grandfather?

Jamal shrugged. What did he care? Right now he wanted to get to the top of the city wall before the call to morning prayer.

Faheema Isaam was already up, lighting the oil lamps and setting out bowls of dates, figs, and almonds for those in the household who arose before the first call to prayer. Only two more days in the month of Ramadan; only two more days of the daily fast. Jamal grabbed a handful of nuts, took a long swig of water from the jug, and scurried out of the house before his mother could ask where he was going so early.

At the end of their narrow street, where it opened into the square, Jamal could hear squads of Legionnaires marching toward the city gates. A few other men and boys spilled out into the gray light of almost-morning, their *jellabas*, caps, and sandals a contrast to the dark jackets, billed hats, and white uniform pants tucked into black boots of the Legionnaires. One of the short figures ran over to him. "I knew you'd come if you heard the soldiers," Hameem half-whispered gleefully.

"We can see better from the wall! Come on!" Jamal led the way as the two boys darted through several streets and alleys to the stairs leading to the top of the wall that encircled Sefrou. They jostled their way through the growing crowd of men and boys who had the same idea and took up a position on the north section of the wall. The sky was beginning to lighten, and they could make out groups of soldiers and officers on horseback heading northeast—toward Taza.

Just then the call of the *muezzin* floated from the top of the minaret of the mosque behind them: "Allah is great! There is no God but Allah!"

But Jamal and Hameem stood transfixed at the sight before them. The soldiers they had heard in the square were the last of the regiment leaving Sefrou. To their surprise, a regiment of cavalry, their horses sleek and champing at their bits, had joined the infantry soldiers who had been staying in Sefrou the past couple of weeks. Had the foot soldiers been waiting to defend Taza until the cavalry had arrived?

Jamal felt a thrill of fear and excitement. Would the French forces hold Taza against Abd el-Krim's desert horsemen? Or would the Desert Prince defeat the French and push them back to Sefrou?

The boys watched until the last company of soldiers had disappeared. By now the sun had started its journey over the horizon and the shadows of night had been exchanged for the muted colors of sandy roads, whitewashed walls, and gray donkeys loaded with bundles of brightly colored cloth and brass and copper.

Jamal and Hameem looked at each other with the same thought: They had both missed morning prayers. Hameem swallowed. "Maybe nobody noticed."

Jamal made a face. "What's the worst that could happen? We might have to make *fidya*." Fidya was compensation for missing or wrongly practicing the required acts of worship. "That's not so bad—we'll just have to donate money or food to the poor."

Hameem shrugged his shoulders gloomily. "Yes, but I will have to ask my parents for the money or food. Then I will have to work it off—double."

Jamal chewed his lip. He was sure to hear about it, too—after all, his father was the *imam* who led the daily prayers. Mirsab Isaam would say Jamal had to be an example to the other boys. But somehow missing morning prayers and having to make *fidya* seemed trifling worries compared to the trouble he *could* be in if his treasure chest was found.

The treasure chest . . . suddenly Jamal remembered. He'd been with Hameem almost an hour already and hadn't told him about his midnight raid at the French garrison. "Hameem! Let's go straight to school—no reason to go home now, anyway. Besides, I have something to tell you on the way!"

Jamal knew Hameem was torn between drop-jaw admiration of his midnight exploit and sheer envy. But when Jamal suggested that the book was worth *twenty* points because of the risk involved, Hameem wouldn't budge. "Ten. That's what we agreed on if we took something from the person of an infidel." All morning long they mouthed words to each other when the teacher's back was turned: *"Twenty." "Ten!" "Come on. Twenty!" "No! Ten."*

The rest of the schoolboys were also abuzz with excitement. The teacher used his cane frequently but couldn't stop the whisperings and restlessness. Finally he gave up and let the boys ask questions. Hands shot up all over the room.

"Are all the French soldiers gone?"

"No. They left two or three platoons to 'guard' Sefrou." The sarcasm wasn't lost on the students.

"Who do you think will win the battle?"

A smile. "We submit to the will of Allah."

"Will the Desert Prince come to Sefrou?"

A pause. "Only Allah knows. But if the rebellion takes Taza . . ." Eyes and ears waited expectantly, but the teacher just said abruptly, "No French lesson today. Let's repeat our verses today from the Koran."

No French lesson? Jamal grinned at Hameem. Even the teacher had his own way of rebelling against the French.

The noontime prayers followed the usual liturgy for Ramadan, but in their hearts, all the boys were praying that Allah would give victory to the Desert Prince.

Sure enough, as the boys came out of school, they saw French soldiers on the walls of Sefrou and stationed at the city gates, and small squads of Legionnaires patrolling the marketplaces. As Jamal and Hameem wandered idly through the basket *suq*, they also saw something else: the two American men were preaching Christianity again.

Instinctively, Jamal glanced toward the old vacant barbershop, half expecting to see Miss Cary sitting in the doorway, telling stories to a crowd of children. But the door to the shop was closed, half hanging on its hinges. Leaving Hameem in the crowd of Christians, Muslims, and Jews to listen to the lively debate, Jamal wandered over to the barbershop and peered through a crack in the door. Maybe, just maybe, Miss Cary had left some of the postcard pictures behind.

A movement inside startled him and he jumped back. Then he felt foolish. Probably just a rat! Who was scared of a stupid rat? Sefrou had hundreds of them. He pulled the door open and glanced inside. A piece of paper was lying on the floor halfway back; could it be one of the Jesus pictures? Stepping up into the abandoned shop, he pulled the door shut behind him and headed across the floor. The crack in the door let in a long finger of light, just enough to point him toward the piece of paper.

He grabbed it and held it up to the finger of light. He was right! It *was* one of the Jesus pictures, one he didn't have yet. Could there be more? He crept farther back into the shop, his eyes adjusting to the darkness as he searched the floor.

Thud! Jamal tripped over something and went sprawling. He started to pick himself up, but just then a strong hand shot out and grabbed him. Jamal opened his mouth to yell, but a voice whispered in French, "Shh! Shh! *Je ne vais pas vous blesser!* I'm not going to hurt you!"

Jamal twisted to see who his captor was and found himself staring into the face of the Jewish soldier—the one whose book he had stolen. For a long moment, both the boy and the young soldier stared at each other. Then Jamal tried again to pull free, but the soldier held tight.

"*S'il vous plaît!* Please! I'm not going to hurt you. I'll let you go. Just . . . don't tell anyone I am here."

Jamal's mind was spinning. Had the soldier recognized him last night and followed him to get his book back? But how could he know that Jamal would come by this marketplace and look inside the old, vacant barbershop? And why was he still in Sefrou? Hadn't most of the soldiers marched out into the desert that morning for the battle at Taza?

With sudden clarity, Jamal blurted in French, "You are a deserter!"

"I beg you, do not tell!" whispered the soldier.

Or what? Jamal thought. Would the man report him? It would not be hard to prove—he had the book in his treasure box at his house! The French had brutal ways of dealing with thieves and traitors. But did the soldier know Jamal was the culprit?

Jamal felt the soldier let go of his arm, and before the soldier had time to change his mind, the boy scrambled across the floor of the "vacant" shop and out the lopsided door.

"Oh, there you are!" said Hameem's voice. "I've been looking all over the marketplace for you. What were you doing in that old shop?"

Jamal's heart was pounding, but he tried to shrug casually. "Nothing. Just looked in. Uh, why do you think Miss Cary is not here to tell stories today? Doesn't she usually come to tell stories when the American men preach in the marketplace?"

Hameem shrugged. "I don't know."

"Well, come on. Let's go find out." Jamal walked quickly away from the old barbershop and smiled smugly to himself as Hameem huffed and puffed to keep up with him. At least he had diverted Hameem before his friend had time to ask more questions about why he was in the empty shop.

"Just don't make me late for midafternoon prayers," Hameem grumbled as the boys navigated the streets toward

Miss Cary's house. "I'll be in enough trouble already for missing morning prayers."

Jamal was having his own doubts. The last time he was at the missionary's house, he had burned her Jesus paper and stomped out of the class. Part of him was still glad he had defended Islam, but part of him regretted what he'd done. She had always been so kind to him, and he would have liked to hear more of the Jesus stories she told.

But now . . . he wasn't likely to find a welcome anymore. He had just about decided to turn back, when he saw a cart piled high with household belongings standing in front of Miss Cary's door.

He stopped, startled. "Look, Hameem. Miss Cary is leaving!"

Hameem's eyebrows shot up. "That is *mosh bikair*—not good. Maybe the French commander doesn't want the Americans in Sefrou if the Desert Prince attacks. Or maybe she's afraid—"

Just then Miss Cary, dressed in her usual pale blue caftan, came limping out of the front door with her arms full of blankets. Catching sight of the boys, she called in Arabic, "Jamal! Hameem!" as she piled the bundle on the cart. "I'm so glad to see you! I was afraid I'd have to leave without telling you good-bye."

Miss Cary's voice was so warm and friendly that Jamal forgot his uneasiness. He ran to the cart. "Where are you going, Miss Cary? Why are you leaving?"

Miss Cary blew a wayward strand of brown hair off her forehead and smiled wearily. "I received a letter saying my elderly parents are very ill. I need to go and take care of them until . . . well, until they don't need me anymore."

"You're going home? To America?"

Miss Cary smiled again, but Jamal did not think she looked very well herself. Sweat beaded her forehead and her hands shook a little. "To America, yes. But Morocco is home to me now." Her eyes got misty. "When I came to Morocco twenty-four years ago, I didn't think I would ever leave. But my parents need me for a little while."

Twenty-four years ago? That was twice as long as Jamal had been alive! "But, why? I mean, why did you come to our country in the first place?"

"Why? Because I wanted to tell the Moroccan people the truth about Jesus. How could I keep such good news to myself?"

Jamal frowned. Truth? Wasn't Christianity just another religion? Grandfather Hatim told him that each religion thought its own beliefs were the "truth," but a person should be loyal to the religion you were born into. He squirmed. Why did he always have such mixed-up feelings when Miss Cary talked about Jesus?

To cover his confusion, he blurted, "Do you need help, Miss Cary? We are strong"—he poked Hameem—"and could load this cart for you."

"*Shokran gazillan*, Jamal—thank you very much." Again Miss Cary warmed him with her smile. "But I think I need to lie down for a while." Indeed, her pale skin looked even whiter than usual. "Mr. Enyart and Mr. Swanson will be coming along soon to help me after they finish preaching in the marketplaces. . . ." Her voice trailed off, and a bit unsteadily she walked back into the house. In the doorway, she turned and gave the boys a brief wave of her hand, and then the door closed.

Jamal just stood there, staring at the closed door. Why did he have such an empty feeling? Miss Cary said she was coming back, but . . . .

"Jamal?" Hameem was exasperated. "Come *on*! You're going to make me late!" He pulled Jamal back down the street. "I've fasted for twenty-nine days . . . only one day to go," muttered Hameem. "Don't want to lose the good I've gained keeping Ramadan just because *you* want to help an infidel load her luggage."

CHAPTER 7

THE HIDING PLACE

Mirsab Isaam gave Jamal a stern lecture about missing morning prayers and strict orders to stay at home as the family observed the weekly Holy Day that started at sundown that evening. Jamal cast his eyes down respectfully; inwardly he breathed a sigh of relief. It could have been worse.

On Friday—April twenty-fourth on the infidels' calendar; the last day of Ramadan on the Muslim calendar—Jamal obediently accompanied his father and grandfather to the mosque in the square, made up quiet games to entertain his little sisters, and tried not to think about the feast his mother was preparing to celebrate the end of Ramadan. When Jasmine and Jawhara fell asleep for their afternoon naps, Jamal slipped away to the privacy of his sleeping room. But his body and mind were restless. Was the French Foreign Legion deserter still hiding in the vacant barbershop? Surely he would have fled by now! But Jamal desperately wanted to go see for himself.

But that wasn't the only thing that made him feel unsettled.

As yet there had been no word from Taza. How had the battle gone? If the Desert Prince gained control of Taza, would he rout the French from Sefrou, too? Everybody seemed to be holding their breath while they waited to hear Taza's fate.

And Uncle Samir . . . he had been gone two days now. Where was he? Why hadn't he come home? Surely he would be home for *Id-al-Fitr,* the three-day Feast of Fast Breaking, which began on the first day of the month of Shawwal. Father and Grandfather acted like nothing was strange about his absence, so maybe Uncle Samir was just doing business in a distant village. But the midnight meeting Jamal had witnessed between his uncle and the light-haired soldier *had* been strange. What did it all mean?

And Miss Cary was going back to America. Jamal didn't know why he felt unhappy to see her go. After all, he'd only known her a few weeks. But she was kind and friendly and had helped him a great deal with his studies. Uncle Samir and his father would probably say, "Good riddance." They called the Christian missionaries "meddlers." But almost every time Jamal had attended her classes, a woman or child had come to her door for medicine to help a stomachache or cough or fever and often went away with a sack of food, as well.

No more Jesus stories? He had so many questions he wished he'd asked! At least he had the collection of pictures.

After checking the courtyard below to make sure no one was about, Jamal pulled his treasure chest from under the low table and opened the latch. He took out the postcard-sized pictures and spread them all out on the floor. The light in the room was too dim to see well; Jamal jumped up and pulled back the heavy tapestry that covered the one window at the back. Now the light was better.

It was the first time Jamal really had a chance to look at the new picture he'd found on the floor of the barbershop. It looked like the shepherd man—probably Jesus—was cooking fish over a fire beside a lake. Out on the water, several men in a fishing boat were desperately trying to haul in a net crammed full of fish. The net was so full it looked like it was going to break. Some of the men were looking at Jesus, some were looking at the bursting net—but all of them looked astonished.

Curiosity licked the edges of Jamal's thoughts. Why did the men look so surprised? And then he saw something in the picture he hadn't noticed at first: Jesus had wounds—holes— in both hands. Wounds in his hands? Casting a quick eye over the rest of the pictures, Jamal snatched up the picture of Jesus hanging on the cross. Big, fat nails had been hammered through his hands into the wood.

Jamal rocked back on his heels. Oh, how he wished he could ask Miss Cary to tell the story. What was it about? What did it mean?

————

Uncle Samir still had not returned by *Id-al-Fitr*. But Jamal's mind was fixed on the huge, steaming bowl of *couscous* in the center of the low table. In another bowl, a soup of lamb broth, diced lamb, chickpeas, onions, and spices thickened with beaten eggs, tantalized his nose. Bowls of fresh figs, olives, and dates kept the children's hands busy as they waited their turn to dip into the bowl of couscous with freshly baked flatbread. Sweet fig cakes stuffed with raisins and nuts followed.

Jamal was so full by the end of the meal he wasn't sure he even had room for the sweet mint tea that his mother poured. But if he had hoped to hear news as the men leaned back against the cushions and sipped their tea, he was disappointed. His father and grandfather were strangely lost in thought.

But not Faheema Isaam. Jamal's mother was already hard at work in a frenzy of cleaning the next morning as Jamal pulled on his blue-and-white cap. "Come home right after school," she ordered. "I will have chores for you. Do you understand?"

Jamal sighed. After spending the Friday Holy Day at home, he had hoped to be free to tally up the points for The Game, which he and Hameem had agreed to do right after Ramadan.

The first day of Shawwal often took on the atmosphere of a festival after the long month of daily fasts. But as Jamal trotted to school, the usual marketplace banter as the merchants set up their stalls was missing. Even the donkeys pulling their carts through the busy streets looked glum. The French soldiers patrolling the walls and the city gates were tight-lipped, their bodies tense, as though they did not know where the enemy would appear—from the desert or within the walls.

But right in the middle of reciting that day's verses from the Koran, the students inside the Islamic school heard the familiar *tramp, tramp, tramp* of soldiers' boots. The boys looked at one another, wide-eyed. Were the French soldiers returning from Taza? What did it mean?

Even the teacher strode to the door of the classroom and looked out. But after only a brief pause, he raised his voice and continued his lesson. "Recite! Sura 64:8: 'So believe in God and His messenger and the light which we have revealed.' "

" 'So believe in God and his messenger and the light which we have revealed,' " murmured a dozen boyish voices.

"What is the 'light' that has been revealed?" the teacher demanded.

"The Koran, our Holy Book!" chorused the boys.

The teacher worked hard to keep the students' minds on their work, in spite of the sounds that invaded the classroom:

boots on cobblestone and waves of murmuring voices and running sandals. Jamal also noted that they had a French lesson that day.

As soon as midday prayer was over, the boys spilled eagerly out into the square, then stopped short as they saw the columns of Legionnaires threading their way into the city, uniforms dirty and torn, faces taut and tired, led by officers on horseback. But not every soldier returned on his own feet. Many lay on litters carried by four soldiers, heads, arms, chests, and legs bound in bloody bandages. And then came the carts carrying the dead.

Jamal knew his mother expected him to come right home, but he dragged his feet, hugging the edges of the crowds of Sefrou citizens to pick up the murmured reports:

"The French managed to hold Taza. . . ."

"But look at the dead and wounded! The battle must have been fierce."

"I heard they lost the element of surprise. Abd el-Krim knew French reinforcements were coming."

"They suspect a spy—from Sefrou—warned the Desert Prince."

"Is the rebellion dead?"

"Far from it, my brother! El-Krim has regrouped and headed for Fez."

"Fez! A royal city!" Ironic laughter. "So! Insignificant Sefrou is safe for the French . . . for now."

Jamal ran the last hundred yards to his door and scurried inside. By the evening meal, his father and grandfather would have weeded out rumors from real reports. But of this he could be sure: The French Legion had returned, and they weren't running for their lives. His thoughts darted to the old barbershop. If the Jewish soldier really was a deserter, had he managed to get away from Sefrou? If not, what a fool! It would be harder now that the Legion had returned.

"Jamal!" Faheema Isaam swept through the courtyard, which had been scrubbed to a sparkle, and thrust a bundle into his hands. "Nadirah and her daughters already picked up the washing and have taken it to the river. But I forgot my favorite caftans! You must take them to her quickly, or I will have to wait a whole week to wear them again!" Nadirah Serraj had done the Isaam family washing as long as Jamal could remember.

"But I'm so hungry!" Jamal had gone without food during the day for thirty days. He didn't want to miss the noon meal on the very first day of Shawwal.

His mother looked momentarily irritated but then disappeared into the main family room. She quickly rolled up handfuls of spiced, shredded chicken in some soft flatbread, wrapped the rolls in banana leaves, and tucked them into his cloth sash. "And here—take this flask of water. That should keep you." Then she pushed him back out the door with the dresses and head coverings in his arms. "The way you eat, you will soon look like your Uncle Samir!"

Jamal shifted the dirty clothes to one arm and with his free hand unwrapped one of the meat rolls and ate leisurely as he ambled in the general direction of the city gate closest to the river. Then suddenly it occurred to him: He was out! He was free! He could even take a small detour through the basket *suq* to make sure the soldier had gotten away.

The basket sellers were doing a brisk business—almost as if, now that the uncertainty of the battle of Taza was over, Sefrou was in a hurry to get life back to "normal." The din of voices bartering over the price of the woven baskets and the thick crowd gave Jamal good cover as he casually pulled open the door of the old barbershop and stepped up onto the raised floor. The dark, vacant stall stank like a barnyard, but the finger of light from the crack in the door showed nothing, and Jamal was thinking, *Of course he is gone . . .* when a hoarse whisper from the far dark corner made him jump.

"*Vous êtes revenus!*—you came back."

Jamal almost turned and ran. Had the soldier figured out who had stolen his book? But blatant curiosity kept him rooted to the spot. "*Pourquoi?* Why didn't you leave?" he whispered in the best French he could muster.

The dark figure in the corner grunted grimly. "I tried. But it was late at night when the *suq* was finally deserted—and by then the city gates had been locked. And there was no way I could get out during the day—not with this uniform on." The soldier's voice sounded desperate. "*S'il vous plaît!* I need water and food . . . and a place to hide until I can get away."

The soldier was begging! Jamal snorted. "Why should I help you? The French are not my friends."

"Ah! But *I* am your friend." Jamal had to strain to hear the hoarse whisper against the bellowing voices outside. "I do not want to fight your people. I am not even French! I was born in Poland. Joining the Foreign Legion was a big mistake . . . but that's a long story. Please. Do you have water in that leather flask?"

With sudden sympathy, Jamal stepped closer and handed the water flask to the outstretched hand. Fasting from sunup till sundown had been hard enough—but two days *and* nights with no food or water? As an afterthought, he dug into his sash and pulled out the second banana leaf wrapped around the flatbread and chicken.

"*Merci!*" The soldier hungrily made short work of the bread and chicken and drank thirstily from the leather skin. Jamal's eyes had adjusted to the dim light, and he watched as the soldier ate. His mind was spinning. The soldier wasn't very old—maybe twenty. Should he help him? Even if he wanted to . . . how? And why? Muslims were supposed to help their Muslim brothers, but this soldier was—what? A Jew? From Poland!

Besides, turning in a deserter was worth twenty French francs! That was a lot of money! On the other hand, if he turned him in, would that be helping his enemies? Hadn't el-Krim himself aided a deserter, the infamous Sergeant Klem? But if he didn't turn him in, what would the soldier do if he found out it was Jamal who had stolen his book?

Suddenly Jamal felt like laughing. He had collected and hidden many things belonging to the infidels, but never an infidel *himself*—a deserter. A shiver of danger prickled his skin. That ought to be worth a hundred points in The Game! But . . . how?

His thoughts were interrupted by the hoarse whisper. "*Quel est votre nom?* What is your name? Mine is David—'Dudzik,' in Poland." The soldier extended his hand. "David Hoffman."

Jamal took the soldier's hand. "Jamal Isaam." Suddenly Jamal looked at his mother's caftans he was carrying. "Here! Put this on." He thrust one of the roomy woman's robes at the slightly built soldier. "And wrap that scarf around your head. You can't stay here. I know where I can hide you."

Uncle Samir was gone. Why couldn't he hide the deserter in his room? No one would think to look for him there!

CHAPTER 8

WANTED: A SPY

In the thick crowds of the marketplace, no one really noticed the heavily veiled "woman" following Jamal Isaam. At the last minute, Jamal had realized the boots were a dead giveaway and made David Hoffman take them off. He wrapped them in his mother's other caftan, along with the soldier's cap, and told the disguised soldier to carry the bundle, just as any ordinary Sefrou woman might walk through the marketplace with a basket or bundle or child on her hip.

"Do not follow too closely and do not speak," Jamal had warned in a whisper. He wasn't too worried about smuggling the deserter through the crowded marketplace. And once the soldier was safely stowed away in his room, he would have bought some time to scout out the city gates to see which one was the least heavily guarded. But he hadn't figured out how to handle the biggest problem—getting David Hoffman into his house and up to the second floor. Well, he'd figure that out when he got there.

The unlikely pair waited to leave the old barbershop till Jamal heard the call to midafternoon prayers ring out from the top of the mosque's minaret. He set out for home and did not even look to see if the disguised soldier was following him until he reached the corner of his own street. Then he simply held up his hand to signal, "Stay here," and casually walked to the blue door and slipped inside.

"Jamal!" His mother's high voice stopped him in his tracks as he entered the courtyard. "What are you doing back so soon?"

Jamal opened his mouth, then closed it again and swallowed. What should he do now? If he left the deserter out in the street too long, someone might get curious—or suspicious.

"Well, good," his mother rushed on. "I wanted to go to prayer at the mosque, but the girls are asleep and I didn't expect you for another half hour at least. But now you can stay here with them until I get back." Faheema Isaam's voice faded as she disappeared into another room, then reappeared with a long head scarf in her hand, which she wrapped around her head and across her face. "I'm glad you got back sooner—I might stop by the bakers' *suq* and pick up some special bread for tonight's meal. Don't let the girls eat too much when they wake up."

Jamal blinked as his mother sailed out the front door, turned toward the square at the other end of the street, and disappeared.

Then he smiled. He couldn't have planned it better if he'd thought about it all day!

Jamal waited a few minutes, then peeked out the front door. His mother was gone. He looked the other way and saw a figure in a woman's caftan sitting in a doorway several doors down. He beckoned. The figure rose and came swiftly toward him.

The boy put a finger to his mouth and motioned the "woman" inside. Keeping an eye on the door that led into the room where his sisters were sleeping, Jamal quickly led the way across the courtyard, up the stairs to the second-floor balcony, and toward his room.

Just outside the open door, Jamal stopped abruptly in a moment of panic. Behind him, David Hoffman in his stocking feet nearly ran into him. Jamal had been presuming Uncle Samir was still gone—but what if he had returned?

Taking a deep breath, Jamal peered into the room. It was empty.

———

David Hoffman was exhausted. As soon as he shed the caftan and head covering, the young soldier lay down on Jamal's sleeping rug and fell fast asleep.

But now that he'd gotten the deserter safely into his room, Jamal realized he still had a host of other problems. What if someone came up to his room? Where could the soldier hide? He pulled the heavy drape over the window, shrouding the room in shadows, and stuffed the soldier's cap and boots on the foot-wide window ledge. *That* would make a good hiding place—as long as no one looked up from the alleyway below.

But he couldn't keep the soldier long. He *had* to get him out of the city tonight or tomorrow at the latest.

Jamal picked up his mother's caftans and long scarves. Should he keep them for the soldier to wear again as a disguise? But what if Nadirah Serraj brought his mother's washing back tomorrow, and the favorite caftans he was supposed to deliver to her were not among them? No, he still had to complete his errand or it would raise too many questions.

As Jamal pondered his options, a plaintive cry from the courtyard sent him scurrying to the balcony railing. Three-year-old Jasmine, dark hair framing her tiny face, stood wailing in the courtyard, crying for her mother. Jamal rushed down the stairs, but within moments, her crying had woken Jawhara, too. Jamal groaned. He had hoped the girls would stay asleep until his mother returned.

The girls' tears, however, stopped immediately when they discovered they'd been left in the care of their big brother. Jasmine begged to be picked up while Jawhara pulled on his shirt. "Take us to the river, Jamal, *min fadilak*—please?" the seven-year-old begged. "You promised!"

"Yes! Yes! The river!" echoed Jasmine, clutching Jamal's neck.

The river? When did he promise to take his little sisters to the river? Probably in a moment of desperation, to get them off his back, he'd said that *someday* he'd take them to play at the river. But not now. He had too many—wait. The *river*? Maybe Nadirah and her daughters were still at the river doing the washing! Now he had a perfect excuse to go again!

He swung Jasmine around and around as she squealed. "Yes! We'll go to the river, little flower—right now!"

———

Faheema Isaam was busy with the evening meal when Jamal returned with the girls, and she seemed extra pleased that he had taken them off her hands for most of the afternoon. At the riverbank, he had made little boats out of twigs and banana leaves to float at the edge of the river, and his sisters barely noticed as he wandered over to where the mothers and daughters were still scrubbing clothes and hanging them on the bushes to dry. Nadirah Serraj, her head covering fallen loosely about her shoulders after hours of scrubbing clothes on the smooth rocks, had grunted with exasperation when he handed her two more garments to wash, then took them with a shrug. After all, more washing, more money.

Shedding himself of his sisters, Jamal made a quick check on the "visitor" in his room, showed him where the covered chamber pot was located, and agreed together in whispers that David should hide on the window ledge behind the heavy curtain if he heard anyone come close to the room. Then Jamal deliberately spent the rest of the evening downstairs—going to evening prayers, lingering with his father and grandfather after the evening meal, and keeping his ears open.

Id-al-Fitr was normally a festive time. But the Isaam family was not the only family who chose to stay at home and mull over the reports from the battle of Taza. Much of what Jamal had heard on the streets was true: The French had held their control of Taza, but their casualties had been great—greater than the French commander had expected. When the Desert Prince realized that the French had brought in reinforcements to keep their hold on this border town, he had called off his mounted warriors, regrouped, and headed northwest—toward Fez.

Jamal listened patiently with half his attention. The other half toyed with his number one problem: how to get David Hoffman out of his house and out of Sefrou without getting caught. During a lull in the conversation, he asked casually, "When do we expect to see Uncle Samir again?"

His father shot him a sharp look. "Your uncle's business is his own." And that was the end of that.

Finally the oil lamps were blown out and the family retired

for the night. Stuffing as much food as he could carry in his wide cloth sash and filling the leather water flask, Jamal finally tiptoed into his room. The room was dark . . . and empty.

"David?"

His whisper seemed to stir the window curtain, and the young Legionnaire slipped back into the room and smiled. "See? Your plan works."

Jamal put a finger to his lips and let his visitor eat until the household seemed deep in its slumber.

"You said joining the French Foreign Legion was *une erreur*—a mistake," Jamal finally whispered as the shadows in the room deepened into a smooth, velvet darkness. "*Pourquoi?* Why?"

The question seemed to pull a stopper from the young soldier's soul. The words poured out, and Jamal struggled to keep up with the French language and Polish accent.

"I was born in a small village in Poland—surrounded by a lush forest, flocks of sheep and herds of cows, and many gardens. My grandfather lived with us, and he led our family in the many rituals of our Jewish faith. Then came the Great War. I was only seven." David Hoffman swallowed. For a few minutes the young Legionnaire could not continue. Jamal simply waited till he drew a breath and continued.

"During the Great War, my village was destroyed and my family scattered. We did not know what happened to my grandfather. My father took us to Warsaw, but my mother died, and it seemed that all the comforting stitches that had held my young life together had fallen apart, like a ragged quilt."

Jamal listened in the dark in rapt attention. He had never before thought of a French soldier as a child or with a family like his own.

"Then one day my grandfather appeared! He had been

searching and searching for us. But he was shocked that my father no longer practiced the Jewish faith, and the older grand-children—my brothers and sisters—were caught up in parties and friends and cafés. So my grandfather took me under his wing and began to teach me to read the Torah. I loved study-ing with my grandfather and began to study the Talmud, also. My grandfather began to dream that one day I would become a rabbi."

David Hoffman took a swig of water from the leather flask to wet his dry lips and throat. "But my father was dead set against it. To him religion was worthless. I felt pulled between my father and my grandfather, until I thought I was going crazy. So as soon as I was old enough, I left home. I hardly knew what I believed any more."

"But why the French Foreign Legion?" Jamal asked. "Why Morocco?"

David gave a short, mirthless laugh. "Why, indeed? I thought the excitement of battles might give me the satisfaction I was looking for . . . or maybe I would get killed in battle and bring *some* honor to my family, who thought I was worthless. But joining the Legion was a big mistake." The young soldier shook his head. "It would be one thing to defend my own country from an enemy, but why should I, a son of Poland, fight for the *French* to keep their hold on Morocco, an *African* country? I realized it was crazy!"

Coughing in another part of the house shushed the whis-pered conversation until all was quiet again.

"How could I go fight against this . . . this man they call the Desert Prince, when it's *his* country? That's when I decided to desert the Legion. Besides," David muttered, "I've heard how the Berber tribesmen cut off the heads of their enemies and stick them on poles. Frankly, I'd like to *keep* my head—at least until I find something worth dying for. I just . . . I just want to go home."

As Jamal digested the soldier's story, he realized he liked this David Hoffman. But this realization tossed his mind in confusion. The deserter was an *infidel*.

Still, he was curious. "If . . . when . . . you get home, will you become a rabbi?"

David shrugged. "I don't know. I feel like my heart is searching for something—something to believe in. A Christian missionary in Fez gave me a Hebrew New Testament—that's the Christian Bible, but written in the Jewish language. I've been reading the stories about Jesus, the one the Christians claim is the Jewish Messiah, or Savior. I've really been thinking about those stories. But . . ." He shrugged sadly, ". . . someone stole it."

Prickles ran up and down Jamal's spine. So *that's* what the book was he had stolen from the soldier's backpack—not a Jewish holy book, but the Christian Bible written in the Jewish language! It was obvious that David did not suspect Jamal as the thief. Should he give it back?

Misunderstanding Jamal's silence, David said ruefully, "So which is the worst sin for a Muslim to hide in his home—a Jew? Or a Christian?"

———

The next day, Jamal had to wait till after school before he could scout out the French garrison to find out which city gates were guarded. Should he go home first to make sure that the soldier had not been discovered? He decided against it. His mother might easily find something for him to do and keep him from going out again.

Jamal said nothing to Hameem about the deserter he was

hiding in his own house—time enough for that when David Hoffman was safely away from Sefrou—but Hameem came along willingly when Jamal said he'd like to hang around the French garrison and find out what was happening.

As the two boys neared the French garrison, they saw a couple of Legionnaires nailing posters to doors, posts, even donkey carts. "Huh," Hameem snorted. "Why do they keep putting those 'Wanted' posters up around here? Do they really think that German deserter, Sergeant Klem, is hanging around Sefrou?"

But something about the posters was different than the ones Jamal had seen before. He sidled closer after the Legionnaires had moved on with their bundle of papers and hammer and nails. The poster was written in French and Arabic, and the words seemed to jump off the paper and hit Jamal between the eyes: "WANTED! Deserter, Traitor, and Spy!" And below that a young, familiar face stared off the paper with a name in bold letters: "Private David Hoffman, 2nd Régiment Étranger d'Infanterie."

Jamal's blood went cold. The French thought *David* was the spy who had tipped off the rebellion that the French were sending extra troops to Taza!

He had to warn David—now!

CHAPTER 9

CAUGHT!

Leaving a bewildered Hameem hollering, "Jamal! Where are you going?" Jamal took off like a horse heading for its stable. He had to warn David Hoffman! Even more, he had to get the deserter out of his house. What had he been thinking? How stupid he'd been to let The Game go this far!

His feet flew over the uneven cobblestones; his mind raced even faster. David Hoffman, a spy? Impossible! Hadn't he been hiding in the old, vacant barbershop for two days? No way could he have gone to Taza and back by the time Jamal had found him the first time . . . unless—unless he'd gone on the last day of Ramadan, the Friday Holy Day, when Jamal was unable to go back to see if he was still there.

Now panic forced his breathing into ragged gasps. Jamal had worried that *he* might get in trouble if his family discovered their unwelcome "guest." But if the French found their "spy" in the Isaam household . . .

Jamal rounded the corner of the narrow street he lived

on—and nearly collided with two men arguing in heated voices just outside the Isaam home.

"Whoa, whoa, whoa!" barked a familiar voice as a hand shot out and pulled Jamal up short. "What is your hurry, nephew?"

Jamal stared up into the dark, intense eyes. Uncle Samir!

"The galloping colt looks as if he has seen a ghost," smirked Uncle Samir's friend Mateen.

"Go on," said Uncle Samir, giving Jamal a little shove toward the blue door. "Tell your mother I am home and have a guest for the evening meal."

Jamal's heart was pounding with alarm and confusion. On top of everything else, Uncle Samir had come home! Had David already been discovered? No, Uncle Samir would have said something. But instead of hours to get the deserter out of the house, now he had only minutes!

Slipping off his sandals, Jamal scurried barefoot through the passageway, across the courtyard, and up the stairs. Quickly . . . quickly . . . before his mother heard that he was home . . . he had to warn David . . . only a few more steps . . . ah! He'd made it to his doorway—

Jamal stopped short in the doorway and stared. David Hoffman was standing in the middle of the room, holding Jamal's treasure box. The lid was open.

Anger washed over the panic and urgency he'd felt just seconds ago. "Give me my box!" he hissed. "How dare you open it! How dare you touch my—"

The soldier in his rumpled uniform calmly reached into the treasure box and pulled out the small book. "*My* book. So it was *you* . . . *you* are the thief who stole my New Testament." He cocked his head slightly. "Why? Are *you* a Christian?"

Jamal was jolted by the question. "A Christian? Of course

not! My family is Muslim! 'There is only one God and Allah is his name and—' "

"I know. 'And Mohammed is his prophet.' " David rummaged in the open box and pulled out some of the Jesus pictures. "Then explain *these*."

In that moment, Jamal forgot he had rushed home to warn David that the French Foreign Legion suspected him of being a spy. Forgot that Uncle Samir was standing outside the house that very minute and likely to come up to the sleeping room shortly. "Give me that box!" he snapped, grabbing for the wicker treasure chest.

He had expected David to resist. But as he grabbed, the box suddenly flew out of both their hands and went crashing to the floor. The contents spilled all over the rug, and some of the items—the shell casings, the pocket comb, the button— bounced off the rug, skittered out the door onto the balcony, and dropped down into the courtyard below.

"What is that?" yelled a voice from below, followed by loud thumps as heavy feet took the stairs two at a time. Sheer panic rooted Jamal to the spot where he stood, and the next moment Uncle Samir loomed large in the doorway. But his eyes only focused on Jamal, then at the pictures scattered on the floor, and back at Jamal.

His heart pounding, Jamal turned his head slightly and took in the room at a glance. David was gone! But where? The window?

"Where did these come from?" Uncle Samir spit out the words, pointing at the pictures. "These have nothing to do with Islam! These are pictures from the infidel Bible. Are these yours, Jamal? You—you have blasphemed our house to bring them here! You—"

"*Ils sont les miens.* They are mine."

77

To Jamal's shock, David Hoffman stepped from behind the heavy tapestry that covered the back window of the room. He knelt on the floor and began to pick up the pictures. Jamal was speechless. David was giving him an excuse! But . . . but why?

Uncle Samir's face had turned purple with rage. "What are you doing in this house, you arrogant infidel?" His hand moved to the knife he wore in his cloth belt under his *jellaba*.

"*Pardonnez-moi*. Forgive me. I did not mean to desecrate your home. I . . . was hiding. The boy caught me, and in my haste to get away, I stumbled over this box and dropped my pictures." David gathered up the last of the pictures and stuffed them in the pocket of his shirt under his uniform. "I will go now."

Uncle Samir drew out his knife. "Not by that window you won't." Roughly grabbing the front of the young soldier's uniform jacket, the big man yanked David toward the doorway. What was his uncle going to do? For a brief instant, Jamal's hopes rose. Maybe he was just going to throw him out into the street.

But as they reached the balcony and the daylight from the open courtyard, the big man suddenly stopped and peered closely at the soldier's pale face. "Wait! I have seen your face— yes! On the new poster! Ha, ha, ha, ha!" Uncle Samir's laughter startled Jamal.

"The French deserter, are you? Ha, ha, ha, ha!"

A sly smile played on the big man's face. "The French commander is looking for you. Ha, ha . . . your fate is just what you deserve." With a quick move, Samir pressed the knife to David's neck and pushed him out of the room and down the stairs.

Jamal still stood rooted to the spot. He was off the hook. His uncle believed David! But he hadn't told David that the French suspected him to be a spy—a traitor! The French executed spies and traitors! Would David have risked getting caught if he'd known?

Jamal rushed to the balcony that overlooked the courtyard below. Mateen had a grip on David's other arm, and Jamal's uncle was still laughing—a dark, gleeful laugh. "Maybe I should thank you, foreign pig. Once they have *you*, they will not keep looking for their spy. Ha, ha, ha, ha, ha!"

———

As the front door closed, Jamal scurried down the stairs and gathered up his fallen treasures. But back in his room, the implications of Uncle Samir's last words settled on Jamal like sand after a desert dust storm. It couldn't be! Uncle Samir . . . was *he* the spy who had warned the Desert Prince? So! That was what he was doing at the garrison that night! That was why he had disappeared for the past few days!

Jamal's legs suddenly felt like cooked noodles. He sank down onto the floor and aimlessly began putting the items he had collected for The Game back into his treasure box. But it felt strangely empty without the pictures.

His emotions fought with each other. Relief that he had not gotten into trouble with Uncle Samir mixed with anger that David Hoffman had taken his Jesus pictures. Was David paying him back for stealing his book? The book was gone, too—David must have slipped it into his pocket, as well. Jamal could hardly complain about the soldier taking his own book. But the pictures—they were *his*, fair and square. Miss Cary had given them to him—he hadn't even stolen them. Even though she'd given them out to other boys, he was sure no one had kept more than one or two. He had made sure of that, darkly hinting that it would be blasphemy to keep them. But even if they had, surely no one had a whole collection of Bible pictures like his.

Under the relief and anger, another feeling rose to the surface—a sense of loss. The pictures had come to mean a great deal to Jamal. He had liked to spread them out on the floor and look at them, recalling the Jesus stories he'd heard from Miss Cary. There was something about Jesus, the things he said and the way he made people feel loved and important, that made Jamal hungry to know more. But now even the pictures and the stories they represented were gone.

And so was David . . . the enemy who had become his friend.

Shaking himself, Jamal jumped to his feet, casting about for his sandals. Where had Uncle Samir taken the deserter? To the French garrison, no doubt. But what was going to happen to him? He had to find out!

———

Once more Jamal's feet flew over the cobblestone streets of Sefrou, past the square and the mosque, through the rest of the Muslim section of the town, and finally to the clump of sun-baked buildings that had been taken over as French headquarters. Stepping into a doorway where he had a view of the main quarters, Jamal searched vainly for some sign of his uncle or David Hoffman. There were a good many Legionnaires standing about, some stiffly on guard outside the headquarters, others looking this way and that and talking to one another in anxious tones as if something had just happened.

As Jamal watched from the shadows, the door of the headquarters office was flung open and two armed guards marched out, followed by two more—with David Hoffman between them. Jamal's throat tightened. The young Polish soldier shuffled along as best he could in the leg irons that circled his ankles where his boots had been, his hands bound behind him. His jacket was gone; all he wore was a shirt and his pants.

Another man—a colonel—appeared in the doorway. "Take him to the stockade!" the officer roared. "He won't be there long!" His eyes roamed over the other Legionnaires who had gathered to stare at the prisoner as he was led away. "Watch and learn what the French Foreign Legion thinks about spies and traitors!"

CHAPTER 10

THE DILEMMA

Faheema Isaam had heard the commotion as Uncle Samir and Mateen dragged the deserter out of the house that afternoon, and peppered her brother-in-law with questions that evening. "How did that infidel get in this house? Why did he come here? What if you hadn't caught him, Samir? Why, he might have killed Jamal—or all of us!"

Jamal dipped his bread into the spicy food in the middle of the low table and listened as his uncle answered with brief, almost impatient, replies. Once or twice he gave a hard look at Jamal, as if telling him to do the same.

Grandfather Hatim and Jamal's father took the news as just an unfortunate incident that ended well. "Now, nothing serious happened, Faheema," chided her husband. "No use worrying about something that's over and done."

Over and done? Jamal stuffed more bread into his mouth, even though he wasn't very hungry. It wasn't over and done— not for David Hoffman.

Jamal excused himself from evening prayers and went to bed early, but he could not sleep. He was still awake when Uncle Samir came into the room with a candle, got ready for sleep, then blew it out. He was still awake when his uncle's steady snores punctuated the darkness.

What was going to happen to David Hoffman? Just the night before, in this very room, David had been telling him about his family and boyhood in Poland . . . that he didn't want to fight for the French to keep Morocco, how he just wanted to go home.

Now he was in prison for deserting . . . and even worse, they thought he was a traitor and a spy.

The French Foreign Legion was tough. Some soldiers thrived on the discipline and comradeship that made brothers out of men from diverse backgrounds and countries. In the Legion, a variety of adventurers, misfits, and even former criminals found a career. But desertion was common—and the Legion was hard on those it caught. Jamal remembered the soldiers he'd seen outside the walls of Sefrou, stripped of their weapons and uniforms, making bricks in the hot sun under the sharp eyes of guards. It was common knowledge that deserters were expected to make one thousand bricks a day—and if they failed to meet their quota, they got no food that night back in the stockade.

Jamal kicked off his blanket and sat up, sweating. If the French officers thought David was a spy, he would not be making bricks. They'd put him in front of a firing squad.

But he wasn't a spy! Jamal had seen him the same day the French marched for Taza—he couldn't have gotten there and back. But if Jamal admitted that he knew where David had been for the past few days, he would be admitting that he had hidden him. That would get him in big trouble. And even if he told, would anyone believe him? He couldn't prove David wasn't a spy—unless Jamal told what he suspected about his uncle.

Jamal's clothes were soaked in sweat. Getting up quietly, so as not to waken his uncle, Jamal pushed aside the heavy curtain hanging in front of the window and sat on the wide ledge, trying to cool off.

This was where David had been sitting when Uncle Samir came rushing into the room just a few hours earlier. He could have stayed behind the curtain and maybe never been discovered. But David had risked his freedom to come to Jamal's aid. Now David was going to die for it!

But Jamal knew the truth. What was *he* willing to risk for the truth?

————

The next morning, the third day of Shawwal, the school was once again abuzz with news coming into the town with merchants and travelers. Abd el-Krim and his mounted horsemen were camped outside the gates of Fez. Would there be a battle? Would Fez, one of the royal cities, fall into the hands of the Desert Prince? Or would el-Krim be pushed back into the desert once and for all?

But Jamal, tired and irritable from his sleepless night, sat woodenly on his bench, hardly hearing the whispers around him. He felt caught in a web, like the flies that twisted and turned in the gauzy nets spun by Sefrou's large spiders in the corners of the room.

After school, he just glared at Hameem when he demanded to know why Jamal had run off without a word the previous afternoon. Hunching his shoulders, Jamal wandered aimlessly through the various markets. What should he do? How did he get himself into this mess?

"In the name of Allah!" whined a beggar, thrusting a tin cup under his nose. Jamal just brushed past and kept on walking. "Curses on you, then!" shouted the beggar after him.

Maybe he was already cursed. Everything was going wrong.

Looking up, Jamal realized he'd wandered into the French military quarters. And he realized what he wanted to do. He wanted to see David Hoffman. He had to talk to him!

Taking off his cap—he'd seen the French do this when they wanted to show respect—he cautiously opened the door of the headquarters office. The man at the desk barely looked up. "Hmph?"

Jamal swallowed. His mouth and throat were dry. French, he had to speak French. "Could I see *le prisonnier* . . . uh, David Hoffman?"

This time the man looked up. "*Pourquoi?* Why?" He didn't wait for an answer. "No one is allowed to see the prisoner."

Jamal crammed his cap back onto his head and backed out of the office. "Hey!" shouted a voice. "Watch where you're going."

Jamal jerked his head around to see a frowning lieutenant trying to come in the door he was backing out of. "*Excusez-moi,*" he mumbled.

The lieutenant's boots thumped on the wooden floor as he went inside. "The colonel wants to see me?" he asked the man at the desk. He pushed the door shut, but not before Jamal heard the other man say, "Yes. He wants you to handpick the men for the firing squad."

A cold hand seemed to clutch Jamal's heart. The firing

squad! Now he was more determined than ever. He *had* to see David Hoffman. And he had an idea that might work!

———

Immediately after midafternoon prayers, Jamal asked his mother if he could prepare a basket of food. Faheema Isaam looked puzzled. "Why?"

"For the prisoner." He said it simply, but his thoughts were anything but matter-of-fact. Why had he asked his mother for the food? What if she said no? He could have managed to sneak some food out of the house. And why did he tell her whom it was for? His mother had been very upset to learn that an infidel had been hiding in her own house!

But he was tired . . . tired of weaving a web of lies and half-truths and secret plans. He hadn't really thought about what to say. The truth just came out.

Faheema Isaam took her son's chin in her hand and lifted it, looking deep into his eyes. He looked back at her, unblinking. They stood that way for a long moment, then she dropped her hand. She seemed satisfied. "Take whatever you want—just don't take the fresh chicken I'm soaking for supper tonight."

Surprised, Jamal lost no time packing a small basket with flatbread, cold meat wrapped in banana leaves, pomegranates and tangerines from the fruit bowl, and some almonds. He wasn't sure his idea was going to work, but it was worth a try. When a local citizen got arrested, he only got fed if his family brought food on a daily basis to the jail. The Legion probably fed its own prisoners—but maybe the guards wouldn't care who brought it.

Jamal's many scouting expeditions to the French garrison with Hameem paid off as he skirted the headquarters office and headed for the squat building he knew held the stockade.

He walked among the throngs of Legionnaires as if he had business there, and no one questioned him. As he expected, a guard leaned against the wall next to the door of the stockade, holding his rifle at ease.

"What do you want?" The guard's voice was mostly bored.

"Food for *le prisonnier*—Private David Hoffman." Jamal tried to say it matter-of-factly, even though his heart was racing.

"Food? All right. I'll send it in." He took the basket from Jamal. "Poor devil," the guard muttered as he disappeared inside.

The moment the guard's back was turned, Jamal scurried out of sight around the side of the building, then crept along the wall until he got to the back corner. What if they had guards stationed at the back, too? But the tiny alley at the back of the stockade was empty. Guess the French weren't worried that the Desert Prince would come to rescue *this* deserter. The rebellion had already moved their forces and laid siege to Fez.

"Hey! Hoffman! Somebody brought you some food!"

Jamal's ears pricked up. He could hear the words clearly. But which barred window? He hunched over and crept beneath the first window, then the second. Talk, somebody, talk!

"Food? For me?" That was David's voice. "Who brought it?"

"*Un garçon*—a boy. Can't open the door, but I'll hand the stuff through the bars."

Aha! The voices were coming from the third window. Hardly daring to breathe, Jamal waited until he thought he heard the guard moving away. Then he waited another long minute. He was just about to risk raising his head and looking in when he heard a low voice right above him.

"Jamal?" David's voice!

Jamal rose from his crouch to see David Hoffman's face

peering out through the bars of the window. A smile creased the young man's face as the boy's head popped into view.

"I *knew* it must have been you who brought the food! Who else would—"

"*Pourquoi*, David?" The words tumbled out of Jamal's mouth as if they would no longer remain bottled up inside him. He had no time for chitchat. He had to know. "Why did you risk getting caught just for me?"

David Hoffman was quiet for a moment, then disappeared from the window. A moment later he was back and pushed a stack of postcard-sized pictures through the bars. They were Jamal's Jesus pictures. David tapped the one on the top. "That's why."

Jamal took the pictures and stared at the one on top. It was the picture of Jesus hanging by nails in His hands on a rough cross of wood. He looked up at David. He didn't understand.

The prisoner shrugged. "You hid me when I asked for help; you gave me food when I was hungry. I couldn't let you get in trouble on my account."

"But they think you are the spy, the traitor who warned el-Krim!" Didn't David realize that the trouble *he* was in was ten times worse than anything he'd saved Jamal from?

David gave a little snort. "Almost funny, isn't it? They think I'm guilty of daring exploits, and I'm just a homesick coward."

Jamal shook his head. "You are not a coward. You let yourself get caught to keep me out of trouble."

David's eyes were surprisingly calm. "It doesn't matter. Maybe that's the one good thing I've done with my life. And that's not very much compared to what He did." David pointed to the picture.

Jamal was confused. "What do you mean?"

David beckoned Jamal closer, and the boy and the prisoner bent their heads as close as the barred window would allow. "I had started to read the Hebrew New Testament the missionaries gave me before you . . . um, took it."

Jamal felt his face flush. *Stole* it was more like it. He was nothing but a thief.

"But last night in my cell," David went on, "I started to look at some of the pictures that I kept from your treasure box. And I recognized some of them as stories that I'd read in the New Testament: Jesus as a boy talking to the religious elders in the temple . . . Jesus commanding the storm to be still . . . Jesus healing the blind man . . ."

But, David said, even though he had seen the crucifix in the garrison chapel and vaguely heard Christians refer to Jesus dying on a cross, he'd never read the whole story. "So last night, sitting in this jail cell, I read the story of Jesus' death and resurrection."

"Resurrection!" Jamal hadn't ever heard that word. "What do you mean?"

"Wait a minute. I'm not there yet." David almost seemed to be reasoning with himself. "Even non-Christians admit Jesus was a good man. And *He* claimed to be the Son of God—yet He let himself be killed as a common criminal. If He was God, why didn't He even try to defend himself? And they crucified Him along with two common thieves. One thief made fun of Him, but the other one expressed sorrow for his crimes—like he was asking Jesus to forgive him."

David paused, as if digesting his own story. Jamal kept silent, willing his new friend to go on. Finally David said, "Not only that, but hanging there on that cross, Jesus asked God—

called Him 'Father'!—to forgive the people who wanted Him dead."

David's voice got husky. "I couldn't understand that kind of love—willing to forgive the very people who kill you? But during the night, I had a dream—oh, Jamal! It was so real, like a vision. Jesus was standing in my jail cell, and He showed me the nail scars in His hands. 'I did it for you, David,' He said. 'I did it for you.' "

David turned his head away from the window and listened. Jamal strained to hear, too, and heard the sounds of voices and footsteps within the stockade. The young prisoner looked back and smiled at Jamal. "You better go, my friend." He didn't seem afraid. "Don't worry about me, Jamal. It's going to be all right now."

The voices from within grew louder, and David disappeared from the window. Jamal stumbled away, his pictures once more hidden in his cloth belt. But his mind was screaming, *No, no! It isn't all right!*

CHAPTER 11

FACING THE TRUTH

Jamal felt more mixed up than ever. He wanted to burst into Legion headquarters and make them listen to him. David Hoffman wasn't a spy! But how could he do that without casting suspicion on Uncle Samir, or getting himself—and maybe the rest of his family—in serious trouble for hiding a deserter? Whose side was he on, anyway—Morocco's French "protectors"? Or his own people?

Unsure what to do, Jamal stumbled out of the military compound and wandered aimlessly through the streets of Sefrou. The Game seemed so unimportant now. He scarcely noticed the pungent smell of saffron and garlic and the sweet smell of cinnamon and mint as he pushed his way through the crowded *suq* that sold spices. The din of voices hawking their wares, chickens protesting in their wire cages, and the jangle of bells the beggars used to attract attention became a mere background to his own confused thoughts.

He wished he could talk with someone—but who? Not

91

Uncle Samir! . . . even though his uncle probably knew more than anyone the truth of the matter.

His father? Mirsab Isaam was a smart man who knew how to get along in a fractured society and refused to dwell on injustice and anger like his brother, Samir. He was happiest when his children did what they were told and caused no grief that kept him from his responsibilities as *imam*.

No, no, his father would not understand. And even though it had been several years since Jamal had tasted the end of a leather strap, his father might not think him too old yet for a thrashing.

Grandfather Hatim? Maybe. The old man was wise *and* patient, willing to listen. But even his grandfather would be shocked that Jamal had deliberately brought an infidel into their home. Jamal knew his grandfather loved him—but he loved Islam more.

His mother? The way she had looked at him when he asked for the food . . . did she know in her heart? But Jamal knew his mother would be hurt by the confusion and questions that plagued him. She only wanted her family to live in peace, to keep the traditions of their faith.

Hameem? Ha. Hameem was no smarter than he was.

Suddenly Jamal went sprawling. "Watch where you're going, boy!" yelled a voice above him. Jamal scrambled out of the way to avoid being trampled by the camel and driver he had just run into, then spit out the gritty dirt in his mouth and surveyed the raw scrapes on his hands. He needed someplace safer to think!

Jamal ducked out of the crowded market into a quieter street, then stopped abruptly. Miss Cary's street! Why had he come this way? Well, he might as well turn back. The missionary teacher was gone now—

Just then, the familiar door opened, and a woman in a blue

caftan with a black scarf draped around her head stepped out of her house. Jamal's mouth dropped in astonishment. It couldn't be . . . but as he watched the woman place a box tied with rope into a pushcart, then straighten with a hand on her hip as if it hurt, he was sure. The woman was Miss Cary herself!

"Miss Cary!" Spurred by this discovery, Jamal ran toward her open doorway. "Miss Cary!"

The American woman, shielding her eyes against the bright afternoon sun, broke into a smile. "Jamal Isaam! My goodness! Didn't we already say good-bye?" she teased in Arabic.

"Yes, but . . . why are you still here? I thought you were going back to America!"

"I am, I am." She laughed ruefully. "But I came down with another case of Malta fever and had to go to bed. Better now— but I still had a few last-minute things to pack. Sure could use a cup of tea, though. How about you?"

Jamal nodded eagerly. Ramadan was over—he could drink tea with Miss Cary with a clear conscience. But he didn't really care about tea. Running into Miss Cary felt strangely like being thrown a rope after falling into the river. Could he . . .? Would she . . .?

He watched as she scooped mint tea into a tall teapot, then poured hot water over the fragrant leaves and let them steep. She didn't speak, just moved comfortably about the nearly empty room, setting out two small cups, a spoon, and a small bowl of sugar cones on top of a box.

As Miss Cary sipped her hot tea, the quietness between them was like an invitation, and Jamal found himself telling her everything that had happened in the past few weeks. He blurted out the whole story—about The Game he and Hameem had made up to defy the infidels by collecting their personal stuff . . . about his collection of Jesus pictures . . .

about always looking for something more risky and exciting to earn more points.

Jamal watched Miss Cary closely when he told her he had come to her school primarily to collect the infidel pictures to get points for his game. Her eyebrows went up, but she didn't seem angry. So he took a big breath and told her about stealing David Hoffman's Hebrew New Testament the same night he ran into his uncle on a mysterious midnight errand. Then discovering David had deserted when the Legion marched to Taza . . . hiding the deserter in his room . . . David getting himself caught to protect Jamal when Uncle Samir found the pictures.

"Now David has been condemned as a traitor and a spy! But I *know* he can't be the spy they're looking for, and . . . and I think my uncle knows it, too." Jamal stopped and gulped. He couldn't say what he thought, that the real spy might be his uncle! He stared miserably at his toes, his untouched tea getting cold in its cup.

Miss Cary nodded thoughtfully but let the silence stretch once more between them. She poured herself another cup of tea and sipped it, her gentle eyes watching him.

That wasn't all that was on Jamal's mind—something he'd wanted to ask Miss Cary but thought he'd missed his chance. "Miss Cary, what did David mean about the picture? About Jesus saying, 'I did it for you'?"

"Ah!" Miss Cary seemed to come alive. Setting down her teacup, she rummaged in a big cloth bag and pulled out her own well-worn Bible and some Scripture portions written in Arabic. "Long ago, in the days of Abraham and Moses," she explained, "God gave mankind rules to live by. But again and again people turned their backs on God and disobeyed His laws."

Jamal nodded. He knew how difficult it was to keep all the rules of Islam.

"God is holy, but sin is the opposite of holy. Obedience to God leads to life, but sin leads to death."

Again Jamal nodded. This was true in Islam, too.

"In Old Testament times, people who wanted to ask God to forgive their sins sacrificed a perfect lamb or other animal that had no blemishes. Something had to die to pay the penalty for sin. But God had an even greater plan—to send His own Son, Jesus, to earth to become the ultimate sacrifice for our sin. Here—read this from the New Testament."

Miss Cary handed Jamal some Bible verses written in Arabic. He read the one she pointed to: " 'For God so loved the world, that he gave his only begotten Son, that whosoever believeth in him should not perish, but have everlasting life.' "

Miss Cary smiled. "See? That's what your friend David Hoffman realized—that Jesus died on the cross for *his* sins."

Jamal's eyebrows came together in a frown. He had always been taught that a Muslim must earn a place in heaven by faithfully keeping the five basic tenets of Islam: declaring that Allah is God; prayer five times a day; observing the fast of Ramadan; giving to the poor; and making a pilgrimage to Mecca. How could someone else do it for you?

As if in answer to his own question, he remembered asking David outside his cell window why he'd let himself get caught just to protect Jamal from the consequences of his own actions. That was like . . . why, that was like—

"Did you say David Hoffman was reading a *Hebrew* New Testament?" Miss Cary's question interrupted Jamal's thoughts. "Hmm. If, as you say, David was taught the Jewish faith by his grandfather, he must have known the ancient prophesies of a Messiah who would come to save all people." She leaned close to Jamal and gazed into his eyes. "Jesus is that Messiah, Jamal, the Lamb of God. And He paid the death penalty for all of our sins—yours, mine, David's—so that whoever believes can live in heaven with our holy God when we die."

Jamal was so startled by what Miss Cary was saying that he nearly fell off the stool he was sitting on. All his life, he had thought that Jews and Christians and Muslims had nothing in common—that everyone who did not follow Islam was an infidel, even if all three religions did share Abraham as a common ancestor. But could the promises God gave to Abraham really be meant for *all* of them? If Jesus was the promised Messiah . . .

This was too complicated for Jamal! A more immediate problem pressed on his mind. "But what about David *now*? He isn't a *spy*. But if I tell what I know, I will be speaking against my own uncle. My own family!"

Miss Cary nodded in sympathy. "You are a bright boy, Jamal. What does the Koran say about speaking the truth?"

The missionary teacher stood and started to load the last of her things into the pushcart outside the front door. Jamal followed her, thinking about all the Koranic verses drilled into him in school. No doubt about it. A "good" Muslim should be honest and upright—something he had failed at miserably of late.

Hot tears suddenly blinded Jamal's eyes. Embarrassed, he turned his back to Miss Cary and pretended to retie a rope around one of the boxes in the cart. He had fooled himself into thinking he'd only been playing a game—but it had led him to steal and lie and . . .

He felt Miss Cary's gentle hand on his shoulder. "Jamal, look at me."

Jamal swiped his eyes and nose with the back of his shirtsleeve and turned around slowly, still staring at his toes. But Miss Cary tilted his chin up.

"Jamal, all the great religions teach their followers to be

truthful. But Jesus *is* Truth." Miss Cary dug in the cloth bag again and pulled out her Bible. "In John's gospel, chapter 14, verse 6, Jesus said, 'I am the Way, the Truth, and the Life. No man cometh unto the Father, but by me.'" She smiled, a hint of sadness in her eyes. "That's why I came to Morocco, Jamal, to share that Good News. If you remember nothing else I've taught you, remember that."

Miss Cary stuffed her Bible back into the cloth bag and added it to the boxes and bundles on the pushcart. "There! That's that. There's a truck waiting for me outside the city; will you help me get this old cart to the south gate, Jamal? I'm heading for Casablanca tonight." She chuckled with good humor. "I hear Fez isn't exactly a safe haven for 'infidels' these days."

Jamal gladly grabbed the handle of the pushcart and pulled it behind him while Miss Cary steadied the load. As the cart rumbled through Sefrou's rough cobblestone streets, a parade of children began to collect behind them, both Muslim and Jewish, calling, "Good-bye, Miss Cary! Good-bye!"

Sure enough, an ancient truck, covered with a thin coat of grimy sand, stood waiting outside the south gate, its driver asleep in the shade of the undercarriage. But with a little prodding and an extra coin, he crawled out to load Miss Cary's things into the back of the truck while she clambered into the cab.

"Good-bye! Good-bye!" The gaggle of children waved and waved as the truck headed south toward Casablanca in a cloud of dust. But Jamal was already running back through the gate as fast as his legs would take him.

He had to get to the French garrison! He wasn't sure what he was going to do, but he had to do *something* before it was too late!

CHAPTER 12

HE DID IT FOR ME

Jamal knocked on the door of the French Foreign Legion office, his knees trembling. What was he going to say? He glanced up at the sky and realized the sun had dipped below the western horizon. Had he already missed evening prayers? He couldn't remember even hearing the call of the *muezzin*. His mother would be worried if he didn't show up for the evening meal.

Why wasn't anybody answering? Jamal knocked again, harder this time. He heard a chair scraping and boots on the wooden floor, then the door jerked open. "You again?" The man he'd seen behind the desk earlier that day had a napkin tucked in his shirt collar and bits of beef hanging from his mustache.

"I—I need to see the colonel." Jamal had no idea who "the colonel" was, but that's who the lieutenant that had come in behind him had asked to see.

"Colonel Maire is eating his dinner. Go away." The man started to close the door.

"No! Wait!" Jamal stuck his foot in the door. "I have information about the—the accused spy, David Hoffman. It's urgent."

The man's beady eyes locked on Jamal. "What information?"

Jamal willed his knees to stop shaking. "My information is for the colonel's ears only—and he'd be mighty upset if you kept me from seeing him," he said with more confidence than he felt.

"Hmph." The soldier hesitated. "Wait here."

Shadows were filling the surrounding streets and oil lamps lit first one window, then another, and another, with thick yellow light. After a few moments, the man with the napkin at his neck reappeared. "Come along."

Jamal followed the soldier past the front desk, through a door and a short hallway, then into a small inner room. At the last minute he remembered to snatch off his blue-and-white cap.

"Colonel Maire? This is the boy asking for you."

An officer with iron-gray hair and colonel's insignia pushed a plate away from him on his desk and looked up. "Well?"

Jamal hesitated and glanced at the soldier who had brought him in.

The colonel sighed. "Leave us, Laval."

"Hmph," grunted the soldier and pulled the door shut behind him.

The colonel's eyes narrowed. "You have information about the spy? You'd better not be playing games with me, young man."

Jamal swallowed. He couldn't back down now. "That's just it, sir—David Hoffman *isn't* a spy *or* a traitor. I can prove it!"

"How?" The word popped more like a challenge than a question.

"Because, sir, I accidentally stumbled across him right here in Sefrou the same day the Legion marched for Taza."

The colonel's face remained hard, passive. "What time?"

"Uh, between noon and midafternoon prayers. I know because I had just come from school. He was hiding in an old vacant shop in the basket *suq*."

"So. You admit he deserted his regiment." Colonel Maire's eyes snapped fire. "A deserter *is* a traitor, young man! What is your name?"

"Um, Jamal, sir." He would leave his family name out of this as long as possible. "But a deserter who just doesn't want to fight is different than a spy who betrays his fellow soldiers and helps the other side—isn't that true? David Hoffman couldn't be your spy, because—"

"Why not?" Colonel Maire got to his feet, leaned over his desk, and pointed a finger at Jamal. "If Private Hoffman left right after roll call the night before, if he had a swift horse, he could have gotten to Abd el-Krim by dawn, spilled our plans, and gotten back here by the afternoon—when you found him."

Jamal was taken aback. What craziness was this? Why would a deserter come *back* to Sefrou once he'd gotten away? It made no sense! Besides . . . Jamal *knew* David had not left after roll call the night before, because David had still been in his bed after midnight. Jamal should know—he was there, creeping beside David's bed to steal his book!

But Jamal felt like a desert cat, caught with a boulder at its back and hunting dogs yapping in its face. If he admitted he had snuck into the soldiers' quarters that night, he would surely be arrested for trespassing and thieving!

"I don't know why you are trying to protect this prisoner—but I don't have time for this nonsense. Hoffman was the only soldier who deserted that day and *someone* warned el-Krim that reinforcements were coming, and from where." The colonel strode to the door and opened it. "Corporal Laval?" he yelled. "Show this boy out."

The soldier from the front desk sneered at Jamal as he took the boy's arm and hurried him from the office and out the front door. As the door slammed shut behind him, he sank miserably onto the ground beside the door, his head in his hands. What was he going to do? If the colonel didn't believe him, David was going to die!

Something he'd tucked in his cloth sash dug in his side as Jamal sat hopelessly outside the Legion office. He dug out the packet of Jesus pictures David had given him through the cell window earlier that afternoon. He almost felt like flinging the whole lot to the ground. Who cared about the stupid game now?

But instead he held them up to the fading light and squinted at the one on top. It was the picture of Jesus hanging on the cross with nails in His hands and feet. What was it David claimed Jesus had said to him in his dream? "I did it for you."

Suddenly Jamal's mind began to clear. Miss Cary said Jesus came from heaven to sacrifice His life, to pay the penalty for our sin, so he—Jamal Isaam—could live eternally with God.

Jamal straightened and stood up. If Jesus was willing to do that for him . . . if David was willing to get caught so Jamal wouldn't get in trouble for having the pictures . . .

With a surge of determination, Jamal marched back through the front door, right past the surprised corporal who had his feet up on the desk, down the hall, and to the colonel's office. The door was open, so Jamal let himself in. Before the colonel could say anything, Jamal blurted, "I know David Hoffman did not leave Sefrou that night because I saw him with my own eyes in his bed just past midnight." There. He'd said it. Now the colonel would have to admit that even with the swiftest horse, there was no way a foreign legion soldier could have ridden to Taza and back by noon the next day.

A firm hand quickly grabbed the back of Jamal's shirt. "I'm sorry, sir! The boy barged right in before I could stop him."

To Jamal's surprise, the colonel waved the man out of the room. But he wasn't surprised by the colonel's next question. "And *pourquoi*, may I ask, were *you* in the soldiers' sleeping quarters in the middle of the night? What mischief were you up to?"

Jamal steeled himself. There was no way to avoid trouble now. Almost unconsciously he sent a prayer heavenward: *Jesus, help me!* He startled himself. Why did he pray that? All he knew was that Jesus would understand.

As briefly as he could, Jamal admitted sneaking into the sleeping quarters to steal David Hoffman's book to get points for the game he'd invented.

"Likely story! Did anyone see you who could prove you were there?" the colonel demanded.

Jamal shook his head, thinking about the sleeping soldier. "But," he said, a little proudly, "I did steal his book. Just ask David Hoffman."

"No one saw you? Then you could be making this all up. As for David Hoffman—sure, he's going to agree with your story if it lets him off the hook. Now go away. I'm busy."

Jamal was shocked. The colonel still didn't believe him! His mind scrambled. He *had* been seen . . . by his uncle. But then the colonel would want to know what his uncle was doing hanging around the French garrison at midnight! Jamal was willing to risk his own neck, but he couldn't tell on his uncle. Besides, he didn't really know his uncle's business with the bearded sergeant—

"Wait! There *is* someone who saw me. One of your soldiers—a sergeant. He had light-colored hair and beard. Maybe he was on guard duty that night. He grabbed me as I was running past this office, but I got away. Ask him! He will tell you I was here. He'll know what time it was."

The colonel frowned. "Could be a dozen such men in this unit. Anything unusual about him?"

Jamal shrugged. "Not really. He swore at me in German. But he must be very good at languages. I heard him talking to someone else in one of the Berber dialects."

The colonel's eyes glinted. "You say he spoke *Berber*? But he swore at you in German?" The colonel opened the drawer of his desk and pulled out a picture. "Is this the man who saw you?"

It was the sergeant Jamal had seen that night. "Yes, yes! That's the man."

The colonel's face darkened in anger, and he spit out just one word: "Klem!"

Jamal was bewildered. Klem? Why was that name familiar? And then he remembered: *Sergeant Joseph Klem*, the infamous deserter who had joined ranks with Abd el-Krim, the Desert Prince, and aided his successful march against French outposts all that past month. So! It was Sergeant *Klem* who had come into Sefrou to spy out the Legion's plans and sped back to Taza to tell el-Krim. What role his uncle played, Jamal didn't know. They had been talking together, but at least he didn't have to tell on his uncle to save David Hoffman.

"The nerve of that traitor!" Colonel Maire snarled, banging a fist on his desk. "Using his uniform—the uniform he has desecrated—to walk right in here unnoticed!" He seemed to have forgotten Jamal. Striding into the small hallway, he roared: "Corporal Laval!" The soldier at the front desk scurried to the colonel's side. "Get me the officers who served on the military tribunal. Now!"

"But . . . but, sir, they're off duty. I don't—"

"Fool! We have a firing squad at dawn tomorrow morning that needs to be stopped. You have one hour!"

———

Weak with relief, Jamal put on his cap and started out the door, confident that justice would be done. But the colonel nailed him with a piercing glance. "Where do you think you're going? I need your testimony. Sit."

Jamal sat. He knew his family would be worried about him by now. He'd missed both evening prayers and the evening meal. What in the world was he going to tell them?

And then he realized it was simple: He would just tell them the truth . . . about The Game . . . about sneaking out of the house and stealing David's book . . . about hiding David in his room . . .

He'd just leave Uncle Samir out of it. Uncle Samir would have to be responsible for himself. It was going to be hard enough owning up to all the things *he* was responsible for.

Three officers showed up, irritability mixed with curiosity evident in their faces. David Hoffman was brought from the stockade, his hands and ankles in chains, and the hearing began.

Once again Jamal had to tell his story. A small smile played on David's face as he listened. The officers pelted Jamal with questions, much like the colonel had, but his answers were the same. And, like Colonel Maire, the officers were furious when they realized that Sergeant Joseph Klem—the Legion's

"Most Wanted" deserter—had been prowling the garrison the night in question.

The tribunal conferred; it didn't take them long to reach a verdict. "Private David Hoffman, the charge against you for spying and delivering classified information to the enemy has been changed to simple desertion, and your sentence of death by firing squad has been commuted to two years of prison and hard labor." *Crack!* went the gavel.

Two years of prison and hard labor! Jamal's elation turned to dismay. But before he had time to catch David's eye to see how David felt about it, one of the officers said, "One moment. Colonel Maire, what about bringing charges against the boy? By his own admission, he is guilty of trespassing and stealing."

Jamal felt the hair on the back of his neck stand up. He'd known he was taking a risk by telling the truth, but—

"As far as I'm concerned," Colonel Maire growled, "the boy has kept us from committing a grave injustice. I'm not inter-ested in pressing charges for trespassing. As far as the charge of stealing—that's up to Private Hoffman. Hoffman?"

A huge grin stretched ear to ear on David Hoffman's angu-lar face. "No, sir! But I would like to talk to Jamal a moment before I go back to the stockade."

With a curt nod, the colonel and the other officers left, leaving only a guard with David and Jamal.

David's eyes were moist, but his smile was nonstop. "*Merci*, Jamal. You have literally saved my life! But, *pourquoi*? You took a great risk."

Jamal grinned, too. "You already know the answer!" He pulled out his packet of forbidden pictures and pointed to the picture on top—Jesus on the cross. "Because He did it for me."

CHAPTER 13

EPILOGUE

"Miss Cary is back!" "Miss Cary is back!"

The word spread like wildfire among the children of Sefrou as a middle-aged woman wearing a "foreign" dress that hung several inches above her socks and sensible shoes—modest by American standards in 1928—climbed out of the battered truck cab and resettled her hat. With one hand holding on to her hat and the other shielding her eyes from the brilliant April sun, the woman tipped her head back and took a big breath, as if drinking in the musty smell of the camels and goats tethered outside the city gate. "Oh, Jamal! It's so good to be back home!"

A tall young man of fifteen swung down off the back of the truck, grinning. "Me too, Miss Cary! Two years of school in the big city is enough for me!" Jamal Isaam, taller now but still sporting a boyish grin, began helping the truck driver unload bundles and boxes from the back of the truck. But even before he had time to locate a pushcart, Muslim and Jewish children were swarming out of the gate and around the American missionary.

"Are you going to teach classes again, Miss Cary?"

"Will you tell us some more Jesus stories?"

Some of the older boys saw commercial opportunity. "I'll help pull that cart, Miss Cary—only a small coin."

Somehow all the bundles and bags got loaded precariously onto a single cart, and the strange procession began winding its way through the familiar crowded streets. Jamal's happiness at being back home was tinged with some anxiety. So much had happened in the last three years!

Jamal's parents and grandfather had been astonished and dismayed to hear about The Game and all its consequences. The Jesus pictures had been destroyed and all the items belonging to the Legion returned—though recalling the puzzled expression on the colonel's face when he was handed a button belonging to *"le prisonnier"* gave the Isaam family many good laughs.

It didn't take long for the Desert Prince and his tribal warriors to push almost to the gates of Fez—but they had hesitated, fearing a trap. Those months had given the French time to regroup, and the following spring Abd el-Krim was driven back as quickly as he had advanced and was forced to sign a document of surrender. El-Krim was exiled and the rebellion had crumbled. Morocco as a "Protectorate" was once again firmly in the hands of the French, and Mohammed V had been appointed as the new sultan.

Once the siege of the royal city had lifted, Jamal had been sent to school in Fez to study Islamic law in hopes that he would quit all the nonsense that had been put in his head. Jamal had studied hard—he knew his family hoped he would follow in the steps of Grandfather Hatim—but he often thought about Miss Cary and the stories she'd told, and the Jewish soldier and his Hebrew New Testament. These two people were hardly the infidels—the enemies—he'd been led to believe foreigners to be.

While Jamal was at school, he was glad to read in the Moroccan newspaper that Sultan Mohammed V supported the nationalist movement for a free Morocco. *That* would give something for the French to worry about. But deep in Jamal's spirit, even though he didn't yet have the words to express it, a free Morocco also meant a free heart to seek the truth about God.

To his surprise, the two American missionaries he'd seen debating in the marketplace in Sefrou—Mr. Enyart and Mr. Swanson—showed up in the marketplaces of Fez! He stopped to listen and was invited to come to the Gospel Missionary Union house in Fez to study the Bible in Arabic. It was here he heard that Miss Cary, after burying her parents in Kansas, was returning to Morocco. He had asked—and been granted—the privilege of accompanying her from Fez back to Sefrou.

As the procession ended up at the door of Miss Cary's house—as everyone called the modest house that had waited for her return—Maude Cary handed out coins to her helpers and candy to the little ones and shooed them away. "Come back tomorrow!" she laughed. "Right now I need to get off my feet."

The children scurried away as Jamal helped the missionary unload the cart. He noticed that her limp was worse than usual and insisted she sit down while he finished bringing in the boxes and bundles.

When he brought in the last of the bundles, she had a fire going in the brazier and a pot of water heating for tea. She sat on a box, hands on her knees, and gave Jamal a tired smile. "Oh, Jamal, see how hungry the children are? Back home our churches are full of young men and women with strong backs who call themselves Christians. Isn't it a shame that I have had to come back here alone? Oh, how we need workers—especially young men! There's so much I can't do—"

She was interrupted by a loud knock on the front door. "I'll get it, Miss Cary," said Jamal. "You just rest."

Jamal opened the front door, expecting to see more curious children—but his mouth fell open in delight. There stood Hameem, stocky as ever, solid as a man; behind him stood a soldier in a French Foreign Legion uniform. "Hameem!" he shouted, slapping his old friend on both arms. "Ha ha! How did you know I was home?"

Before Hameem could answer, the soldier stepped forward and held out his hand in greeting. "*Bonjour,* Jamal. Remember me?"

Jamal's eyes widened. "David Hoffman." He swallowed, trying to find his voice. "You are no longer *le prisonnier*. But what are you doing here?"

"I heard that a Christian missionary had returned to Sefrou; Hameem offered to show me where she lives. You see, Jamal, I believe in Jesus from reading this book"—he held up the well-worn Hebrew New Testament—"but I want to learn more about Him."

From the small courtyard within, Jamal heard the plaintive voice of Miss Cary. "Are you going to keep my guests all to yourself, Jamal?"

Laughing and talking, Jamal ushered the two visitors into Miss Cary's courtyard. Miss Cary insisted they sit down—"Will the floor do? I haven't any chairs or cushions yet!"—and offered them sweet mint tea in cups she'd dug out of a box. Hameem squirmed and shook his head—then his eyes widened as he saw Jamal lift the teacup to his lips.

"Jamal! What are you doing? It's the fast of Ramadan!"

Jamal looked at Miss Cary for support, drew a deep breath, and said quietly, "I no longer keep the fast of Ramadan. I have become a Christian."

Hameem's mouth fell open. Then he hunched his shoulders and stared at the floor for a long moment. He looked up. "Does your family know this?"

Jamal shook his head. "Not yet. But today . . . today I will tell them."

Hameem looked genuinely frightened. "Jamal! Do you know what this will mean? You could be disowned by your own family! No one will give you a job!"

Jamal nodded soberly. Oh yes, he had thought about this many times. "But, Hameem, I cannot be a secret Christian. Because Jesus is the Truth."

David Hoffman, sitting cross-legged on the floor, had been intently listening to this exchange. He set down his cup and sighed. "I am ashamed. You see, Miss Cary, my grandfather is a very devout Jew, but my father no longer believes anything. I have never written to my family back in Poland about my belief in the Messiah because I am afraid they will disown me—will never let me come home." He looked with new respect at the younger boy. "But if Jamal has the courage to tell his family and face the persecution he is sure to suffer right here, I must find the courage to do the same."

Hameen hung his head. "I have wanted to believe, too— ever since I heard the stories Miss Cary told," he said in a small voice. "But I was afraid."

A well of happiness started deep in Jamal's spirit and grew until he felt like shouting. Instead, he reached into the folds of his *jellaba* and pulled out a picture of Jesus on the cross, a new one given to him by the missionaries in Fez.

"Here, Hameem, keep this. Think about why Jesus died. Because . . . He did it for you."

MORE ABOUT MAUDE CARY

In 1901, twenty-three-year-old Maude Cary sailed for Morocco with four other young Americans—all single—to help bring the Gospel to the Muslim people. The Gospel Missionary Union worked in cooperation with four other Protestant missions in Morocco to put the unwritten language of the nomadic Berber tribes into writing, to translate portions of Scripture into Arabic, and to reach Muslim men with the Gospel in the marketplace and the women in the home. Summer months were spent doing evangelism among the many villages.

Maude's early years as a missionary were difficult. She out-scored one of her male peers in language study, and her "gaiety, friendliness, and laughter" and "pride of dress" brought criticism down on her head that she was worldly, lacked meekness, and was too flighty. The mission board suggested she go home—but she clung to her calling, refusing to go unless they actually sent her away. Soon she was assigned to the mission in El Ksar. Other missions were opened up in Meknes and Sefrou.

Many years passed, filled with language study, translation of the Scriptures, and sharing the Gospel to a polite but indifferent people, with no conversions among the Muslim people—only several Jewish boys. Outwardly polite, Moroccans despised the missionaries on two levels: because they preached the Christian Gospel, and because of the foreign nations they represented. Colonialism was at its fever pitch in Africa at the turn of the century, and the French had been pushing for a toehold in Morocco for years to help keep its hold on neighboring Algiers. Although the sultan was the official ruler of Morocco, he held only a nominal control of the fertile coastal area west of the Atlas Mountains. Elsewhere, especially among the fiercely independent Berber tribes to the east, the sultan's rule was largely ignored.

In 1907, French forces occupied Morocco, launching their offensive from Casablanca, and in 1912, Sultan Hafid signed the Treaty of Fez, making Morocco a French protectorate.

Meanwhile, several single men and women of the Gospel Missionary Union became married couples, and this was Maude's dream—to not only be a missionary but a wife and mother, as well. George Reed, secretary of the mission, asked her to be his wife—but the prolonged engagement was broken in 1913 when George left Morocco to establish a GMU mission in the Sudan. Maude's heart was broken, but at least now she knew where she stood. She had nothing to hold her back from giving one hundred percent to mission work.

As the men of the mission pushed into new frontiers, Maude was often left to take care of things by herself in Meknes and Sefrou—teaching classes to boys, teaching Arabic to new (often young) missionaries, and assisting at births and bedsides of sick missionaries, even though her own health often failed. She divided much of her time between the two locations: In Meknes, the sultan donated a house to the missionaries, which they called "Three Derb Skat"; in Sefrou, the mission house was known simply as "Miss Terri's house" ("Terri" possibly being a mispronunciation of "Cary").

In 1914, war broke out in Europe and many French battalions were recalled to France. Those soldiers who were left in Morocco were bitter and restless. They were prevented from fighting in "The Great War" and also forbidden to do anything in Morocco except "hold" the territory already occupied. The French Resident General, Marshal Louis Lyautey, threw himself into public works: building roads and harbors, establishing schools and infirmaries, even setting up a merry-go-round in Fez! "Much was done *for* the Moroccans, but little done *by* them," wrote one biographer.

After the war, the French and the unruly Berber tribes engaged in "bush warfare." The French would advance in the spring and summer, build a blockhouse in the new area in the fall, then leave a few Legionnaires to hold the fort till spring. These forts were regularly ambushed by rebel forces among the Berbers. French morale was at an all-time low.

As for the missionaries, by 1924 there were five baptized believers among the tribespeople—the fruit of a quarter of a century of work! Persecution from tribe and family was relentless, but the believers held firm. In Sefrou, Maude had reason to be encouraged. She had the respect of the local women— they appreciated the simple medicines with which she doctored them, and she did all she could to alleviate hunger and poverty. Dozens of Jews also came to hear the Word preached and debate matters of religion.

In April of 1925, a serious rebellion developed among the tribespeople under the leadership of Abd el-Krim—aided by a French deserter, Sergeant Joseph Klem, as advisor. El-Krim steamrollered his way south across the country, capturing nine French border outposts, while another thirty were evacuated. French forces rushed to hold Taza, a small town not far from Sefrou. El-Krim turned his forces and pushed all the way to

Fez, one of the royal cities, but hesitated, fearing a trap. This gave the French time to regroup.

Maude had been in Morocco twenty-three years without a break (the missionaries had come for life), but she finally took a furlough to assist her aging parents. She stayed with her elderly parents for three years, but when they died, she returned in 1928 to her beloved Sefrou in Morocco. To her joy, two young men—formerly boys in her classes—took their stand as Christians: Mehdi Ksara and Mohammed Bouabid, even though it meant fierce opposition from their families.

Around this time another young man appeared at the mission door: Leon Hoffman, another French deserter. He had been caught, but while in prison, he read a Hebrew New Testament and one night saw a vision of Christ holding out his nail-scarred hands, saying: "I died for *your* sins." Leon was so moved that he determined to find some Christians to help him understand what it all meant. Realizing the spiritual hunger of the young Legionnaires in Morocco, the GMU missionaries set up special meetings to reach out to them with the Gospel.

Like Mehdi and Mohammed, Leon was also disowned by his relatives back in Poland. All three young men became faithful workers with Maude Cary and the Gospel Missionary Union. (Leon came back to Morocco after his tour of duty with the French Foreign Legion was completed.)

Maude Cary took a second furlough in 1936 and returned a year later. Health problems and family needs had taken a toll on many of the GMU missionaries. As the world prepared for another war, two more single women missionaries slipped into the country before the door slammed shut—leaving only Maude and three other women to maintain three mission houses (Meknes, Sefrou, and Khemisset) and carry on the work. Rather than huddle together for support, they spread out—and when the war was over, the work was still alive, thanks to these courageous women!

After World War II, Maude prayed "for at least ten men" to work among Muslim men. But even after her prayer was answered, Maude didn't slow down. At the age of seventy-one, she opened a new mission at El Hajeb, in spite of poor health and much opposition. "The work is prospering," she quipped, "as one can tell by the battered front door."

The undercurrents for Moroccan independence exploded again in 1953. The French sent Sultan Mohammed V (Sidi Mohammed Ben Yousef) into exile, but it only fanned the flames of rebellion. In 1955, Mohammed V was brought back from exile—just as Maude Cary, who was very ill, took her final trip back home to the United States. The next year the sultan negotiated independence from France and gave himself the title of "King."

In 1967, Maude Cary died at the age of eighty-eight in Kansas—just as all missionaries were ordered to leave Morocco. They were given eight days to pack and get out. Mission houses had to be abandoned. After seventy-five years of service, there were no GMU missionaries (or any Christian missionaries) in Morocco. Now the Gospel was in the hands of the Moroccan Christians like Mehdi Ksara and Mohammed Bouabid.

FOR FURTHER READING

Stenbock, Evelyn. *"Miss Terri!": The Story of Maude Cary, Pioneer GMU Missionary in Morocco.* (England: Back to the Bible Broadcast, 1970).

TRIAL
BY POISON

MARY SLESSOR

Authors' Note

The main characters and major events in this story are true. However, certain events (such as the trading expedition and Etim's accident) do not follow the actual timeline. In the same way, certain minor historical characters have been left out of the narrative to simplify the story. In particular:

The woman named Inyam was indeed a relative by marriage to Chief Edem, and her teenage daughter (whom we have named Imatu) was a cousin of Etim, the chief's son. The real names of Mary's two foster sons (whom we call Okot and Udo) are not known.

The incident of Imatu breaking a taboo by entering the boys' yard is based on an actual incident in another village in which two sixteen-year-old harem wives entered the boys' yard on a lark, and would have been given a hundred lashes if Mary Slessor had not intervened.

We have merged the incident of finding the baby in the bush with the events surrounding Etim's funeral; it actually took place later, and the child was "heard" by village women on their way to market.

Finally, the time frame for the first communion service, which actually took place on Mary Slessor's fifteenth anniversary in Okoyong, was shortened by about half for the purposes of our story. Also the story tells only about one set of baptisms; the next day eleven younger children were also baptized, among them six of Mary's adopted children.

CONTENTS

CHAPTER 1

THE WHITE MA AND THE ROYAL CANOE

Pressing her body against a twisted mangrove tree, Imatu peered around the trunk. There. She could see the goat a short distance away, flicking its tail and munching the grass along the riverbank.

I'll catch you now, Imatu thought grimly. A light rain was falling steadily through the forest, covering any noise she might make.

But before Imatu could move, the goat threw its head up, gave a startled leap, and disappeared into the wet, dripping bushes.

"Wicked goat!" Imatu fumed, stamping her foot in frustration.

She had been trying to catch the runaway since noon and had followed it all the way to the Calabar River. At first she'd been glad her mother had sent her after the missing goat—that meant she didn't have to go to the funeral in Ifako, the next village. Imatu hated funerals. All the drinking made everyone crazy, and the witch doctor was sure to accuse someone of casting a spell on the person who had died.

But the light was slipping away in the late, rainy afternoon, and Imatu didn't want to be in the forest after dark. She'd been so close to catching that goat! She knew she hadn't made any noise. What had startled it?

Then she heard it. Chanting . . . coming from the river.

The chanting grew louder, accompanied by the steady *swish, swish* of paddles dipping into the water. Who was coming up the river? Imatu's heart beat faster; she was tempted to turn and run back to the village. But curiosity moved her feet quietly through the wet grass, stepping over gnarled tree roots and tangled vines, toward the edge of the river.

The girl crouched behind a bush and listened. She could make out some of the words now . . .

> *Ma, our beautiful, beloved mother,*
> *Is on board.*
> *Ho! Ho! Ho!*

And then the canoe came in sight. Imatu gasped. She had never seen a canoe like this one! It was twice as long as the fishing canoes the men of her village hollowed out of fallen tree trunks. From front to back, strong paddlers lined either side—more than she could count!—their dark skin glistening in the rain. A steersman stood in the back, beside a pole with a long banner flying out behind. But strangest of all was the little "hut" in the middle of the canoe, covered on top by palm leaves, with brightly colored cloth curtains fluttering on all sides.

The canoe shot past her, on up the river. Imatu ran after it, safely hidden among the bushes and trees of the forest. This was no fishing canoe. It couldn't belong to an ordinary village chief. This must be a *king's* canoe.

Whump! A hidden tree root sent Imatu sprawling on the ground. She scrambled to her feet but she could no longer see the canoe, though she could still hear the chanting . . . *Ho! Ho! Ho!* Ignoring her stinging toes and knees, Imatu ran faster. She had never seen a king before—the Okoyong people had no king. So where did this king come from? And where was he going?

Suddenly the chanting stopped. Coming over a little rise beside the river, Imatu quickly crouched down. The canoe had pulled up onto a little strip of sand. The front paddlers hopped out and pulled the canoe halfway out of the water and started to unload bags and boxes. But Imatu's eyes were riveted on the little hut.

The curtains parted and a young boy and girl crawled out. Right behind them, an older boy about Imatu's age came out, holding a small child on his hip. The children scrambled over the side of the big canoe, squealing, obviously glad to stretch their legs after being cooped up in the little hut.

But where was the king?

The curtains parted again and a woman came out, holding a baby. Imatu shook the rain out of her eyes; the fading light must be playing tricks on her! She squeezed her eyes shut, then opened them and stared again.

The woman's skin had no color! It was as white as the goat Imatu had been chasing all afternoon. And her hair! It was reddish orange—as orange as the yams Imatu and her mother dug out of the ground to roast and eat.

Imatu had never seen a white person before. What was a white woman doing in a king's canoe? Imatu's heart thudded so loudly in her chest she was afraid the people from the canoe could hear it, too. Had this strange woman brought warriors to attack her village while everyone was away at the funeral? Everyone, that is, except Imatu's mother and a few slave women. . . .

Just then the strange white woman called out to the oldest boy: "Okin! Gather the children and follow that path." Imatu was startled; the woman was speaking in Efik, her own language! "And, Akani," the woman said to the steersman, "the children and I are going ahead. You organize the bearers and bring the supplies. We need to get to Ekenge before dark . . . about four miles into the forest."

Ekenge! That was Imatu's village. The white woman *was* going there!

Imatu jumped quietly to her feet, still careful not to be seen, and ran as fast as she could through the tangled underbrush toward her village. When she thought she was well ahead of the strangers, she found the path that led from the river to the village. The rain had slowed to a drizzle, but the path was wet and slippery.

Daylight was almost gone when Imatu stumbled into the nearly deserted village. Ekenge, like other Okoyong villages, was a loose cluster of family compounds. Each compound consisted of several huts grouped together behind a rough bamboo fence for a man, his wives, their children, several slaves, and assorted animals. Tonight the compound fires were cold—except for one.

Slipping in the mud, Imatu made her way toward the single fire flickering in the drizzling rain. Her mother, Inyam, was stirring a mush made of cornmeal under a palm-thatch shelter, while two old women—slaves of the chief—sat in the doorway of one of the huts.

"Mem! Mem!" Imatu called out, gasping from her run.

"Imatu? Did you find the goat?" her mother called back. Inyam was a handsome woman, large boned and strong.

"No . . . the goat . . . not important . . . woman coming . . ." gasped Imatu.

"What?" said Inyam angrily. "You came back without the goat? Go! Go now and find it, or the chief will beat us when he returns."

"Wait! Wait!" pleaded Imatu. "I came to warn you . . . a woman with many warriors . . . coming!"

"Woman? What woman?" frowned her mother.

"A *white* woman! In a king's canoe!"

Inyam grabbed Imatu by the shoulders and gave her a shake. "You're talking crazy! Who gave you gin to drink?"

Suddenly they heard the sound of children crying, coming from the forest path. Imatu's mother stared in astonishment as the white woman with short, red hair marched barefoot and hatless out of the brush and into the muddy clearing, carrying a year-old infant. Clinging to her skirts were two children crying lustily. Imatu saw that the boy called Okin was right on her heels, carrying another whimpering child.

The two old slave women gave a fearful cry and scurried into the hut. But Inyam walked slowly toward the pathetic little group standing in the middle of the village. Imatu crowded close behind her, peeking around her mother's back.

"Oh! I'm so glad to see you!" said the stranger, shifting the baby to her other hip. "I'm looking for Chief Edem, village of Ekenge."

Inyam looked the woman up and down. "You have warriors?" she asked.

"Warriors? No, no," the woman shook her head, trying

vainly to shush the tired, wet children. "I come as a friend. I am a Jesus teacher."

Inyam frowned at the strange name. "Jesus teacher? Is he the king of the canoe?"

"The king of the . . . what?" Then the woman laughed. "Oh, the canoe! No, no. The canoe belongs to my friend, King Eyo Honesty VII of Creek Town. The king loaned me his canoe because I had no way to come up the river—"

Just then a man ran out from the forest path into the village clearing. Inyam tensed; Imatu recognized him as the steersman of the canoe.

"Ma! Ma Slessor!" the man cried, panting from his run. "The paddlers will not bring your supplies tonight. They say it is too dark; they are afraid of the evil spirits in the forest. They will come tomorrow."

For a moment the white woman's shoulders seemed to sag. Then she lifted her head. "No, tomorrow is Sunday, God's day of rest. I cannot ask them to work for me tomorrow. It must be tonight. Here," she said to a startled Inyam, handing the baby to Imatu's mother. "Will you please take care of my children until I get back? It seems I must go shake the men myself. Come, Akani." And with that the woman plunged back into the now-dark forest, the steersman at her heels.

Inyam just stared after her, openmouthed, the baby screaming in her arms. Imatu tugged at her mother's skirt and pointed to the pot of cornmeal mush still cooking on the sputtering fire. "We can feed them," she suggested, suddenly feeling sorry for the children, who had just been abandoned by their "mother" . . . or whoever that white woman was.

In a short while the five children were greedily stuffing cornmeal mush into their mouths and being fussed over by the two old slave women who had come out when the white woman left.

"No milk to drink," Imatu said, shrugging her shoulders at the boy named Okin. "I lost the goat."

Imatu woke with a start. The rain had stopped, the baby was asleep in Inyam's arms, and the white woman's other children had curled up on mats inside the hut. But she saw the dancing light of many torches approaching the village and heard drums beating and drunken singing. Was it the white woman returning? . . . No, the torches were coming from the direction of Ifako. The villagers must be returning from the funeral.

Inyam had heard the commotion, too, and was trying to lay the baby down without waking it up when a tall man in a flowing robe strode toward their still flickering fire.

"Inyam!" he bellowed angrily. "Why did you not go to the funeral? You dishonor me and our sister village by your absence!"

Imatu's mother scrambled to her feet, her eyes cast down. "I didn't mean to dishonor you, brother-in-law," she said. "The goat that my dead husband left us—it ran away. Imatu and I had to find it, so that we do not presume further on your generous hospitality."

"A likely story!" roared the man, who was obviously drunk. "You probably untied it yourself to have an excuse not to go to the funeral, you insolent woman! And . . . what is this baby? Whose orphan did you snatch from the forest? Do you think our poor village can feed another mouth? I won't have it! I—"

"Chief Edem!"

A powerful woman's voice carried through the night, over

the babble of voices slurred with strong drink. All eyes turned in the direction of the path that led to the river, and voices suddenly ceased. Into the circle of torchlight marched the white woman with red hair, followed by a line of unhappy-looking men carrying all sorts of boxes and bundles.

"Chief Edem," said the woman again in the Efik language, addressing Inyam's brother-in-law. "The baby is my adopted child. I am Mary Slessor; do you remember me? You and I talked in a big *palaver* once before, almost two years ago, and you invited me to come to your village and teach 'book.' Well, I am here."

The drunken chief's eyes bugged and his mouth opened and shut, but no sound came out. Imatu felt like giggling but dared not. And then in the silence she heard a forlorn "baaaa."

Attached to Mary Slessor's wrist was a braided vine, and at the other end of the vine was the missing goat.

CHAPTER 2

"RUN, MA! RUN!"

Chief Edem was so astonished to see Mary Slessor that he forgot his anger at Inyam and Imatu. He said no more about the runaway goat, which Imatu tied up next to her mother's hut. The drunken chief merely stalked away, and Mary and the canoe men were left to sleep among her boxes and bundles as best they could.

Early the next morning, the red-haired woman fed the canoe paddlers from her supplies, then sent them off to return King Eyo's canoe. While the chief and most of the people were sleeping off the effects of their drinking binge at the funeral, Imatu saw the Jesus teacher do a strange thing: She covered one of her boxes with a pretty cloth on which she laid a book and a bouquet of purple orchids and yellow jasmine picked from the edge of the forest. Then she started talking to the handful of children and slave women who had gathered around curiously.

"This book is called the Bible," explained Mary. "It is God's

Word to *all* people—white people like me and black people like you. It tells the story of God the Father, who loves you. In fact, He sent His Son Jesus to take the punishment for all of our sins. Today is Sunday, the first day of the week, a day God set aside for us to worship Him and thank Him for His love."

She was speaking in the Efik language, but the words were very strange to Imatu. Whatever was she talking about? The only gods Imatu knew about were angry spirits, putting curses and spells on people and requiring blood sacrifice to satisfy their anger. Imatu was afraid of gods, and she didn't trust this new one, either. But she liked the woman's gentle smile as she spoke.

Imatu milked the goat and brought the milk in a clay bowl for Mary's children to drink, along with some boiled yams and rice that her mother had cooked. The strange family had set up "camp" among their boxes and bundles, and Imatu squatted nearby, watching as they ate. Then, shyly, she pointed at each of the children in turn and looked quizzically at Mary.

Mary smiled and nodded. "This is Annie," she said, giving the baby a playful shake. Then she tapped the two younger boys, who had cooked yam smeared on their faces. "Okot is three years old and Udo is eight. Janie . . ." Mary gave the little girl, who was about six years old, a big hug. "Janie has been my own sweet adopted daughter since she was a baby, just like Annie. And then there is Okin . . ."

The older boy looked embarrassed.

"Okin is on loan to me," Mary went on, "because his mother wants him to be trained in God's ways. I couldn't manage without Okin—he's the man in our family, even though he is just eleven."

"I am twelve," Imatu spoke up proudly. "My father died

last year—that's why my mother and I live in my uncle's compound. But my uncle doesn't . . ."

Imatu's voice trailed off and her eyes widened with alarm. A sober Chief Edem was approaching the little group, accompanied by a very large woman and a boy about sixteen. The three of them were wearing their best clothes, and the boy had a drum slung over his shoulder on a snakeskin strap.

Had her uncle heard her?

But Chief Edem ignored Imatu and spoke to his guest. "We welcome you, Ma Slessor!" he boomed, as if she had just arrived. "This is Etim, my oldest son, who will be chief after me. And this is my sister, Eme Ete. She will show you a hut for you and your children in the women's yard of my own compound. You are our honored guest."

Mary Slessor thanked the chief warmly and followed his very large sister into the chief's compound as Etim beat importantly on his drum. Now that the chief had officially welcomed the white woman, all the other villagers crowded in, too, not wanting to miss anything that this strange person might do. The children pinched her skin to see if it was the same as theirs; the women touched her straight red hair and laughed. But "Ma Slessor" just smiled and laughed along with them as she dragged her boxes and bundles behind the chief's bamboo fence.

———

The next morning Imatu woke up to discover Ma Slessor and an amused Eme Ete—whom everyone called "Ma Eme"— vigorously sweeping out the filthy hut with palm branches, repairing the sagging roof with fresh palms, and hanging a curtain of cloth in the doorway. The boxes and bundles all went inside the hut—though at night, they all had to come out again, so that the white Ma and her children could sleep inside.

Imatu left the frenzied cleaning and took the four goats from Chief Edem's compound into the forest in search of sweet grass to eat—her daily job. Today she kept the braided vine around the neck of her mother's goat to make sure it didn't run away. When she returned in midafternoon, Ma Slessor was talking to her mother and several "lesser" wives and slave women of the chief.

" . . . to learn to read 'book,' " the white woman was saying.

"But we are women," Inyam protested. "Surely the chief will not let us."

"And we are slaves," several other women snorted bitterly.

"It doesn't matter," Ma Slessor insisted. "I talked palaver with the chief. If one person learns to read, all must be able to learn to read, whether chief or slave, man or woman or child. That is my rule."

Sure enough, a curious crowd of about thirty men, women, and children, both slave and free, gathered around the missionary in the village clearing for their first reading lesson. Ma Slessor held up a slate with a funny mark on it and made a sound. Everyone repeated the sound. Then she turned the slate over and scratched a new funny mark on the other side and made a different sound. Everyone repeated the second sound. Back and forth they went between the two marks, each representing its own sound.

"She is teaching the Efik alphabet," Okin whispered to Imatu.

Imatu was excited. Would she really be able to learn "book"? Just then she glanced up and saw her cousin Etim, the chief's son, standing off to the side with his drum, smirking. He didn't say anything, but she could read his sneer: *Huh! Reading is for slave women and children. You won't catch the chief's son doing such a "womanish" thing.*

Imatu looked away. She didn't care what stupid old Etim thought.

———

Reading School was held in the early evening after the slave men and women got back from tending their masters' or mistresses' "farms"—plots of land scattered in forest clearings where each extended family grew yams and cassava roots, red peppers and corn, beans and rice. The children in each compound milked the goats and fed the scrawny chickens that provided eggs and sometimes meat to flavor a pot of vegetables. Men and boys also went fishing in the Calabar River to supplement the meager food supply.

Ma Eme still had a farm near her old village, where she had lived with her husband before she became a widow. Several days after Ma Slessor arrived, when the August rains had slowed a little bit, the chief's sister announced that she was going to the farm to check on one of her slave women, who was pregnant and about to have a baby. Ma Slessor politely asked if she could go along. Ma Eme was pleased, and together with baby Annie and Ma Slessor's three boys, they set off.

But six-year-old Janie had stepped on a thorn and couldn't walk such a distance, so Imatu quickly volunteered to take care of her. The older girl carried the younger girl on her back, following the goats to a nearby clearing, where the rainy season had created a carpet of rich grass. As noontime came and went, the goats lay in patches of welcome sunshine, chewing their cud.

"Where's your *real* mother, Janie?" Imatu asked, weaving tiny orchids into the little girl's hair.

The little girl looked confused. "Ma is my mother," she said.

"But she's a white woman. Her people must live across the sea."

Janie brightened. "Oh, yes. Ma is from Scotland. It's cold and rainy there, and all the houses are made from wood and stones, all crowded together in a big city. . . ."

Imatu's eyes widened. "How do you know?"

Janie's white teeth flashed a big smile in her pretty, dark face. "She took me there when I was a baby. I wore English dresses and learned to talk English, too. And we had tea and biscuits every morning for breakfast. I don't remember going there—but I do remember coming back to Calabar on a great big ship across the ocean."

Imatu thought about this. She could hardly believe that little Janie had been on a big ship, bigger than the king's canoe, and had gone across the ocean to a country named Scotland full of pale people with red hair.

"But where's your *Calabar* mother and father?" she finally asked.

Janie shrugged. "I don't know. They didn't want me, I guess. But Ma did."

Then the little girl, her head crowned with a wreath of little orchids, looked curiously at her new friend. "Your mother lives in Chief Edem's compound like his other wives. Is Chief Edem your father?"

Imatu scowled. "No, he's my uncle. . . . Never mind. It's time to take the goats back to the village."

———

After that day, Janie Slessor often begged to be allowed to go with Imatu to take care of the goats. Imatu didn't mind; it was like having a little sister to play with and talk to. She had felt very lonely ever since she and her mother had moved away from their own village a few months ago. For some reason the other children in Ekenge seemed to ignore her when they were playing games or telling secrets. But now Okin and his "brothers" and "sisters" were her friends, which raised her status in the eyes of the other village children.

Even though Okin was a year younger than she was, Imatu was impressed at his friendliness and helpfulness toward everyone—not like her cousin Etim, who was always playing his stupid drum and would barely speak to Imatu. And Okin was a good worker, just like Ma Slessor had said. Even Ma Eme decided to send him on an errand to her farm one day because she was feeling "poorly" and didn't want to make the trip.

That evening as Reading School began, Okin still wasn't back from Ma Eme's farm. Imatu was disappointed because Okin had been helping her review the alphabet sounds she had learned. This evening, Imatu was struggling by herself with two new alphabet sounds when she thought she heard someone shouting in the forest. A moment later, Okin came running out of the trees, calling frantically, "Run, Ma, run!"

Dropping her slate, Ma Slessor ran to meet him, followed by half the Reading School.

"The babies . . . the babies . . ." he gasped.

The crowd around Okin parted as Ma Eme shouldered her way to the boy. "Is it my slave woman? Did she have her baby? What has happened?" the big woman demanded.

Okin looked frightened and turned toward Ma Slessor. "It's . . . it's twins. You have to run, Ma, or they will kill them!"

Ma Eme let out a roar. "Twins! That evil woman! She has

been dancing with the devil and pretending all is well. And after I have treated her like my own daughter . . . what? Where is Ma Slessor going?"

At the word "twins," Ma Slessor had taken off into the forest like a startled deer with Okin hot on her heels. The rest of the villagers milled around, muttering angrily to one another.

Imatu was frightened. Among the Okoyong people, a twin birth meant the father of one of the babies must be an evil spirit, and that twin would grow up to be a monster if allowed to live. But since no one ever knew which twin was cursed, both were usually killed or put out in the forest to die, and the mother was driven out and shunned because of her great sin.

So what was the white Ma going to do? The whole village wanted to know. As darkness fell torches were lit, and everyone kept watch. One hour, then two went by. Then they heard the *thwack, thwack* of machetes cutting down vines and bushes. One of the village men trotted into the forest, then came back and reported: "It's Ma Slessor. She has the twin mother with her! But she is having Ma Eme's slave men cut a new path so the twin curse will not pollute our path to the village."

Imatu could tell the adults were upset and bewildered. Ma Slessor was bringing the twin mother to Ekenge? She was having a new path cut so that they didn't lose their own path into the forest? What did it mean?

Soon Ma Slessor came out of the forest, carrying a wooden gin case piled high with household cooking pots, followed by Ma Eme's slave woman, stumbling and frightened. Chief Edem cried out, "No, Ma Slessor! Don't come into our village with that twin woman!" But Ma Slessor marched right into the village with the box, into Chief Edem's compound, and into her hut.

The villagers crowded around—but not too close. Would their village be cursed if the twin mother stayed? What was Ma Slessor going to do?

A little while later, Ma Slessor came slowly out of her hut, carrying the box. But the cooking pots were gone. Instead, a small bundle wrapped in a cloth lay at the bottom of the box.

Ma Slessor looked around sadly. "Twins were born today at the farm of Ma Eme to a good woman, a good slave. She did nothing wrong. But she has been driven off the farm, all her belongings have been broken, and the babies were stuffed into this box along with her cooking pots. I brought her to my hut for safety. No one may touch her there."

The villagers were quiet, staring, wondering.

"One twin, a girl, still lives," Ma Slessor continued. "But the other twin, a boy, is dead . . . his head smashed by a cooking pot."

Imatu winced and looked over at Ma Eme. The chief's sister stood off to the side, a scowl on her wide face.

"I am going to give this baby a Christian burial. We can commit his soul to the tender mercies of the Heavenly Father, even in the wake of this great tragedy."

With that the Jesus teacher walked solemnly toward the forest edge. Several men stepped forward and broke up the ground with their machetes, then scraped aside the loose dirt. Chop, scrape, chop, scrape went the machetes. Finally a small hole was dug. Ma Slessor laid the bundle into the ground, and dirt was pushed back over the little body.

Immediately villagers began to wail and shout, but Ma Slessor yelled, "Stop!" Startled, everyone was quiet. Then, in a calm voice, Ma Slessor began to sing in Efik:

Be still my soul: the hour is hastening on
When we shall be forever with the Lord,
When disappointment, grief, and fear are gone,
Sorrow forgot, love's purest joys restored.
Be still my soul: when change and tears are past,
All safe and blessed we shall meet at last.

Stunned by the strange, quiet little funeral—so different from the drunken orgy at the village of Ifako last week!—the people walked quietly back to their compounds. But Imatu could hear angry murmurs about "the other twin" and "the twin mother."

"I don't know what everyone is upset about," Okin whispered in Imatu's ear as he came up alongside Imatu. "After all, Janie is a twin . . . and everyone seems to accept her."

Imatu stared at Okin, fear leaping up into her throat. Janie Slessor was a *twin*? Why had no one told her? She and Janie had played together, hugged each other, even eaten from the same dish.

If Janie was under a twin curse, had the curse come on Imatu, also?

CHAPTER 3

THE PRANK THAT
BACKFIRED

Imatu didn't know what to do. If she told her mother that Janie was a twin, Inyam might forbid her to play with the little girl. But Imatu was afraid of the twin curse; no one was supposed to associate with twins or the mother of twins. So when Janie called out to her the next day, begging to go along to feed the goats, Imatu pretended she hadn't heard and hurried the goats away without her.

As the goats filled their stomachs with the sweet grass from the small clearings in the forest, Imatu had time to think. So *that's* why Janie didn't know about her mother and father. Ma Slessor had probably rescued her from being killed at birth, just like she had rescued this new baby. Janie was already six years old and so pretty and sweet—she certainly didn't seem to have a twin curse on her. And Ma Slessor and the other children who related to Janie didn't seem to suffer any effects of the twin curse. . . .

Imatu had a sudden thought. The witch doctors said that only *one* twin is fathered by an evil spirit, but no one ever knows which one, so both are usually killed, just to be sure. But since Janie seemed no different than other children, the curse must have been on Janie's *twin*—not Janie herself.

That was it! Imatu was so relieved to figure it out that she rounded up the goats and headed back to the village earlier than usual. When she arrived, a crowd of men, women, and children were peering through the bamboo fence into the chief's compound. Okin saw Imatu return with the goats and ran over to her.

"Ma Eme and Ma Slessor are talking in the yard; they won't let anyone else in until they're done," he said excitedly.

But just then Ma Eme came out of the gate, her large bulk nearly filling the opening. Right behind her came Ma Slessor, her face beaming. Ma Eme stood with her hands on her hips and looked around at the curious faces.

"I have decided . . ." she said slowly, obviously not in a rush to satisfy the crowd's curiosity. "I have decided," she began again, "to take back my slave woman. She is a good woman and *if* . . ." Ma Eme let the word hang in the air for a moment. "If an evil spirit begat one of these twins, it wasn't the slave woman's fault." A noisy murmur went through the crowd, but Ma Eme glared at them, daring anyone to disagree with her. "But . . ."

The murmur stopped.

"But I will not take the twin baby that lives," sniffed Ma Eme. "Ma Slessor and I have made a compromise. I will take back the slave woman, and she will keep the baby. If the baby is cursed, the curse will be on her house and hers alone."

At this, the babble of voices rose to a high pitch. But Ma

Slessor held up her hand, and again the crowd managed to quiet down.

The red-haired woman smiled happily. "I have named the baby Susie, in memory of my sister Susan—just as Janie is named in memory of my youngest sister. I am full of joy today that a precious life has been saved. And I promise you all that I will be a good mother to this child."

The crowd slowly drifted away, shaking their heads and muttering to one another. The white Ma certainly had some strange ways. Who ever thought that their village would allow a twin baby to stay alive—in the chief's compound at that!

———

The slave mother went back to Ma Eme's farm, taking some new household things, a gift from Ma Eme. The newborn Susie—so tiny that she made baby Annie look huge!—thrived on cans of milk that Ma Slessor had among her many boxes. The rest of the villagers eyed the baby suspiciously but gradually accepted her presence, as long as Ma Slessor didn't ask anyone else to take care of her. So Janie and Okin now toted baby Annie about with them while Susie was rarely out of Ma Slessor's arms.

The little hut that Chief Edem had given her was much too crowded for a family of seven. "Chief Edem," Ma Slessor said to him one day. "I am deeply honored that you have given me a hut in your own compound. But would you give me a plot of land near the village where I can build a larger mission house? It would make your own compound less crowded," she said diplomatically.

The chief frowned thoughtfully and walked away. A few hours later he was back. "Ma Slessor, I have good news for you. I would like to give you a plot of land where you can build a larger mission house," he said, as if he had just thought of the idea. "I am honored that you have shared my compound, but you need more room for your growing family. This we would like to do to show our appreciation to you for coming and teaching us 'book.' "

When Okin told Imatu what the chief had said, he added slyly, " . . . *and* it gets the twin baby out of his compound." Imatu laughed. Okin had read her thoughts exactly!

True to his word, the chief gave Ma Slessor a plot of land—though he did not offer to help her clear it or build the house. Undaunted, Ma Slessor tied baby Susie on her back with a long strip of cloth, and for a few hours each day—when the rain stopped long enough—she and Okin whacked at the forest bushes, vines, and small trees with machetes to make a clearing.

The rest of each day, Ma Slessor went from compound to compound in the village, visiting with each of the women in turn, helping to pluck a chicken or weave a basket from tough grasses as they talked. The women were amazed and pleased that the Jesus teacher seemed genuinely interested in them and were soon chatting away about their babies, complaining about their husbands or children, or showing her new herbs to flavor the Okoyong diet of cornmeal and beans and hot peppers and fish.

All except Imatu's mother. Whenever Ma Slessor sat down by Inyam's hut to talk, the young widow became nervous and said little.

But one day, when Chief Edem, his son Etim, and some of the other village men were gone fishing, and Ma Eme had gone to visit her farm, Ma Slessor again came and sat down by Inyam's hut.

"Why are you afraid, my sister?" Ma Slessor said gently, touching the handsome woman gently on her arm.

Imatu was surprised to see her mother's eyes fill with tears. And then the whole story just seemed to spill out.

"My . . . my husband was the brother of Chief Edem's head wife," Inyam said, her voice quivering. "We lived in the village of Akpo—about five miles from here—and I was the only wife to my husband, but my sister-in-law did not like me. When my . . . my husband drowned in a fishing accident, I was forced to take the *mbiam* oath to prove I had not put a curse on him and caused the accident. A chicken was slaughtered, and if it fluttered one way, I was innocent; if it fluttered the other way, I was guilty."

Imatu felt like putting her hands over her ears and running away. Her mother's words brought back the feelings of grief and terror following her father's death, like ripping open an old wound. But . . . it also felt good to have her mother tell Ma Slessor. Imatu wanted her to know! She wanted her to know about the sadness and fear and loneliness of living here in Ekenge. . . .

"I passed the test," Inyam went on. "So now by tradition my husband's relatives have to provide for me. This makes my sister-in-law angry. She has turned her husband, Chief Edem, against me. By Okoyong law, he has to give me protection in his compound, but he took all my inheritance as 'payment' for his hospitality."

Inyam's eyes narrowed and the tears stopped. "He treats me no better than one of his slaves, yet he expects me to be grateful. I hate him. *I hate him!*"

There. It was out. What would Ma Slessor say?

Ma Slessor sat beside Inyam silently for a long time.

Then she said quietly, "It is not right. You have been treated unjustly."

Inyam looked startled. She had expected the Jesus teacher to tell her she ought to be grateful to her benefactor.

"But, dear sister Inyam," Ma Slessor continued, "your hate only hurts you. You must forgive your brother-in-law. That is the way of Jesus."

Inyam shook her head and got up abruptly. "*Never.* I will never forgive him. He looks for ways to humiliate me. And one day . . . one day he will find a way to get rid of me—or kill me."

———

The beating of Etim's drum irritated Imatu. Several nights a week her cousin sat in the doorway of the boys' yard—where the older boys and unmarried young men lived when they got too old to live in the women's yards—and beat his drum. Usually the young men had been drinking gin, and they danced and laughed until late at night.

"Where do they get the gin?" Ma Slessor asked the chief crossly.

"Why, Ma, you know. The white traders sell us guns and slave chains and gin," the chief said, shrugging.

"What do you trade in return?" she demanded.

"Palm oil . . . a little rubber." The chief shrugged again. "We don't have much to trade."

"Nonsense!" Ma Slessor got all steamed up every time she and the chief had this conversation. "You have many rich resources in this delta between the Calabar and Cross rivers. And they have many good things you could trade them for besides gin!"

It was Ma Slessor's opinion that the young men drank

because they were bored and didn't have enough to do. Okin grumbled to Imatu that Etim and the others just stood around and watched and drank while he and Ma cleared the little plot of land for the mission house.

But Imatu had her own reason for being upset when the young men drank: because they became insulting.

"Hey, chicken-legged girl!" they called out when Imatu went by with her goats. "You will have to stay in the fattening hut a whole year before anyone will marry *you*." Then they laughed, and her cousin Etim laughed hardest of all.

Imatu put her nose in the air and pretended not to hear them. But their insults hurt. She knew she was skinny, and that Okoyong men liked a fat wife best. What if no one wanted to marry her? Secretly, Imatu was glad she was skinny; she didn't want to get married anyway. But the boys' taunts also worried her. A single woman without a husband's protection was easy prey in the jungles of Okoyong.

"I wish I could take Etim's stupid drum and throw it in the river," Imatu complained to Okin one evening. Reading School was over, and the drumming and drinking and dancing in the boys' yard had begun. "He thinks he's better than anyone else."

Okin nodded in agreement . . . and then a slow grin lit up his face. "Why not?" he whispered. "We could sneak into the boys' yard when they fall asleep and take Etim's drum and hide it. No one would know what happened to it! That would teach him a lesson."

A thrill of excitement prickled the back of Imatu's neck. No girl was *ever* allowed in the boys' yard. But they all snored like sick cows after they'd been drinking. No one would ever know. And what a great trick to play on that stuck-up Etim!

It was hard to stay awake that night till the drumming and

dancing stopped. But finally Imatu heard a quiet clicking sound outside her hut—Okin's signal. Hardly daring to breathe, she crawled out of her hut and followed Okin out of the chief's yard, across the village clearing in the darkness, to the gate of the boys' yard.

The gate was closed and Imatu suddenly got cold feet. They should go back to their own huts now, before they got caught! But Okin had already figured out how to unfasten the gate, and pulled it open before Imatu could run. He stepped inside the yard and motioned her to follow.

The moon was hidden by a thick blanket of clouds, and it was very dark inside the boys' yard. Imatu had never been inside the fence, but she thought she knew which was Etim's hut. Sure enough, Etim's spear that he had proudly decorated with colorful bird feathers was lying carelessly outside one of the huts. But no drum.

Okin motioned to Imatu to wait while he crept inside the hut and found the drum. Her heart was pounding so loudly in her ears she was sure it would wake up the whole yard! *Why* had she and Okin planned such a stupid trick?

After what seemed like hours, Imatu saw a movement at the door of the hut. Okin was handing out the drum! Just as she took hold of it, however, she heard a big "Humpf!" from inside the hut . . . and then Etim's voice crying out loudly, "Wh—what? . . . Thief! Thief!"

Imatu turned and ran for the gate, the heavy drum thumping against her legs as she clutched the snakeskin strap. Was Okin behind her? She couldn't wait to find out! She had to get—

Whump! A dark figure jumped in her way and she crashed right into him.

She was caught!

CHAPTER 4

THE CURSE

Etim kept screeching, "Thief! Thief!" and soon the whole village was awake and stumbling into the clearing to see what was the matter. By the time Ma Slessor and Inyam arrived, torches had been lit, revealing the frightened faces of Okin and Imatu in the grip of Etim and one of the other young men who lived in the boys' yard.

"What is the meaning of this?" demanded Chief Edem, half-awake and bleary-eyed, wearing only a long sleeping shirt.

"These two—two *animals*," sputtered Etim, "came into my hut and stole my drum! See? The girl still has it in her hand!"

"Okin! Whatever put such a thing in your mind?" said Ma Slessor.

Okin hung his head. "We were only going to hide it—for a joke on Etim."

The other villagers, relieved that a real thief had not snuck into Ekenge, smiled and nodded. It was only a prank, a joke.

"Prank or not," scolded Ma Slessor, "you should never have done it." She turned to the chief. "I apologize for the behavior of my foster son, Chief Edem. I will see that he is punished."

Chief Edem seemed not to hear her but stood with his arms crossed, a scowl on his face. Finally he spoke. "A childish prank can be forgiven. But a more serious crime has been committed this night. The *girl*—this unruly, ungrateful girl that I have taken into my own compound—has violated a taboo: She has entered the boys' yard, which is expressly forbidden by Okoyong law!"

All the villagers turned and stared at Imatu. Suddenly she was very frightened; she wanted to run to her mother and hide her face in her skirt, like she used to do as a little girl when she was afraid. But the young man who had captured her still had her arm in a firm grip.

"Does everyone agree that the girl is guilty of entering the boys' yard?" asked the chief, looking around at the spectators.

There was a murmur of agreement.

"What is the penalty for violating this taboo?" asked the chief.

Imatu's whole body was shaking.

One of the older men stepped forward and cleared his throat. "The penalty for a female entering the boys' yard is one hundred lashes."

There was a stunned silence. Then Imatu's mother screamed. It took Ma Eme and another woman to hold her back as she writhed and sobbed.

"*One hundred lashes?*" cried Ma Slessor. "For a childish prank? The penalty is too severe! The child would die under that many lashes. *Two* lashes is enough—a lesson she will remember."

"Two? You make a joke! All the children will disobey the taboos if we don't punish the girl."

"Punish her, yes," argued Ma Slessor, hands on her hips, standing face-to-face with the chief. "But a punishment fit for a child."

Imatu was so terrified she could not utter a sound or even think. All she knew was that tonight she was going to die.

Back and forth the chief and Ma Slessor argued. The villagers looked at one another. Had anyone ever dared argue with the chief about a penalty for breaking a taboo? This was an amazing woman, this Ma Slessor!

Finally the chief snapped, "*Ten* lashes for breaking the taboo—and I will not give one less!"

———

Imatu's whole body shook with sobs as she lay on a mat in her mother's hut. Her back felt as if it were on fire from the ten lashes. She flinched when Ma Slessor gently put some cool ointment on the cuts and welts.

"Do you see now?" said Inyam in a voice thick with anger. "The chief hates us. One day he will kill us."

Ma Slessor did not answer right away but continued to treat Imatu's wounds. Then she said, "But a taboo *was* broken. The chief would have given a penalty to any girl who entered the boys' yard."

"Bah!" spat Inyam. "Taboos are broken, and sometimes they are punished, and sometimes the chief looks the other way."

"Yes, but when the whole village knows what has happened?" asked Ma Slessor gently. "Besides, he did finally agree to give only ten lashes instead of a hundred."

Inyam's temper flared. "You *agree* with lashing a young girl? Look at my daughter! She will have scars her whole life!"

"Agree? I certainly do not!" cried Ma Slessor. "It's an evil custom, and I will fight it with every ounce of my strength! But *ten* instead of a hundred is a giant step in the right direction. We must be grateful."

Inyam was silent as she squatted by the mat and stroked Imatu's head. Finally she spoke. "I *am* grateful to you, Ma, for standing up to the chief and demanding a lesser penalty. Only you could have done such a thing. He respects you. He respects this Jesus God you teach about. But I am *not* grateful to Chief Edem. That is exactly what he wants . . . to beat me down so low that I will be grateful when he 'only' beats my daughter ten times instead of a hundred!"

Imatu's wounds healed fairly quickly, and within a few days she was able to tend the goats as usual, but Okin would not be comforted. He could barely look Imatu in the eye. "It is all my fault, Imatu," he said gloomily on a visit to her hut with Ma Slessor and baby Susie. "I am the one who suggested we sneak into the boys' yard and take the drum."

Imatu struggled with her feelings. She resented the fact that both she and Okin had taken Etim's drum, but only she was given a whipping. Even worse than the terrible pain of the lash was the utter *humiliation*. Every time she saw her cousin Etim, he was mocking her. Right now Imatu didn't feel like having anything to do with boys at all—or anyone else for that matter—so she avoided Okin whenever possible. But she could see the sorrow in his eyes.

———

The rainy season finally ended in late October, and the warm, sunny months of the dry season were a welcome relief. Okin and Ma Slessor had almost finished clearing a place for the new mission house. The next step was to cut bamboo poles for the structure and find good mud to daub all over it.

But then Chief Edem developed an abscess—a festering sore on his back that made him very sick.

Immediately, Ma Slessor dropped everything else to nurse the chief. She bathed his body with cool water to bring down the fever. She used some of her precious canned milk to get nourishment down his throat when he refused to eat. She boiled medicinal herbs, soaked rags in the brew, and applied poultices to the abscess, assisted by the large, comforting bulk of Ma Eme.

When her supply of herbs was all used up, she begged some from the other women in the chief's yard. But Inyam was reluctant to donate any of her own herbs. "Let him die," she muttered.

"Inyam!" Ma Slessor was shocked. "You must never say anything like that. Revenge is not the way of Jesus. Besides," Ma's voice became anxious, "someone might hear you."

"Well . . ." Inyam considered. "Imatu picks herbs for me when she goes with the goats. Maybe she could show you where to pick the ones you need."

So the next day, Ma Slessor left Ma Eme and the chief's head wife with instructions on how to put poultices on the chief's back, and went with Imatu and the goats to pick a fresh supply of herbs. All the Slessor children went, too, from Okin down to baby Susie.

At first Imatu felt awkward with Okin. She wanted to be his friend again, but she didn't know how to say it. When the goats stopped to eat, Udo and Okot and Janie ran on ahead, and Okin dropped behind with Imatu.

Okin spoke first. "Will you forgive me, Imatu, for getting you in trouble?" he said hopefully.

Forgive? Imatu wasn't sure what that meant. "It wasn't all your fault, Okin," she said slowly.

"But I *am* sorry, and it wasn't fair, and I want you to forgive me. That is the only way to make something right again—that's what Ma says. Just like Jesus forgives and washes us all clean inside when we are sorry for our sins."

Clean inside. How Imatu wished she felt clean inside! She was tired of all the anger and fear and loneliness.

"Yes, I—I forgive you . . ." she faltered, "and . . . and I want you to forgive me, too. For keeping you away."

A big grin spread over Okin's face. "I do! I forgive you!" And he laughed.

It was a wonderful day for Imatu. She had not realized how terribly lonely she'd been the past few weeks, not playing with or even speaking to the Slessor children. But now she pointed out the herbs Ma Slessor was looking for, milked one of the goats to give the children something to drink, and even carried baby Susie. She didn't even care that Susie was a twin.

When the happy little group trudged back into the village, however, they were met by an anxious Ma Eme.

"Careful, Ma Slessor," the big woman said under her breath. "Witch doctor has come." And then the chief's sister hurried away as quickly as she had come.

Ma Slessor gave baby Susie to Janie and hurried toward the chief's hut. The witch doctor was sitting smugly outside the door, his face and body smeared with gray ashes. When the red-haired woman approached, he stood up and held out a bag.

"See what I have taken out of the chief's back?" he said accusingly, dumping the contents of the bag onto the ground. Ma Slessor and the children stared in amazement. There on the ground lay bird bones, animal teeth, pieces of eggshell, gun shot, various seeds, and a carved toothpick.

"Nonsense!" protested Ma Slessor. "Impossible."

"Very bad medicine," said the witch doctor, clucking his tongue. "Someone . . . someone has put a curse on him—"

"What?" protested Ma Slessor. "What are you talking about? Who called you to come? Who—?"

Just then the little group saw the chief's head wife slip away behind the hut.

"Never mind," sighed Ma Slessor. "But you must let me in to see the chief. I have fresh herbs to make poultices to draw the infection out of the abscess. Now step aside."

"You are mistaken!" scowled the witch doctor. "The chief will not get better until we discover who is to blame! Go away! You are not wanted here now." And he stood in the doorway, preventing Ma from entering. There was nothing Ma Slessor could do for the moment.

When time came for Reading School, only Imatu and Okin showed up. The rest of the village was milling around the witch doctor, wondering what he was going to do.

It didn't take long to find out. Some of the men built a fire in the middle of the village clearing. The witch doctor shuffled around it, chanting and mumbling to himself. Then he threw some powder into the flames; the fire sputtered and shot out sparks.

"Aiiieee!" cried the witch doctor. "The fire speaks. Someone is guilty of witchcraft . . . but who? Who makes an accusation?"

There was a hush. Then a voice cried out, "Inyam did it! The widow of my brother! She has no love for our chief!"

Imatu felt as if the breath had been knocked out of her. Why was the chief's head wife accusing her mother?

Two others were accused: a new slave woman and one of the chief's lesser wives. Immediately some of the warriors hurried into the chief's compound and dragged out the three women accused of witchcraft.

"Ma! Ma! What is happening!" screamed Imatu. "Stop them. They are putting chains on my mother."

Ma Slessor marched right past the witch doctor and the three prisoners and into the hut of Chief Edem.

"Chief! What is the meaning of this outrage?" she demanded. The chief was lying on his side, surrounded by smoking pots and feathers and necklaces of teeth—charms scattered around by the witch doctor.

"Go away, Ma Slessor," the chief moaned. "You mean well, but you do not understand these things. Have I ever had an abscess before? No! Someone has put a curse on me, and I will not get better until that person has been found out and punished."

"This is ridicu—"

"Get out, I say!" cried the chief, "or I will have you thrown out. Out! Out!"

Ma Slessor left, but she did not stay out. The next morning she was in the chief's hut, witch doctor or no witch doctor, pleading for him to release the prisoners. Twice more that day, she attempted to see the chief, to make him see the folly of chaining up prisoners instead of letting her treat his abscess with the fresh herbs.

The next time she came to the chief's hut, however, Ma Eme stood in the doorway. "You must stop pestering the chief, Ma Slessor," said the chief's sister, not unkindly. "He will see you no more."

"I will not stop!" cried Ma Slessor. "There are three innocent women chained to a pole in the middle of the village—and the chief's abscess is growing worse. Something is terribly wrong here!"

Ma Eme shrugged helplessly and did not move.

Imatu was afraid. She wanted to stay with her mother during the night, to make sure nothing happened to her, but the guards chased her away. So Ma Slessor took her into the crowded Slessor hut and let her sleep on a mat with little Janie.

Early the next morning, however, Imatu crept out to take some water to her mother. A few minutes later she was back, shaking Ma Slessor frantically. "Ma! Ma! Wake up!" she cried. "They are gone! My mother . . . the other prisoners . . . the guards . . . they have all disappeared!"

CHAPTER 5

EXILED

Ma Slessor scrambled out of her hut, followed by the older children. It was true; the village clearing was completely empty—no prisoners, no guards. The missionary hurried to the chief's hut to demand an explanation and made another startling discovery: The chief, his head wife, their son Etim, and the witch doctor were gone too! But where?

Running to Ma Eme's hut, Ma Slessor breathlessly told her friend about the missing persons. But the chief's sister just shrugged.

"My brother is stubborn," she said, calmly slicing a plantain into some sizzling palm oil over her breakfast fire. "He was tired of being pestered by you, so he took his family and the prisoners to his farm." The bananalike fruit turned crisp on the outside, mushy on the inside, and smelled delicious. Imatu's mouth watered, in spite of her anxiety about her mother.

But then the tone of Ma Eme's words changed. "He forbids you to follow him, Ma Slessor, or *all* the prisoners will be killed," she warned, shaking her finger.

Without a word, Ma Slessor turned and went back to her hut. *Is she going to give up so easily?* thought Imatu, scurrying along behind the slight, red-haired woman. She watched anxiously as Ma Slessor got the other children up, washed their hands and faces, put on fresh clothes, and fed them a breakfast of cold rice and dried fish. But just when Imatu had decided that Ma didn't care that her mother had disappeared, Ma Slessor took her and Okin aside.

"Okin," she said quietly, "I want you to go with Imatu and the goats today. Head in the direction of the chief's farm. When you find a good, grassy clearing, braid some vines and tie the goats so they can eat and lie down. Leave the goats while you find Chief Edem's farm and spy out what is happening. Then come and tell me. But be careful! Don't get caught."

Imatu was glad to have a plan—and glad for Okin's company. When they found a good spot for the goats to graze, they braided strong vines and tied the goats to some sturdy palm trees—not too close together, so they wouldn't get tangled up—just as Ma instructed. Then they headed in the direction of Chief Edem's farm.

Ma Eme had been speaking the truth. When the children finally located the chief's farm after a two-hour trek through the forest, Imatu could see her mother and the other two women prisoners, still in chains, harvesting cassava roots in one of the chief's garden plots. Okin crept closer to the huts but couldn't get close enough to hear anything.

That evening they reported what they'd seen to Ma Slessor.

"Hmm. If they are using the prisoners to work the farm, your mother does not seem to be in any immediate danger,

Imatu," she said. "You must go each day, however, and bring me word. In the meantime, we must keep on with Reading School each evening, as if everything is normal."

For two more days, the children spied on the chief's farm and saw Inyam and the other prisoners working in the chief's garden. But on the fourth day, the prisoners were chained together near one of the huts. And this time they saw the witch doctor chanting and scattering charms all around another hut.

"What does it mean?" Imatu asked anxiously.

"I don't know," Okin said. "But we must go tell Ma— quickly."

As they had agreed, the children met Ma Slessor in the little cleared plot of land that the chief had given her for a mission house, so that no one would overhear them. When they described what they had seen that day, Ma Slessor paced back and forth. "The chief's abscess must be worse," she murmured, thinking out loud. "If he dies, they will kill all the prisoners and not bother to find out which one is supposedly 'guilty.' "

Imatu's heart seemed to crawl up into her throat.

The red-haired missionary kept pacing and thinking. Finally she stopped. "Okin, do you remember the Christian Calabar woman in Old Town who knows herb medicine?"

Okin nodded.

"This woman has treated many abscesses with much success," she explained to Imatu. "She may be our only chance. Okin, you must take a fishing canoe and go downriver to Old Town and persuade this woman to come with you. Say Ma Slessor asks her to come. Then take her straight to Chief Edem's farm. Do you think you can find it from the river?"

Again Okin nodded, his eyes shining with adventure.

"But do not take her all the way to Chief Edem's farm.

The last mile she must go by herself, and just say she has heard that the chief is ill. Do you understand?"

That very evening, on the excuse that she was sending Okin to Old Town to purchase more canned milk for baby Susie, Ma Slessor packed some dried fish, fruit, and a cooked yam in a skin bag, gave him a few coins for the milk, and waved good-bye as the boy headed down the path toward the river.

Ma figured that, if all went well, Okin could arrive at Old Town by morning. He would need to rest, persuade the herb woman to come with him, and then paddle back upriver—which would take another day and night. Then the walk through the forest to the chief's farm . . . then back to Ekenge.

Two nights and two days . . . if all went well.

Sick with worry about her mother, Imatu found it hard to milk the goats, take them to the grassy places, boil rice and beans for her supper, and concentrate on the reading lesson during Reading School.

One day went by. On the second day, Imatu was tempted to tie up the goats and run through the forest to the chief's farm to see what was happening. But Ma Slessor had told her she absolutely must not do that. Her job was to wait.

Okin had not returned to Ekenge by the time she got back with the goats that afternoon. He was still not there when it was time for Reading School. But just as Imatu was getting ready to curl up on Janie's mat for the night, she heard whis-tling coming from the direction of the river path.

It was Okin! And he was carrying a box of canned milk on his head.

All had gone as planned. The Christian Calabar woman from Old Town had agreed to come with him, and he took her as close as he dared to Chief Edem's farm. Then he went back to the river to get the milk from the fishing canoe. And that was all. But one thing he knew: Imatu's mother and the other prisoners were still alive.

Now they had to wait.

Two more days went by. Then three. Still no word from Chief Edem. Imatu tossed and turned on her mat at night, worried about the fate of her mother. The only good thing was that Etim was also gone, and there was no annoying drumming coming from the boys' yard.

By the fourth day, Ma Slessor was as anxious as Imatu. "Okin, you must go with Imatu again today," she finally said, frowning. "Tie up the goats out in the forest once more and spy on the chief's farm."

Relieved to be able to *do* something besides wait, the two children did as Ma Slessor asked, and after tying the goats to graze, they crept close to the edge of the forest from where they could see the gardens and huts of the chief's farm in a sunny clearing. To their surprise, they were greeted by a flurry of activity. Bundles were being packed, fires put out . . . and the chief was standing up and walking around! Imatu looked around anxiously for a glimpse of her mother—and found her and the chief's lesser wife coming out of one of the huts carrying small bundles.

Okin poked Imatu. "Look!" he said, grinning. "No chains."

Imatu was weak with relief. But just then a movement on the far side of the clearing caught her eye. Out of the forest came two tall warriors. They did not look like Okoyong warriors, however. Where were they from? And what were they doing?

They watched one of Chief Edem's men go into a hut and bring out the third prisoner, the slave woman, still in chains. Chief Edem and the strange warriors met and talked, and then the tall warriors led the woman away.

Imatu's mouth went dry. "I think those were *Aros* warriors," she whispered to Okin.

"Aros? Who are they?" asked the boy.

Imatu swallowed hard. "From the north . . . they're cannibals. They eat people."

————

Ma Slessor went over again what Okin and Imatu had seen that day at Chief Edem's farm. "The chief looked healthy? And it looked like they were packing to come home?" The children nodded. "Praise to the Father of Light, who is stronger than the powers of darkness!" Ma exclaimed. "But . . . you say the slave woman was taken away by Aros warriors?"

More nods.

"I wonder what that rascal chief is up to," Ma Slessor muttered.

Chief Edem and his party walked into the village just as Reading School was finishing that evening. The chief smiled broadly at Ma Slessor. "See, Ma?" he said cheerfully. "I am better now. The old ways are best, you see?" And without waiting for a reply, he retired to his hut.

With a grateful cry, Imatu ran to her mother and gave her a big hug. "Oh, Mem, Mem, you have returned safely!" she cried.

But Inyam did not smile. She loosened Imatu's grip and pushed her back so that she could look at her. "We are being sent away," she said dully.

"What?" cried Ma Slessor, who had also come over to greet Inyam. "Sent away? But why?"

Inyam just picked up a bundle with one hand, took Imatu's hand with the other, and walked toward their hut. Bewildered,

Imatu looked back over her shoulder at Ma Slessor, Okin, and the other children. What was happening?

That night Imatu lay on her mat, listening to Etim's drum coming from the boys' yard. She had thought that when her mother returned home safely, everything would be all right again! But something was wrong. What did her mother mean, "sent away"?

Maybe Imatu had misunderstood. Maybe she meant that the slave woman had been sent away. That must be it.

But the next morning Inyam told Imatu to begin rolling their sleeping mats as she packed their cooking pots, baskets, and clothes. Ma Slessor, with baby Susie on her hip, watched the pile of bundles growing outside Inyam's hut, then marched over to the chief's hut.

"Chief Edem!" she called. "I have missed you. Now that you are well, let's sit and have a *palaver*—so much has happened while you were away; there are so many things to talk about."

Looking relieved that Ma Slessor did not seem to be angry with him, the chief came out of his hut and sat down on one of Ma Slessor's stools that she brought out of her hut. Several other villagers gathered around to hear the chief and Ma talk. Imatu slipped away from her mother's packing and crept close to the *palaver*.

Ma expressed her happiness that the chief was feeling better and had returned to the village. She then described her plans for the mission house she was building—the dimensions had been marked on the ground, and the next step was to gather bamboo for the frame and mud for the walls. The chief nodded his approval.

Ma offered to tutor the chief personally so that he could

catch up with the rest of the Reading School now that he was well. Again the chief seemed pleased.

"But, Chief Edem," the missionary said abruptly, "you went away with three prisoners and only two have come back. What happened to the other slave woman?"

The chief squinted into the morning sunlight, as if he hadn't heard her question. After a few minutes, however, he said, "Oh, she ran away. But she was a worthless slave anyway, so I let her go."

Imatu shot a sharp look at Okin. Ran away? They knew better! Then she realized that Ma Slessor could say nothing about the slave woman being given to the cannibal warriors or the chief would know someone had been a spy—and suspected spies would be subjected to the poison bean ordeal!

Ma Slessor changed the subject. "Why are you sending away the woman Inyam and her daughter Imatu?"

The chief squirmed a little—then lifted his chin defiantly. "Because I am chief and must do what is best for the whole village! The kinswoman of my wife does not appreciate what I have done for her, taking her into my own compound and giving her protection. Already there have been two incidents threatening the well-being of my family—"

"*Two* incidents?" Ma Slessor interrupted. "If you mean taking Etim's drum, that was an innocent joke! And the girl has already been punished enough. As for the abscess you suffered, it was a natural infection that has now healed. You *know* that Inyam did not cast any witchcraft spell on you!"

Chief Edem stood up in frustration. "Ma, you mean well, but you do not understand these things. Sickness and accidents—these things are not natural! A wise chief must get rid of evil influences. The woman and the girl must go—today!" With that, the chief stalked away.

Ma Eme, who had been standing nearby, stopped Ma Slessor from running after the chief. "My brother has spoken," she warned. "At least Inyam is leaving with her life. You have influenced him more than you know."

Ma Slessor sighed and caught Imatu's eye. The girl's face registered her shock and dismay.

"Ma! What does he mean? Where will we go? What about Reading School?" Tears welled up in Imatu's eyes.

Ma Slessor shook her head and walked over to Inyam, who continued to stack her belongings outside of the hut. "Where will you go, Inyam?" she said gently to the handsome woman. "What will you do?"

Inyam straightened, her face betraying no emotion. "We will go back to Akpo, our old village. My sister's husband may be willing to give me some land to farm. Imatu and I know how to work hard. We will survive. Maybe it is best. I do not want to live where I am not wanted."

———

Okin handed Imatu the braided vine tied around the neck of the goat. "I will miss you, Imatu," he said awkwardly.

Imatu dug her toes into the dirt. A big lump tightened her throat, and tears threatened to spill down her cheeks. She didn't want to say good-bye. Ma Slessor and Okin and little Janie were the only friends she had.

No one else from the village had come to the edge of the forest to say good-bye to Inyam and Imatu. Only Etim leaned against a tree in the distance, a mocking smile on his face, idly thumping his drum. Imatu looked at Ma Slessor holding little Annie on one hip and baby Susie on the other. Three-year-old Okot and eight-year-old Udo were clinging to her skirts. But . . . where was Janie?

"Good-bye, Inyam," said Ma Slessor softly. "Good-bye, Imatu. The God of love will go with you."

Inyam just said, "Come on, Imatu. We must leave."

Imatu tugged on the vine and started down the path after her mother with the goat in tow.

"Imatu! Imatu! Wait . . . wait!" cried a familiar voice. Janie came flying around the edge of the village. Her arms were full of flowers—orchids and jasmine and orange blossoms.

Panting, the little girl tucked the lush bouquet in a fold of Imatu's skirt. "For you," she said shyly. "I love you."

The tears finally spilled over. No one had ever said "I love you" to Imatu before. And the sweet words had come from Janie—a twin supposedly under a "curse."

CHAPTER 6

BASKETS AND
MORE BASKETS

Imatu straightened up and stretched her aching back. The tropical sun shone hot and unrelenting in the little clearing where she and her mother were planting rows of beans. Mopping her face with her head scarf, Imatu thought longingly of the shady forest where she used to take Chief Edem's goats when they lived in Ekenge. But now. . . .

It had been four months since she and her mother had been exiled from Chief Edem's village. Their old village of Akpo had been reluctant to take them back. Two more women's mouths to feed! But Inyam had been determined to pay her own way. She rented a patch of land from her sister's husband, promising to pay him with part of the first crop. Then she begged small amounts of seeds from several families until she had enough to plant a few rows of beans, corn, yams, cassava root, and even some rice in a swampy patch near a creek—enough to feed her and Imatu. In the meantime, Inyam hired herself out to various village farms in exchange for food until she could harvest her own meager crops.

"Hurry up, Imatu!" called Inyam impatiently, loosening the ground ahead of Imatu with her machete. "There will be time to rest when the seeds are in."

Imatu sighed and retied her head scarf. It was April—time for the wet season to begin, and they had to get the seeds planted before the rains came. She poked several beans in the ground and made a little mound where the bush would grow, then she took a few steps and poked several more beans in the ground.

"Hello-o-o! Hello!" called a voice. "Inyam! Imatu!"

Imatu jerked her head up. That sounded like Okin! She jumped up and scanned the edge of the forest. Sure enough, there was Okin running down the path carrying a bundle, and behind him she could see Ma Slessor—barefoot and hatless, as usual—with baby Susie tied on her back.

A big grin spread on Imatu's face. Ma Slessor had not forgotten them. At least once a month she and some of her children had walked through the forest the five miles from Ekenge to Akpo to see them. Old Chief Akpo—after whom the village was named—had heard that Ma Slessor was a wise woman and a fair judge. He welcomed her visits and invited her to judge family disputes or cases when Okoyong law was broken. And at each visit, Okin had tried to teach Imatu what they'd been learning in Reading School—but Imatu felt frustrated and sad that she couldn't be learning every day.

Today Ma Slessor immediately began helping Inyam break up the ground with her own machete. "I'll help you plant the beans," Okin said to Imatu. Imatu knew her mother would be pleased, even if she didn't say so. That was Ma Slessor's way: When she visited any family, she always pitched right in and helped with the work, so that her visit was a help instead of a hindrance.

With four people working, the rows of beans were soon planted, and the little work party collapsed in the shade at the edge of the forest. Inyam laid out some flat bread and beans seasoned with red peppers that she had brought for their noon meal; Ma Slessor and Okin contributed two juicy mangoes and some dried fish.

"It's a picnic!" laughed Ma Slessor, bouncing baby Susie on her lap. "Just like we used to have back home in Scotland."

"Speaking of Scotland," said Okin slyly, "I have a treat for you, Imatu—it came in the missionary box from Ma's home church."

He unwrapped some hard, round, pink things and put them in Imatu's hand. "Suck it," he urged.

Imatu put one of the hard things in her mouth. Oh! It was so sweet and good!

Okin grinned. "It's peppermint candy! The children in Scotland sent them for Ma Slessor's children—*and* our friends."

"And I have a present for you, Inyam," said Ma Slessor, pulling a smaller bundle out of Okin's bag. "It's cotton cloth—to make clothes for you and Imatu."

Inyam's eyes grew big. She gently touched the soft, green cloth. It had pretty pink and gold flowers scattered all over it. She held it close to her body, where it made a sharp contrast with the drab, brown, tattered garment she was wearing.

"That came in the missionary box, too," Okin said.

"But that is not the real reason I came," Ma Slessor said, her tone becoming very businesslike. "I want to talk to you, Inyam, about trading Okoyong goods with the people of Calabar along the seacoast."

Inyam gave Ma Slessor a puzzled look. "Trade? You mean

like the white traders who come up the Calabar River and trade guns and gin and slave chains for some of our palm oil and rubber?"

Ma Slessor put her hands over her ears and gave a little screech. "That is exactly what I want to change!" she cried. "Bullets and alcohol and chains only make your lives more miserable! But there are many things the Okoyong people could trade for that would give you a better quality of life—cloth and tools and household goods and cooking utensils and medicine and even doors and windows for your huts! And there are wonderful resources here in the rain forest that you could use for trade: rubber and palm oil and peanut oil and woven baskets—"

"Baskets!" snorted Inyam. "Every woman weaves her own baskets to hold the yams she digs or to carry clothes down to the creek to wash. No one would trade beautiful cloth like this"—she held up the soft material Ma Slessor had given her—"for my plain old baskets."

"But you're wrong, Inyam," said Ma Slessor. "Your baskets are beautiful and well made. The women in the towns downriver don't have time to make their own baskets. They have to help their husbands in the marketplace or clean the fish their husbands catch at sea. They would rather trade or pay money for good-quality baskets to use at home or in their shops."

Inyam stared at her.

Ma Slessor got up, brushing dirt and grass from her skirt. "Will you think about it, Inyam? I must also go talk to your chief. If the young men from Ekenge and Ifako and Akpo work hard to get the sap from lots and lots of rubber trees, they can trade for many things that would help their villages—*and* they won't have so much time to drink gin and get into fights with each other!"

———

The stack of baskets inside the hut was growing. Each day after hoeing their little farm plot and milking the goat, Imatu would go hunting for sturdy, long reeds and grasses, which Inyam wove into baskets of different shapes. Then her mother would soak the finished baskets in water and let them dry until they were tight as a drum.

Some of the other women in Akpo thought Inyam was crazy. "Why do you make so many baskets? You will not be able to give them away!" they laughed.

Inyam ignored their comments. "My daughter and I are working like slaves, even though I am a free woman," she retorted. "If Ma Slessor is right, I will be able to trade for things we need and won't have to work night and day just to put a little food into my daughter's belly."

One day when Imatu was out in the forest hunting for reeds, she popped some juicy berries into her mouth . . . then stared thoughtfully at the red stain they left on her fingers.

"Mem! Look at this!" she cried when she got back to their hut. She unfolded a large leaf and poured out a handful of berries into a clay bowl. She pounded the berries with a stone, making a thick, red liquid. Then, dipping a green twig into the red liquid, Imatu carefully smeared the red color along one of the woven rows on a basket.

Her mother watched, fascinated. "Do another," she urged.

Imatu painted another ring around the basket. Inyam was pleased—and so was Ma Slessor the next time she came to visit and saw all the different designs and colors Imatu had painted on various baskets. "This is wonderful!" she exclaimed. "You must both come with me when we go downriver to trade in

Creek Town. Yes—it's about time to set up our first trading expedition and go to meet King Eyo!"

———

The constant summer rains had made the path through the forest from Akpo to Ekenge slippery with mud. Monkeys screeched in the treetops as Inyam and Imatu carefully picked their way through the dripping bushes, ferns, and rotting leaves on the forest floor. Both the woman and the girl carried a large bundle of baskets tied together with vines.

Imatu was excited. Tomorrow they were going by canoe downriver to Creek Town—and would meet King Eyo Honesty himself! And in just a few hours she would get to see little Janie Slessor—as well as Okin and the other Slessor children.

But as they got closer to Ekenge, Imatu's excitement changed to worry. "Mem . . . Mem!" she called, trying to keep her balance as she stumbled on a large tree root. "What if Chief Edem is angry that we are returning to his village? What will he do to us?"

"You heard Ma Slessor," Inyam reminded her. "She told us to come straight to her new mission house on the edge of the village. The mission house is a refuge—no one will dare hurt us there."

Even though Okin had told Imatu that Ma Slessor had finally built a two-room mission house on the piece of land Chief Edem had given her, Imatu was still surprised to see the large, rectangular hut sitting on the little clearing. Janie and Udo and Okot came squealing down the path to meet them. Ma Slessor stood smiling in the doorway, baby Susie on her hip as usual.

"Guess what?" Okin whispered to her as they put down their big bundles of baskets. "Etim is getting married. He's actually clearing land to build himself and his new wife a hut!"

Imatu just made a face. She didn't care what her cousin Etim did—although it would be a sight to see him actually *working*.

"Such a fine house," Inyam murmured as she walked slowly through the two-room mud house, stepping over an old, sick woman lying on a mat in the sleeping room and gently touching Ma Slessor's sewing machine, which the missionary used to sew simple garments for the village women and children.

"And look!" Janie pointed proudly. "A dish cupboard and something to sit on!"

Imatu was amazed. One mud wall had been scooped out to make several flat shelves for Ma Slessor's dishes and cooking pots. A fireplace in one corner had a mud chimney so the smoke could go outside. But most amazing of all was a mud "bench" built right against a wall, with a soft pad on the seat that Ma Slessor had sewn. A runaway slave woman nursing her year-old baby was occupying this wonderful piece of furniture.

Ma Slessor nodded. "We are very grateful to have this house . . . but as you can see, it is already too small. I am thinking of building on more rooms—or even making it two stories high! Many come who are sick or need refuge."

Imatu was only half listening. On the wall hung a photograph of a handsome white man, a pretty white woman, and two children. "Who is it, Ma?" she asked.

Ma Slessor started to answer, but Okin jumped in. "That man was a mean bully when he was my age. He tried to scare Ma to keep her from teaching the Bible to orphans on the street in Scotland—"

"And he swung a heavy stone on a cord closer and closer to her head, but she didn't run away!" Udo interrupted.

"Is that true, Ma?" Imatu asked.

Ma Slessor smiled and nodded. "I made that bully a deal. If he couldn't scare me, then he had to listen to my Bible lesson! When the stone scraped my forehead, he was so ashamed that he made his whole gang come to my Bible class. Now he's all grown up, and he sent me that picture of his family to thank me for introducing him to Jesus. I keep it there to remind me how Jesus can change a young person's life—even someone as young as you, Imatu."

Ma Slessor gave Imatu a warm hug, then bustled around organizing supper for her huge household—twelve adults and children tonight! "We must get to sleep early—we have a long journey tomorrow," she said. "Several chiefs and men from all three villages will be going along bringing goods to trade."

Imatu shivered even though the damp evening was warm. She was both scared and excited. Whoever thought she would see Creek Town and meet the king who had loaned Ma his royal canoe!

CHAPTER 7

THE ACCIDENT

Early the next morning, the whole village of Ekenge gathered at the riverbank in the rain to send off the people going to Creek Town. The chiefs of Ifako and Akpo were also there, along with several men from each village taking things to trade.

Okin was being left behind to take care of Udo, Janie, Okot, and the mission house guests—under the watchful eye of Ma Eme. There was some muttering about why the woman Inyam was going, but Ma Slessor made it clear that Inyam had no husband to support her, so she must represent herself. As for Imatu, Ma Slessor needed help with the babies—Annie and Susie—and that settled that.

Everyone was yelling advice.

"Put all the goods in one canoe and tow it behind the other."

"Idiot! Each canoe needs its own paddlers. Chiefs in one, women in the other—and divide the paddlers."

"Don't stack those baskets that way! Any child can see you have to do it like this."

"Bring back cloth for dresses!"

"No! We need more weapons."

In spite of all the advice, both canoes were finally loaded to the rim with a barrel of palm oil, large balls of raw rubber, baskets of yams and plantains, a bag of palm kernels, some gifts for King Eyo, and Inyam's baskets. But as the men stepped forward to get into the canoes, Ma Slessor shouted, "Stop!"

She looked the men up and down. Each one was wearing a sword or carrying a spear or gun. "*No weapons,*" she said firmly. "We are going as peaceful traders—not warriors. Leave them behind."

There was an immediate uproar. "What? No Okoyong man goes to a strange place without his weapon!"

But Ma Slessor sat down on the riverbank and said stubbornly, "We don't leave until the weapons stay."

For an hour the men argued. "You want to make women of us, Ma!" they complained. Mary Slessor just sat. Another hour went by. Some of the men stalked off angrily, including Chief Akpo, to the cheers of the crowd.

But finally Chief Edem, the chief from Ifako, and the remaining men reluctantly laid down their weapons and got in the canoes. One of the canoes was so overloaded that it immediately tipped over, causing another uproar until all the trade goods had been fished out of the river, the canoe drained, and everything repacked.

As Ma Slessor got into one of the canoes, she noticed several spears sticking out of a long bundle hidden on the bottom. Grabbing the spears, she pitched them out onto the riverbank. "I said no weapons! And I mean no weapons!"

Finally, to the wails and shouts of those being left behind, the two canoes were pushed away from the bank. Imatu sat in the middle of one with baby Annie. Her mother and Ma Slessor sat in the middle of the other, taking turns caring for baby Susie and using a paddle.

They were off.

––––––

The trip down the Calabar River to Creek Town took twelve hours, and it was dark before they pulled the canoes up onto the narrow beach. A runner had alerted King Eyo that Ma Slessor and the Okoyong visitors were coming, so they were met at the beach by men with torches to light the way to the king's house.

The king's house was not made of mud but of wood and stone, with tiles on the roof instead of palm branches. Imatu had never imagined such shiny floors—and real furniture to sit on! They were all given fresh fruit and chicken and plenty of rice to eat and a blanket to sleep on for the night. But Imatu was too excited to sleep much.

The next day they met with the king. Imatu hadn't expected the king to be a dark Calabar man dressed in European clothes and a top hat. He was accompanied by several Calabar chiefs, dressed in traditional, full robes and brightly colored hats.

King Eyo and Ma Slessor exchanged warm words and handshakes, then Ma politely introduced each individual who had come along on the trading expedition. Chief Edem was so delighted to meet the king that he jabbered away nonstop for ten minutes about the king's fine house and his unusual clothes and how the king must *come* to Ekenge in his royal canoe for a visit. Then, to impress the king, he bragged about how many wives and slaves he had, how many hunts he'd been on, and how he was the most important chief in Okoyong because Ma Slessor had chosen to live in his village.

Imatu noticed that the fancy Calabar chiefs were whispering and chuckling at Chief Edem's foolish talk. The king noticed also and scolded them gently. "The Gospel, which has made you what you are, has only recently been taken to Okoyong by our dear Ma. These are our guests, and we must honor them for the sake of our Lord and Savior."

King Eyo then graciously invited the Okoyong visitors to come to the Calabar Christian church in Creek Town that evening, where he himself preached. Afterward, Imatu overheard the Ifako chief telling Chief Edem: "Ma Slessor has been wanting to build a church school in Okoyong. I will donate land near Ifako, and it will be a church for both our villages. What do you say, eh?"

Two days later, as the Okoyong canoes headed upriver, Imatu's head was full of all the sights and sounds of the trading expedition to Creek Town. The marketplace had been wonderful! Besides local fruits, vegetables, and live animals to trade, there had also been goods from other countries—cloth and shoes and chairs and tea and spices and tools and glass windows. Her mother's baskets sold quickly, and many people grunted approvingly when they saw the designs that Imatu had painted on them. Many people paid in coins. At first Inyam didn't know what to do with them and was afraid she was being cheated. But then Ma Slessor showed her how she could take the coins and buy things she wanted in the market.

Imatu nudged the bamboo cage at her feet that held the four hens and one rooster her mother had purchased. Now they would have eggs to eat along with their beans and rice and yams! Her mother had also bought or traded for some more cloth, seeds to plant, and a large metal pot.

Imatu sighed contentedly, careful not to disturb little Annie who lay on her lap, lulled to sleep by the *swish, swish* of the canoe paddles. She had so much to tell Okin and Janie! Of course, they had seen it all before, but now she could share it with them.

The trip upriver took longer than the trip down, and it was the middle of the night before the two canoes nosed up on the little landing beach in Okoyong. It wasn't easy unloading the canoes in the dark, but the job was almost finished when Ma Slessor spoke. "What is that? I hear something."

Everyone stopped and listened. Then they saw it—a light bobbing toward them down the path from Ekenge. And then they heard a voice calling: "Ma! Ma Slessor! Oh, Ma, come quickly!"

Within moments, a small figure carrying a torch ran out of the forest and down the riverbank.

"Okin!" cried Ma Slessor. "What is it? What is the matter?"

Okin's eyes were wide with fright. "There's been an accident! It's . . it's Etim! A log fell on him and he can't move!"

———

Ma Slessor sank onto the mud "bench" in the mission house and wearily closed her eyes. She had been up the rest of the night with Etim and had only come back to the house to get some fever medicine from her supplies.

"Here, my friend, you must eat something," said Inyam, handing Ma Slessor a cup of goat's milk and some corn mush that she had prepared for all the children. While Chief Edem and Ma had kept the long night vigil with the paralyzed Etim, Inyam and Imatu had put the babies to sleep in the mission house and comforted the other children, who were frightened by all the confusion.

"Etim is supposed to marry a girl from Ifako next month, you know," Okin had tried to explain. "He was chopping down a tree to build his new hut when something happened . . . the log slipped and hit Etim on the back of the neck. When the men pulled it off, Etim couldn't move. They carried him back to the village . . . and . . . and I was sent to tell the chief and Ma as soon as the canoes got back."

Imatu was upset by the news. She didn't like Etim very much, but she had never wanted anything so terrible to happen to him. But other feelings competed with concern for her cousin. She felt resentful that her excitement about the trip to Creek Town and meeting King Eyo and trading their baskets for many new things seemed unimportant now. And underneath all the other feelings was a vague, unsettling fear. . . .

"Thank you, Inyam," sighed Ma Slessor, handing back the empty bowl and cup. "I'm sorry our trip has ended this way. But . . . I think you should go back to your own village right away. Etim is very bad, and if he dies there's going to be trouble. The chief believes no violent death happens except by witchcraft. I don't know what will happen—but I think it'd be best if you weren't here."

Inyam seemed relieved to have permission to leave and quickly began packing her things.

"But," Ma continued, "I have a favor to ask. Could Imatu stay with me for a few days? I must stay close to Etim . . . and Imatu could be a big help with the babies. That is," she turned to Imatu, her eyes pleading, "if you would be willing, Imatu."

Imatu looked uneasily at her mother. She felt pleased that Ma Slessor wanted her help . . . and taking care of Annie and Susie was a lot more fun than chopping weeds on their farm plot. But she felt afraid—afraid to stay in Ekenge near an angry Chief Edem, afraid to be away from her mother.

Inyam was silent for several moments. Then she nodded. "You have done much for us, Ma Slessor. We will do this for you." She picked up the cage of chickens in one hand, slung the bundle of her other goods from Creek Town over her back, and with a brief wave, disappeared quickly into the forest.

———

Imatu knew there was going to be trouble when the witch doctor arrived.

Two weeks had passed, and Etim hung between life and death. Most of the time he was unconscious or delirious. The red-haired missionary stayed by the injured boy's side almost constantly day and night. Daily she tried to feed him a nutritious broth, but most of it ran out of Etim's mouth.

And then the witch doctor arrived. That night the drums began beating. The villagers built a huge fire in the village clearing and began to drink a great deal of gin.

Exhausted, Ma Slessor was persuaded by Ma Eme to get a few hours sleep. But listening to the drums, Ma was anxious. "Keep watch," she urged Okin and Imatu. "Wake me if anything happens."

Imatu and Okin crept to the edge of the village clearing, where they could watch the fire without being seen. The witch doctor danced slowly around the fire while the worried chief and many of the villagers watched and drank. The chanting and dancing went on for hours, it seemed. And then suddenly the witch doctor shouted some words that Imatu didn't understand.

A few minutes later, four men appeared carrying something between them. Imatu almost cried out. It was Etim! The men laid the young man down on the ground near the fire. The witch doctor and several of the older men began shouting in

Etim's ear, trying to wake up his spirit. They sucked on pipes and blew smoke up his nose. Then they dipped their fingers into a bowl and rubbed something into his eyes.

"Get Ma—quick!" Imatu whispered fiercely into Okin's ear. With her heart beating wildly, she continued to watch from the shadows. Suddenly Etim's body began to convulse violently. And then—just as suddenly—the convulsions stopped.

The drumming and the dancing and the shouting stopped. There was dead silence.

Then a bloodcurdling scream pierced the night air. "He is dead!" shrieked Chief Edem. "My son is dead! Sorcerers have killed him, and they must die!"

At his words, all the village men and women who had been watching disappeared. No one's life was safe when a witch-hunt was declared. In the middle of the clearing, Etim's mother—the chief's head wife—threw her body on top of her son, wailing with grief.

A cool hand touched Imatu's shoulder, and the girl nearly screamed with fright. She looked up into the worried face of Ma Slessor, who put a finger to her lips.

Meanwhile the witch doctor was shaking a leather bag. With a flourish he shook out several small stones and studied the way they fell on the ground. He raised his arms high, casting a long, dancing shadow in the firelight. "The stones do not lie!" cried the witch doctor. "Someone in a nearby village has cursed the chief's family, and now his son is dead."

Hearing his declaration, a few of the villagers crept back into the circle. One of the men said, "Chief Akpo was angry when Ma Slessor told us to leave our weapons behind when we went to Creek Town. He left and did not return."

Heads nodded and voices murmured angrily. Then someone else spoke up. "Akpo! That is where the chief's sister-in-law lives since he sent her away!"

Imatu began to tremble. She heard voices shouting her mother's name. "Inyam! Yes! Yes! Inyam returned to trade with us at Creek Town . . . and then the accident happened!"

"Akpo! That is the village responsible for our trouble!"

Imatu felt Ma Slessor's arms go around her, and then she breathed urgently into Imatu's ear, "You must run, Imatu—run to Akpo and warn your mother. Warn the whole village!"

Imatu's heart seemed to leap into her throat. "But it is night! The dark . . . the wild animals . . . it is five miles—"

"Go *now*! Your mother's life depends on it!"

Stifling a frightened cry, Imatu ran toward the yawning mouth of the forest.

CHAPTER 8

THE REGAL CORPSE

Driven by terror, Imatu's feet flew over the path toward Akpo. She could hardly see where she was going, but she stumbled blindly along, pushing aside vines and bushes that seemed to slap her face and tear at her clothes.

After the first headlong rush into the forest, Imatu knew she couldn't run all five miles. She slowed to a walk, trot . . . walk, trot. *Don't think about Chief Edem's threat, she told herself. Don't think about the dark forest. Just keep walking fast.*

Somewhere in the forest a panther screamed. Raw fear threatened to freeze Imatu in her tracks, but she forced herself to go on. She mustn't think about wild animals . . . she mustn't think . . . she mustn't think. . . .

Imatu jumped at a strange, small sound—almost like a baby's weak cry. Maybe it was the panther's cub, whimpering for its mother. If so, she must keep going . . . walk, trot . . . walk, trot . . . mile after mile. . . .

Just when she thought she must have taken a wrong turn,

the path spilled out of the forest into a large clearing. A damp smoke from a dozen smoldering fires hung over the sleeping village of Akpo. And there was her mother's hut, sitting by itself on the edge of the village, and the goat, penned in its little yard.

"Wake up! Wake up!" shouted Imatu, running through the village. "Warriors are coming! You must run . . . run! Into the forest! Wake up! Run, run!"

Villagers stumbled out of their huts. "What warriors?" they demanded. "What has happened?"

"Chief Edem's son . . . is dead," Imatu gasped. "They think Akpo . . . is guilty of putting a curse on him!"

"Look! Look!" someone yelled. "They're coming now!" All eyes turned toward the forest, where the darkness now glittered with the bobbing light of approaching torches.

There was immediate confusion. Fathers and mothers grabbed sleeping children and ran into the forest. Goats bleated and chickens squawked. People were running . . . stumbling . . . grabbing weapons and clothes and food—whatever they could carry.

Imatu ran to her mother's hut. It was empty.

The young girl panicked. Where was her mother? But she couldn't wait to hunt for her—the bobbing torches were almost to the village. Maybe her mother already got away. Without looking back, Imatu ran into the forest.

Behind her she heard the Ekenge warriors give a shrill war cry, followed by the shouts and shrieks and cries of the villagers.

A few minutes later, a brilliance lit up the forest. Imatu stopped running, circled back cautiously, and peered through the leafy bushes into the clearing.

Akpo was burning.

The Ekenge warriors were setting all the huts on fire. She could see people still running and screaming, being chased by warriors. Some were caught and herded together in a group away from the village.

Imatu's heart beat loudly in her ears. Where was her mother? Did she get away?

On the edge of the village, Imatu could see her mother's hut—the hut Inyam had worked so hard to build—burning brightly along with the others.

Imatu slumped to the ground, hidden by the bushes and the night. She suddenly felt very alone and scared.

———

Imatu woke with a start. Her body felt stiff and cramped. Daylight had come, but the only noise was the squawking parrots and chattering sunbirds in the treetops overhead.

The village of Akpo lay silent . . . or what used to be the village. All that remained were charred bamboo fences and smoldering lumps of palm branches that had caved into the mud huts.

Then Imatu heard another noise . . . a familiar bleat. Blinking her eyes against the sunlight, she watched as a goat wandered out of the forest, looking confused and unhappy. It stumbled around the edge of the smoking village, bleating now and then as if to say, "Is anybody here?"

Imatu waited. Five minutes . . . ten minutes. But she saw no one else. Cautiously, she crept out from under the bush and stepped into the clearing.

Was it her mother's goat? Imatu wasn't sure. But because she didn't know what else to do, she braided a vine, tied it around the goat's neck, and started back down the path . . . back to Ekenge.

Imatu led the goat the five miles to Ekenge in a kind of daze. Her mad run through the night . . . had it done any good? Had she warned the people in time? Some people had been caught . . . but what about her mother? Had she gotten away? The need to know kept Imatu's feet plodding ahead, one after the other, even though she was afraid of what she might find when she got back to Ekenge.

Even before she reached the village, Imatu could hear the death drums and a great commotion—wailing and loud shouts. Avoiding the main path, she stayed sheltered in the forest until she circled around to Ma Slessor's mission house. Tying the goat at the forest's edge, Imatu ran for the missionary's door.

"Imatu!" cried Janie, flinging herself into the bigger girl's arms.

Imatu looked around the hut quickly. Udo and Janie were there, watching Okot, Annie, and Susie. "Where is Ma?" she asked. "Where is Okin?"

Janie pointed to the main clearing of the village. With her heart racing, Imatu left Ma's house and walked slowly toward the drums and wailing. The villagers were milling around, muttering to one another, gesturing with their hands, watching. But no one seemed to notice or care as Imatu crept closer.

Then she saw Okin standing with others around the edge of the main clearing. She touched his arm. A wide smile lit up his face. "You are safe!" he whispered. "We were so worried when . . . when . . ." the boy jerked his head toward the center of the clearing, " . . . when the warriors brought back prisoners from Akpo."

Imatu craned her neck to see. In the center of the clearing a group of prisoners—maybe a dozen—were chained to several posts. She could see one of Chief Akpo's wives . . . several slave men and women, some holding infants or children . . . a couple of free men and . . . and Inyam, her mother.

Hot tears blurred Imatu's eyes. Her shoulders shook as she cried silently. She had been too late. Her mother had been captured. And now . . . maybe she would die.

Okin awkwardly patted her arm. "Don't give up," he said kindly. "Pray . . . pray to Jesus. Ma has been praying all night. She says God gives her strength to fight the evil ways. Look." He pointed to the prisoners.

Imatu wiped her eyes with her hands. Blinking rapidly to hold back the tears, she saw the red-haired missionary in a familiar stance: hands on hips, feet apart, facing Chief Edem and the witch doctor.

"You must let these prisoners go, Chief Edem," she was saying. "Killing them will not bring back your son."

"But the son of a chief must be accompanied to the spirit world," said the chief stubbornly.

"You are full of sadness . . . you have lost your son and heir," Ma said, her voice full of sympathy. "But killing these men and women will not make you glad. It will only bring more sadness and grief to the families of Akpo."

"A chief's son must be buried with honor!" interrupted the witch doctor.

"Yes . . . yes, you are right. We must honor him," Mary Slessor agreed, "but not by killing." She stood her ground thoughtfully for a few minutes, then suddenly went running back to the mission house, taking several village men with her. They returned a short while later carrying one of Mary's armchairs, a large umbrella, and an armload of fine cloth and a suit of clothes.

"I was making these clothes for *you*, noble Chief Edem," Ma Slessor explained. "But now we will use them to honor

71

your son." The chief stared after her, perplexed and curious, as she disappeared into the women's yard where the dead boy's mother was moaning over her son.

An hour later, the gate to the yard was swung open, and the villagers were invited to look into one of the huts. Mouths dropped open and eyes popped at the amazing sight before them. The corpse was sitting regally in the armchair, dressed in a brightly colored shirt, an ornamented vest, and loose trousers, over which went a flowing robe, similar to the ones Chief Edem had admired on the Calabar chiefs in King Eyo Honesty's court. The dead boy's hair had been shaved into intricate patterns, painted yellow, then covered with a silk turban. On top of the turban sat a tall black and red hat with plumes of brightly colored feathers.

A whip and a silver-headed stick had been tied to the young man's hands—symbols of his position as heir to the chief. Beside him stood a small table on which had been placed the treasures of the chief's house: jewelry, a comb made from bone, decorated dishes, a skull taken in war, several candles. As a crowning touch, an enormous English umbrella was propped open behind the dead boy's head.

The villagers were delighted at the spectacle and immediately began to chant and dance about. To Ma Slessor's dismay, casks of gin were rolled out, and a long afternoon of drinking added to the merriment and mayhem. But she kept quiet. "Strong drink is a fight for another day," Ma muttered to Okin and Imatu. "Today we fight for the lives of the prisoners."

As the celebration moved into the evening with no sign of letting up, Imatu finally worked up the courage to walk past the guards and creep close to her mother, who sat unmoving among the other prisoners. "Mem?" she whispered. "See? I have water for you."

Inyam looked up dully, took the gourd and drank, then let her head and shoulders sag once more, staring at the ground. Imatu sat silently with her mother as the long evening dragged on, her eyes getting heavier and heavier. . . .

"Wake up, Imatu!" said Ma Slessor, shaking the girl gently. Imatu sat up with a start. She had fallen asleep, her head on her mother's lap.

The village was quiet once more, and most of the villagers had fallen into a drunken sleep in their huts. But as Imatu scrambled to her feet, she realized the guards were unlocking some of the chains and prodding the prisoners to get up.

Her heart lurched with hope. Were they being released? But Ma Slessor shook her head. "The prisoners are being moved into the women's yard where it is more secure," she said. "But nothing will happen tonight. You must go back to the mission house and help Okin take care of the little ones . . . and get some sleep yourself."

"Are you coming, Ma?" Imatu said, watching as a guard pulled Inyam to her feet and prodded her into the women's yard along with the others.

Mary Slessor shook her head. "No . . . I will stay with your mother and the other prisoners. Someone needs to keep watch."

CHAPTER 9

BABY IN THE BUSH

Imatu was wakened the next morning by the frantic bleatings of the goat. Uh-oh. She had forgotten the goat, left tied at the edge of the forest and unmilked the night before. Quickly she brought the goat close to the mission house and milked its swollen bag. The other children were beginning to awaken, so she and Okin prepared a breakfast of cold rice and goat's milk, sweetened with sugarcane.

As soon as she could get away, Imatu hurried back to the women's yard. She found Ma Eme trying to persuade Ma Slessor to go back to her house and get some sleep.

"Ah, here is Imatu," said Ma Slessor gratefully. "Yes, if Imatu will keep watch, I will sleep awhile."

"Do not worry," grunted Ma Eme in her crusty way. "I will send the girl to get you if anything happens."

Imatu wasn't sure she could trust Ma Eme. Ma Slessor counted her as a friend, but Ma Eme *was* the sister of Chief

Edem and Etim's natural aunt. Whose side was she on, anyway? The girl decided to keep her own eyes and ears open.

Imatu tried to avoid looking through the hut door at the body of Etim, sitting stiffly in the chair, dressed in the fancy clothes. The situation was so weird: a group of moaning prisoners, chained together on one side of the yard, while a dead body in fancy dress sat in the hut on the other. And all around, the women who lived in the yard went about their morning chores: making their fires, grinding cornmeal, feeding their children.

Imatu shivered. What was it like to be dead? Ma Slessor said that when a Christian dies, that person's spirit goes to a happy place called heaven to live with Jesus for ever and ever. But the Okoyong people were afraid of the spirit world. Funerals were frantic rites designed to pacify the angry spirits . . . so unlike the peaceful little funeral for baby Susie's unfortunate twin.

Imatu's thoughts were interrupted as one of the prisoner's mumbled, "Water . . . please, water." She jumped up and ran to one of the village water jars that caught the rain. Back and forth she went several times, bringing gourds full of water for the thirsty prisoners.

But on one of her trips to the water jar, Imatu stopped short. There on a grinding stone sat a handful of black beans. Imatu looked closer and her mouth went dry. Those were not ordinary beans. They were the dreaded *eséré* beans.

Poison beans.

Dropping the gourd of water, Imatu ran to the mission house and burst in the door. "The poison beans . . . I saw the poison beans!" she cried, shaking the sleeping missionary.

Immediately Ma Slessor got up and followed Imatu back to the women's yard. Taking one look at the grinding stone, Ma scooped up the beans and marched to the chief's house.

"You were very pleased with the way we honored your son last night, Chief Edem," she said, eyes blazing. "Why are you planning to still give the trial by poison to the prisoners?"

"Ma . . . Ma," soothed the chief. "Do not be worried. As you know, only the prisoners who are guilty will die from the poison . . . the rest will go free!"

"Nonsense," said Ma Slessor, her voice shaking. "Poison is poison—it can kill innocent people. Would you be willing to drink the poison bean, Chief?"

The chief's eyes narrowed. "Do not insult me, Ma. We are talking about the murder of my *son*. I would not murder my own son."

"It was not murder . . . it was an accident," Ma Slessor insisted. "But if you force the prisoners to take the poison bean ordeal, then you *will* be guilty of murdering innocent people. And," the red-haired woman tilted up her chin defiantly, "you will have to give it to me first."

With that, Ma Slessor turned on her heel and walked away. Sitting down in the gate to the women's yard, she only let the women and children in and out—no one else.

Chief Edem's head wife, Etim's mother, was furious. "If we give the trial by poison," she screeched at Ma Slessor, "it will all be over and we can bury my son. But if you stand in the way, the body will soon stink! His spirit will wander alone in the spirit world! And," she said, shaking her finger in Ma's face, "who will feed all these prisoners? Soon they will die of starvation, eh?"

Ma did not answer. But when the angry woman stalked away, Ma called to Imatu, who was sitting with her mother. "Etim's mother is right about the prisoners," she said quietly. "We must feed them or they will die of hunger. But where are we to get food for so many?"

"Maybe . . . maybe there is food at Akpo," Imatu said. "My mother harvested beans from her garden . . . and yams could still be dug out of the ground."

Ma Slessor's face lit up. "A great idea, Imatu! But you will have to go alone. I need Okin to take care of the children so I can stay with the prisoners . . . and none of the villagers will help you. I hate to ask you to make the trip once more . . . but will you go? Maybe you could take Udo with you. He is big enough to help carry some food."

Imatu nodded. Of course she would go. Wasn't her mother a prisoner? Didn't Inyam sit there as if her life was already gone? Imatu was glad to do something . . . anything except sit and wait, sit and wait.

Within a half hour Imatu and Udo were walking swiftly along the path to Akpo, each carrying long strips of cloth for carrying back whatever food they could find. At least it was daytime and the forest held fewer fears and threats, Imatu thought.

They walked without speaking. But when they had gone about two miles down the path, Udo called out, "Hush! What was that?"

Imatu kept walking. She did not hear anything.

"Wait!" Udo called again. "I hear a baby crying!"

A baby? Imatu stopped and listened. Again she did not hear anything.

"You are imagining things," she snapped at Udo. "We must keep walking. This is not a game we are playing." Besides, she wanted to get out of there. She did not like it when the forest made strange sounds.

They walked the remaining three miles to Akpo, keeping up a quick pace. As they came out of the forest into the clearing, Imatu thought she saw someone—or something—run into the forest on the other side of the burned-out village. She stopped so suddenly that Udo bumped into her.

"Shh," she hissed. They stood still in the shadows at the edge of the forest, scanning all sides of the clearing. Nothing moved.

Finally Imatu ventured out into the clearing with Udo close on her heels. Still nothing moved. She went first to her mother's hut and stepped into the charred remains. A big lump formed in her throat. Everything her mother had worked so hard for . . . gone.

The girl shook her head as if to get rid of the sad thoughts. She must find food . . . that was all she must think about.

The mud walls of the hut were still standing, open to the sky and breezes above. The palm-thatch roof lay in ashes inside. With a stick she poked among the charred baskets, blankets, and three-legged stools. Then suddenly the stick hit something that made a metallic *ping*. She peered closer. It was the metal pot her mother had brought back from the Creek Town market! Imatu snatched off the lid. It was full of beans.

Three hours later, Imatu and Udo were trudging along the path back to Ekenge. Between them they were carrying a bag of rice found in one of the partly burned huts, Inyam's beans, and dozens of yams dug out of the ground, wrapped in the long cloths they had brought with them and tied on their backs.

When they reached the halfway point, Imatu stopped to rest. The food was heavy and both children were breathing hard. But when they started walking again, Imatu noticed that Udo seemed to be listening for something. She walked faster, forcing him to trot to keep up.

"Wait, Imatu!" the boy called out. "There it is again. Don't you hear it? A baby is crying!"

Imatu listened. Yes, now she heard a noise . . . a faint

whimpering, somewhere out in the bush. But it could be any-thing . . . a panther cub, mewling for its mother . . . a parrot mimicking another animal's cry.

"It's nothing," Imatu said impatiently. "Ma expects us back right away—we mustn't stop for anything. It's already getting dark."

"But—" Udo protested. But Imatu was already out of sight down the path.

The late summer light was fading when Imatu and Udo finally unwrapped their bundles in the mission house yard. Okin had milked the goat and baked some yams in the fire. Imatu drank and ate greedily. Then she stopped. The prisoners must be hungry, too. How could she eat when her mother had had nothing to eat for two days?

Working quickly, Imatu, Okin, and Udo soaked some of the beans to cook the next day, made a pot of rice flavored with peppers and onions and other vegetables, and carried it carefully to the women's yard, where the prisoners were still chained.

Some of the village women looked on, neither hostile nor friendly, as Ma Slessor and the children fed the prisoners. The villagers were simply curious how this strange situation was going to turn out.

Inyam ate hungrily. When the food was gone, she looked at Imatu with sad eyes. "You are a good daughter," she whis-pered.

Ma Slessor was also pleased. "I knew you could do it," she said proudly, giving both Imatu and Udo a hug. "But I'm glad you got back before dark. I was beginning to get worried."

Udo sighed. "I guess Imatu was right. I heard a baby crying in the bush, but Imatu said we mustn't—"

"What?" hissed Ma Slessor, grabbing both Udo and Imatu

and jerking them away from the others. "A baby? What are you talking about? Shh—don't let anyone hear . . . but tell me—*now*."

"B-but it was probably nothing," Imatu stammered, trying to whisper. "Just an animal or . . . or something. I thought I heard the same sound when I ran to Akpo to warn the village . . . but it was nothing."

"But it sounded like a baby," insisted Udo.

"Don't be silly, Udo," said Imatu crossly. "A baby couldn't live that long in the bush."

Ma Slessor ignored her. "Where?" she demanded in a fierce whisper.

Udo tried to explain where he had heard the sound along the trail.

Ma Slessor paced back and forth in the women's yard. Then she sent Udo back to the mission house and took Imatu and Okin outside the women's yard.

"You must both stay here with the prisoners. Don't leave, even for a minute, and don't tell anyone that I am gone. They will think that I have simply gone back to the mission house to sleep. In fact, I will probably be back before anyone even misses me."

"B-but where are you going?" Imatu said.

"Where? To find that baby, of course!" said Ma Slessor. And the next moment she disappeared into the thick darkness.

CHAPTER 10

TRIAL BY POISON

Imatu looked around fearfully. What would happen if Chief Edem or the witch doctor discovered that Ma Slessor was gone? Most of the prisoners, their stomachs full of rice, had fallen asleep in their chains. But Imatu couldn't sleep. Her whole body was tense.

Outside the women's yard in the central clearing of the village, the witch doctor was building a bonfire. Many of the villagers, both men and women, began gathering around. Chief Edem opened some casks of gin, and the people began drinking and dancing slowly around the fire.

The fire leaped up taller than a man. The flickering light and weaving figures cast strange shadows. Inside the women's yard, Okin and Imatu looked at each other anxiously. The shadows looked like spirits, Imatu thought, darting through the fence and out again . . . in and out.

Someone looked in the gate of the women's yard, then disappeared. Man or woman . . . Imatu couldn't tell. But shortly after that, the commotion around the fire seemed to get louder.

Why was Ma taking so long? Imatu thought angrily. She should be here, protecting the prisoners, not out searching the darkness for some . . . some abandoned, half-dead baby. If it even was a baby. Maybe the "crying" in the forest was just a sick animal. What if something happened to Imatu's mother because Ma Slessor was out hunting for . . . nothing at all?

Okin interrupted her angry thoughts with a poke on the arm. Imatu looked up . . . into the face of the witch doctor. His eyes darted this way and that. "Where is the white woman?" he demanded.

Imatu's tongue seemed to stick in her mouth. But Okin piped up, "She went to get something and will be back any minute."

The witch doctor grunted, then disappeared as abruptly as he had come. But now Imatu was really frightened. *Please, please, Jesus God*, she found herself praying, *bring Ma Slessor back quickly*. The minutes seemed to drag by, as if time had slowed to the crawl of an insect.

Suddenly several warriors with torches burst into the women's yard, pushed Imatu and Okin aside, and began to unlock the long chain fastening the prisoners together. With their torches they peered into the faces of the now-terrified prisoners until they came to Imatu's mother. Then they pulled Inyam to her feet and pushed her out of the yard toward the fire.

"No, no!" screamed Imatu. "Don't take my mother!" She ran after the warriors but was stopped by the large bulk of Ma Eme, who stepped in her way.

"Hush, girl," said Ma Eme bluntly, holding Imatu by both

arms. "You will only make things worse for your mother. You can't do anything to help her now."

Imatu squirmed in Ma Eme's grasp until she could see what was happening around the bonfire. A warrior had forced Inyam to kneel in front of the witch doctor, who was holding a bowl of liquid out in front of him. The drunken shouts and mutterings of the crowd suddenly quieted.

"The murder of young Etim must be avenged!" cried the witch doctor. "His spirit cannot rest until the person who put a curse on him is found. The trial by poison will discover who is guilty . . . and who must die!"

"No-o-o!" screamed Imatu, struggling in Ma Eme's arms. She saw the bowl being held to her mother's lips . . . the fire and the witch doctor and the gawking crowd seemed to spin around and Imatu thought she was going to faint . . . when a loud shout broke the uneasy silence.

"STOP!"

A slight woman's figure in long skirts and bare feet strode quickly through the crowd and knocked the bowl out of the startled witch doctor's hands. Then Ma Slessor immediately whirled toward the crowd of villagers and held out a small bundle she was carrying, wrapped in what looked like Ma's petticoat.

"Look! Look what I have found . . . a baby which has survived several days and nights lying alone in the bush. A miracle baby! Only God the heavenly Father could have kept the leopard and the snakes away and protected this child. See? . . . See?" Ma Slessor walked around the crowd, holding out the tiny child for the villagers to see. The women especially craned their necks and made clicking noises of amazement.

Inyam and the trial by poison had been momentarily forgotten.

Chief Edem, however, quickly tried to regain control of the situation. "Ma . . . Ma Slessor," he said angrily. "You must not keep interfering. We cannot delay—"

"Interfering?" Ma Slessor looked shocked. "I am trying to keep you from doing something you will deeply regret. See this baby?" And she held out the infant toward the chief. "It is a sign! *A sign of life!* God has protected this baby, alone and helpless in the forest, to show us that human life is precious. Saving life—not taking it—is what God wants us to do."

Some of the villagers nodded their heads and murmured to each other. But the witch doctor pointed an accusing finger at the baby Ma Slessor held in her arms. "Why was the child left in the forest?" he sneered. "It must be a monster child . . . a twin . . . fathered by an evil spirit. If you allow it to live, this village will be cursed!"

To Imatu's surprise, Ma Slessor burst out laughing. "The people of this village know better than that," she said, scoffing. "We already have two twin children living among us—baby Susie, the slave woman's child, and my own sweet Janie—and no one who takes care of them has been harmed in any way. The twin taboo is a big lie."

The villagers immediately began arguing and gesturing among themselves, some siding with the witch doctor and others agreeing with Ma Slessor, who continued to show off the tiny infant to each curious person. In the hubbub, Ma Eme let go of Imatu and nodded toward Inyam. Immediately Imatu was beside her mother, helping her stand.

Chief Edem gave a sigh of resignation. "Take the prisoner back to the women's yard," he told one of the warriors. "We will *palaver* tomorrow."

———

Imatu watched as Janie and Okin and Udo and Okot fussed over the new baby—a girl. Even little Annie toddled about clapping her hands and saying, "Baby!" She was a tiny thing, with a pinched face and scrawny body from days without food. Ants and insects had bitten her nose and mouth and ears. But everyone shook their heads in amazement and agreed: It was a miracle that the baby was still alive.

Imatu felt confused by all the mixed-up feelings she had inside. She was grateful that Ma Slessor had saved her mother's life from the trial by poison . . . but she was angry that Ma had left the prisoners alone in the first place. What if she had arrived one minute later? It was too close . . . much too close.

And Imatu was glad Ma said that the baby she found in the bush was a sign of life . . . but going to find the baby had almost cost Inyam *her* life.

Imatu also felt guilty that she had ignored the baby's cries when she and Udo heard it on the path. And even though Ma Slessor had not said so, Imatu wondered if the red-haired missionary was mad at her.

Still, she resented all the attention the baby was getting. Didn't everyone realize that Inyam was still in chains, her body and clothes dirty and smelly from three days without being able to wash?

When the morning rain had stopped, Ma Slessor marched over to the village clearing with the new baby, followed by Janie and Okin carrying Susie and Annie, with Okot, Udo, and Imatu bringing up the rear.

"Chief Edem!" she announced pleasantly. "I am ready to *palaver*."

The witch doctor was noticeably absent. He had been deeply offended the night before and had gone away, taking his charms with him. No one seemed too upset. Most of the villagers considered it an honor to have Ma Slessor living among them, and if it was a choice between her and the witch doctor . . . well.

The chief sat on his leather and bamboo stool and rubbed his chin. "The headmen and I have been talking, Ma," he said thoughtfully. "We'll agree to release the prisoners if that will make you happy—"

"Yes, that would make me very happy, Chief Edem," said Ma Slessor with a big smile.

The chief held up his hand. "I am not finished. All the prisoners . . . except for two: the wife of Chief Akpo and my kinswoman, Inyam."

For a moment hope had flickered in Imatu's heart, but it died again.

"But why?" cried Ma Slessor. "Why not release them all?"

"I am trying to be patient, Ma!" said the chief gruffly. "I have listened to you! We will release ten prisoners—isn't that enough?"

Ma started to protest, but the chief held up his hand to silence her. "I will tell you why. Chief Akpo—he ran away, did he not? Doesn't that suggest that he is guilty of putting a curse on my son? Wasn't he angry that you wouldn't let him take weapons to Creek Town? He probably wanted revenge."

"Then why punish his wife?" argued Ma Slessor. "She is innocent . . . let her go."

The chief was silent. Ma Slessor always outtalked him, ruining his good arguments. Finally he said, "All right, I will make a deal. I will let the woman go, but only on one condition: If Chief Akpo is captured, he must face trial to see whether he is innocent or guilty of cursing my son."

"Agreed!" said Ma Slessor happily. Imatu knew that the chief was probably thinking of trial by poison . . . but Ma was thinking of the "talking" kind of trial, where witnesses presented evidence and a judge—usually Ma—decided the verdict.

"What about Inyam?" Ma Slessor pressed.

The chief stuck out his chin stubbornly. "Enough! Be content that only one prisoner stays. Now go away. My heart is grieving for my son." And the chief picked up his stool and went into his hut.

Before the chief could change his mind, Ma Slessor motioned for the guards to unlock the prisoners' chains. "Go quickly," she said to the men and women, who stood up shakily, rubbing their sore wrists and ankles. "Go to the mission house. We will give you each some food to take with you. Now go . . . go."

Only Inyam remained chained to the post in the women's yard.

It was too much for Imatu. She fell on the ground, beating her fists in the dirt and weeping. Inyam just looked away.

Okin knelt down beside his friend. "Don't cry, Imatu," he said anxiously. "Don't cry. There is still hope. See how many prayers Jesus has answered? He can answer one more. . . . Please don't cry."

———

Imatu stayed beside her despondent mother the rest of the day, leaving only to get her water or food. Everyone left them alone . . . even the guards left.

That evening, the chief, his head wife, and several of the headmen of the village came to sit with the body of the dead boy, still dressed in his fancy clothes, sitting under the large umbrella.

Finally the chief stood up. "We cannot wait any longer,"

he said. "We must bury the boy tomorrow. *All* will be done tomorrow."

And he walked out of the yard with the others following behind him, without giving Inyam a glance.

"That is a good sign," said Ma Slessor. "Nothing will happen tonight. He made no threats. . . . Whatever is going to happen won't happen until tomorrow. I think we should all get a good sleep."

But Imatu refused to leave her mother. Together they curled up on the ground as the night sank into an inky darkness, the moon and stars hidden by the ever-present clouds of the rainy season.

Sometime in the middle of the night, Imatu thought she heard something. Without moving her position, she opened her eyes but could see nothing. By her mother's deep breathing, she knew Inyam was still asleep.

There—she heard it again . . . as if someone was stealthily moving in the women's yard. Imatu's heart started beating faster, but she was too frightened to move.

Out of the corner of her eye Imatu saw a large, dark shape bend slowly over her mother. She heard a small metal click . . . then another. And then the shape was gone.

CHAPTER 11

NO MORE VENGEANCE

Imatu held her breath. There was no more movement in the yard. Slowly, carefully, she sat up, peering into the darkness. Who was it? What had he—or she—been doing?

Standing up, she crept quietly to where the shape had stood beside her mother, and she bent down as she had seen the shape bend down. Reaching out her hands she felt the iron chains that bound her mother's wrists and ankles.

They were unlocked. Imatu wanted to shout! . . . but she swallowed the urge and gently shook her mother's arm. Inyam started, but Imatu pressed her hand against her mother's mouth and hissed, "Shh." With deft fingers, she wiggled the unlocked chains off her mother's wrists and ankles and helped her stand. Then, clinging to each other, trembling with the desire to run, mother and daughter stealthily opened the gate to the women's yard.

Five minutes later, Imatu knocked softly on the door of

the mission house. "Ma! Ma!" she called in a low voice. "Let us in . . . quickly!"

They heard noises rustling inside, and then the door opened. "Praise to the Lord in heaven!" exclaimed Ma Slessor, clad only in her nightdress, as she pulled them inside.

When the door closed behind her, Inyam sank to the mud floor and began shaking and crying with relief. Even Imatu's knees felt wobbly.

"What . . . how . . . ?" Ma said in amazement, looking from one to the other.

Imatu told about the dark shape coming into the yard, then finding the chains had been unlocked. A slow smile spread over Ma Slessor's face. "I think Ma Eme may have been our angel tonight," she said. "But we must never mention our suspicions to anyone else."

———

Dawn was just beginning to lighten the sky when Imatu heard a shout outside the mission house.

"Ma Slessor! Where is the prisoner!"

It was Chief Edem's voice.

Ma Slessor quickly pulled on her skirt and a shawl, and stepped outside.

"The woman Inyam is in my house, Chief," Imatu heard her say pleasantly. "But as you yourself have declared, my house is a house of refuge, and she is safe here."

Imatu heard other voices and murmurings that she couldn't make out. Then the chief said, "It is time to bury my son. Will you and your household join the procession?"

"Of course," Ma Slessor agreed. "Give us a little time to get ready."

Ma Slessor quickly woke the older children, fed them some

fruit and cold corn bread, then washed and dressed them in their best clothes. "Imatu, will you watch the three little ones while we are gone?" Ma asked. Imatu nodded gratefully. She knew Ma was giving her an excuse to stay with her mother and not attend the funeral.

As Ma Slessor and her brood started to leave for Etim's funeral, the new baby—who had been named Mary—began to cry in her weak little voice. Immediately Inyam picked her up from the padded box where the baby had been sleeping and began to pat and soothe her.

Ma looked pleased. "You are not afraid of the twin curse, Inyam?" she asked.

Inyam shrugged. "This child is not a twin. Three days before . . . before the warriors came to Akpo, a woman died in childbirth. Her husband did not want to care for it, so the child was thrown away in the bush."

Ma stared at Inyam, opened her mouth as if to say something, then thought better of it and hurried the children out the door. Imatu knew Ma was shocked and angry that a baby could be thrown away like that.

As Imatu fed baby Susie and played with the mischievous Annie, she felt ashamed of how angry she'd felt when Ma ran off to rescue the baby in the bush. To Ma Slessor, every human life was worth fighting for—whether it was an abandoned baby, or a slave, or . . . or a powerless widow like Inyam, or even crusty old Chief Edem.

When Ma Slessor and the children returned several hours later, Inyam had stripped off her smelly garment, washed all over with water and Ma's soap, and put on one of the dresses from the "mission box" from Scotland. Janie ran over to the shy woman, wrapped her arms around Inyam's waist, and looked up into her face. "You are *beautiful!*" she said, her eyes wide.

Everyone laughed.

Okin couldn't wait to tell all the details about the funeral. He described the villagers dressed in their finest clothes and jewelry and hats and feathers, the flute and drum music, and the long procession that wound into the forest to the burial place. "But," said Okin, his eyes dancing, "there were no prisoners to kill to send along with Etim on his journey to the spirit world . . . so they killed a cow instead and put it in his grave!" And the boy rolled on the mud floor, holding his sides as he laughed.

"Stop it now, Okin," chided Ma Slessor. "We mustn't make fun. The old customs and superstitions die hard; at least the cow was a step in the right direction by saving a human life. And Chief Edem seems resigned to the fact that Inyam has taken refuge here."

"Well, if you ask me," said Okin, folding his arms knowingly, "Chief Edem wanted Inyam to escape. That way he could say he didn't give in to all Ma's demands, but Ma would be happy and leave him alone now because Inyam is safe. Why else did he take away the guard and announce to everyone that the funeral would be 'tomorrow'?—to give someone time to help Inyam escape."

Ma Slessor chuckled. "You may be right, Okin . . . but that'll be our secret, all right?"

———

Inyam waited until Ma Slessor had sung lullabies to the little ones and kissed them good-night. Then she came and sat down beside the missionary.

"Ma . . . you have been a good friend to me," said Inyam. "Thank you for saving my life and giving me refuge in your house. But . . ." Inyam stopped and wrung her hands nervously.

"But?" said Ma Slessor gently.

"I have been inside the mission house for three weeks! I dare not go outside—I am still an escaped prisoner and could be captured again. But . . . but I can't stay cooped up here forever. I must go away . . . far away!"

Imatu looked up from the cooking pots she and Okin were scrubbing by the fireplace. She liked staying at the mission house with Ma Slessor and Okin and Janie and the other children. She didn't want to leave . . . besides, where would they go? The village of Akpo was just a pile of ashes.

Ma Slessor echoed Imatu's thoughts. "But where would you go, Inyam? Maybe I should talk to Chief Edem—"

"No! No," said Inyam, shaking her head vigorously. "I don't want to live in Ekenge, even if Chief Edem said yes—which he won't. I—I'll go find my sister and her husband . . . the people of Akpo are hiding *somewhere* in the valley."

Ma Slessor frowned. "Yes . . . but I worry about your safety in the forest alone. And what about Imatu?"

Inyam looked at her daughter, who was staring anxiously back at her.

"She is safe here with you . . . if you will let her stay," said Inyam finally. "And I know she is eager to attend Reading School again. I will leave the goat to help pay for her food. Maybe later, when I find a place to live . . ." Her voice trailed off.

"Of course she can stay. She is a big help to me," said Ma Slessor. "But let's talk about it more in the morning. We can make some plans. We'll begin asking around the area if anyone knows where the Akpo refugees are."

But the next morning, when Imatu heard the goat bleating, begging to be milked, her mother was gone.

———

The rainy season ended early in October and the dry season began. Three months . . . four months . . . five months passed, and Imatu heard nothing from her mother. A few times she and Okin walked the trail to Akpo, to see if anyone had returned. But the walls of the roofless mud huts were crumbling, and weeds and grasses crowded the abandoned garden plots.

Then one day in early March, Ma Slessor came back full of news from a visit to villages farther north. "As I was walking back along the trail," she said to Ma Eme, who had been staying at the mission house in her absence, "I passed a small group of huts hidden in the forest. I thought I heard someone call my name . . . and then suddenly a familiar face peered through the bushes. Who do you think it was?"

Imatu's eyes widened. "Not . . . my mother?"

Ma Slessor laughed. "Yes! It was Inyam! And her sister's family . . ." Then Ma's smile faded. "But she did not look like the beautiful Inyam who left here six months ago. She is thin and dirty . . . life in the forest is very hard. Chief Akpo was there, too—but he has been ill. He is afraid to come home, because Chief Edem insisted he would have to face trial."

Ma Eme lifted her bulk off the mud "couch," and started out the door.

"Where are you going?" asked Ma Slessor in surprise.

The big woman beckoned. "Come. Bring all the children. I think it is time you talked to my brother."

They made a strange procession: Ma Eme moving like a steamship through the village with Ma Slessor and all her children trotting to keep up right behind her. Chief Edem, sitting in front of his hut, smoking a clay pipe, looked up in surprise as Ma Eme and her entourage came to a stop in front of him.

"Ma Slessor! I heard you had returned from your visit north. I am glad to see you well," said the chief.

For a few minutes the missionary made small talk with the chief until Ma Eme cleared her throat impatiently.

"Chief Edem, it has been six months since you buried your son," said Mary Slessor. "Don't you think it is time to bury old grievances as well? Five miles from here a once-thriving village sits abandoned and broken. Old friends and neighbors are living like wild animals in the forest because they are afraid to come home. It is our loss as well as theirs."

Chief Edem puffed on his pipe and looked at the red-haired woman thoughtfully.

"God's Book says that anyone can love his friends—that's easy," Ma Slessor continued. "But it takes a truly great person to love his enemies."

Chief Edem continued to puff on his pipe. Finally he took it out of his mouth. "Very well, Ma. You can tell Chief Akpo that all thought of vengeance is gone from my heart, and if he wishes to return to his own village or live in your home or go anywhere among the Okoyong, he is at liberty to do so."

"And Inyam? And the other people who were chased away from Akpo?"

Chief Edem gestured with his pipe. "All can come home. I give my word, no harm will come to them."

Imatu could hardly believe her ears!

But it was a bittersweet homecoming. Ma Slessor had to go three times to the little huts hidden in the forest to persuade Chief Akpo, Inyam, and the others that it was safe to return. And when they finally did straggle into their old clearing, they were met by the ruins of their once-vigorous village.

That same day, however, the refugees were surprised to see half the village of Ekenge coming out of the forest, carrying bamboo and palm leaves to help rebuild the huts. Mats, blankets, baskets, and cooking pots were donated to help the villagers of Akpo get back on their feet. Chief Edem himself was with them, bringing bags of seeds to plant.

Imatu went back to Ekenge for one more night, to get the goat and say good-bye to Okin and Janie and all the other Slessor children.

"Why are you going away, Imatu?" asked Janie, her eyes brimming with tears. "Don't you like living with us?"

"Oh, yes," said Imatu, blinking back her own tears. "But I must go help my mother plant new crops and . . . and make more baskets to sell in Creek Town."

"We will go see Imatu often," Ma Slessor assured the children. "Maybe we will even start a Reading School in Akpo!"

"The chief of Ifako has finally started to build the church that he promised," Okin spoke up. "When it is finished, everyone from Ekenge and Akpo and Ifako will be invited to worship there."

"Yes! I will come," said Imatu, almost fiercely. "Someday I want to read God's Book for myself." Imatu wanted to see if God's Book really said to love your enemies . . . or if Ma Slessor had just made that up to get Chief Edem to change his mind.

Just then they heard Chief Edem calling Ma Slessor from the mission yard. This was unusual; the chief rarely came to the mission house. Ma went outside to greet him while the children stared from the doorway. The chief was alone in the twilight.

To their surprise, Chief Edem knelt down, his forehead touching the dirt, his hands holding Ma Slessor's feet. "Thank you . . . thank you, Ma," he said humbly. "You have done a brave and wonderful thing. You kept me from killing other people when my son died. You told me to forgive my enemies. I am weary of the old ways . . . the fear and fighting and superstitions . . . which always end in death."

Ma Slessor hardly knew what to say. "Dear friend," she said kindly, helping the chief to his feet, "it is the love of God that has the power to bring life instead of death."

That night as Imatu fell asleep for the last time in the mission house, with Janie cuddled against her, Ma's words tumbled over and over in her mind. *The love of God . . . life instead of death . . . the love of God . . . life instead of death . . .*

CHAPTER 12

MOVING FORWARD

The church school in Ifako was filled to overflowing with young and old from neighboring villages. Several years had passed since Mary Slessor had first come to live among the Okoyong people in Ekenge; this was Ma's anniversary celebration.

Imatu, now a handsome young woman, sat nervously at the front glancing over the people as they jostled each other for space to sit or stand on the hard mud floor. Ma Eme was there, sitting regally on a wooden box, fanning herself with a colorful paper fan, a treasure from the "mission box." But her brother, Chief Edem, had died of smallpox during the epidemic that had wiped out half the population of Ekenge and many people from other villages . . . including Imatu's mother, Inyam.

Sitting on the ground in the front row under the watchful eye of Janie, now a young woman herself, were Mary Slessor's family of children: Annie, Alice, Mary, Maggie, Dan, Whitie, and Asequo. Imatu felt a familiar lump in her throat when she thought of baby Susie, who had died at fifteen months after being accidentally burned by a spilled pot of boiling water. As for Udo and Okot, they had returned to their own families in Creek Town after being trained by Ma Slessor for several years.

Imatu could hardly believe Okoyong was the same place she had lived before Ma Slessor had come. So much had changed: There was no more human sacrifice . . . and very little twin murder . . . raiding and plundering of other villages had stopped . . . disputes were settled in tribal court with Ma as judge . . . and trading had improved their lives—raising their standard of living and giving people productive work to do rather than wasting time drinking and fighting. . . .

The talking and shuffling died as Mary Slessor stood up to welcome everyone. Though she was wearing her "best" dress from the mission box, Ma was still hatless and barefooted, as were her black sisters sprinkled throughout this amazing congregation—the first of its kind among the Okoyong people. Imatu realized that the red hair had deepened to a dark brown, and the missionary's skin was like weathered parchment.

"Dear brothers and sisters," Ma Slessor began in the Efik language, "I am deeply moved to be here with you today. Today is a special day . . . the happiest day since I came to live among you . . . because today we are going to baptize seven young men and women who are dedicating their lives to the one true God."

Imatu flushed and glanced nervously at the other six "young men and women" sitting on either side of her. The young men had white shirts on, and the young women wore colorful blue dresses that Ma had sewn herself.

Okin, who was sitting beside Imatu, gave her a little grin.

"Relax, Imatu," he whispered, "or I will have to pinch you, and won't *that* cause a scene!"

Imatu stifled a giggle. Her childhood friend still knew how to make her laugh.

"This is also a special day," Ma was continuing, "because our guest today is Reverend W. T. Weir, who has come from Creek Town to conduct the baptism, and to receive these new converts as the first members of the Okoyong Christian Church!"

Ma sat down, beaming, as the packed church clapped enthusiastically. A spontaneous song started, and for ten minutes the thatched roof shook with a joyful noise. But the singing and clapping died to a rustle as Reverend Weir—a serious-looking white man—took his place before them.

He got right to the point. "Will the candidates for baptism please stand?" he said in Efik.

Imatu, Okin, and the others stood up.

"Okin, will you come forward and kneel?" said the missionary.

Okin knelt in front of Reverend Weir.

"Do you confess your faith in Jesus Christ, the Son of God, as your Savior and Lord?" the man asked.

Okin nodded. "I do, gladly," he said in a strong voice.

Imatu saw that Ma Slessor was blowing her nose in a handkerchief.

"Do you confess your sins and accept the forgiveness Christ offers by His death on the cross?"

Again Okin said, "I do."

Reverend Weir lifted a pitcher of water. "Then I baptize you in the name of the Father, the Son, and the Holy Ghost." And he poured water—lots of water—over Okin's head. It ran down the young man's face and shoulders, soaking his white shirt, and his smile glistened with happiness.

Imatu was watching Okin so intently that she was startled when someone poked her and whispered, "He called your name."

Imatu's knees shook as she walked a few paces and knelt in front of the missionary from Creek Town. The man asked her the same questions he had asked Okin. She wanted so much to answer strongly and clearly from her heart, but her voice seemed to squeak in her own ears. Then she felt the water pouring over her head and shoulders . . . and suddenly Imatu felt as if she might burst from happiness. All the pain and anger and fear of the old ways seemed to wash away. And she knew it was true: The love of God had the power to bring life instead of death.

Warm tears of happiness mingled with the cold water dripping from her head as Imatu got to her feet and stood beside Okin. One by one the other five young men and women were baptized and pronounced members of the first Christian church in Okoyong.

But the celebration wasn't over yet. Because Reverend Weir was an ordained minister, Ma had asked him to serve the Lord's Supper to all the Christians in the house—including Imatu and the others who had just been baptized. Imatu took the small bit of flat bread and sip of wine, which symbolized the broken body and spilled blood of Christ. "Eat and drink this together in remembrance of Me," Reverend Weir said, repeating Jesus' words to His followers.

"Christians do this all over the world," Ma had explained to Imatu. "Besides reminding us of Jesus' sacrifice in our place, the Lord's Supper also reminds us that we belong to the family of God all over the world!"

101

As she chewed the bread and swallowed the wine, Imatu thought how wonderful it was to belong to a new family—God's family. She had felt so alone when her mother died of smallpox . . . but Ma and Okin and Janie truly seemed like her family, too. "That's because you too have become a child of the heavenly Father," Ma had smiled when Imatu told her how she felt.

After the Lord's Supper, all the people sang Psalm 103, which Ma had taught them in the Efik language—though the tune was a Scottish melody:

> *He forgives all my sins*
> *And heals all my diseases.*
> *He keeps me from the grave*
> *And blesses me with love and mercy.*

The service had been long, but even the children were quiet and still as their beloved Ma finally stood up and spoke directly to the young men and women who had just been baptized. "What has happened here today is not my doing," she said seriously. "Give God all the glory! I am only His hands and feet. In fact, the people of Okoyong now look to you more than me for proof of the power of the Gospel. Whether I am here or not, the church of Jesus Christ must carry on His work—and you are that church."

Something in her words troubled Imatu. Afterwards, as the people moved outside and set up the feast they had prepared for the occasion, Imatu looked for a chance to speak to Ma Slessor alone. But everyone wanted to shake Ma's hand and greet Reverend Weir and congratulate the newly baptized young people. Only hours later, when the people finally began to drift home to their various villages and Ma was collecting her children, did Imatu see her chance.

"I will walk home with you," she offered. Imatu fell in step with Ma as the Slessor family walked the trail to the mission house.

"Ma . . . what did you mean when you said, 'Whether I am here or not'?"

Ma did not answer for a few minutes. But finally she said, "I am feeling restless, Imatu. There are still so many villages farther inland that have never heard the Gospel . . . like the Aros people."

Imatu was shocked. "But, Ma! The Aros are cannibals!"

Ma gave a little laugh. "All the more reason they need the Gospel of peace, eh?"

"But, Ma," Imatu protested, "aren't you afraid?"

"Oh, yes," Ma Slessor admitted.

"Then you must have more courage than . . . than even the Okoyong chiefs, who never venture among the Aros if they can help it."

Ma shook her head. "Not courage . . . faith. Faith in our God. What is courage anyway, but faith conquering fear?"

The two women walked silently for a while, watching the children skipping ahead on the trail in the twilight. Then Ma said, "Imatu, when I was a lassie about your age—still in my twenties—a great missionary to Africa died. His name was David Livingstone. In many ways he was my hero . . . I wanted to be like him. I especially remember one thing he said: 'I am ready to go anywhere, provided it be forward.' "

Ma Slessor stopped and turned to Imatu. "It is time for me to move forward . . . time to leave my work here in hands like yours."

"*Me!*" gasped Imatu. "But . . . but . . ."

"Yes, you and Okin and the others. There is so much you can do! You can teach the Reading School and care for those who need refuge in the mission house and tell the Jesus stories to the little ones . . . oh, there is much you can do."

A funny feeling stirred inside Imatu. Yes . . . yes, she could do those things. Hadn't she been helping Ma for several years now?

"But I could never take your place—no one could," Imatu said quietly, looking at the ground.

"Of course not!" Ma laughed, lifting Imatu's chin with her finger. "You must take your own place . . . while I find the next place God has for me."

Ma looked down the trail. All the children except Asequo, who was snoring gently on Imatu's back, had disappeared.

"Come on," Ma said laughing. "We must catch up or they will all hide and jump out at us and scare us half to death. Cannibals are one thing . . . but mischievous children are an entirely different matter."

And grabbing Imatu by the hand, the two women ran laughing down the trail.

MORE ABOUT MARY SLESSOR

Mary Mitchell Slessor, a red-haired Scottish "lassie," was born in Aberdeen, Scotland, in 1848. She was the second of seven children, the daughter of a shoemaker. Though her childhood was marked by hardship and hunger because of her alcoholic father, Mary took a keen interest in missions early in life.

Poverty forced the family to move to Dundee when Mary was ten, and the next year she went to work in a weaving mill while still attending school. By age fourteen, she was working full time in a factory to help support the family. Converted at a young age, she was active in her local Presbyterian church, volunteering to teach Sunday school among rowdy street kids.

When Doctor David Livingstone, famous missionary and explorer in Africa (see *Escape From the Slave Traders*, the first story in this book), died in 1874, his life and work inspired many—including Mary Slessor. She applied to the Calabar Mission, which had been in Calabar, Africa (what we know today as southern Nigeria), for thirty years. When she was accepted, she made arrangements for the care of her mother and sisters, and sailed in late summer 1876 for Calabar. She was twenty-seven.

As Mary was waiting to board her ship, the *Ethiopia*, she saw many casks of gin and rum being loaded on board for sale and trade in Africa. She shook her head sadly and said, "Scores of casks and only one missionary."

Mary's first assignment was to the mission station in Duke Town along the Calabar River, under the guidance of veteran missionaries "Daddy" and "Mammy" Anderson. Her basic duties were to teach in the mission school, learn the Efik language, and simply "visit" with the Africans, establishing relationships and learning their beliefs and their ways.

But Mary was essentially a pioneer and impatient to move beyond the well-ordered work of the established mission. When she returned from her first furlough in 1880, she was reassigned and given charge of the work in Old Town, three miles upriver. Uncomfortable with the discrepancies in lifestyle between the European missionaries in Africa and the native peoples, Mary chose to live very simply, eating native food and living in a mud hut African-style—with a few personal touches, such as a real door and windows. This enabled her to send much of her salary back to Scotland in support of her family.

But Mary also realized that much of African life was rooted in pagan customs and beliefs—such as witchcraft, twin-murder, polygamy, buying and selling of slaves, and even cannibalism— that needed to be changed if the ethics of the Gospel were to take effect. One superstition she confronted head on was that the birth of twins was a curse. It was thought that an evil spirit fathered one of the children; usually both twins were murdered or left out in the jungle to die, and the mother of the twins was driven out of the village and shunned (often to die).

When Mary returned to Scotland for her second furlough in 1883, she took along a six-month-old twin she had rescued, whom she named Janie after her youngest sister. (She had failed to save Janie's twin brother.) Janie was the first of several twins who became her own "family" of adopted orphans, while she rescued and cared for many more who were then placed with sympathetic families. After twenty-two years in Calabar, Mary, by her own count, had rescued fifty-one twins from death!

Shortly after returning to Calabar in December 1885, Mary received word that first her mother, and then her last surviving sister, had died. Though she was grief stricken, she set her face even more resolutely toward the interior of Africa, which had never heard the Gospel; "There is no one now who will be anxious for me if I go," she said.

Her destination was the Okoyong people, who were related to the Bantu race of Central and South Africa. They were a tall, regal people, but addicted to witchcraft and human sacrifice, fighting and warring, thieving and plunder. Nonetheless, noting her courage to come alone, they welcomed the "white Ma" to live among them.

She settled in the village of Ekenge about four miles inland from the Calabar River, also establishing a school and "meeting-house" in Ifaku village two miles away. She believed that "school and the Gospel" went hand in hand. The people were eager to learn "book," and she insisted that all people, young and old, slave and free, could come to her school. And in every human interaction she never let an opportunity go by to share the Gospel.

With unbelievable courage, in spite of sometimes weakened health and bouts of malaria, Mary—or "Ma" as she was called by everyone—confronted the chiefs and the people in their pagan practices. She stood up for justice in their dealings with one another, and her reputation as a peacemaker soon brought chiefs and people from neighboring villages to seek her counsel and advice. The Okoyong people viewed her as their unofficial magistrate, making judgments between disagreeing parties—or even warring villages. In 1892, the British designated her as the official vice-consul for the area, a position she held for many years; and in 1894 she helped oversee an agreement between the local chiefs and the British consul, Sir Claude Macdonald, at which time the chiefs agreed to quit their "murderous practices" (such as human sacrifice at the death of a chief); in return Macdonald declared them a free people.

Mary stayed among the Okoyong people for fifteen years (minus two furloughs). Her accomplishments at the midway point were considerable. Raiding, plundering, and the stealing of slaves had stopped. People were as safe traveling, visiting, and trading among the Okoyong as in Calabar. The people did not want a king (black or white), but they did ask Ma to serve as consul in their tribal court. When she had arrived, the only trade had been guns, gin, and chains, but Mary encouraged the people to increase their agricultural efforts in palm and peanut oil, yams, cassava root, rubber, etc.—not only to raise their standard of living but to use their idle hours more productively as one way to decrease wanton drinking and fighting. Human sacrifice at funerals and to avenge sickness or accidents had ceased; twin-murder had decreased, and in general there was a new regard for human life.

After her third furlough, Mary moved her mission headquarters to Akpap, a market village farther inland. Finally in 1902, after fifteen years among the Okoyong people, the first Communion service was held and eleven young people were baptized. Seven of those eleven were her own adopted children: Annie, Alice, Mary, Maggie, Dan, Whitie, and Asequo.

But Mary was restless. There were still tribes who had never heard the Gospel of Jesus Christ! And Mary was at heart a pioneer. Others could take over the church she had established; she must push on. She was due for another furlough in 1904; instead, Mary spent her own time and her own money to search out a new mission base in order to reach the fierce Aros and Ibibios tribes along Enyong Creek, who had long been dominated by "The Long Juju," a mysterious and powerful witchcraft.

She finally settled on the village of Itu at the junction of the Cross River and Enyong Creek as a mission base. Because of its strategic position, Itu had formerly been a slave market; under Mary's supervision, a medical center was established there, which was eventually named the Mary Slessor Hospital. Several years later, in 1913, she was awarded the title Honorary Associate of the Order of St. John of Jerusalem (an order dedicated to the relief of the sick and suffering) for establishing the hospital at Itu and other humanitarian work in Calabar.

Even though her health was deteriorating, still Mary pushed on. She alternated between several villages farther north, traveling in a rickshaw-type cart pulled by young boys. Beloved and respected by slaves and chiefs alike, she continued to settle quarrels, nurture unwanted babies, teach men and women and children to read "book," and preach the Gospel of Jesus Christ.

Finally on January 13, 1915, at the age of sixty-six, she succumbed to fever and dysentery for the last time, with this prayer on her lips: "*O Abasi, sana mi yok*" (O God, release me). But her spirit and influence lived on. As Carol Christian and Gladys Plummer said in concluding *God and One Redhead*, their biography of Mary Slessor:

> *Yet wherever along the lower reaches of the Cross River, and particularly the Enyong Creek, an African woman earns her own living; wherever a mother of twins rears her children and her husband stands loyally by her; wherever parties to a quarrel seek the mediation of the courts instead of leaping for their machetes, something endures of the spirit of a slight, red-haired woman who in the midst of this region was whirlwind, earthquake, fire, and still small voice.*

FOR FURTHER READING

Christian, Carol, and Gladys Plummer. *God and One Redhead: Mary Slessor of Calabar.* Grand Rapids, MI: Zondervan, 1970.

Livingstone, W. P. *Mary Slessor of Calabar: Pioneer Missionary.* London: Hodder and Stoughton, 1915.

Miller, Basil. *Mary Slessor: Heroine of Calabar.* Minneapolis: Bethany House Publishers, 1974.

AMBUSHED IN JAGUAR SWAMP

BARBROOKE GRUBB

Authors' Note

Barbrooke Grubb first met Kyemap as a "young lad" in his native village of Yitlo-yimmaling, and it wasn't long before the boy went to live at the mission station to help Grubb. However, Kyemap was probably older than thirteen when this story took place.

The first reports to reach the mission station concerning the attack on Grubb said that he had been killed and named his attacker, and there soon developed a great deal of superstitious confusion about whether Grubb was dead or alive. We added the element of mystery for the sake of the story.

Though Kyemap went to Grubb's aid with Robert Graham and Sibeth, the second private trip is fictional.

Two events are chronologically out of order. Kyemap's baptism actually occurred in June 1899, and the showdown with the witch doctors took place in 1900, some three years after the main events of this story. It involved an attack on Kyemap's house and Grubb's response as described in this story but under more complicated circumstances.

The names of Richard Hunt's and Sibeth's wives are not known, so we have called them Mary and Hannah. We also shortened Kyemap's name from Kyemapsithyo, the mission station's name to Waik from Waikthlatingmangyalwa, and Poit's village to Namuk from Namukamyip. Grubb sometimes did the same in his writings, but have some fun trying to pronounce the longer names . . . at least once.

The "alligators" of the Chaco were probably caimans, a South American reptile similar to alligators and crocodiles that can exceed fifteen feet in length.

CONTENTS

CHAPTER 1

SLEEPING WITH A GHOST

Sparks sprang into the violet sky, chased by flames that erupted when Kyemap dropped an armload of sticks on his small fire. He whirled around and stared toward the bushes that surrounded his small clearing. What had screamed? Was it the harmless paca rodent with its bloodcurdling cry . . . or was it a ghost?

Watching the dimly lit bushes for any sign of movement, the young boy carefully leaned down and drew a large stick from the fire. Small flames flickered from its other end. With two quick steps and a strong overhand, Kyemap flung it toward the bushes, blue smoke looping behind. He did not care if the bushes caught on fire. In fact, a small brush fire would end this frightening ordeal. The villagers would come running to put it out, and his test would be forgotten.

The stick landed with a rattle and a thud, and then some small animal scampered off through the dry leaves. Kyemap peered into the darkness a few moments longer—the scream must have come from a paca—and then he turned with a sigh and sat back down under the bottle trunk tree near the fire. He wrapped his blanket tighter around his shoulders and stared into the flickering flames.

This was a foolish test he had agreed to. Ever since the missionary Mr. Grubb had come to the Chaco, that vast wilderness plain of Paraguay, the witch doctors had been buzzing like cicadas in a tree on a hot night. At first they said the white man who told stories of Jesus was a fraud, and they would drive him away with their magic. But when their spells had no effect on him, they changed their tune and said that *he* was a witch doctor, too. "We witch doctors have special powers," Pinse-Tawa, the chief witch doctor, warned. "The evil spirits don't hurt us because our powers are so strong. But the rest of you had better be careful. They can steal your soul and cause you to die."

But Mr. Grubb had only laughed. "They are just trying to frighten you," he said to the Indians in the Lengua language. "When you are afraid, they have power over you, and you will do what they tell you to do even though they are not chiefs. Jesus will free you from that fear."

The debate had gone on and on as Mr. Grubb traveled around the Chaco visiting the different Lengua villages. On his third visit to Kyemap's village, Mr. Grubb had announced that he was building a mission station at Waik on the north bank of the river Negro. "Anyone who wants to come and learn about Jesus can live there," he said. "I will also teach you better ways to plant your crops and raise sheep and cattle."

Kyemap was tempted to laugh at the white missionary's terrible accent and use of the wrong Lengua words sometimes. But the rules Mr. Grubb made for anyone coming to live at the mission station were plain enough to understand.

1. No babies are to be killed.
2. No beer is to be brewed or drunk on the station.
3. Feasts are to continue no longer than three days.
4. People must work when asked to help.
5. No cattle are to be killed without Mr. Grubb's permission.

Kyemap had been one of the first people to settle in the village that quickly sprang up outside the mission station. "Go and discover the truth about this white man," Kyemap's father had said, "so that all our people may know." Soon almost two hundred came from far and wide to live in the village. Among them were Pinse-Tawa and two of his assistant witch doctors. "Every village needs a witch doctor or two or three," they said. But when they were reminded that they had claimed that Mr. Grubb was a witch doctor, they shrugged and said, "But he's a foreign witch doctor."

Foreign or not, Kyemap soon grew to like the tall white man with the bushy eyebrow on his lip. The Lengua people did not have beards, and when two or three hairs would occasionally sprout from a man's chin, he would quickly pluck them out. Grubb, however, had hair all over his face, far too much to pull it out, so he shaved it off every day with a sharp knife . . . except on his upper lip. There he let it grow like an extra eyebrow. All the Indians laughed when it wiggled as he talked.

In spite of the rules against killing babies at Waik, the witch doctors managed to kill some of them anyway to maintain the people's superstition. Whenever twins were born, the witch doctors said to kill them because one would be weak. And if the first child born to a couple was a girl, she would be killed because the witch doctors said she would bring bad luck. The same thing happened if a baby was born with unusually dark skin or if the father deserted the mother before the child's birth.

These practices brought much grief to the people, but the witch doctors controlled them. In fact, there were so many reasons for killing babies that the whole tribe was in danger of dying out. "This killing of your babies must stop!" Mr. Grubb shouted after the third child had been killed at Waik. "The witch doctors are telling you wrong!"

Just that afternoon Mr. Grubb had invited all the Lengua people who had been learning about Jesus to come to his house. Being only thirteen years old, Kyemap did not know if he was welcome, but he had been coming to Mr. Grubb's classes. So he stood at the back of a group of twenty or so Lengua people as they gathered before the verandah of Mr. Grubb's house. Pinse-Tawa came, too. He stood with his blanket wrapped tightly around his thin, crooked body. A deep frown etched his pock-marked face, and his uncombed hair was full of ashes.

Five other foreigners joined Mr. Grubb on his veranda. They were Richard Hunt, his wife, Mary, and Andrew Pride—English missionaries who had come to assist Grubb at the Waik station. To the side stood Sibeth, a German cart-maker, and his wife, Hannah, who had begun working for the mission the year before, in 1895. Sibeth built and drove the big-wheeled carts that carried supplies to the mission. Hannah was the daughter of a German colonist who had settled about sixty miles east along the Paraguay River near the town of Concepción.

After greeting everyone, Mr. Grubb asked in a confident voice, "What is the thing the Lengua people fear most?"

He looked around at the Indians until one said, "The bones of a dead horse?"

Grubb shook his head. "No, no. That won't do. Horse bones may be scary, but they're not that bad. Why, one time I saw

Chief Mechi walk right across the bones of a dead horse. What's more frightening than horse bones?"

"The darkness," offered another Indian.

"Ah yes, but why?" asked Grubb.

"Because the spirits of the dead roam the night," answered the Indian.

"And isn't the grave of a recently killed baby the most frightening place of all at night?" asked Grubb.

Kyemap nodded his head while other Indians murmured their agreement. Then, before Kyemap realized what was happening, Mr. Grubb pointed at him and said, "What do you say, Kyemap? Why is the grave of a baby the most frightening place of all?"

Kyemap shrank back until the man standing in front of him hid him from Grubb's view.

"Come on, now. Speak up," said Grubb as he moved to the side where he could see the boy. "I really want to know."

Finally, Kyemap mumbled, "It is because a baby is too small to know who killed it, and so its ghost will haunt anyone who comes near, especially at night."

"Is that right?" asked Grubb, looking right at Pinse-Tawa.

The old witch doctor nodded his head and looked down as he scuffed his feet in the dust. "It is very dangerous to go near a grave at night. I don't like to do it myself, and I am the most powerful witch doctor of the Lengua people."

"Good," said Grubb. He rubbed his hands together as though he were warming them on a frosty morning. "Then if you think a baby's recent grave is the most scary place at night, I will prove it is powerless. Kyemap, you are only thirteen, the youngest person here this afternoon and therefore the least skilled in magic. I want you to do something for me, and I promise you that you will be completely safe."

Kyemap's knees almost folded when Grubb selected him. The "proof" Mr. Grubb wanted him to provide was to spend the night by the grave under the bottle trunk tree where the body of the murdered baby had been buried that very morning. If nothing happened to him during the night, then everyone would know that the witch doctors had lied.

That was how he had ended up alone out here in the dark with nothing but his blanket and a small fire to protect him.

The scream in the dark came again, this time from the other side of the clearing. Kyemap turned that way, his forehead wrinkled, his eyes wide to see into the night. Maybe it wasn't a paca after all. How could a little rodent get all the way from one side of the clearing to the other so quickly? He had heard something scamper off through the leaves when he threw the stick, but wouldn't a ghost pretend to be something else if it was trying to fool you . . . if it was trying to get close enough to grab your soul?

This was a terrible mistake!

"O great Creator of all things, Jesus, the God Mr. Grubb tells us about. If you exist, if you are good, if you care about me, please do not let the ghost of that poor baby take my soul," whimpered Kyemap as he stared at the edge of the clearing.

And then under the edge of the bushes, he saw movement in the grass. He jumped to his feet and was almost ready to flee for the village when a paca sat up on its haunches and chattered at him through its buckteeth. Kyemap jumped toward it, waving his outstretched arms. The little creature screamed again, and ran off into the night.

"A paca. Just a paca, a silly paca!" he repeated to himself again and again as he paced back and forth beside his fire, not realizing that he was almost stepping on the new grave. "A ghost might make the sound of little feet in the leaves in order to fool me, but no ghost would take on the form of a paca." Then he slowed, "Or would it? A ghost is supposed to be hard to see. But if you could see it, would it look like the baby? Or . . . ? No, I'm sure I saw a paca!"

He walked back to the tree and sat down again. He stared at the little grave on the other side of the fire. Then he looked back toward the brush and frowned. On the other hand, in the dark one might mistake a baby for a large paca. It had looked like a paca because it sat up and chattered and ran off into the brush . . . but a ghost, could a ghost do that? How could he know?

Kyemap tried to calm his trembling body. He would not give in to panic. Mr. Grubb had warned him that he would have to resist fear. He had prayed, and that was just before he had actually seen the . . . the—could he believe it had been only a paca? Mr. Grubb had talked about faith, believing that God loved you and heard your prayers. Had God shown him the paca as an answer to his prayer?

"O God, I want to believe it was you who showed me the paca." The night was so long, and he was so tired. Kyemap closed his eyes and leaned forward, resting his head on his arms on his knees. "I want to believe it was you. I want to believe it was you." He kept whispering the prayer. . . .

The sky was turning pale yellow and his fire was nothing but glowing ashes when he awoke. He stood up and wrapped his blanket around him and looked around the clearing. He was alive after all! No ghost had attacked him. Though everything was still a shade of gray, he could see clearly. He had thrown the stick in the bushes over that direction. In the opposite direction he had seen the . . . yes, it must have been a paca.

He touched some dry grass to the coals and blew until a flame burst forth. Then he added twigs and sticks until the fire's cheery warmth calmed his shivering. He opened his blanket, stretched his arms with the blanket held by its corners so that he looked like a bat, and took a deep breath. When he wrapped it back around him, he walked slowly to the spot where he had seen the . . . He knelt down and examined the grass. There, like large black seeds, were eight shiny pellets. He crushed one between his thumb and first finger. It was soft and damp. A big grin spread across his face as he stood up.

———

All the people gathered around that morning when Kyemap marched back into the village. Children reached out to touch him, and the adults asked if he was all right. "Of course I am fine," he said confidently. "Mr. Grubb told you the witch doctors were wrong."

"But what happened?" they asked.

"I will tell you when Mr. Grubb has finished his breakfast," he said.

Mr. Grubb did not wait to finish his breakfast when Kyemap arrived at his house. Instead, he took his cup of tea and went outside where he rang the mission bell, inviting the whole village to gather and hear Kyemap's report. The witch doctors came sullenly; Pinse-Tawa was frowning darkly.

Kyemap told his story slowly, not leaving out any detail as he described the scream in the dark and the scurrying feet through the leaves. "Then there was another scream from the other side of the clearing," Kyemap said in a hushed voice. "I was so afraid that I prayed to the Creator God as Mr. Grubb told me to do. And then . . . and then, guess what happened?" He stopped and looked around. "A paca popped its head up out of the grass and chattered at me. That was right after I prayed.

"And, of course," he concluded, "you can all see that I have returned home safely. So Mr. Grubb must be right. There is nothing to fear." He glanced toward Pinse-Tawa.

The old witch doctor just closed his eyes and shook his head, but one of the younger witch doctors spoke up. "You are very foolish to mock the spirits," he warned. "They may have had mercy on you this once, but now *everyone* may be in danger. I think we should all leave this village."

"Why should we leave when I have proved there is nothing to fear," said Kyemap in a challenging voice.

Pinse-Tawa cleared his throat and said, "You speak too quickly. Ghosts can make noise in leaves that sound like an animal scampering away. They can even look like a paca."

"Yes, I thought of that," said Kyemap, "but can they eat?"

"Of course not." The witch doctor spat on the ground. "Everyone knows that."

"Is that so, Mr. Grubb?" asked Kyemap.

The missionary shrugged. "I don't even believe in ghosts, but . . . " Then he smiled. "After Jesus rose from the dead, His disciples thought He might be a ghost, so He ate some fish with them to demonstrate that He was alive. So I guess that proves ghosts—if they exist at all—can't eat."

Kyemap grinned broadly, stood taller, and tilted his chin toward the witch doctor. "Then I'll go sleep out there again tonight."

Pinse-Tawa shook his head. "You tempt the spirits, foolish boy. I rattled my gourd all night to make powerful magic to keep that ghost away from you, and now you mock me." Then his eyes got very big and he leaned toward Kyemap. "In the dark of the night, how can you be so sure that what you saw was a paca and not the ghost of the baby?"

"Because of these," Kyemap said as he held out his hand with the dark pellets in it for everyone to see. "If ghosts cannot eat, they cannot make droppings!"

CHAPTER 2

THE FROG TALKER

Kyemap slept out under the bottle trunk tree the next night and was not even awakened by a paca. He was so tired after being scared the night before that he didn't wake up until the sun was high above the scrubby trees of the Chaco.

When he returned to the village, people nodded their heads knowingly and smiled at him with respect. But the witch doctors scowled. Kyemap did not understand the witch doctors' anger until he heard people repeating what he'd said. He was hoeing weeds in the pumpkin patch that afternoon. One woman stood up, drew her dirty hand across her sweaty forehead, and said to another, "Do you think it will finally rain tonight?" The other woman looked at the sky where only a few clouds had gathered and answered, "If ghosts cannot eat, they cannot make droppings." Then they both laughed.

Kyemap didn't understand what they meant. What did ghosts—or pacas—have to do with rain? But in the next few days, he heard the saying several times.

14

"Will One-Eye marry that White-Partridge girl now?" gossiped some girls gathering sticks for cooking fires. "If ghosts cannot eat, they cannot make droppings!" came the lighthearted answer.

A woman said admiringly, "Isn't Short-Blanket a good hunter?" Her husband snorted, "If ghosts cannot eat, they cannot make droppings."

The phrase had become a new saying among the people, meaning, "No way," "Not a chance," or "It'll never happen." Every time the people said it, they laughed and remembered how the witch doctors had been wrong.

Kyemap knew that was exactly what Mr. Grubb had hoped for. The power of the witch doctors had been reduced, and the people were less afraid. Maybe the baby killing would stop . . . at least at Waik. But Kyemap also knew the witch doctors would not quickly forget who had made them look like fools.

The young boy shrugged it off. He was enjoying the daily Bible classes Mr. Grubb taught to villagers who were interested. Even more important, Mr. Grubb had just invited him to be his personal assistant, working in his house so that he could learn more about God. "Each day I'll give you a Bible lesson, and when you are ready to follow Jesus, I will baptize you as a Christian," said Grubb.

———

Mr. Grubb had been sick with the fever again. As Kyemap hurried to the missionary's house with some of Mrs. Hunt's good broth to build back Grubb's strength, he saw a familiar figure walking into Waik. "Oh no, not Poit," muttered Kyemap.

Poit was Kyemap's distant cousin. The young man lived on the western frontier of Lengua country near the borders with the Toothli and Suhin tribes. Poit was a small-time trader, traveling a good deal and often carrying news from one village to another.

"Well, if it isn't my little cousin from the swamp," Poit said when he saw Kyemap. "Take me to meet this white man I've been hearing so much about. How did you get to be his personal helper? I didn't realize you were old enough to start your own fire."

Kyemap grimaced and rolled his eyes. Of all his relatives, why did Poit have to show up? It seemed like he never missed a chance to try to make Kyemap look foolish. Kyemap was tempted to call him "Poit, Poit, Poit." After all, that was how he had gotten his name. His first words as a toddler had copied the croak of the little green tree frog: *"Poit, poit, poit."*

"I hear this foreigner is some kind of a witch doctor. How did you manage to work for him?" asked Poit as they walked through the dusty village.

Not knowing whether his cousin would use his report as another way to make fun of him, Kyemap reluctantly told of his nighttime vigil under the bottle trunk tree.

But to his surprise, Poit did not laugh. "That wasn't my private hunting lodge, was it?" he said with a scowl. Poit had hollowed out a bottle trunk tree near the Sievo River where he sometimes stayed when hunting in the area. Once he had shown it to Kyemap.

"No, no. This tree is very close to the village," assured Kyemap. "You can see it from the sheep pens right over there."

"It better not have been my hunting lodge. You know what'll happen if you ever tell anyone. It's private!" he warned. Then after a moment, he dropped his angry tone and changed the subject. "I've never had much use for those witch doctors myself. They're always begging for food and never do any work. If this foreigner is more powerful, maybe it is good for you to

16

become his friend, cousin. But Pinse-Tawa's not going to like it." Just then Poit looked up at the crooked figure approaching them from the side. "Speaking of the devil's own," he whispered, "look there."

Pinse-Tawa was walking toward them with a great limp—something the old witch doctor did on occasion, Kyemap thought, just to get people's attention and sympathy. "The people are so glad you have come!" Pinse-Tawa said, holding his left hand out toward Poit as he got closer.

Poit stopped. With his hands on his hips and his head tipped to the side, he said flatly, "Why is that?"

"They have been waiting for you to come and rescue your poor cousin here."

Kyemap jumped forward, but Poit held out his hand and calmly said, "Rescue my little cousin or rescue you, you old fleabag? What are you talking about?"

Pinse-Tawa slapped his head with his left hand in a display of great surprise. "Have you not heard? He is in great danger. All the people are talking about him. The missionary forced him to spend two nights out on the Chaco alone—" he paused for emphasis and then whispered as though he were sharing a secret—"near the new grave of a poor baby who died under, uh, unfortunate circumstances."

"Unfortunate circumstances? I can imagine," said Poit.

"Well!" Pinse-Tawa rolled his eyes. "The boy has lost his mind. He came completely under the spell of this foreign witch doctor, and we can't do a thing with him. That is why we are so glad you have come to take him home to his parents. How they must grieve! I feel so bad that we couldn't help, but these foreigners are very powerful."

"If you weren't as sneaky as a rattlesnake, I might pay attention to you," Poit said. "But you won't poison me with your crazy schemes. I'll meet this man and make up my own mind. Come on, Kyemap. Don't you have some broth for this Mr. Grubb?"

Kyemap glanced out of the corner of his eye at his older cousin. Poit had always been a schemer and certainly not his favorite relative, but he didn't appear to be under the power of the witch doctors. Maybe it was good that he had come.

Grubb was slouched on the veranda of his house, still weak from the fever. But as soon as Kyemap introduced Poit and said that he came from a village on the western frontier, Mr. Grubb perked up. "I've always wanted to make contact with the Toothli and Suhin tribes. Could you help me, Poit?"

All afternoon Poit and Mr. Grubb talked about the distant tribes. Finally, as the cousins were leaving, Grubb said, "There are legends that tribes of giants and pigmies are living in the forests to the west. Do you know about this?"

Poit laughed. "No. Those were just stories to scare the Spaniards away. Do you know that they never succeeded in exploring the Chaco? Even with all their guns, we always chased them away before they got very far."

That night as Kyemap and Poit sat by the fire outside Kyemap's hut, Pinse-Tawa and two other witch doctors came and sat near them. Kyemap wanted to get up and walk away; given the sour look on Poit's face, he figured his cousin felt the same way. Only politeness prevented them. "Why are you interested in this foreigner?" challenged the youngest witch doctor.

Poit ate a pumpkin seed and spit out the hull. He ate another and another, spitting the hulls into the fire before he answered. "Two moons ago," he said without looking at the witch doctor, "I met a very old wise man in the West who was dying. He told me a prophecy that has been passed down from generation to generation among our people. Possibly you know of it since you are so smart," he said sarcastically, "but I had not heard it before." Poit stopped and put another seed into his mouth. Slowly he cracked the hull, spit it into the fire, and chewed the meat.

"How should we know whether we have heard the prophecy if you don't tell us what it is," said the young witch doctor impatiently.

Kyemap noticed a twinkle in Poit's eye as he teased the witch doctors. "I thought your magic might be powerful enough to know what I was thinking without me saying anything," he mocked.

Pinse-Tawa snorted and looked away.

"No?" said Poit. "Well, the prophecy said that someday foreigners will come to our land who will reveal the mysteries of the spirit world, and they will help our people. But it also included a warning: If we reject the message of the foreigners, we will cease to exist. Have you heard of that prophecy?"

The two younger witch doctors shrugged and looked at each other. "Who can tell what some wrinkled old goat might say? Why should we pay attention?" They did not look at Pinse-Tawa, who was about as wrinkled and old as a person could be.

Pinse-Tawa frowned at their disrespect. "Well, I have heard of that prophecy," he growled, "but foreigners have tried to enter our land since the time of my grandfather. They came only to steal and kill."

"That is true," admitted Poit. "The foreigners have cheated and robbed us, and they brought men with guns who sometimes killed our people. But this Mr. Grubb—is he not different? I have heard that he has traveled in the Chaco for five years now, and he has never killed anyone. I have heard that he and the missionaries with him do not cheat or rob. I have heard that he does not hide behind armed soldiers when he travels. I have heard that he sometimes travels completely alone in the wilderness. Is that not true?"

"You have heard a lot," said Pinse-Tawa scornfully. "But I think he is here to steal our way of life."

Kyemap spoke up. "The only thing he will 'steal,' as you put it, is your power to frighten and control the people."

Pinse-Tawa shrugged, and everyone sat silently until the fire needed another stick.

Kyemap got up and put on some more wood, but he remained standing. He had listened long enough to not be rude. Even though he was the youngest person present, it was his hut and his fire and therefore his right to signal when the conversation was over. Slowly, the witch doctors rose and nodded their good-byes. As they were leaving, Kyemap said quietly, "What if the old prophecy is true, and Grubb and his assistants *are* the foreigners who bring the *Tasik Amyaa* [Good News]? What will happen if we reject it?"

———

Days passed, but Poit did not build a hut of his own. "Why build a hut when I can sleep in yours?" he said to Kyemap. "Besides, I have more important things to do. I am talking business with Mr. Grubb. He's going to give me a herd of cattle, and I'll become very rich. You'll see." Indeed, by the time Kyemap got to Mr. Grubb's house each morning, Poit and Mr. Grubb were so busy talking that there was no time for Kyemap's Bible lesson. Kyemap did his work in the house, then went out to the garden to harvest melons or sweet potatoes or manioc root. Sometimes he repaired the pen for the sheep.

Traditionally, the Lengua people allowed their sheep and goats to roam freely, and wolves or even a jaguar often killed them. Mr. Grubb said that such helpless animals should be kept in pens near the village, but Kyemap thought it was a lot of work repairing the fences. He stood up from weaving new sticks into the animal pen. It was so much hotter out in the sun than it was back on Mr. Grubb's veranda with a cool glass of tea.

He wiped his brow and looked toward the mission station. Why was Mr. Grubb spending all his time with Poit and none with him? He was the one who braved the ghost under the bottle trunk tree at night! He was the one who helped Grubb reduce the power of the witch doctors! What happened to his Bible lessons?

He swung around to go get more sticks and bumped into one of the witch doctors who was walking past. "Watch where you are going," snapped Kyemap, still feeling upset. "You've got the whole Chaco to walk on, so why do you need to walk down this fence as though it were a narrow trail in the forest?"

The witch doctor ducked his head and raised a hand like he was warding off a blow and hurried on without saying a word. "Wait!" Kyemap called after him. "You've walked past here several times today. What are you doing? You lazy dogs never leave the shade of your palm tree unless you have some purpose. So why are you bothering me?"

But the witch doctor hurried on. Then Kyemap noticed Pinse-Tawa standing at the other end of the fence smoking a pipe. Kyemap looked around. It was very strange for anyone to smoke a pipe alone without sharing it with others. Why was he standing out here by the animal pen as though he enjoyed the scenery?

The sticks Kyemap needed were in a pile beyond Pinse-Tawa, so he headed for them. "Good day, Old One," he said as he approached the witch doctor.

Pinse-Tawa grunted. But as he passed, Kyemap noticed a quick movement out of the corner of his eye. He turned in time to see the witch doctor step away from the fence and plant his misshapen bare foot right where Kyemap had walked.

Kyemap flinched, thinking the old man intended to hit him, but he didn't raise his hand. Then Kyemap saw what he was doing. He was stepping on Kyemap's shadow. The witch doctors were working magic on him.

CHAPTER 3

THE MAGIC SHOW

Mr. Grubb shook his head in bewilderment. "I don't understand," he said in Lengua. "So what if he steps on your shadow? What harm can that do?"

"It's magic," said Kyemap. "They are trying to kill me!"

Grubb threw up his hands. "How can stepping on your shadow possibly hurt you?"

Kyemap shrugged, but his wide eyes still revealed his fear.

"Look," said the missionary. "If we were going on a journey, walking side by side, I would be stepping on your shadow and you would be stepping on mine all day long. What difference would it make?"

"Yes, but we wouldn't be using any magic on each other," said Kyemap.

"Exactly, because there is no power in their foolish spells and superstitions. Didn't you prove that yourself the nights you spent under the bottle trunk tree?"

Kyemap stood looking down at the floor.

Finally, Grubb said, "Alright, alright, so you are afraid. Let's approach this another way. Why do you think they might be wanting to kill you?"

Kyemap shrugged.

"Poit," Mr. Grubb said, "do you have any idea why these witch doctors are upset with this boy?"

"They probably want to get rid of him. They've tried every day since I got here to get me to send him home, but so far"— Poit flipped his hand out, palm up, in a careless gesture—"they can't pay enough."

"Pay?" said Grubb. "You would accept a bribe to send your own cousin home?"

"Why not?" laughed Poit. "I'm learning business. But as my little cousin says, 'If ghosts cannot eat, they cannot make droppings.' Witch doctors have no money, so I don't send him home. That's why they have turned to magic."

"Well, how do we get them to leave him alone?" said Mr. Grubb.

"Use greater magic," offered Poit.

"Magic?" Grubb shook his head. "After all the time we've talked, do you think I came here to practice magic?"

"How should I know?" Poit retorted.

————

That night the witch doctors said that they wanted all the people to meet in the small field between the village and the mission buildings. They had something very important to say to the people.

Mr. Grubb did not ring the mission bell to announce this meeting, but he and his assistant, Andrew Pride, came nevertheless and stood with the villagers.

24

After everyone had gathered before a large bonfire, Pinse-Tawa stood up and said, "The spirits have shown us that Kye-map must leave this place. He has been away from his home village for too long, and his spirit is in danger of getting lost."

Mr. Grubb stepped forward. "That is a lie. What has happened is that he has weakened your power, and to get it back, you want people to forget about him," he said.

"No," said Pinse-Tawa in a solemn voice. "It is the will of the spirits, not us."

"Spirits?" challenged Grubb. "You do not speak for spirits. Where is your authority?"

"You challenge my authority?" roared Pinse-Tawa in a voice that surprised everyone. "You watch this!"

At that moment he threw off his blanket and began dancing around the bonfire, shaking his rattle violently. All the villagers shrank back as his dancing got wilder and wilder, and then he stopped and faced the open Chaco in the direction where no one sat.

He leaned far forward, pursing his lips, and then spat something out into the knee-high grass.

"Is there a small child who saw where that seed landed?" he asked.

Three little hands shot up, and he picked a girl about four years old. "Go see what you find there," he said.

The girl looked at her mother and then ran into the grass, almost to the edge of the firelight. "A pumpkin," she squealed with delight, as she picked up one about the size of her head and brought it back.

The old witch doctor spat out three more seeds, and other children found a pumpkin where each landed. "Oos" and "ahs" from the villagers showed they were impressed.

"Stop," said Grubb. "Don't anyone move!" Then he walked

over to one of the assistant witch doctors and pulled off his blanket. Two more pumpkins fell to the ground. Grubb also walked out into the grass and found three more pumpkins in the dark.

Coming back to the fire, he challenged, "When Pinse-Tawa was dancing around so wildly that you were watching his every move, these other fakers walked out in the grass and dropped the pumpkins for the children to find. It's a nice trick, but that's all it is. Seeds do not turn into pumpkins unless you plant them and wait a few weeks."

The villagers clapped their hands. "If ghosts cannot eat, they cannot make droppings," shouted one of the villagers from the back of the group. Everyone laughed, and Kyemap breathed a sigh of relief. He had not seen the assistant witch doctors hide the pumpkins in the grass, and until Grubb revealed their trick, it had looked like magic to him.

"You'll have to do better than that," said Grubb as he went to take his seat with the other villagers.

An angry scowl contorted Pinse-Tawa's face. "You want big magic? I will show you big magic!" Then he slowly walked to the other side of the fire and sat down with his back to the fire and all the people. Beside him stood his two assistants. For several minutes he sat there chanting. Then he spun around, creating a little cloud of dust. But he still sat on the other side of the fire from the crowd of villagers.

"Come here," he ordered, pointing to the little girl who had found the first pumpkin. Shyly, with her thumb in her mouth, the girl walked around the fire to the old man. He had her lie down in front of him as he continued his chanting and waved his hands above her body. Then he grabbed her bare stomach so that she cried out and sat halfway up. "Lie down," he shouted at her, and suddenly in his grimy hands there was a small kitten, meowing loudly and waving its paws with claws extended.

The witch doctor dropped the kitten on the ground, and it scampered away into the night. Then he grabbed the girl's stomach again. It was hard to see exactly what was happening through the smoke and flames, but suddenly he lifted up another kitten. He tossed it aside, and it, too, ran off.

This he repeated a third time, and then he slowly stood up and stepped back beside his assistants. The girl lay on the ground whimpering for a few minutes, then got up and ran to her mother.

Everyone sat in stunned silence.

Kyemap stole a glance to see what Mr. Grubb was doing. He was just staring at the ground. But finally he stood up and said, "Well, I can't top that, and I can't explain it, but I assure you all that it was just a trick. I've learned some tricks in my day, too. Now, I'm not a witch doctor as some of you may think, and what I'm going to show you will prove it takes no special power to perform a good trick."

He stepped out in front of the people but not behind the bonfire. Then he whistled to call a dog over to him. The dog came, cautiously sniffing, and Grubb held up a small piece of paper for everyone to see. When he offered it to the dog, the dog quickly ate it, licking its nose and thrusting its head forward slightly as it swallowed the paper.

"Now," said Grubb, "watch very closely." He grabbed the dog's tail and pulled the paper from the tip of the tail. "You like that?" he said, holding the paper up for everyone to see.

They all clapped—all except the witch doctors—and Grubb did the trick again.

"Does anybody know how I did it?" he asked.

Everyone shook their heads.

"Kyemap, come here," he said. Then speaking to the villagers he added, "Any one of you could do this same trick, and I'll show you how.

"I put some chicken fat on the paper, which is what made the dog eat it. Here, Kyemap. Here's some paper and a little bit of fat. You try it, but make sure everyone can see what you are doing."

There was nothing unusual about a dog swallowing a small piece of paper with some tasty fat on it, and the dog proved it in one gulp.

"In my other hand," said Grubb, "I had hidden a second small piece of paper that looked very much like the first piece of paper. It was easy to fold up so no one noticed it. A few moments later, when I was holding the dog's tail, I unfolded the paper and made it appear as though it came from the tip of the dog's tail. Here, Kyemap, you try it." He handed the paper to Kyemap, then said, "Show the people how the paper is hidden in your hand. Now grab the dog's tail and unfold the paper."

Everything worked just as he said, and soon everyone was clapping and cheering.

"Yes, that was fun, wasn't it? But it was just a trick. Let's all go home and get a good night's sleep."

As the people departed, the children chased the village dogs to see if they could do the trick, too. The witch doctors, however, walked off alone into the dark.

———

In the middle of the night, Kyemap was awakened by a terrible commotion. People were running around and yelling. Something crashed into the back of his hut, and suddenly portions of the roof began flying off.

Kyemap jumped up and tripped over his water gourd as he tried to scramble out to see what was happening. Dogs were barking, and by the time he got outside, people were running past his hut yelling that they had seen a ghost.

He grabbed a small bundle of straw and held the end of it against the dimly burning coals of his fire. He blew on it until it ignited into a torch. Kyemap examined the backside of his hut, and sure enough, whole sections of the roof had been flipped off and lay several feet away on the ground.

"What's happening out there?" came the voice of Poit from inside.

"I don't know," said Kyemap.

By the time Poit joined him, several other villagers had torches and were surveying the damage. "It must have attacked the sheep," said a man standing at the edge of the village, peering off into the darkness. "I can see where they broke out of their pen. It looks like most of them ran off into the night. But I'm sure not going out there to try to find them in the dark."

"I know that I saw a ghost," said a frightened woman between sobs. "It was floating around above the roof of your hut, Kyemap. I think you've made the spirits angry."

Soon everyone was examining the torn-up roof of Kyemap's hut and shaking their heads. Some backed away from him as though he were the ghost.

"Now maybe you won't mock the spirits anymore," said one of the young witch doctors.

"Now maybe you'll go home to your own village," said the other. But Pinse-Tawa was nowhere to be seen.

No one slept the rest of that night, and by the next morning, Kyemap had decided to return to his home village. He gathered his few belongings together into a small bundle. He looked over toward Mr. Grubb's house and shook his head. "I suppose I should at least tell him that I am leaving," he said as he walked slowly from the village to the mission station.

He expected the missionary to be angry with him as he explained what had happened during the night and his decision to leave. But instead, all Mr. Grubb said was, "I have had a little touch of the fever again, so I haven't gone out this morning. Would you please find Pinse-Tawa and bring him here to my house? I want to talk to him, and I want you to hear what I have to say."

Kyemap shrugged. If Mr. Grubb was sick, then obviously he had to help him. He went looking for Pinse-Tawa and found the old man outside the village sitting under the bottle trunk tree near the baby's grave. No one knew for certain, but it was probably Pinse-Tawa who had killed the baby. Parents seldom did the deed themselves. When the witch doctor said it had to happen, the new parents usually paid the witch doctor to do the killing.

As he approached the old man, Kyemap said, "I see you are not afraid of the baby's ghost."

Pinse-Tawa looked up in surprise. "No, no. I have charms that protect me . . . at least during the day." Then he changed the subject. "Will you be leaving Waik?"

"I plan to leave today," admitted Kyemap, looking at the ground. "But first Mr. Grubb wants to talk to you. He waits at his house. Will you come?"

The witch doctor got up and followed in silence.

Back at the mission station, Mr. Grubb met them on the veranda and said, "Come in, both of you. I want you to see something." He led them through the general room and out onto the dining and sleeping veranda that extended across the whole back of the house. It had a wall halfway up and screens above that on all three sides.

Grubb casually walked over to his bed and then removed one of the screens so as to create an open window facing the Lengua village. "I understand," said Grubb to Pinse-Tawa, "that there was a great disturbance in the village last night."

"Yes," said the witch doctor. "Many ghosts."

"And a few devils, no doubt," said Grubb. "Well, we can't let the village be disturbed like that again, can we?"

"No. They attacked this poor boy's hut. I think they are angry with him," said Pinse-Tawa.

Grubb grinned so that his mustache spread out flat under his nose. "I have a plan that should put an end to it. See my rifle here? If tonight—or any other night—those ghosts bother his hut, I'll just fire a few shots over there and scare them off. You think that will work?"

Pinse-Tawa's eyes got very large, and he began shaking. Finally, he muttered, "I don't think they will bother him anymore."

"Good," said Grubb. Then he turned to Kyemap. "Then I don't see any reason why you need to leave. Our great witch doctor here is quite certain that you won't be bothered again. Is that good enough for you?"

CHAPTER 4

ALLIGATOR STEW

When he had finished the work in Mr. Grubb's house the next day, Kyemap decided he would just stay there unless Mr. Grubb told him to go out to the garden. He went out onto the veranda, where Poit and Mr. Grubb were talking.

"Let's go tomorrow," Poit was saying to Grubb when Kyemap sat down. "You want to take cattle to the Suhin and Toothli people as gifts? We can take the cattle as far as Namuk; I know of a good pasture for them not far from my village. Then I will take you to the Suhin and the Toothli people."

"I'm afraid I can't," said Grubb reluctantly. "In ten days, I have to go away, far away across the big water to my country of England. I have not had a furlough, a—" he fumbled for the right word, "—a vacation . . . Oh, you wouldn't understand that, either. Anyway, I have to go away. There is not enough time between now and then to visit the Suhin and the Toothli."

"That doesn't matter," said Poit. "I will be glad to look after the cattle for you at Namuk while you are gone. Then when you come back, you could make Namuk your base camp and visit the Suhin and Toothli."

Kyemap frowned. It wasn't like Poit to offer to look after livestock. His cousin liked to be free to travel whenever he felt like it.

But Mr. Grubb seemed to like the idea. "Well," he said, rubbing his chin thoughtfully, "we would have to take an oxcart with supplies and things to trade, and we'd have to build a house to store the supplies in until I come back." He brightened. "Yes, maybe that would work. I could drive the cart if you would help with herding the cattle."

"Of course," said Poit. "We could take my little cousin here. He ought to be good for herding cattle, and that would get him out of the way of these foolish witch doctors."

Kyemap looked away toward the Chaco, where a dust devil spun its way across the dry ground. He felt like a dust devil was spinning in his stomach the way his cousin always treated him like something extra that needed a reason to exist.

———

Early the next morning, Sibeth, the German cart-maker, had two oxen hitched to a large-wheeled cart that he had loaded with all the items Mr. Grubb had ordered. With a small herd of seventeen cattle, Mr. Grubb, Poit, and Kyemap set out. Travel proved much slower than they expected. The early days of March 1896 seemed to evaporate as they cut a trail through scrub brush, forests, and swamp.

When they finally arrived at the Sievo River not far from the village of Paisiam—about fifteen miles south of Waik— Mr. Grubb pulled the oxcart to a stop along the edge of the steep riverbank some six feet above the water. He looked back toward Kyemap and Poit, who were following with the cattle, and yelled, "We're never going to make it to Namuk in time. I think we'd better build some kind of a storage hut in Paisiam. Chief Mechi is a good man. He will look out for our supplies and prevent anyone from taking them."

"But what about the cattle?" called Poit.

"Well, I suppose . . ." said Grubb, but the ox closest to the riverbank was pawing the soft ground so hard that the loud *thud, thud, thud* made it hard to talk. Grubb got down and walked back toward Kyemap and Poit. "I suppose you could take them on to Namuk, but are you sure you have a good pasture there? You can't turn cows out into a swampy area or they'll get disease, but they must have access to water at all times." Poit was nodding his head eagerly as Grubb spoke. "You've seen the pasture near Waik. Do you have something like that at Namuk?"

The ox that had been pawing the ground had loosened the dirt enough to kick it up onto its flanks in an attempt to drive off the tormenting horseflies. It kept pawing and kicking.

"Oh yes, much better," said Poit. "Namuk is built on a little hill with a lake all around. It is beautiful, and there is always water and good grass. Our goats and sheep do very well there."

"Sheep? But if too many sheep graze a pasture, it's no good for cattle," worried Grubb. "They eat the grass too short."

"No, no," said Poit. "Our grass grows tall." And he demonstrated with his hands a height of six or seven inches.

Suddenly, a commotion from the cart caused the three travelers to turn that way just in time to see the edge of the bank give way and the ox that had been pawing the ground slip over the edge, bellowing in horror as it scrambled to stop itself.

Terrified, the other ox pulled away from the crumbling edge with all its might; because the two were joined by the strong yoke, this was just the help the fallen ox needed to finally crawl back up the bank. Snorting and lunging with its eyes wide, the beast finally made it up onto flat ground, but its effort broke off more huge wedges of dirt. The last piece of the bank to cave in extended under the front wheel of the cart.

Kyemap, Poit, and Mr. Grubb ran toward the slowly toppling cart and grabbed its near side. Together with the oxen, they kept it from tipping into the river. But in the course of the tussle, the tongue of the cart broke. The loud splintering of the wood frightened the oxen even more.

"Steady those oxen!" yelled Mr. Grubb as the cart teetered on the brink. "Don't let them run away!"

Kyemap grabbed the reins and pulled with all his might to stop the frightened animals. The commotion, however, had startled the cattle, and they bolted away through the brush in several directions, their tails high and their hooves kicking behind them.

Poit and Grubb were barely keeping the cart from going over the bank. Once Kyemap had the oxen under control, Mr. Grubb grunted, "Now, wrap those reins around that stump and carefully get the rope out of the back of this cart."

Kyemap quickly tied up the oxen and then rummaged in the cart, taking care not to do anything that would push it over the edge. Once he had the rope, he tied it securely to the cart and then to the oxen's yoke. "Good, good," said Grubb. "Now slowly urge the oxen forward—we can't hold this thing much longer!"

Indeed, Mr. Grubb and Poit were straining their muscles so hard that their arms shook, and sweat dripped freely from their faces. The oxen, which were still frightened, refused to pull together. When one pulled, the other thought that it was being pushed toward the river. As soon as Kyemap got that one settled, the other shied away.

"Forget the reins!" yelled Mr. Grubb. "Grab their nose rings!

They've got to know you are in control and that you are not trying to pull them toward the river."

Kyemap did as Grubb said, and sure enough, the oxen calmed down and finally pulled together. The rope tightened until it vibrated like the wings of a hummingbird. If it broke, Kyemap knew the ends might whip around and injure someone. But slowly, their huge muscles straining, the oxen managed to pull the cart up onto level ground and away from the crumbling bank. Poit and Grubb fell panting to the ground.

When they'd caught their breath, the cousins started the task of rounding up the scattered cattle. An hour later, Mr. Grubb called to Kyemap and Poit from the river. He was standing up in a dugout canoe waving to them. "I borrowed this canoe from Chief Mechi!" he yelled. "I'm going to go across the river to that grove and find a nice straight sapling I can cut down to make a new tongue for the cart. I'll be back soon."

As Grubb paddled across the river, Kyemap sat down on the bank where the sparse shade of a tree fell, but Poit walked away from the river's edge and crawled into the shade under the cart to escape the heat of the afternoon sun.

———

Kyemap did not know how long he had dozed when the sound of the wooden canoe awoke him as it scraped ashore on the grassy sandbar that hooked out into the river a short distance downriver. He saw Grubb stand up and, using his paddle like a cane to steady himself, walk toward the front of the tipsy canoe. Suddenly, what had looked like an old brown log half-buried in the grass rose up and charged Grubb.

"Alligator!" screamed Kyemap in warning, but Grubb had already seen the reptile and was jamming his paddle into its gaping mouth. The huge monster crunched the paddle into matchsticks and kept hissing at Grubb, taking a step closer each moment.

"Poit, come quickly!" yelled Kyemap to his cousin, who was already running toward the riverbank. "We've got to help him!" he said, pointing toward Grubb.

But instead of hurrying downstream to where the gentle slope out onto the sandbar would make it easy to run to Grubb's aid, Poit stood riveted, watching the struggle, his hand outstretched toward Kyemap as if to stop him.

Kyemap couldn't understand why his cousin hesitated, but by the time he looked back at Mr. Grubb, the missionary had picked up the pole he had cut to make a new cart tongue and rammed its pointed tip down the alligator's throat. Then he began hammering on the other end with his ax to drive it deeper. The alligator roared like a sick cow and began flipping its tail around to break free, but Grubb kept on hammering the pole until he drove it into the monster's vital organs, and the creature ceased to fight.

Kyemap's mouth dropped open. "Can you believe that?"

But behind him, his cousin had not moved an inch. Poit was staring at the missionary as though he had seen a vision. "Poit!" snapped Kyemap. "What's the matter with you? Why didn't you go help Mr. Grubb?"

Poit muttered something under his breath, but Kyemap caught the words: "They might find a man's bones out here in the Chaco, but who could prove how he died?" Then, abruptly, he began walking along the bank and turned down onto the sandbar.

"What do you mean, Poit?" demanded Kyemap, running to catch up. "Why didn't you go help him?"

"Forget it," Poit said with a wave of his hand. "It doesn't matter now; he killed the dragon alone. We will help repair the cart."

———

The red sun was falling into the shimmering edge of the Chaco as Grubb climbed onto the cart and urged the oxen toward the village of Paisiam. Kyemap and Poit came along behind, driving the cattle they'd rounded up from the surrounding brush. Across the top of the cart was tied the huge body of the alligator, the largest Kyemap had ever seen. "It will make a good gift to Chief Mechi for having left his canoe down here," said Grubb.

"And for breaking his paddle," added Kyemap. They all laughed.

Late that night in the village of Paisiam, everyone feasted on alligator stew.

———

The next morning, after several villagers had helped build a storage hut and Chief Mechi had promised to care for Mr. Grubb's supplies, the missionary turned to Poit. "Take good care of these cattle for me," he said. "But remember, they are not your cattle. They belong to me. You are just their caretaker until I get back. Then we will use them to benefit your people and to contact the Suhin and the Toothli people."

Poit nodded but did not answer or look at Mr. Grubb. "Poit!" Mr. Grubb said sharply. "Are you listening to me? You are not to kill any of them. They belong to me."

Still, Poit did not look at him. "What's the matter?" asked Mr. Grubb. "Are you upset that I'm taking Kyemap back to Waik? You said you could find someone else to help you herd the cattle on to Namuk. What is it—another sixty miles?"

Finally, Poit answered. "Yes, yes, that's fine. You can take him. I will take the cattle." But he still refused to look Mr. Grubb in the eye.

CHAPTER 5

THIRTEEN MOONS
OF WAITING

Kyemap felt like an ant clinging to a witch doctor's rattle as he tried to stay on the seat of the empty oxcart as it bounced over the dry Chaco on its way back to Waik. To keep their insides from turning to jelly, he and Mr. Grubb took turns walking beside the cart until they came to a marshy area where the softer ground cushioned their ride.

"You've been helping me for quite a while now," said Mr. Grubb when Kyemap climbed back up on the cart beside him. "What have you learned?"

Kyemap looked at the missionary as they rolled along. Was this some kind of a test? How could he list everything he had learned over the past few months! And what if he forgot to mention the most important lessons? Finally, he said, "I have learned much, and I thank you for letting me work in your house. I've even been learning English: *Good morning. Good evening. Would you like some tea?*"

"Good, good. But what have you learned from the Bible? Have you decided to follow Jesus with your life?" asked the missionary.

Kyemap watched the rolling muscles under the hide of the oxen as they plodded step by step—one, two, one, two. They had taken twenty steps since Mr. Grubb had asked his question, and Kyemap knew he had better answer pretty soon. One, two, one, two, one two . . . He had learned a lot about Jesus, but what could he say? Making such a decision would make him the first Lengua to convert to the Christian faith. He didn't much care what the witch doctors thought. He had become convinced that they were powerless compared to Mr. Grubb's God. But would God really care for a young Lengua boy, or would Kyemap be left alone without even the traditions of his people?

"Do you pray like I taught you?" asked Grubb.

"Sometimes," mumbled Kyemap.

"Good," said the missionary. "You keep asking God to show himself true to you."

After a few moments Grubb continued. "I will be gone for thirteen months—thirteen moons—but I will return. Maybe when I get back you will be ready for baptism."

———

Mr. Grubb left for his trip on March 24, 1896. The date meant nothing to Kyemap, and he had no idea where England was. All Mr. Grubb could tell him was that it was far down the river Negro and far down the river Paraguay (which Kyemap had never seen, but had heard about) and far across the big salt sea where summer was winter, and winter was summer.

Sometimes on the Chaco, shallow saltwater ponds collected after a long rain. When the hot sun dried up the water and baked the mud until it was hard and cracked, the Lengua people scraped white crystals off the top. It was good for preserving meat. But Kyemap knew nothing of a salt sea or big canoes that, like thistledown, caught the wind and sailed away.

The work of the mission station was carried on by the other missionaries: Richard and Mary Hunt, and Andrew Pride. Gardens were planted, sheep tended, cattle fed, and the missionaries taught Bible classes. Kyemap attended and listened quietly for one moon and then two and then three, but finally he lost interest. Mr. Grubb had said he would return in thirteen moons, but that was nearly forever.

Then one very hot and dry evening Poit returned to Waik. "Where is Mr. Grubb?" he asked Kyemap as he sat down beside the boy's fire. "I must warn that foreigner."

"Warn him of what?" asked Kyemap.

Poit looked around to make sure no one else was listening. "I have had a dream," he said in a whisper. "In it Mr. Grubb drowned. I must warn him."

"He is not here," said Kyemap. "He told you that he would not return for thirteen moons, and so far only six moons have passed. Besides, it hasn't rained in so long, there isn't a puddle deep enough for drowning."

"Nevertheless," said Poit with a shrug, "if I cannot warn him, he will surely die."

Kyemap eyed his cousin closely. When the alligator had almost killed Mr. Grubb near Paisiam, Poit had hesitated to go to his aid. Now Poit was again acting like he didn't care whether Mr. Grubb lived or died, so why had he come so far to warn Mr. Grubb? Finally, Kyemap asked, "Was the water in which Mr. Grubb drowned salty or sweet?"

"How should I know?" said Poit. "Do you think I tasted it in my dream?"

"I only asked because he is traveling on salty water. If the water in which he drowned in your dream was not salty, then it was a false dream," Kyemap reasoned. "Besides, Mr. Grubb does not believe in dreams."

Poit snorted in disgust. "How can one not believe in dreams? They tell everything." He tossed a few sticks on the fire and then stared into the flames for a long time without blinking. Finally, he declared, "He is dead. He will never return. These missionaries are not the fulfillment of the ancient prophecy. I will go home and have a feast with his cattle because now they are mine."

"But you can't!" said Kyemap as his cousin stood up. He, too, got to his feet. "You promised to care for his cattle, and thirteen moons have not yet passed."

Kyemap had grown almost as tall as his cousin and stood looking him in the eye. "They are not your cattle!" he said boldly.

"He is dead!" declared Poit. "The cattle belong to me."

Kyemap argued some more, but nothing he said made any difference to Poit. Later, when they had wrapped their blankets around themselves and Poit was snoring softly, Kyemap watched his cousin in the flickering light from his fire. Why did he care what Poit did? Was he afraid that Mr. Grubb would return and be upset with Poit? Or was he afraid that the Lengua superstitions might be true and Mr. Grubb would never return?

Probably a little of both. He wrestled with both questions a long time before he fell asleep.

The next morning, through half-closed eyes, Kyemap watched as Poit got up and roasted a sweet potato in the coals of the fire. After Poit had turned it several times, he stabbed it with a stick and pulled it from the fire. "Well, I'm returning to Namuk," he announced as Kyemap sat up and rubbed his eyes.

Poit wrapped his blanket around himself with a flourish. "I am going to throw a great feast," he said. "Who knows how long it will last? It may go on forever, and the grateful people may make me chief. At least your Mr. Grubb has done something good for me." Poit started to walk away, but then he turned back to Kyemap. "Oh, by the way, since you introduced me to my good fortune, you can come to my feast, too."

Kyemap gritted his teeth as he watched his cousin walk across the bare, dusty ground. A skinny dog got up and followed Poit to the edge of the village, then stopped and gazed sadly after the man. Finally, it turned around and wandered back, sniffing the ground for any potato peels Poit might have dropped. "I know just how you feel," Kyemap said, more to himself than the dog, "living off Poit's crumbs." He spat on the coals, making a loud sizzle. He didn't need a special invitation to Poit's feast. Anyone could go. It was tradition. But somehow Poit had a way of making Kyemap feel as unwelcome as a wildfire sweeping the Chaco's dry grass.

Several months had passed without rain. Every water hole was dry, and only one of the mission wells had drinkable water. Pinse-Tawa, the witch doctor, decided he would try one more time to discredit the Christian God. After one Sunday's worship, he addressed Mr. Hunt in front of all the people.

"I have been trying to make rain," he said so everyone could hear, "but I cannot because everyone knows I need a new duck feather, and all the ducks have flown away." Then he turned to Mr. Hunt. "But you say that your God is good and kind to

His children, that He hears your prayers, and that He is the one who sends the rain. Is that so?"

Mr. Hunt looked uneasy. "Yes."

"Then," said Pinse-Tawa, "why don't you pray to your God and ask for rain so our animals—and even we—won't die?"

Kyemap could see that Mr. Hunt was upset. "God does not like being tested," he said sharply. "But I will pray like the prophet Elijah that you will see God is more powerful than false gods."

Mr. Hunt prayed. He did not pray long, and he did not dance or yell or make a big show as the witch doctors did when they tried to get their spirits to help them. When he finished, he looked at Pinse-Tawa and then at the gathered villagers and simply said, "Now we will see."

The next afternoon, huge rain clouds gathered, but no rain fell. However, that night it rained harder than Kyemap had ever remembered. In the morning every well was full. Every water hole was full. The rivers overflowed their banks. In fact, much of the Chaco had again become a vast swamp. And it was just the beginning of the rainy season.

As Kyemap splashed around in the puddles, he thought to himself that when Mr. Grubb returned, he would be ready to become a Christian.

———

The next morning three visitors arrived at Waik. Kyemap was among many other villagers who gathered to see who they were. One was a red-faced man with a large stomach and straw hat. Like most foreign men, he had hair on his upper lip, but his mustache was whiter than his suit. A pair of spectacles hung from his collar by a gold chain.

The big man talked loudly and waved his arms as if he

were trying to talk to someone on the other side of the river. Finally, he stopped talking and carefully looked from one to another of the mission houses as though examining which one he would choose. He pointed to the Hunts' house with its beautiful little flower garden that Mrs. Hunt tended so faithfully. Kyemap had never understood why she spent so much time growing flowers that no one could eat, but he did understand the fat man when he announced, "That one," and began walking toward it.

Andrew Pride quickly stepped in front of him, shaking his head and saying, "No, no . . ." and many other words in English so fast and urgently that Kyemap did not understand them. Then he introduced the fat man to the Hunts. They shook hands, and finally they all headed off to Mr. Grubb's house.

All this while a small thin man followed the fat man and kept bowing to everyone like a swamp reed bending before a stiff breeze. He was a strange-looking fellow with a face like an armadillo—big ears, beady eyes, and a long, rough nose.

A third newcomer stood back by himself. He leaned against a tree with his legs crossed at the ankles and his arms folded across his chest. Kyemap watched an amused grin flicker across his face as he eyed the big man barking out orders to other people as he moved into Mr. Grubb's house.

The villagers were staring at the newcomers. Who were these men? Why had they come? Flustered, Andrew Pride came back out and announced in Lengua, "Please go to your homes. Come back this evening and we will introduce these visitors to everyone."

CHAPTER 6

THE LUNGFISH
PROFESSOR

When the mission bell rang just before sundown, everyone in the village gathered again in the now muddy field between the village and the mission. Mr. Pride raised his hand for their attention and spoke in the Lengua language. "As you know, we have some guests. This is Professor Kerr of Glasgow University in Scotland," he said, indicating the fat man in the white suit. "A professor is a very important teacher," he explained. "And this is his assistant, J. S. Budgett. They have come to study the lungfish."

Everyone was silent. What was a lungfish? "You know, the *lolach*!" Mr. Pride explained, using the Lengua word for the strange eel-like fish that grew abundantly in the swamps and rivers of the Chaco. It had both gills and lungs. When the swamps dried up—as they often did—the fish burrowed into the mud, leaving a little tube for air, and waited for rain. Some grew three feet in length.

The villagers looked at one another in puzzlement. Why would anyone want to study a lungfish? They caught the ugly creature all the time and ate it, but what could anyone learn from it? Quiet giggling broke out over such a silly idea and spread through the crowd until the people were openly laughing.

"Quiet, quiet, please," said Mr. Pride. "From time to time the professor may need your assistance in finding the fish or with other aspects of their research. I hope you will be willing to help."

Again the villagers laughed, but most also nodded their heads in agreement.

Kyemap then spoke up. "Has he seen Mr. Grubb?" he asked, and everyone became very quiet.

Mr. Pride said something to the visitors in English, and then he turned back toward the people. "Professor Kerr has not had the privilege of meeting with our Mr. Grubb, but this other fellow"—and he indicated the man who had held back that morning, smiling under the tree—"saw Mr. Grubb just before he left England. He is Robert Graham, a new missionary who is joining us."

"Has he drowned?" asked Kyemap.

Everyone looked at him in amazement. They were probably wondering why he had asked such an unusual question. Finally, Mr. Pride said, "You must be concerned because he traveled so far across the sea." He repeated some words to Robert Graham in English. Both missionaries laughed, and then Mr. Pride addressed Kyemap. "Mr. Graham says that our Mr. Grubb is quite dry and well. No need to worry."

Kyemap sighed with relief as the crowd broke up and went back to their huts. Then he stopped and looked back.

Mr. Grubb may be dry and well now, but he still had to come back across the salty sea. Would he drown then?

"Kyemap, wait," called Mr. Pride. Kyemap turned back. "You have worked closely with Mr. Grubb and the rest of us," said the missionary, "and you know a little English. Would you help Professor Kerr tomorrow?"

Kyemap shrugged. Why not?

The next morning, he arrived early to guide the fat professor and his assistant out onto the swamps and lagoons along the river where the lungfish could be found. Aware of the purpose of their trip, several other villagers volunteered to go along, too. With the recent rain, the lungfish would be coming out of their tunnels, and they would be very hungry and active. It would be a great day to catch lots of fish, and there would be a feast that evening.

But Professor Kerr needed more than a guide. He wanted to take all the comforts of home with him. Kyemap had to find two canoes the same size (which wasn't easy) and lash them together, side by side. Then he positioned a large chair with the right legs resting in the bottom of the right canoe and the left legs in the left canoe. In front of this chair the professor wanted a small table. Overhead, Kyemap set up a large umbrella to give Professor Kerr shade—or protection from more rain, should it come. The professor also required writing materials, some large glass jars, and a pot of hot tea. The floating contraption was very unstable, but Kyemap did the best he could.

The sun was straight overhead before Kyemap pushed the craft off from shore using a pole to propel the professor and his floating "laboratory" out into the swamp. Mr. Budgett, the professor's assistant, paddled alongside in a dugout canoe of his own. But by that time of day, most of the other villagers were coming in, having caught all the fish they wanted.

Using sign language and the few English words Kyemap could understand, the professor asked how the fishing had gone that morning, so Kyemap translated. The report from the other fishermen was good, but no one held up their catch for the professor to see.

Unfortunately, Kyemap could not maneuver the canoes well enough to get close to any fish to spear them when they surfaced to breathe, and Mr. Budgett did not have the skill to do it himself. So after three unfruitful hours on the water, the discouraged professor indicated that he wanted to return to shore.

Walking stiffly after having sat so long, he finally waddled into the village, where cooking fires seemed to be going every-where. Mr. Pride had no sooner joined them than the professor realized what was roasting over the fires. Huge lungfish were being turned on spits as they sizzled to a golden brown.

With a liveliness that surprised Kyemap, the professor began doing a foolish-looking dance from one cooking fire to another, waving his hands in the air and spinning around and shouting his foreign words.

"What's the matter with him? What's he saying?" asked Kyemap.

By then Mr. Pride was laughing so hard he had to hold his stomach. "He says," Pride gasped when he could catch his breath, "that he has come all the way from Europe to find these fish, and here you are cooking and eating the valuable creatures. They are larger, and there are more of them, than he ever imagined."

When the feast began, the professor shrugged as if to say, "Might as well join in," and accepted a roasted portion of fish on a large leaf. After a few bites he smacked his lips. With Mr. Pride translating, the professor explained that to the scientists in Europe, a lungfish was worth a month's wages. But now that he had found so many, and since they tasted so good, he might set up a canning factory right there on the Chaco and send canned lungfish back to England.

Yet when Mr. Pride had finished translating, he made a face and rolled his eyes. "I wouldn't pay a penny for a can of that fish," he added. "They taste like mud to me!"

As the weeks passed, Kyemap grew to resent being the professor's personal servant, always ordered about. "Find my slippers, boy." "Fetch me some tea." "Why weren't you here when I woke up this morning?" Kyemap had worked hard for Mr. Grubb, but Mr. Grubb had never taken advantage of him. But, he admitted to himself, there was one advantage to helping the professor: He was learning English. The professor did not know Lengua and made no attempt to learn it, so Kyemap had to do all the learning, and he learned fast.

———

The thirteenth moon had come. Kyemap was worried. What would Mr. Grubb do when he returned—*if* he returned— and found someone else living in his house?

The day Grubb arrived back at the mission station in the middle of April 1897 was a glad day. Kyemap could hardly contain his excitement. Grubb hadn't drowned after all! And the day after his return, Mr. Pride left for his vacation.

"But why should I have to move into his house?" asked the professor when Mr. Grubb asked him how long it would take to get his things transferred into Pride's place. "Why should I move when all of my books and research are set up in your house. I would think that you could camp out in Pride's digs until I leave."

Mr. Grubb's eyebrow went up as if to ask whether the professor now ran the whole mission station. Kyemap put his hand over his mouth and turned away.

"Because, Professor," said Mr. Grubb in an overly pleasant voice, "I have been 'camping out' for thirteen months, and I would like to get back into my 'digs,' as you call them, as soon as possible. The *work* of the mission is spreading the Gospel, not studying the lungfish, and so the Gospel must be our first task. You and your research efforts are welcome as long as it doesn't interfere."

With a look of innocent bewilderment on his face, the professor said, "But how would living in Pride's house for a while interfere with your preaching or whatever it is you do?"

"Look," said Grubb, "if you can't understand, then don't even ask. Get your stuff over to Pride's house by noon." Mr. Grubb walked away but then called back. "And by the way, you should prepare yourself. If the bishop or any other missionaries drop in on us for an extended stay, they will need Pride's house to stay in. We'll set you up in a tent."

———

Several months passed at the mission station while Mr. Grubb used the Lengua dictionary that Mr. Hunt had been working on to prepare Bible lessons in the Lengua language. Kyemap was grateful that with Mr. Grubb's return, he no longer had to work for the professor. The professor was forced to hire various other Indians to help him make his trips gathering information about the lungfish and other creatures of the Chaco.

During this time, reports reached Waik that Poit had killed

several of Mr. Grubb's cattle and had been providing nonstop feasts for anyone who wanted to attend. Kyemap was sure that Mr. Grubb must have heard the rumors, but the missionary never mentioned it to Kyemap.

One day Professor Kerr marched into the mission station sweating and as red as a dusty sunset. "You have a thief wandering around out there," he panted to Mr. Grubb. "And I want something done about it!"

"What are you talking about?" asked Mr. Grubb.

"I met some fellow on the trail who said he was a friend of yours," blurted Professor Kerr. "We were so shorthanded that I let him drive the cart, but then this morning when we broke camp, he had disappeared. And he took my new Winchester rifle with him!"

Mr. Grubb frowned. "How do you know?" he asked.

"I used it just yesterday to shoot at a peccary—a wild pig. I missed, but afterwards I put the rifle in the cart, and now it's gone," explained Kerr.

"Are you sure it didn't jostle out? It's pretty rough traveling out there," said Grubb.

"No, no. The case is still there—it's just the rifle that's missing. He took it; there's no other explanation," said Kerr.

"I'm sorry about your loss, Professor," said Mr. Grubb. "We'll put the word out. There are few enough guns here on the Chaco that if someone finds a Winchester and starts using it, word will soon get around."

The professor was not satisfied, but there wasn't anything he could do.

Later, when Mr. Grubb and Kyemap were planing lumber for a new medical clinic, Mr. Grubb asked, "What do you think about the professor's lost rifle? Has Poit come around lately?"

Kyemap shook his head. "I haven't seen him."

"What do you know about these rumors that he has given feasts?" he added.

Kyemap stopped his work and looked up. His cousin would be very angry if he told on him. "Who can tell about rumors?" he said. After thinking for a few moments he added, "He told me that he thought you were dead. Maybe he thought the cattle were his."

Mr. Grubb stopped planing the wood. "But I'm not dead! I came back in thirteen months, just like I promised. If he has killed some of my cattle, he's going to have to—" He did not finish his threat.

After a few moments, Kyemap spoke again. "Maybe that's why he hasn't come to see you. He's probably afraid."

CHAPTER 7

DEAD MAN WALKING

Professor Kerr and his funny-looking assistant finally left the Chaco and returned to England. They were happy with all the research they had done on lungfish. However, Mr. Grubb did not think they would be back to set up a fish canning factory.

Weeks later, Kyemap was sweeping the steps when Poit and three strange Indians walked up to the missionary's house. "Well, if it isn't my favorite cousin," Poit announced. "You still working here for nothing?"

Kyemap stopped sweeping and wiped the back of his hand across his sweaty forehead. If he was Poit's "favorite," he'd hate to see how Poit treated an unpopular cousin.

Mr. Grubb came out onto the porch, letting the screen door slam behind him. Kyemap looked around to see a frown on his face. "Poit!" Grubb said gruffly. "I hear that you—"

"Mr. Grubb!" Poit interrupted. "Mr. Grubb, I have brought

you three Toothli Indians who would like you to come visit their tribe in the West."

Mr. Grubb's frown melted into a smile. "Toothli Indians? Welcome! Welcome! Kyemap, would you please go make tea for everyone? Then come and join us under the mesquite trees out back."

Kyemap shook his head as he walked into the house. Poit's diversion had worked. That rascal could get away with anything. Kyemap knelt down and opened the door on the small black iron stove and blew on the coals. Then he checked to see that there was enough water in the kettle on top.

A few minutes later, when he went out to the chairs under the trees carrying the tray with a pot of tea and cups for everyone, Poit was in busy conversation with Mr. Grubb, translating what the Toothlis were saying . . . or that was what he was claiming to do. But who knew? Maybe his cousin was making it all up in order to interest Mr. Grubb and keep him from asking about the cattle or the professor's rifle. The Lengua and the Toothli languages were similar, but Kyemap could only understand a few words, and it was obvious that Mr. Grubb couldn't catch any of it.

The Toothli visitors had to leave that afternoon. But it was decided that as soon as Mr. Grubb could make arrangements, he and Poit would travel west to visit the Toothli people. "Tell them that we'll stop on the way at Namuk and pick up some of my cattle and bring them as gifts," Mr. Grubb said, smiling at the Toothli men.

Kyemap was watching Poit and saw his face turn gray and his eyes flicker with fear at the mention of cattle. But Poit recovered quickly and began speaking to the visitors using a lot of excited hand gestures. Again, Kyemap could not follow what he said, but he did not hear the word "cow," which he should have been able to recognize, even in the Toothli langauge.

———

A disease had recently killed many of the horses in that part of the Chaco, and those who hadn't died had been greatly weakened by the disease. Mr. Grubb decided that the trip to the West should be made on foot. But at the Sunday service when he said that he wanted to hire several Indians to help carry supplies, the villagers began urging him not to go. One old woman stood up and said sadly, "Please, Mr. Grubb, I have had a dream about you. If you go to the West, you will leave your bones along the road to whiten in the sun."

"Thank you for your concern," said the missionary kindly, "but you know I don't believe in superstitious dreams. This is an important trip to reach the Toothli tribe. Poit will be my guide, but I need five more men to carry supplies. Today is December 12, and I want to get going tomorrow. Who will go with me?"

Reluctantly, five men raised their hands, but as the villagers left the service, several were shaking their heads and muttering, "He should not go. He has been traveling too much and should stay home."

Light was just spreading up the eastern sky when Kyemap arrived at Mr. Grubb's house the next morning. The idea was to get in as much traveling as they could before the hot sun forced them to stop. But when the missionary came out onto his porch, he said, "I'm sorry, Kyemap, but you will not be going with me this time. Robert Graham needs help with the Lengua language. I know he's new, but he seems to be having an awful time. You could be a big help to him."

Kyemap didn't mean to make a face at the missionary's

request, but he was tired of "lessons"! Even in the gray dawn Mr. Grubb must have seen his displeasure because he quickly added, "You don't have to sit around with him as though you were in a class. He needs help in the mission store; someone stole $28 from there the other day. So just answer his questions, and for goodness' sake, help him get his accent right. He talks like he has a chicken bone in his mouth."

Half an hour later, Kyemap watched with a heavy face and sagging shoulders as his cousin gave orders to the other Indians about what order they should walk in—with himself in the lead beside Mr. Grubb, of course—and how they had all better "keep up" or he would withhold their pay. Kyemap's eyes narrowed. How had *he* become boss? Then the little procession headed out of Waik until their blue shadows disappeared into the rosy mists of the early Chaco morning.

———

Nine days later as Kyemap was closing up the little store in the evening, a messenger came running into the mission station from the direction of the setting sun. He had been running so long and hard that he collapsed on the ground and was barely able to gasp, "News! . . . Grubb . . . dead!"

Kyemap had no idea how the word spread, but within moments all the missionaries and thirty or forty villagers had gathered around the sweating man who had finally raised himself to a sitting position as he panted for breath.

Robert Graham was pulling on Kyemap's arm. "What did he say? I couldn't understand him. What did he say?"

In his faltering English, Kyemap told the new missionary what the man had said.

"What do you mean, 'dead'?" demanded Richard Hunt, bending over the runner. "How can that be?" Then, because their house was closest, he turned to his wife. "Mary, would you fetch a cup of water? The man has exhausted himself."

"Are you sure it was Grubb?" said Sibeth, the cart driver.

Once Mrs. Hunt brought the water and the man drank a little, he tried to explain. "Somewhere in Jaguar Swamp . . ." he panted for more air, " . . . possibly twenty-five miles west of Poit's village, . . . Namuk, . . . not far from Toothli territory . . ." He stopped and reached again for the cup of water.

"Just tell us what happened, man!" demanded Mr. Hunt.

"Jaguar! Grubb and Poit were attacked by a jaguar," he blurted.

"But how did you find out?" said Hunt.

The man was finally recovering his breath. "Poit—he managed to escape. But Grubb died, and Poit was unable to retrieve his body from the huge cat."

A great hubbub went through the growing crowd. Sibeth growled, "If he didn't get his body, how can Poit be sure Grubb was dead? Maybe he was just badly injured. Maybe he needs help. Did anyone else go out to check?"

"I don't know," said the messenger, starting to cough. "All I know"—*cough, cough*—"is what the last runner told me."

"Well, I'm going after him!" declared Sibeth. "If there is any chance of retrieving his body for burial, someone has to go."

"Me too," added Robert Graham.

Dozens of the villagers joined in, saying that they were going, too. They would catch that "deceitful Poit," as they called him, and find out why he hadn't taken better care of *their* Mr. Grubb. But the missionaries urged them to calm down and wait patiently. They had only heard the first report from the scene, and no one knew for sure what had happened. Sibeth and Graham could handle whatever needed doing.

This time Kyemap decided that he was not going to be left behind.

There were only two horses left in the mission station that were healthy enough to ride, and sometimes, when the fever struck them, even they wobbled like newborn colts. It was midnight when Sibeth and Graham rode out of Waik. Kyemap watched from the shadows of the huts at the edge of the village until they were out of sight, and then he followed quietly.

It was not hard to keep up with the weak horses, but Kyemap kept his distance until dawn when Graham and Sibeth arrived at Paisiam. Chief Mechi and all the villagers came out of their huts to see if the foreigners had any more news. Graham and Sibeth, of course, were wondering the same of the villagers. Sibeth knew the Lengua language better than Graham, but still there were immediate problems of communication. That's when Kyemap stepped forward.

"Kyemap! What are you doing here?" asked Graham.

"I thought you might use some help translating," suggested Kyemap. "So I followed along."

The two foreigners frowned but quickly asked Kyemap if the villagers had any more news about Mr. Grubb.

There was no new information about Mr. Grubb, but someone did say that Poit was traveling toward them. "He is on his way back to Waik," said the villager. "If you hurry, you may be able to meet him at the village of Mopai by nightfall."

Mopai was another thirty-five miles west. Tired as they were, the possibility of hearing directly from Poit about what had happened urged Sibeth, Graham, and Kyemap on. As they left Paisiam, Kyemap looked with longing at Chief Mechi's horse in its palm-shaded coral. It was the healthiest-looking horse he'd seen on the Chaco since the horse disease had come, but the chief did not offer it for him to ride. Probably he knew three couldn't ride one horse, and Kyemap could certainly walk as fast as the weakened beasts Sibeth and Graham rode.

———

Kyemap had never walked so far in one day in his entire life. When the party from Waik finally straggled into Mopai, several people gathered around them, but it was an old woman who offered information. "Yes, yes. Poit is here, but he is hiding in a hut and will not talk to anyone." Then, after a long pause, her wrinkled face brightened and she waved her finger from side to side. "But Mr. Grubb is not dead!"

"W-what?" stammered Kyemap.

"He is not dead—not yet!" she added.

This information created a great deal of confusion as Kyemap tried to get the story straight and explain it to Graham and Sibeth. Apparently, said the woman, Mr. Grubb had been severely wounded but had managed to crawl to a trail where an Indian found him and took him to a village on the Lengua frontier. "But he will die soon," said the women solemnly. She had gotten her information from a second news runner who had arrived after Poit. "Mr. Grubb lost much, much blood. He is not dead yet, but by now, he is no more than a dead man walking."

She then led the three people from Waik along with several local people to the hut where Poit was hiding. Kyemap could hardly believe what he found inside. The filthy, wide-eyed creature that cowered in the corner looked very little like his proud elder cousin. For some time, Poit only grunted responses to their questions.

"Come on, now, man," urged Graham, "speak up. Is Mr. Grubb dead or alive?"

After Kyemap translated the question for the fifth time, Poit finally said, "He *was* dead."

"What do you mean, 'He *was* dead'? They say he is alive. They say he crawled away. Why did you leave him?" pressed Sibeth in an angry voice.

"I *thought* he was dead," pleaded Poit like a whimpering child. "I saw him go down. There was nothing I could do."

After Kyemap translated, Sibeth shouted, "Why didn't you get some Indians from the next village and go back for him?"

"I don't know! I don't know!" protested Poit. "I was afraid. . . . I didn't know where I was. I barely escaped with my own life. The jaguar was very fierce!"

"Jaguar?" said the old woman, who was still standing in the entrance to the hut. "The runner didn't say anything about a jaguar. He said Mr. Grubb had been shot in the back with an arrow!"

CHAPTER 8

GHOST OF THE CHACO

No, no!" Poit protested in a panic-stricken voice. "That can't be true. We were attacked by the jaguar."

Sibeth understood enough of this answer not to need translation. "Then where are your arrows?" he demanded, pointing at the bow that lay in the dust beside Poit.

In the dim light of the hut, Poit frowned as though he was trying to remember something. Then he began speaking as though he were in a dream. "I had five arrows . . . yes, five arrows, and I shot them all at the jaguar." But the more he spoke, the more excited he became. "I wounded that great cat, making it all the more dangerous—that's why I couldn't go to Grubb's aid. I had no weapon!" he said as though he had finally discovered the answer to an important puzzle.

"But if Mr. Grubb was wounded by an arrow in the back," challenged Graham, "then it must have come from you. *You* shot him, and if he dies, you will have killed him!"

"No, no, no!" protested Poit as he dissolved into sobs. "I couldn't have killed him."

They talked on and on with the confused Poit until he finally admitted that one of his arrows *might* have hit Grubb accidentally. "But by then," he protested, "he was so severely mauled by the jaguar that it wouldn't have made any difference. He was dying. What could I do?"

"What could you do?" said Kyemap with disgust. "The least you could have done was to go for help." It was the first comment Kyemap had made on his own that had not been the translation of another's question.

Poit jumped to his feet. With hands on his hips and his nose just inches from Kyemap's face, he snapped, "Who are you to challenge me, you half-grown grasshopper? I did not kill Mr. Grubb! The jaguar killed him, and I did everything I could to defend him. I shot all my arrows at that enormous cat. The cat was wounded by my arrows, and everyone knows that it is impossible to approach a wounded cat!"

With that he pushed his way through the people and out the door of the hut. As he stalked through the dusty village, his pace got faster and faster until he ran out the other side and into the forest north of Mopai.

———

It was Saturday, Christmas Day, when the three from Waik—hoping now to be Mr. Grubb's rescuers—arrived at Namuk, Poit's village. Poit, of course, was not there. He had disappeared into the jungle, but the rescuers didn't care because they were looking for Mr. Grubb.

"Yes, yes," the villagers said, "Mr. Grubb slept here last night. He came to us staggering—sometimes crawling—from a village many miles west of here, but he would not stay with us.

He insisted he had to get back to Waik. We gave him our only remaining horse. It could barely walk, and so we sent two men to walk alongside to keep Mr. Grubb from falling off. But . . . he will die soon," they said sadly, and everyone nodded their heads in sad agreement.

"Something's not right," said Graham after hearing the villager's story. "They are not telling the truth. How could we have missed Mr. Grubb if he were on his way to Waik? We have just come from that direction."

But when Kyemap questioned the villagers, they pointed down a different trail. "It was getting so hot, that our old horse could never have traveled across the open Chaco. So we sent Mr. Grubb through the forest."

It was a likely explanation. The temperature had already climbed to 110 degrees in the shade. Without taking time for rest or refreshment, the rescue party headed down the trail indicated by the villagers.

Walking ahead of the missionaries, Kyemap found fresh hoofprints on the forest trail. "They can't be far ahead now!" he announced to Sibeth and Graham following behind on the sickly horses, whose heads hung almost to the ground.

Ten minutes later, they came out of the trees and into a marsh with grass that was five feet high. "Can you see them?" asked Kyemap anxiously.

Sibeth stood in his stirrups, looking out across the plain. "No," he said. "How could they have disappeared? . . . No, wait! . . . I see something, straight ahead! Grubb must be down, because the grass hid them all."

They hurried forward to an opening where a wheezing horse, down on its side, had flattened the grass. A couple feet away were three men. Mr. Grubb sat in the ankle-deep marsh water with an Indian supporting him on either side. Blood and drool dripped from his mouth as he coughed weakly, trying to get his breath.

Kyemap arrived at his side only seconds before Graham and Sibeth had time to drop from their horses and sprint the last few yards.

"We're here; we're here, brother," Andrew Graham said in English as he replaced the Indian on the other side of Grubb.

Grubb looked hollowly from one to the other of his rescuers. Feebly, he pointed to Kyemap on one side as he spoke to Graham on his other side, "Hasn't . . . this boy . . . taught you Lengua yet? What have you two . . . been doing with your time?" His weak laugh at his own joke turned into a coughing fit that brought up more blood.

———

Somehow the rescue party managed to get Grubb back on one of the horses, and they returned to Namuk, where they tried to make him as comfortable as possible. He had only one wound, a deep and terrible hole in his back that looked far more like an arrow wound than anything a jaguar could have done. When Kyemap pointed this out to Graham and Sibeth, they shook their heads. "Let's not question him about what happened just now," said Sibeth. "There'll be time enough for that later . . . if we can get him safely back to Waik."

They couldn't have questioned Mr. Grubb if they had wanted to, because by then he was losing consciousness and mumbling gibberish. "We've got to get him back to Waik," said Graham. "He needs medicines and clean bandages."

"At least let him rest until tomorrow," said Sibeth. Kyemap volunteered to stay with Mr. Grubb the remainder of that day and all during the night, bathing him when his fever raged and comforting him with hot rocks wrapped in blankets when he shivered from chill.

Kyemap did not sleep all night, but in the early dawn when Mr. Grubb slept peacefully for the first time, Kyemap left the hut to stretch his legs. Outside, he noticed one of the village hunters talking to a friend and showing off a small bag of money. Could this man be the thief who had stolen the money from the mission store? Kyemap had never seen him at Waik. Nevertheless, he casually walked over to the man and asked, "How did someone way back here in the bush get so much money?"

"It walks across the Chaco," the hunter said through a wide, toothless grin.

"Traveling money, huh?" Kyemap observed. "How much is it?"

The man shrugged but agreeably leaned down and dumped out the coins on a split log. Kyemap quickly counted the coins and realized that they amounted to exactly twenty-eight dollars. "Were you ever at Waik?" he asked.

The man shook his head solemnly.

"Then where did you get this white man's money?"

The hunter just laughed and said, "I sold my iron-tipped arrows, all five of them." Then he walked away.

Kyemap did not have time to consider what this meant because Sibeth was calling to him. Knowing that their two sick horses were almost spent, and fearing that Mr. Grubb might not be able to stay astride a horse anyway, Sibeth had built a travois to carry him. "What do you think of this?" he asked as he led his tired horse to the front of the hut in which Mr. Grubb slept. Two long poles were tied to the saddle, one on each side and dragging on the ground behind. A blanket was tied to the two poles like a stretcher.

Kyemap agreed that it was better than trying to keep Grubb on a horse. "But the going will be slower," he said.

"Not any slower than if this horse gives out . . . or Grubb falls off," Sibeth added.

———

A long day of hard travel brought the bedraggled party to Mopai. Grubb didn't seem to be any worse, but he still hadn't regained his senses enough to know where he was. He did seem to know that he was with friends, though, and often reached out a feeble hand to take comfort in their touch.

After two more days of slow travel, the party arrived at Paisiam. From the point of his attack, Grubb had traveled over ninety miles in his weakened condition. "Hang on, you can make it," encouraged Robert Graham as he walked alongside the missionary. "We'll spend the night here, and tomorrow there'll be only another fifteen miles to go before we get you to the mission station."

But as they entered Paisiam, Kyemap noticed a strange response from the villagers. They all crowded around the slowly-moving travois, but the moment they saw Mr. Grubb, they drew back, some holding their hands over their mouths, others staring at the missionary from a distance. A few even ran to their huts and disappeared inside.

Kyemap looked at Mr. Grubb. His eyes were closed as his head rocked slowly back and forth with the motion of the travois, and his pale face was covered by the dark stubble of a short beard—that strange feature of foreigners—but Kyemap didn't think he looked *that* bad.

Then Chief Mechi came alongside the travois. He stared at Grubb a long time, walking just slower than the horse so that distance increased between himself and the injured missionary. Finally, he turned to Kyemap and said, "Is it really Mr. Grubb?"

"Of course," said Kyemap. "Who else could he be?"

The chief looked this way and that. "Who knows? Mr. Grubb *was* dead, wasn't he? We all heard the reports." Then the chief added confidentially, "Maybe some other spirit took over his body. Maybe . . . he is a ghost!"

CHAPTER 9

THE IRON ARROW

Wisps of a merciless Chaco breeze brushed Kyemap's face like hot feathers as the rescue party plodded into Waik shortly before sunset.

"Did I miss Christmas?" whispered Mr. Grubb from his rickety travois.

"I'm afraid so," said Sibeth. "It's December 29, but you're finally home, so rest easy."

Just as in Paisiam, the villagers of Waik quickly gathered around and elbowed one another aside to get a look at what appeared to float in a little swirl of dust behind the frail horse. Again Kyemap heard the hushed word "ghost" muttered from one person to another as they shrank back from the shadow of a man on the travois.

For two days Kyemap nursed Mr. Grubb before he seemed to fully recover his senses. On New Year's Day the other missionaries and a few of the Indian elders gathered at Mr. Grubb's bedside. "Grubb, can you tell us what happened in the swamp?"

Richard Hunt asked. Kyemap noticed that one of the five carriers who had started the trip with Mr. Grubb and Poit had come with the little group.

Mr. Grubb frowned, as though trying to remember. "From early on," he said, "things didn't go right. We were only a short distance beyond Mopai when for some reason our five Indian carriers lagged behind." He took a sip of water from the glass that Kyemap had placed on the small table beside his bed. "I didn't think much of it. It was hot, and they had heavy loads, so I thought they were picking some fruit or something. Finally, however, about noon, I sat down under a tree and sent Poit back to hurry them up.

"For some reason, Poit took a long time, and when he finally came back, he had a little food and my teakettle, but no carriers followed him. 'One of them ran a long thorn into his foot,' Poit told me. 'They'll catch us by evening.' "

"But . . . that's not right!" said the carrier. "Poit told us to go back to Mopai and wait there. He said it might be two weeks before you came back for us."

"He told you what?" said Mr. Grubb. "But why would we have hired you as carriers only to dismiss you when we were just halfway there? Unless . . ." His voice trailed off.

The Indian carrier raised his palms in a helpless manner. "We couldn't understand why you didn't need your supplies or would go on alone, but Poit said those were your instructions, so . . . we went back."

"Yes, I'm beginning to see," said Grubb.

Richard Hunt leaned forward, putting his elbows on his knees and folding his hands. "Then what happened?" he asked.

"Well, of course the carriers didn't catch up that night, and I was rather upset. But Poit said not to worry. We went on until a couple days later we got to his village, Namuk. The first thing I wanted to do was check my cattle, but Poit kept putting me off, saying they were out to pasture and it would take too long to round them up. I guess I became upset, because I told him to have his relatives round up all the cattle by the time we returned or he would be in big trouble."

Mr. Grubb stopped, and Kyemap adjusted his pillow so he could sit up better. Then he continued. "The next morning I had Poit recruit some men from his village and some sweet potatoes and manioc and other items for trading, and we headed on west to the last Lengua village on the frontier. But that night I had a touch of malaria fever, and the next morning Poit suggested not leaving until the dew was off the swamp grass. We were very close to Jaguar Swamp by then. He sent the new carriers on ahead.

"While we were eating breakfast, I noticed that he had some new iron-tipped arrows and asked him about them. 'Oh, Mr. Grubb,' he said, 'this is jaguar country. My wooden arrows would never do if we met a big cat. So I traded them for these fine arrows back at Namuk.' "

Grubb took several deep breaths, and the listeners waited patiently till he was ready to go on. "Finally," he said, "we got under way, but it was already getting hot. Several times we crossed the river Monte until I asked Poit if he knew where he was going. It seemed like he was getting us lost. 'This is a shortcut,' he said. Still weak from the malaria attack, I was a little short-tempered and told him that if this was a shortcut, I'd rather stay on the trail. I was tired of tramping through bush and swamp.

"But I didn't know the way, so there was nothing to do but keep going. Eventually we entered a forest, but soon the undergrowth got so dense that our path was blocked. Poit then left me, saying he would scout a better trail. A short time later I heard something crackling branches in the thicket ahead, and I began making a lot of noise to scare away whatever it was, especially if it was a jaguar."

"Make noise?" injected Robert Graham, the newest missionary at the station. "I'd be inclined to keep silent and hope no wild animal would find me."

Sibeth snorted. "You never want to surprise a dangerous animal. Most wild animals prefer to get away from humans, but if you surprise one, it's likely to attack, thinking it is defending itself from you. No, making noise was the right thing."

"Yes," said Grubb absently. "Anyway, the crackling stopped, but then in a few minutes I saw Poit looking at me through the thicket with a very strange expression on his face. For a moment I wondered whether he had seen a jaguar, but then he said, 'The trail is clear over this way. Just push on through. It won't take long.' And he disappeared from sight into the foliage.

"After that, I tried to get through the thicket, but it was impossible. Then Poit called out again, 'Wait, I'll come help you.' I kept pushing at the tangle of vines and bushes until I felt this terrible blow to my back. It was so hard that it would have knocked me flat to the ground if the brush hadn't caught me.

"I struggled to regain my footing, I turned around to see Poit standing about five yards behind me with his bow in his hand. Then he yelled, 'Oh my! Oh my!' and ran off toward the river." Grubb stared off into space for a moment and then added, "I never saw him again."

"But was there a jaguar?" demanded Mr. Hunt, pointing his finger toward Mr. Grubb and tipping his head to the side as he asked the most crucial question.

Grubb shrugged. "I don't know, but . . . I don't think so. On the other hand, everything in my memory is a little fuzzy about what happened next."

"But obviously Poit shot you," said Hunt, "so the question is, why?"

"If there was a jaguar, and Poit shot at it, I suppose he could have accidentally shot me . . ." Grubb mused.

As everyone began discussing the possibility of whether Poit had been trying to shoot a jaguar or not or whether there even was a jaguar, Kyemap stepped away from the bed and stared through the screen that surrounded the sleeping porch. He frowned. There might have been a reason for Poit to shoot Grubb. He had told Kyemap that Grubb's cattle belonged to him now, and there had been rumors of big feasts. Also, Grubb said that when they went through Namuk, Poit made an excuse for not producing the herd for inspection. Was Poit so afraid of being found out about stealing Grubb's cattle that he decided to kill Mr. Grubb?

The thought seemed impossible! As much as Poit got on Kyemap's nerves, and even though Poit was a very selfish person, Kyemap could hardly believe his cousin would stoop to murder. That was too much . . . or was it?

Suddenly, Kyemap realized that Mr. Grubb was continuing his story. He turned back just as Grubb was saying, "That arrow was stuck in my back so deep that I couldn't pull it out. And when I tried to reach back there, the pain was so bad that I nearly passed out. I staggered along by the river's edge not knowing what to do until I came to this little sapling that had a Y about chest high. I finally worked myself around until I got the shaft of that arrow wedged between the two branches of that little sapling. When I was sure it was really caught, I just lunged forward and let myself fall.

"The pain was so great that I blacked out. When I woke up, blood was all over me, and I was coughing up more. I knew right then that my lung had been punctured, and I thought for sure that I was dead. But I couldn't just give up and die. I cried out to God to see me through, and then I began crawling."

"Excuse me," said Kyemap. "Did you get a look at that arrow?"

"Oh yes," Grubb said, his eyes going wide. "It was a wicked one, an iron-tipped arrow—one of those he had traded his own arrows for, I suppose. That arrowhead was nearly seven inches long, and the tip had bent over, probably where it had hit my bone. I suppose that's why it was so hard to pull out."

Everyone groaned.

"Anyway," continued Grubb, "I crawled on until I came to the river's edge. There was nowhere to turn, so I had to go through. The cool water refreshed me somewhat, but I kept worrying that if I fainted again, I would certainly drown, so I hung on until I came up on the other side. I struggled on through the forest for I don't know how long until I came across a trail, and then I collapsed. I didn't pass out, but I literally couldn't muster enough strength to go farther.

"But God was with me, because within an hour a man came jogging down the trail. He was returning home to his village—the very one we had stayed in the night before. He recognized me and helped lean me up against a tree and then went for help. Before long several kind villagers arrived and made a stretcher to carry me back to the village."

Robert Graham blew air through his lips as though he had been holding his breath for the last of the story. "I'm sure you were glad that ordeal was over," he said. "Thank God!"

"Thank God, indeed," said Grubb, "but I was far from being out of danger."

"What do you mean?" said Graham. "You said those people were very friendly."

"They were, but the Lengua people are also very superstitious." Grubb took another sip of water. "I was in danger from two of their beliefs. First, they believe that anyone who passes out is dead, so I was even afraid to fall asleep. What if they couldn't wake me? Second, they believe if a person dies in their village at night, his ghost will haunt their village, and they have to move. Isn't that right, Kyemap?"

Kyemap dropped his head. "Yes, sir," he mumbled. Then he looked up at the other people around Grubb's bed. Why should he feel embarrassed about such superstitions? They were not of his making. In a matter-of-fact tone he added, "My grandmother was buried when she was still awake because the witch doctor said she would die that night, and no one wanted her to die in the village after dark." Then he grinned at Mr. Grubb. "But I don't believe in ghosts anymore."

"I sure could have used a few people like you in that village!" said Grubb. "No one even knew how to clean my wound." He paused as though recalling events. "One of the first things I did when I was clearheaded enough to think was send a messenger back here to Waik to tell you about my state. I was so grateful when you three came for me!

"Now, where was I in my story? Oh yes. As you can imagine, I didn't get much rest that night. The next day many people came to visit me, even from neighboring villages. Everyone shook their heads and said they had never seen anyone with such a severe wound who survived—not very encouraging, I can tell you. But they meant no harm." Grubb chuckled. "They told me they intended to take the best possible care of me. They had even selected a beautiful spot under a nice shade tree for my last resting place. That evening, the children kept coming up to me and saying, 'It's getting dark. Are you strong?' You can believe that I did some very serious praying that nothing would happen during the night to make them think that I had lost consciousness. Though I napped a little that night, I did not permit myself to fall into a deep sleep.

"The next morning I forced myself to begin traveling east. I was so dizzy that if I hadn't had the help of some kind Indians, I'm certain that I would have wandered in circles. Sometimes I walked. Sometimes I rested. One of the Indians even offered to carry me on his back, but that didn't work. Finally, with the Lord's help, I made it to Namuk, which is where Sibeth, Graham, and Kyemap found me. And—well, you know the rest."

As Mr. Grubb ended his story, the conversation once again turned to why Poit might have shot Mr. Grubb. Had he missed the jaguar and hit Grubb by accident? Had there even been a jaguar? If not, it looked as though the shooting was intentional, but no one could think of why he would do such a thing. Still, Poit had run off. Why?

There was only one way to solve the mystery: Find Poit and get the truth from him!

CHAPTER 10

THE MANHUNT

While the other people around Mr. Grubb's bed discussed Poit's motives and whereabouts, Kyemap wandered out the front door. *He* could think of a motive for why Poit might have shot Mr. Grubb! Poit hadn't wanted him to find out about the cattle he had killed and the feasts he had held.

In fact, Kyemap had an idea of who had taken the money from the mission store and why. It all fit together! Poit had stolen the money from the mission store to buy the iron-tipped arrows. Then he tried to kill Mr. Grubb to cover his greed in taking the missionary's cattle.

But as much as Kyemap disliked Poit, he was his cousin. Kyemap couldn't condemn his own relative without being absolutely sure of his guilt.

He sat down on the bottom step of Mr. Grubb's house, which creaked loudly with his weight. The cicadas were whining in the nearby mesquite trees, and the air smelled like rain might finally fall from the gold and gray thunderheads that boiled in the sky over the Chaco.

Kyemap picked up a mesquite pod, snapped it open, and began gnawing absently at the sweet pulp inside. Finding Poit could be a problem. He traveled so much that he might have a dozen places to hide. There might even be whole villages that would protect him.

Suddenly, Kyemap threw down the remains of the mesquite pod and got up. There was one place he could look, a place no one else knew about—Poit's private "hunting lodge," the bottle trunk tree he had hollowed out down near the Sievo River. Could he find it again?

Saying nothing to anyone about where he was going, Kyemap stopped by his hut to pick up his drinking gourd, then headed out of the village and across the Chaco.

———

The heavy, damp air felt exhausting. After hours of trying, it had failed to wring any rain from the clouds that were now breaking up in the west to reveal a sunset that looked like pink rose petals thrown on a blue pond. Kyemap slowed his easy jog to a walk. He recognized the grassy plain that bordered the Sievo River. Just a short distance upstream he would find the bottle trunk tree Poit used for his hunting lodge. The sharp grass stung his legs. He would welcome a rest at Poit's hidden lodge.

But when he finally saw the lone tree with its bulbous trunk and spindly, crooked limbs sprayed out from the top of the trunk, he hesitated. What if Poit were hiding there now and didn't want to be found—by anyone? He might be very angry that Kyemap had come. And if Poit had actually tried to kill Mr. Grubb, would he become violent if Kyemap confronted his cousin about the shooting?

The young Indian observed the tree from a distance. There was no smoke coming out of the dark gash down one side, and Kyemap did not see any personal belongings scattered about outside. He waited for a long time, then slowly circled to get a better view.

"Poit, you there?" he called in a tentative voice. He shivered—even though the air was as heavy as steam from a stew pot—and took a few more steps. "Poit?"

There was no response.

He waited fifteen minutes, then half an hour as the sky cleared and the pink clouds that had streaked the West faded to gray. The light on the Chaco dimmed, washing out the browns, yellows, greens, blacks, and whites until everything was either a lighter or darker shade of the same blue. Kyemap crept closer, bending low and letting the tall grass and occasional bush hide his body, and still there was no sign of Poit. He called once more, then stood up straight and looked all around the clearing. Either his cousin was there or not. It was time to find out. He walked directly toward the peculiar tree.

As he put his hand against the tree, he said, "Poit?" one last time before sticking his head into the opening, but by then he knew no one was there. The grass outside had not been trampled by any recent traffic.

Inside there was just enough room for a man to squat down. Kyemap felt around in the dark. Some hunting lodge! Anyone who spent the night in a place as small as this would be so cramped the next morning that a snail could outrun him.

Then Kyemap felt something cold and hard and long. It was metal. It was heavy. Carefully, he picked it up and held it in the dim light that came through the entrance. A rifle. Kyemap rolled it from side to side in his hand, feeling the balance of the gun. Cautiously, he cocked the lever downward under the handle. The rifle was empty. He felt around on the floor of the hiding place and then on the walls in case a bag of ammunition was hanging there. Nothing!

He stepped outside and looked around the clearing as though he expected Poit to return any moment. Then in the better light, he examined the rifle again. He had seen its custom engraved side panels before. It was Professor Kerr's new Winchester rifle, with tiny specs of rust already etching their way into its blue barrel.

Kyemap looked back at the entrance in the bottle trunk tree. The evidence appeared even worse for Poit. Had he stolen the professor's rifle thinking he would kill Mr. Grubb with it only to find it had no bullets in it? When that didn't work out, had he taken money from the mission store in order to purchase the next best weapon, the iron-tipped arrows? "Oh, cousin, I hope this is not true," Kyemap said to the still evening air. "Selfish as you are, I cannot believe you would commit murder!"

Was there any way to prove that Poit had not intended to shoot Mr. Grubb? Had he bought the arrows, as he said, as protection from the jaguar?

Kyemap looked up at the purple sky. A bright moon, two nights beyond first quarter, was just rising. In spite of the clouds that often came up in the afternoons, it had not rained for over a week, since before Mr. Grubb was shot. If it had not rained in the west, either, then there still ought to be tracks in the soft, swampy ground where the shooting had occurred. Jaguars were big, heavy cats. If one had been there, ready to attack Mr. Grubb as Poit claimed, it would leave tracks, and those tracks should still be visible.

He would go and find proof for what really happened. If it was an accident, he would prove it.

———

When Kyemap arrived at Paisiam, only a few miles from Poit's bottle trunk tree, most of the men were already out looking for Poit. It seemed like the whole Lengua people had been alerted that Poit was a wanted man. The missionaries had only wanted to question him, but as Kyemap listened to the Indians talk, it was obvious that many of them considered him guilty of murder.

When Kyemap heard the word *murder* mentioned by a group of women—and a few old men—who were gossiping around a common fire, he slipped away into the dark shadows of the village. This was becoming serious. If Poit were caught and found to be guilty of murder, he could be sentenced to death. If that happened, the Lengua custom was to also kill all immediate family members. It was a harsh but effective way to prevent feuds—no one was left alive who cared enough to take revenge on the executioners.

A knot of fear pinched his stomach. It was unlikely that the elimination of family members would reach as far as Kyemap's family, he reasoned—they weren't that closely related to Poit. But during the past year Kyemap himself had spent a lot of time with Poit. Once people had drunk enough strong beer, it was never certain where the killing would stop. They might think he was close enough to Poit that he would want to take revenge. His life could be in danger, too.

The moon lit his way as Kyemap wove through the village huts until he came to Chief Mechi's home. The old chief was more levelheaded than many people, and Kyemap hoped he could trust him with his plan. "Chief Mechi?" he called softly from outside the hut. "Chief Mechi?"

Someone stirred inside and came to pull back the dusty blanket that served as a door. In the soft moonlight, Kyemap could see the pearly cataracts that blinded the old chief's eyes. "Who is it?" he said.

"I am Kyemap. I come from Yitlo-yimmaling, a very small village in the west, but I think you know my father. He used to hunt with you for tapirs every year."

"Oh yes. Come in," he said, holding back the blanket. "I'm sorry I have no candle or fire. Light doesn't help me much anymore, at least not in my own hut."

Kyemap tripped over a water jug before he found a seat on a mat near the chief's bed. After a respectful silence, he said, "I have come to beg your help and the use of your fine horse. It is the only way I can make the long trip I must make in time to be of any good."

Then he told of his plan to travel west to the site where Mr. Grubb had been shot to see if there were tracks of a struggle with a jaguar or any jaguar tracks at all. "With your horse, I could be back in three or four days; but if I walk, they could find and try Poit before I get back."

The old chief thought for a few minutes and then said, "Finding jaguar tracks may not prove anything. With all that blood there, it is quite likely that a cat came to investigate afterward even if it wasn't about to attack."

In the dark, Kyemap's shoulders slumped. Then after a moment he spoke up. "But if there was some sign of a fight, that would prove Poit was telling the truth, wouldn't it?"

"Yes," said the chief softly. "But it doesn't sound like the cat actually attacked. Poit finally gave up on that story, and Mr. Grubb has no scratches. If there was a jaguar, how will you know whether it was there at the time of the shooting or came later to investigate the smell of blood?"

Kyemap considered. "The only thing I can hope for is if I can find a human footprint on top of a jaguar print. That would show that the cat was there first."

"Yes," admitted the chief. "But even if all Poit said was true, finding such a pair of footprints would be as unlikely as finding a stone on the Chaco." (The chief said this because there were almost no stones in the central Chaco. It was one vast plain of silt and sand, washed down from the Andes.) "Nevertheless," said the chief with a sigh, "you may use my horse. It is better to know than not to know. May God go with you!"

Kyemap stood up, mumbling his thank-yous in surprise. Was the old chief coming to believe in Mr. Grubb's God? Sometimes he did attend the Sunday morning services at Waik. His comment certainly was not a Lengua thing to say. The Lengua tradition did not believe in any kind of a good God who would go with, help, or protect anyone. That was definitely a Christian idea.

CHAPTER 11

ON TRIAL

Two days later, Kyemap rode into the village where the helpful natives had first brought the wounded Mr. Grubb. Arriving on a healthy horse aroused considerable attention. Everyone wanted to know where he got the horse. Soon the man Kyemap was looking for was standing among the children and other villagers who had gathered around his horse. Directions to where the man had found Grubb were simple enough, but the man had no idea where Grubb had crawled from before he collapsed on the trail.

Kyemap thanked them and headed out of the village with children trailing alongside until they grew tired and turned back. However, the closer Kyemap got to the place where the villager had found Mr. Grubb, the more impossible his task seemed. Finally, he reined in his horse in a small stand of palm trees that looked just like the villager had described. Was it the place? Or would there be another grove farther along? Kyemap went to the edge of the trees. Beyond them the land was flat.

As far as he could see, scrub brush extended to the south and swamp to the north. There were no more groves of trees.

He dismounted the horse and began his search. Mr. Grubb had described crossing the river, so he must have come from that direction, from the north, so that is where Kyemap went. There was no trail, but some of the tangles of plants and vines were so thick that no one could have come through them.

At the river, he waded across. Was that how Mr. Grubb had come? How many times had he crossed a river? Had he gone in circles? Grubb had been almost out of his mind with pain and loss of blood. Were any of his memories accurate? On and on, Kyemap trudged through thicker and thicker foliage. Every few feet he waded through swamp water. This was Jaguar Swamp, all right. What if there was a killer jaguar following him even then? Hopefully, the horse that he led behind him would smell it and give him a warning.

He stopped to listen but heard nothing other than frogs and birds. Maybe he ought to give up. How would he ever find the site of the shooting in a tangle like this?

And then, just when he was about to turn around, he spied a sapling with an arrow wedged between its limbs. "That's it," he said aloud. Dark, almost black, blood still smeared the arrow shaft and the iron arrowhead. And like Mr. Grubb had said, the tip was bent over. Yanking it out must have hurt more than Kyemap could imagine.

In the soft ground in front of the sapling, Kyemap could see where the missionary had fallen. There was still blood on some of the grass. Carefully, he began tracing Grubb's tracks back to a thicket where the shooting had taken place. Every few feet along the way, there where human footprints—undoubtedly Mr. Grubb's—but no jaguar prints. Finally, Kyemap discovered where Grubb had been hacking on the vines to get through.

Grubb's machete was stabbed in the ground where it had probably fallen. Still there were no signs of a great cat.

Kyemap stood up straight and surveyed the area. Poit had claimed to shoot all his arrows at a jaguar. If he had done that, and one had accidentally missed and hit Mr. Grubb in the back, then the jaguar must have been beyond Grubb, and Poit must have been shooting from that direction. Grubb had said Poit was only five or so yards away.

Kyemap tied the horse to a bush and carefully walked to the place he had calculated Poit to be. There, indeed, were prints of Poit's bare feet in the soft ground. He turned around to face where Grubb had been hacking at the thicket with his machete. But the more Kyemap looked at the scene, the more impossible Poit's story seemed. If there had been a great cat in that thicket, how could he have seen it through the dense undergrowth? How could he have hoped to hit it with arrows? How could the cat have been in the process of attacking Mr. Grubb? Nothing could have gotten through that dense tangle, at least not quickly.

One thing was certain, there was no sign of a fight with a wild animal. In fact, there were no tracks of a jaguar anywhere. But how could Kyemap be sure? Maybe he was in the wrong spot. After all, both Grubb and Poit had been struggling to get through the underbrush for some time before the shooting. So even though he had found the machete, maybe the shooting had occurred to one side or the other.

Kyemap was turning aside to check out other options when he noticed something under a bush. He reached for the long tan rods and pulled out four iron-tipped arrows.

Kyemap sighed as though all the air he had ever breathed was leaving his lungs. There was no doubt. His cousin Poit had not shot all five arrows at a jaguar as he had claimed.

There had been no jaguar! Poit had shot one arrow at Grubb, intending to kill him.

———

Two years ago Kyemap would have refused to be alone at night out on the Chaco for fear of wandering evil spirits, but Mr. Grubb had helped him conquer that fear. At this point, the thing he feared most was facing other people when he knew his cousin was guilty of trying to kill Mr. Grubb. On his way back to Paisiam, Kyemap rode around villages and settlements and avoided meeting people on the trail whenever he could. At night he camped alone with nothing but a small fire and his striped blanket. Of course, Chief Mechi's horse tethered nearby was some comfort, but still he felt edgy. He knew that an awful confrontation awaited him somewhere ahead, and it wouldn't be with a ghost.

He would have to face his cousin with the truth of what he had discovered. He would have to tell the elders and other villagers about the proof he had found. That might seal Poit's fate. And if it led to Poit's execution, he might be next.

As he rode along the next day over the dry and dusty trail, Kyemap again went over the whole experience in his mind. Poit had come to Waik to discover whether Mr. Grubb was the one the old Lengua prophecies promised, the one who would reveal the mysteries of the spirit world. It seemed that Poit believed what Mr. Grubb said—at least he worked very hard to become Mr. Grubb's "number one man."

Kyemap straightened himself on the horse's back. Poit had stolen that position from him. Nevertheless, he admitted to himself, that was a small matter when his cousin's life was at stake—and maybe his own, too.

Mr. Grubb had entrusted Poit with a herd of cattle while

he went away to England, but Poit had stolen them for himself, probably concluding that Mr. Grubb was not God's messenger after all. When Mr. Grubb returned, Poit had become afraid that he would get in trouble for killing the cattle. And to cover one sin, he had committed a greater one in trying to kill Mr. Grubb.

The hours passed with the miles as Kyemap reviewed again and again what had happened. Why had Poit become so afraid that he would attempt murder? Yes, he would have been in trouble with Mr. Grubb for having killed the cattle, but that would have only been Mr. Grubb's displeasure. Unlike other foreigners who had entered the Chaco or some of the whites that the Indians met along the Paraguay River or in the town of Concepción, Mr. Grubb had never beaten or hurt anyone. All over the Chaco he was known for being kind and fair. So what had Poit feared so much that he thought he had to kill Mr. Grubb?

Darkness was descending and Kyemap was approaching the village of Paisiam when the answer finally came to him. It was greed that had motivated Poit. He wanted to be the most important Indian on the Chaco. When it looked like being Mr. Grubb's assistant would give him that position, he took that route. When Grubb went away, Poit couldn't imagine him coming back, so he decided to use the cattle to become the most important person in the western Chaco. But when Mr. Grubb returned, both plans fell apart. Mr. Grubb was about to discover the missing cattle and would not trust Poit any longer, and he would take away the rest of the cattle. That's when Poit must have decided to kill him. With Grubb out of the way by an "accident," at least Poit could continue buying his importance with the remaining cattle.

Poor Poit! Mr. Grubb would say he was trying to be

something he was not—foolish ambition. Mr. Grubb was eager to help the Indians become everything they could be, but not based on cheating and falsehoods.

———

An orange light from the huge bonfire in the center of Paisiam glowed in the sky over the village as Kyemap walked the horse into Chief Mechi's corral. He closed the gate and made sure there was water in the trough. Then he grabbed a handful of straw and rubbed the horse down before removing the simple halter and giving the animal a slap on the rump. The horse kicked up its heels and then trotted around the corral while throwing its head from side to side celebrating its freedom.

Upset by his discovery in the Jaguar Swamp, Kyemap walked slowly into the village, looking between the huts to see the loud gathering around the fire. The closer he got, the more he could hear people yelling in angry voices. Then, startled, he saw Poit, tied to a post with his arms behind him. He was close enough to the bonfire to see the dark tracks where Poit's sweat had run down his dirty face.

They had found Poit and the trial had already begun!

An elder from a neighboring village took a long drink from his gourd of beer and then yelled in Poit's face so that a spray of beer accompanied his words. "You murdered him, didn't you?"

"No! No!" protested Poit shaking his head vigorously. "I shot my arrows at a jaguar. I was trying to protect Mr. Grubb. I shot all five arrows. If one missed and happened to strike Mr. Grubb, it was an accident. You've got to believe me!"

Another Indian demanded to know why the cowardly Poit left the missionary if it was only an accident. Poit repeated his story that the wounded jaguar was too dangerous and Mr. Grubb was beyond help.

"But he wasn't beyond help! He lived, didn't he?" accused the man.

"How could I know that?" cried Poit desperately.

Kyemap almost stepped forward to contradict Poit with what he had discovered. But he hesitated. He, too, was in danger if Poit was condemned. Maybe they would not need his evidence. After all, his evidence only proved what everyone suspected.

"Even if I did plan to kill him," Poit said defensively, "he didn't die. So you can't condemn me for murder. No one has been killed!" He said it defiantly, like he had finally discovered a way to beat his accusers at their own game.

But the man closest to him spat in Poit's face. "How do we know that Mr. Grubb lives? Many say another spirit lives in his body."

One of the elders shook his finger toward Poit. "If . . . if he is alive, it is no thanks to you," he said through gritted teeth. "Under Lengua law the intent to kill is as serious as the act. You must die!"

Howling in desperation, Poit cried, "The Lengua people have never executed one of their own people for killing a foreigner. You cannot condemn me!"

The same elder took up the challenge. "But Mr. Grubb has become one of us. He is no longer a foreigner. The full Lengua law will be applied to you . . . to you and *all your kin*!" shouted the angry man.

At that, Kyemap panicked and ran back between the huts and out to the corral. He threw open the gate and ran in after the chief's horse. Moments later he was galloping down the moonlit trail toward Waik. There was only one hope remaining.

CHAPTER 12

A PLEA FOR MERCY

Kyemap slipped off the sweating horse to the bare, hard-packed ground of the mission station and walked through moon shadows under the trees to Mr. Grubb's house. The first step creaked in protest as he mounted the porch. Would it awaken Mr. Grubb? Would he come out with his gun to scare away the "ghosts"? Kyemap grinned as he recalled the encounter with old Pinse-Tawa. Hostile witch doctors seemed as pale as the moonlight compared to the blaze of danger that now danced before Poit . . . and Kyemap, too.

He stepped carefully across the porch, through the quiet house, and out back. At one end of the screened-in sleeping porch stood a tent of mosquito netting that glowed dimly orange from the low-burning oil lamp within. Kyemap could see through the hazy netting the form of a man tossing and moaning on the bed. As he approached, he caught a pungent whiff of medicine and noticed beads of sweat glistening on Grubb's sickly-looking forehead.

"Mr. Grubb?" Kyemap said quietly.

Grubb sat up with a start, panting as though he had been having a bad dream, but it was not a dream. The man was sick—sick with a fever that caused him to sway and half close his eyes. "Who's there?" he mumbled, seeing the shadow of Kyemap through the mosquito netting. "What time is it? Is it time to get up? I don't think I can make it today." Then his strength drained away like water from a broken jar, and he melted back onto his pillow with a faint, high-pitched sigh.

Kyemap stepped forward and parted the netting. "Are you all right? Should I get someone?"

Grubb opened his eyes again and stared at Kyemap, slowly bringing him into focus. "Oh, it's you, Kyemap. No, no, don't bother anyone else. Just get me a glass of water, please."

Kyemap sat on the edge of the bed and poured water from a small pitcher on the side table. With a shaky hand the missionary took a sip from the glass and said, "I'll be all right in a day or so. This fever comes and goes." Then he added with a wry grin, "But I always seem to recover." He was quiet for a moment then looked up at Kyemap. "Where have you been the last few days? I haven't seen you around."

Kyemap straightened up. How could he ask a sick man to help him save Poit? Grubb couldn't even get out of bed, let alone travel to Paisiam.

Grubb must have seen the hesitation in his face, because he said, "What's the matter? Has there been more trouble with the witch doctors?"

"No," said Kyemap. And then after a long moment, "It's Poit. They've caught him, and I think they're going to execute him."

Grubb pushed himself up on his pillows. "What's happened?" he said. "What do you know." Kyemap found himself pouring out the whole story, including his trip to the site of the attack and the proof of Poit's guilt that he found there.

Grubb shook his head. "I don't want Poit to die," he said. "Executing him would not solve anything. You must ride back to Paisiam immediately and tell them that I am not dead, and I will be greatly grieved if they execute him. Tell them that is my wish."

When Kyemap hesitated, Grubb said, "Go on, now. You can do it." Then after studying Kyemap's face, he said, "Don't worry about me. I'll be okay. Hunt will look in on me in the morning. Now go." He paused and stared hard into Kyemap's eyes. "What is it? There's something else you haven't told me, isn't there?"

Kyemap took a long breath. "It is the Lengua custom to not let anyone close to a condemned person live so that there won't be any retaliation. I . . . I fear for my life."

"But surely that doesn't include you. You are a distant cousin," said Mr. Grubb.

Kyemap shrugged. "I don't know. The last thing I heard one of the elders say to Poit was, 'The full Lengua law will be applied to you . . . to you and *all your kin*!' I'm afraid that might include me because Poit has been seen with me so often this last year."

Mr. Grubb shook his head. "Some of these customs have got to change," he said. "Look, I don't want anyone to die on my account—not you, not any of Poit's other relatives, not even Poit himself. You've got to go tell them that! Convince them that there is to be no more killing." He watched Kyemap's face for a few moments and then added, "Remember how God protected you that night under the bottle trunk tree? Remember how He gave you courage when you prayed to Him? That's what you've got to do now. You go and pray on the way, and I'll stay here and pray. Now, be off with you."

————

It was nearly noon when Kyemap got back to Paisiam. A foul-smelling smoke hung over the whole village and stung his eyes. Kyemap did not see Poit anywhere, but he soon found Chief Mechi and several elders from other villages sleeping under their blankets in the shade of three palm trees.

Kyemap ground-tied the horse and approached the sleepers. Given the amount of beer they had been drinking the night before, they would probably have pounding headaches and not want to be awakened. In fact, it might be difficult to awaken them. Still, his assignment was urgent, and finally he gently shook the chief's shoulder.

Surprisingly, Chief Mechi sat straight up as though he hadn't been asleep at all. "What do you want?" he said in a clear and firm voice. It was loud enough that some of the other men stirred.

"I-I've returned your horse," Kyemap said tentatively.

"Is that a reason to wake me up?" said the chief with a scowl. "Just put it in the corral, and get out of here before . . ." He looked around with his marbled eyes that saw so poorly as though realizing for the first time how loudly he was talking. He lowered his voice. ". . . before some of these men wake up and find you here."

"But I need to talk to you," said Kyemap in hushed tones. "Poit must not be executed!"

The chief stood up then, and his blanket slid off his shoulder onto another man. That man woke up, and before Kyemap realized what was happening, all the other men were sitting up, rubbing their eyes at him.

"Who's this?" said one of the elders. "Has the killer's cousin come to surrender himself?"

Two of the other elders stood up quickly, at first holding their heads and swaying dizzily. Then they stumbled forward and grabbed Kyemap's arms. "We have him now," said one of the men.

"Wait," said the chief, putting up a hand. "Did you find some proof of your cousin's innocence?" he asked Kyemap.

Kyemap avoided the question and quickly said, "I come from Mr. Grubb. He sends a plea for mercy for Poit. He does not want you to execute him."

"But what did you find on your trip?" pressed the chief. "You did go to the west as you asked, didn't you?"

"Yes, but—"

"Well?" urged the chief. "Did you find the place of the attack?"

Kyemap nodded, then said yes, realizing that the chief would have trouble seeing just his head nod.

"Don't be difficult, boy," said the chief. "What did you learn?"

So Kyemap told about what he had found, ending with, "But I've also talked to Mr. Grubb and told him what I found. He wants to forgive Kyemap."

"Sounds like you are looking out for yourself," muttered the elder who held Kyemap's right arm.

Again the chief held up his hand. "If what you found proves that Poit tried to kill Grubb, why should we not have executed him?"

"Because . . . because—" Suddenly, Kyemap realized that the chief had used the past tense. Had they already put Poit to death? "Because he . . . because Grubb doesn't want *any* killing, none at all!" Though his words were firm, his voice trailed off as he saw in the eyes of the men that the deed had already been done. "Is he already dead?" he asked the chief.

"At first light this morning," said the chief gravely. "But since your findings prove him guilty, then we did right. Besides, he made a full confession." The chief shrugged as though executing Poit was all they could have done under those circumstances. "At first Poit had wanted to use the gun, but there were no bullets. He decided to lead Grubb into Jaguar Swamp. But no cat came, so he shot Grubb thinking that wild animals would quickly devour his body before anyone found it. He was wrong," the chief added matter-of-factly.

"But Mr. Grubb didn't want *anyone* killed for this. He *forgives* Poit," said Kyemap.

"The boy's just trying to save his own skin," said one of the elders.

"That's right," said another. "Whoever heard of forgiving such an evil person?"

"Especially forgiving the person who tried to kill you!"

"God did," said Kyemap, surprising himself. But as he looked around at the Lengua elders, the Gospel that Mr. Grubb had been teaching him began to make sense. "God forgives us all. All of us are evil sometimes. We lie. We grab the best things for ourselves. We are mean to other people. We all do it. God calls that sin, but He forgives us if we will forgive one another." Suddenly, he realized that he was preaching to them like Mr. Grubb did on Sunday mornings.

Surprised by this Good News that most of them had never heard, the elders listened as Kyemap explained how God loved humans so much that He sent His only Son to save them, even though people were so sinful that they killed Jesus.

"If the people killed God's Son," asked one of the men, "how can He forgive us?"

"Because God raised Him from the dead," said Kyemap. "Many people saw Him." Shaking his head earnestly, he said, "This was no ghost. Jesus was really alive again. Many people talked to Him and touched Him . . . and ate with Him," he added, remembering the proof he had discovered that a paca and not a ghost had visited him that night at the bottle trunk tree.

Chief Mechi nodded his head soberly and said to Kyemap, "We must talk. Take my horse to the corral. When you return, we will have made our decision."

With wide eyes, Kyemap looked around at the other men. Decision? What decision were they going to make? Had they really intended to kill him right then? He backed away, stumbling over a stick and almost falling. He recovered, turned, and ran to the horse.

As he walked it back toward the corral, Kyemap slowed, scuffing his toes in the dust. Was he a fake? Had he only been preaching the Gospel to the elders in hopes that they wouldn't kill him? Of course he wanted them to accept it and not kill him, but he hadn't accepted it himself. Oh, he recognized that the things he had been saying were true, but he hadn't done anything about them. He hadn't accepted God's forgiveness for himself. He hadn't decided to give his whole life to God in gratitude for forgiving him. He hadn't asked Jesus to live in his heart. Those were all things Mr. Grubb had said were part of really *believing*, part of becoming a true Christian.

So why had he been preaching to the elders? Was it just to save his own life?

"O God," he prayed quietly, "please forgive me and make my life new. I am sorry for using your Gospel just to save my own life. I want to become a Christian now, no matter what happens. And if my life is spared, I will go straight to Mr. Grubb and tell him that I am ready to be baptized so everyone will know that I am a Christian."

For some reason, Kyemap realized his fear was gone. With new courage he returned to Chief Mechi and faced the elders.

"We cannot do anything about Poit," the chief announced with great solemnity. "He has already been executed. But we have decided to honor the rest of Mr. Grubb's request, and we will not kill any of his relatives. You are free to go."

———

A short time later, Kyemap became the first baptized convert among the Lengua people. With the baptismal waters streaming down his face, he said, "From now on, I would like to be called by the name of Philip, because, like Philip in the Bible, I want to become an evangelist and tell people the *Tasik Amyaa*, the Good News."

And he did.

MORE ABOUT
BARBROOKE GRUBB

Barbrooke Grubb was born on August 11, 1865, at Liberton in Midlothian, Scotland. As a boy he delighted in wrestling and feats of strength and was filled with mischief. He completed his education at George Watson College in Edinburgh, Scotland, where his interest in geography and ancient history led to his study of the habits of primitive peoples. He also took a medical course in which he and a friend both cut themselves accidentally in the dissecting room. His friend died within forty-eight hours, and Grubb remained sick for nearly a year.

In 1884, he met Dwight Moody and Ira Sankey, the dynamic evangelists from the United States, and ended up devoting his life to missions. On his nineteenth birthday, Grubb decided to join the South American Missionary Society and two years later went to the Falkland Islands, where he spent four years. But he always felt called to the Indian tribes of the northern interior.

Nothing pleased him more than his assignment in 1890 to the unexplored interior of Paraguay, known as the Chaco, and the wild tribes of Indians who lived there.

Initially, Grubb employed the unusual (at that time) tactic of going right into the interior, first to explore the territory and make friends, and then to live right with the Indians rather than build a large station on the perimeter of the field to which the Indians came. Though later he did set up mission stations such as Waikthlatingmangyalwa, they were in the heart of the Chaco and were designed for the sake of the Indians rather than the convenience and comfort of the missionaries. At these stations, the Indians learned better agricultural techniques, industry, and the Gospel. Even at the mission stations, Grubb's unusual acceptance by the Indians was based on his willingness to live among them in an unthreatening manner.

Grubb was not very good at foreign languages. Lengua was the only language of the Chaco that he spoke easily, and in that he broke almost all the grammatical rules. But he had a gift for picking up enough essential words and phrases in half a dozen languages to make himself understood. He communicated more by speaking from the heart than as a skilled linguist.

Grubb's fearlessness and Christian love so won the confidence of the Indians that the government of Paraguay appointed him commissioner for the Chaco.

On May 15, 1901, Grubb married Mary Bridges in Buenos Aires. She, of course, joined him in the Chaco, but Grubb never had the assistance of more than four other European missionaries in his work.

Some of his greatest challenges came from the oppressive superstitions of the people promoted by witch doctors who kept the people in bondage while living off their fears. Though Grubb was deliberately contemptuous of the witch doctors (so as to break their cruel power over the people), he nevertheless studied their mysteries and learned secrets otherwise hidden from all those outside their guild. Politically incorrect as it now may sound, he concluded that ridicule was the safest weapon to reduce a witch doctor's power among his own people.

Even though the number of baptized believers in the Lengua church did not grow beyond two hundred during his ministry among them, the general life for the majority of the people was profoundly transformed. Tribal wars ceased, infanticide ended, hunger (from a nomadic lifestyle and failure to plant crops and prepare for the future) was overcome, and the general health of the people was greatly improved. With the help of his assistants, Grubb also translated hymns, prayers, and most of the New Testament into Lengua.

One of his greatest concerns while working among the Indians was that the government had already divided up the Chaco into county-sized lots to sell to land speculators intent on making their own fortunes. Neither the sellers nor the potential buyers had set foot in this wilderness, but they were ready to grab it out from under the Indians for whom it had been home for countless generations. Using his own savings and all the funds he could raise elsewhere, Grubb set about to prevent this theft by purchasing the land in the name of the Indians. It was his vision that the Lengua people would become a self-supporting, self-governing community. His goal was for each family to possess its own livestock and homestead, equipped to engage in agriculture or in the arts and crafts such as woodworking, pottery, weaving, or sewing.

The mission to the Lenguas, which was started in 1890, was fully established by 1910 when Grubb had already begun work with the Toothli and Suhin tribes of the west and the Sanapana in the north. Grubb then moved to northern Argentina and Bolivia, where he established a strong mission among the Matacos of the Bermejo and a prosperous beginning among the people of the Pilcomayo. He also began tentative efforts among the Tobas and converted many among the Tapui Indians of Bolivia. It is no wonder that in his lifetime he became known around the world as the "Livingstone of South America."

Grubb accomplished all this before he died on May 28, 1930.

FOR FURTHER READING

Davidson, Norman J. *Barbrooke Grubb: Pathfinder.* London: Seeley, Service & Co., Ltd., 1924.

Grubb, W. Barbrooke. *A Church in the Wilds.* London: Seeley, Service & Co., Ltd., 1914.

Grubb, W. Barbrooke. *An Unknown People in an Unknown Land.* London: Seeley, Sevice & Co., Ltd., 1914.

Hunt, Richard James. *The Livingstone of South America.* Philadelphia: J. B. Lippincott, 1933.

Don't Miss Any of These Other Exciting TRAILBLAZER Story Collections!

Stow away on a ship to China as you tag along with missionary Hudson Taylor. Experience a dangerous trip on the Underground Railroad with escaped slave and freedom fighter Harriet Tubman. Join an outlawed Ecuadorian boy as he risks his life to team up with Nate Saint to bring peace back to his home tribe.

These and other exciting stories wait for you in the pages of these next TRAILBLAZERS books. Don't miss a single adventure!

TRAILBLAZERS by Dave and Neta Jackson

Trailblazers: Featuring Amy Carmichael and Other Christian Heroes

Trailblazers: Featuring Harriet Tubman and other Christian Heroes

Trailblazers Featuring William Tyndale and other Christian Heroes

Trailblazers: Featuring Martin Luther and other Christian Heroes